THE LOYAL, TRUE, AND BRAVE

THE LOYAL, TRUE, AND BRAVE

A Novel of the Civil War

ROBERT J. SWEETMAN

Charleston, SC
www.PalmettoPublishing.com

The Loyal, True, and Brave

First Edition

Paperback ISBN: 978-1-64990-259-7
eBook ISBN: 978-1-64990-608-3

This novel is dedicated to Karen, for her encouragement and support, and to the men of the Army of the Potomac, from major general to private, famous and unknown, who threw their lives into the breach to save the Union on those crucial three days of July 1863.

We will welcome to our numbers
The loyal, true and brave,
Shouting the battle cry of Freedom;
And although they may be poor, not a man shall be a slave,
Shouting the battle cry of Freedom.

Chorus:

The Union forever,
Hurrah, boys, hurrah!
Down with the traitors,
Up with the stars;
While we rally round the flag, boys,
Rally once again,
Shouting the battle cry of Freedom.
From The Battle Cry of Freedom by George F. Root (1820–1895)

Table of Contents

Part One

Chancellorsville, Virginia

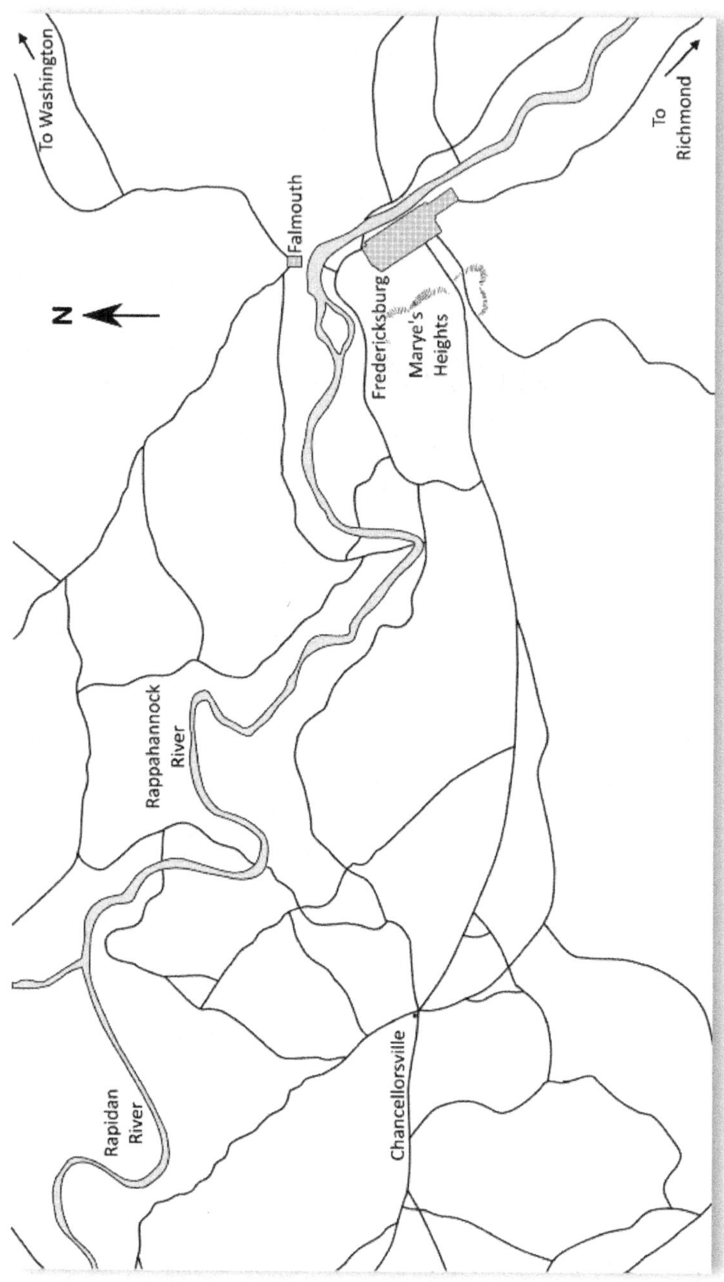

MAP 1—FREDERICKSBURG AND CHANCELLORSVILLE

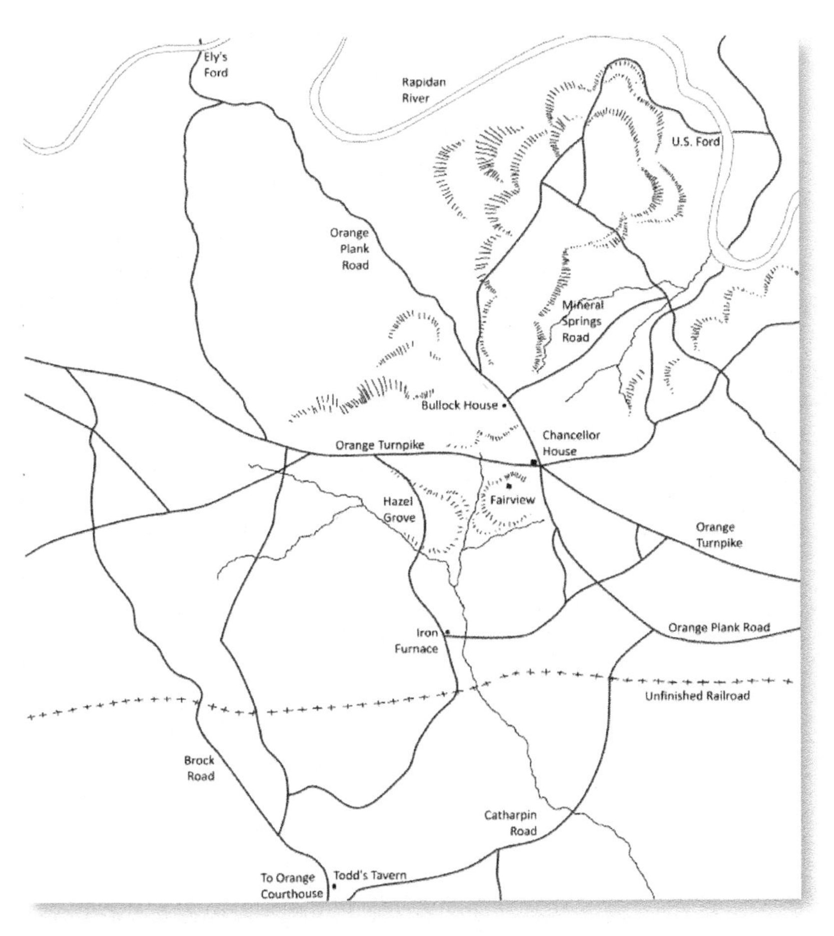

MAP 2—CHANCELLORSVILLE BATTLEFIELD

Chapter 1

May 2, 1863

He could see them clearly with his field glasses—there on that ridgeline about a mile away, white-topped wagons bobbing quickly along some unmarked cow path. Dan Sickles, major general, United States Volunteers, lowered his glasses and scowled. He was a handsome man with chestnut hair and penetrating blue eyes. The bags under those eyes spoke of too much late-night carousing—Daniel Edgar Sickles had spent his share of time in both barrooms and bordellos. Still, he cut quite a figure—short, slight, but well turned out in his major general's frock coat, kepi, riding gloves, and sword belt. He liked to think that he resembled General McClellan in some ways, and a patch of beard under his lower lip, added to a drooping mustache, enhanced his resemblance to the "Young Napoleon."

Sickles lowered his field glasses and looked questioningly at the lieutenant in charge of the observation detail. "How long have they been moving past this position?"

"We first spotted them around eight o'clock this morning, sir," the lieutenant said. "They have been moving past like this ever since with no letup: troops, then artillery, then wagons, and then more troops."

Sickles glanced quickly at his pocket watch. "That's an hour and a half of solid rebels." He made a quick calculation and whistled at the result. "We've seen at least an entire division move past us."

Sickles looked back toward the enemy column. *Why would they be moving across my front?* He shot a glance at the soldier high up in the tree above him. It was one of these lookouts who first had spotted the movement several hours earlier. "Any sign of where they are headed?" he called up to the treetop.

"No, sir," a voice shouted back. "I don't see a thing. There's no dust cloud neither. Must be the ground is too wet under all them trees."

"Right..." Sickles bit his lip and looked through his field glasses again. *A whole division strung out four deep and miles long. It would be so easy to hit the flank of that column, break them up, and drive them from the field.* Sickles imagined the laurels that would come with such a stunning victory.

A voice behind him interrupted his pleasurable thoughts. "It's a shame General Hooker has ordered us to take no offensive action."

Sickles half turned. It was Major Henry Tremain, his chief aide. Tremain was a lot like Sickles: sharp, ambitious, a crafty lawyer, and a man who knew how to pull strings to make things happen. Only twenty-three years old, this self-assured young man had become indispensable—his alter ego in dealing with the army bureaucracy. Sickles had come to rely heavily on Tremain, and he was glad the young major was along on his first campaign as a corps commander.

"Yes," he replied. "If he only knew what an opportunity he was passing up."

"Do you suppose the rebs are trying to move around our right flank?" Tremain asked.

"Hard to say," Sickles replied. He frowned at the thought. "Somehow I doubt it, though." He looked at Tremain and the rest of his aides as they crowded in a little closer to hear his opinion.

"It has all been progressing exactly as General Hooker said it would," Sickles said.

"You mean the part about Lee being forced to meet us on our own ground?" Tremain asked.

"No, it's more than that. It's the whole campaign. Hooker told me his whole plan." Sickles lowered his voice and looked around. The aides crowded even closer. "He strongly believed, and certainly convinced me, that any direct attack on Fredericksburg was doomed to failure. Hooker told me the only way to force the strong defensive line along the Rappahannock was to flank Lee out of his positions. That's why he moved us all upriver to cross where there would be no opposition." Sickles cast a questioning look at his aides. They were all nodding in growing comprehension. "I spoke to General Hooker last night," he said. "He believes the rebels will be forced to withdraw now that we have flanked them out of their works around Fredericksburg. To be sure, he has sent our cavalry down around our right to cut the railroad south of Fredericksburg."

"And without a secure supply line, Lee will definitely be forced to retreat," Tremain said.

Sickles smiled at Tremain's quick grasp of the situation. "Quite correct."

"So what we are seeing is an enemy retreat?" Tremain asked.

Sickles's confident smile wilted just slightly as he shook his head. "I'm not sure...Hooker told me there was a chance that Lee would actually attack us. We really do hope that he will. If we can hold back in a strong defensive position and force Lee to attack, then we can win a great victory by remaining on the defensive."

Sickles turned back to the column and raised his field glasses for another look. Lowering his glasses, he played with his mustache in thought. "Were you able to find that road on a map?"

Tremain slowly shook his head. "It's not on any of our maps. We checked with General Warren at headquarters; it's not on any of their maps either. His best guess is that it connects the road we are on with the Orange Plank Road, which is about a mile to the east from here." Tremain unfolded a map and held it up for Sickles to see.

Sickles considered the map. "It looks to me that all of the roads head south and southwest from here."

Tremain nodded. "In general, that is true, sir."

Sickles hesitated, trying out a thought. "So it may be that the rebs are retreating toward the south after all."

Tremain shrugged. "Well, General, that hypothesis certainly fits the facts as we know them."

Sickles's mood darkened. He turned back to the column and scowled. "We would know for sure if we broke that column up and chased it down the road. Damn it, Tremain, we have to sit here and watch the reb army march in front of us, and we can't do anything about it."

"Yes sir," Tremain said. "If only General Hooker could see what we see now. I'm sure he would reach the same conclusion we have."

Maybe Tremain has an idea there. Sickles was silent for a moment, considering how Hooker might react. The commanding general was the kind of man to snap at an opportunity like this dangled in front of his eyes. Sickles nodded. "Tremain, I want you to ride up to see General Hooker and speak to him personally.

Tell him something important is happening and that I request that he come down here to see for himself."

The major saluted and ran for his horse.

Sickles looked around and sighed. He was on high ground, a hill the locals called Hazel Grove. A dirt road to his left ran off to the south, down the steep slope of Hazel Grove, finally disappearing into the woods to his front. To Sickles's left front, roughly toward the southeast, through a small gap in the trees, was his glimpse of the rebel army. Behind him, to his left rear and across a stretch of low ground, was the brick-walled cemetery of Fairview, and beyond, Hooker's headquarters at the Chancellor House. Everything else was a mass of twisted shrubs and trees, hiding both the terrain and the enemy movement. "Damn second-growth forest," he swore. "Can't see a thing through it!"

Dan Sickles trusted his own instincts, and he resented having to ask permission when he knew he was right. That was the thing he most disliked about the army. It was unavoidable, though, and he finally lit a calming cigar. The teasing glimmer of sunlight reflecting off the rebel guns brought his attention back to the enemy column. Sickles raised his glasses for another look. They were still there, moving quickly toward some unknown destination, on some unknown purpose. *So near and yet so far away.*

"Damn!" Sickles looked away in disgust. *This is one hell of an opportunity. Can't just let it go to waste!*

Dan Sickles knew all about opportunities. He knew how to spot them, he knew how to play them for everything they were worth, and yes, he knew how to squander them away, as he had done with his father's allowance money. In his forty-some years, Dan Sickles had encountered a number of occasions to learn a great deal about opportunities.

Once he had been President Buchanan's protégé, a sharp, young rising-star congressman from New York. The old man was grooming him for a future presidential bid. They all said he had the ability to be president if he could just stay out of the gutter. But Dan Sickles just couldn't stay away from the seamier side of life. Surprisingly, it wasn't his playing in the gutter that brought him down—it was his own wife. Sickles shook his head at the improbability of this. They didn't blame him for shooting his wife's lover. No, that was expected by the Code, and he was quickly absolved of that understandable act of violence. Sickles thought back with a grim pleasure at the novel defense he had cooked up with his attorney, Edwin Stanton. "Temporary insanity" they had named it, and it sounded reasonable enough for the jury to let him off the murder charge.

His real sin was to forgive his wife for her unfaithfulness. They had made him a pariah for that act of compassion, and he was cast into political oblivion, his career seemingly at an end. He achingly remembered the pain and humiliation of being shunned in the House chamber, with all the other congressmen avoiding him as if he had smallpox. So he was forced to suffer in humiliating isolation, riding out his term until he would disappear with barely a ripple in the genteel southern pond that was antebellum Washington. Then, at his lowest point, he was presented with an opportunity—Fort Sumter.

It didn't hurt that he was genuinely outraged by the thought of South Carolina seceding and taking federal property with it at the point of a gun, but Dan Sickles was too much of an opportunist to keep quiet. The opportunity to champion a cause and regain some manner of recognition would have been hard to pass up no matter what the cause. He quickly stepped in to fill the vacuum, and people began to listen to his fiery words on

South Carolina's intemperate actions. With this attention came at least some renewed degree of respectability. He had begun his political rehabilitation.

The war presented him with the biggest opportunity of all. When it started, Sickles instinctively realized that things would never be the way they were before. The old order was being swept away and with it the smug, snooty southern gentry who shunned him. In the New Order, a war hero would be forgiven for many indiscretions. He quickly resigned from Congress and went back to New York City to raise a regiment for the cause. Instead of just a regiment, he managed to raise an entire brigade. Using this accomplishment as ammunition, Sickles parlayed his political connections to win the commission of a brigadier general of volunteers.

And now he was well on his way to becoming a war hero. His friend and army commander Joe Hooker had just appointed him to command the Third Corps—a tough outfit with an excellent war record. Maybe, just maybe, he could be president after all. This rebel column, so tantalizingly close, could be another big step in his long road back from oblivion—if he could only get permission to attack it. Sickles marveled at his luck—a corps commander with an opportunity to hand the rebels a resounding defeat. The newspapers would sing his praises!

A shout disturbed his thoughts. "Sir, here comes Major Tremain!"

Sickles watched as his senior aide rode up. He could tell by the look on Tremain's face that the news was not favorable.

The major halted in front of Sickles and sadly shook his head. "General Hooker says he is much too busy to come here, sir. He is under the belief, based on our reports, that the enemy may be trying to move around our right. He is sending out a circular to all the corps commanders warning them to be on the lookout for such a move. General Hooker did agree, however, that we could use our artillery to harass the enemy movement." Tremain made a face and shrugged in resignation.

Sickles frowned at this news. He had expected Hooker to at least come and see the situation for himself. *This is quite unlike Fighting Joe Hooker,* Sickles thought. "Is that all?" he asked. Sighing, he turned to Captain Randolph, his chief of artillery. "All right, Randolph, bring up some artillery on the double."

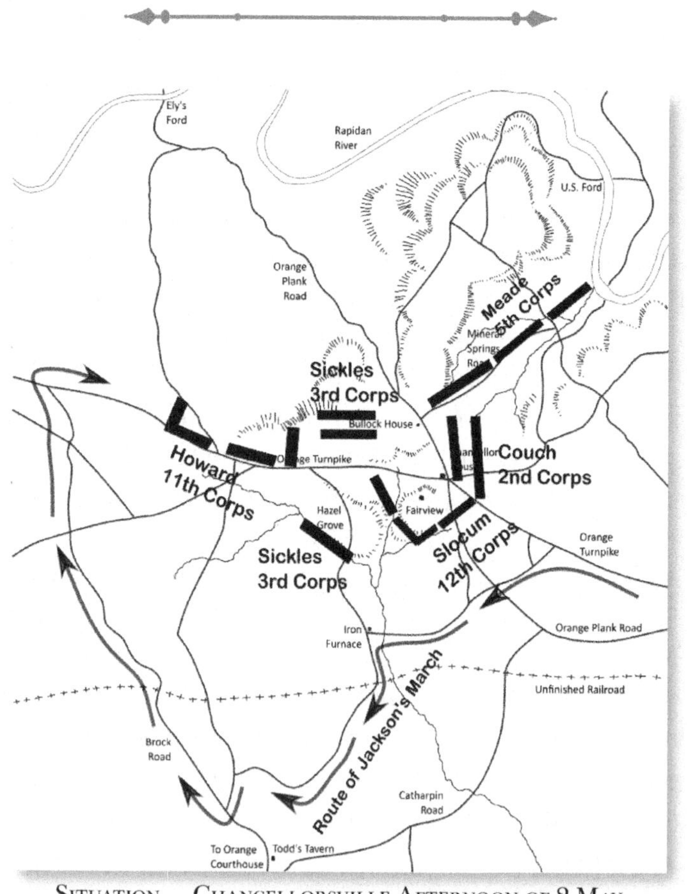

SITUATION— CHANCELLORSVILLE AFTERNOON OF 2 MAY

Major General George Gordon Meade reined in his horse to look over the Fifth Corps line along the Mineral Springs Road. Details of infantry, stripped to the waist, were digging rifle pits. Others were felling trees to construct a breastwork of logs. To his front, toward the east and Fredericksburg, the ground fell off steeply into a ravine with the Mineral Spring Run at the bottom. Pioneers were busy near the bank of the stream felling trees for an abatis—a wall of intertwined logs and branches that would slow any assault to a crawl. The infantry, firing from protected positions in the rifle pits, could send a withering fire into the stalled attackers below. After a long, critical look, Meade finally nodded with satisfaction. Things were being done right—by the book. If the enemy gave him a few more hours, they would pay dearly for an attack on his position.

He was tall and careworn, this commander of the Union Fifth Corps, looking more like a bookish professor than the commander of an army corps. A rumpled blue sack coat with mud-splattered corduroy pants tucked carelessly into long jack-boots furthered this image, and only the major-general shoulder straps indicated his true rank. An old black slouch hat was pulled down on his head, partially concealing his haggard face, but neither the brim nor his glasses could hide the worry marks that spread from the corners of his eyes and ran into his gray pointy beard.

Meade pulled a crumpled map from his case and studied it with the precision of a trained topographical engineer. His finger traced the stream at the bottom of the ravine to the point where it emptied into the Rappahannock River. He tapped thoughtfully at the position's topographical weak point. Stuffing the map back in his case, he nudged his horse forward. This was

General Humphreys's sector, and Meade needed to make sure that Humphreys properly covered this weak point.

Meade found his Third Division commander along the line inspecting the fortifications. He looked up as Meade approached and offered a crisp salute. "Good morning, General Meade," Humphreys called out. "We have an excellent position here. Another half a day, and we will have a stronger position than Malvern Hill."

Meade nodded. They had punished the rebels severely at Malvern Hill when Lee attacked heavily entrenched positions. These works could be every bit as strong—if the enemy would just give him time. Meade dismissed the thought. There was work to do. "I am worried about your left flank, General. If the enemy forces his way along the riverbank, he can turn your left and threaten the US Ford. It's only a mile upstream. We must protect our line of communication at all costs."

Humphreys cocked his head in thought. He was a slight man, very prim with a neat mustache and a fresh paper collar. Meade knew that these looks were deceiving. Humphreys was a real fighter, and Meade was glad to have him as one of his division commanders. Meade always felt a bit uncomfortable giving him orders. Humphreys was older, having graduated from West Point the year Meade entered. His time as McClellan's chief engineer during most of 1862 had retarded Humphreys' promotion opportunities, allowing younger men to rise above him.

Closing his thoughts with a bob of his head, Humphreys looked up at Meade. "You are absolutely correct, General! I will send reinforcements to the left flank, and we will push all the way to the river. We can build barriers all the way down to the waterline and cover them with cannon and rifle fire."

Meade nodded absently and turned away. He was already worrying about his line to the south. Down there somewhere in the woods, his right connected with Couch's Second Corps. They were another tough outfit, and it gave Meade some comfort to have them anchoring his right flank. The problem was the thick woods, which restricted visibility and fields of fire. Meade sighed at the expanse of green and nudged his horse forward.

He pulled up as one of his aides galloped toward him. It was Captain Mason, who had recently joined his staff. "A message from Colonel Webb, sir..."

Meade nodded—Webb was his chief of staff.

At Meade's nod, Mason continued. "General Hooker has sent out a circular to all corps commanders. The Third Corps has spotted an enemy column moving to their south. General Hooker warned the Third and Eleventh Corps to be prepared for a possible enemy flanking movement."

Humphreys had walked up during Mason's report. Meade raised an eyebrow with an unasked question and quickly dismounted. Throwing the reins to Mason, he motioned Humphreys off to where they could be alone. The administration was cashiering senior officers for real or imagined disloyalty. It paid to be very careful who heard your private conversations these days.

Meade turned to face his subordinate. "What do you think of all this, Humphreys?"

Humphreys wrinkled his nose in disgust. "It's a damn mess. I don't like it, don't like it one damn bit. We're too close in. It's just inviting an attack. And look around..." He swept his arm around in a long arc. "We're hemmed in by this goddamned scrub forest. The rebels will be on top of us before we know it."

Meade nodded sadly. "I know...we should have pushed ahead yesterday. There was nothing in front of us that we couldn't have forced our way through. We were almost out of this wilderness. Instead, we surrendered the initiative to Lee. It's strange that Fighting Joe Hooker would do that." He paused and looked out over the ravine. "I can't get over Hooker's sudden caution."

Humphreys shrugged. "Well, I hope it's just caution and not the bottle that is at the heart of his change in tactics."

Meade shrugged. "I saw Hooker last night. His staff was drinking, but he abstained. I don't believe he is drinking. He genuinely thinks we are in a good defensive position and wants the rebels to attack us."

"Well, he just may get what he asked for." Humphreys cocked his head. "What do you make of this report of enemy movement, Meade?"

Meade hesitated. *A good question. Try to look into the head of Bobby Lee. What would he be thinking? Faced with a superior force, would he retreat? Not likely, knowing Lee. If not retreat, what then? Defend along the strongest terrain feature? Possibly, but what is that rebel column doing? Moving around our flank? Why not? Scott did it in Mexico, with Lee at his side. So many questions. It's impossible to solve this problem with so little data.* Meade looked at Humphreys and shrugged. "Hard to say. It could mean a number of things. We just don't know enough right now to say for sure."

Humphreys said nothing. Meade changed the subject. "What's going on in front of you?"

"Mixed signals." Humphreys shook his head uncertainly. "Don't know what to make of it." He made a quick wave of his hand towards the picket line of soldiers out beyond the main defensive line. "My pickets report rebel probing all along the line—like they're looking for a weak point to attack. We've already had one false alarm this morning. We heard bugle calls and orders to advance for an attack. I called the entire line to arms, but nothing happened." He paused to shake his head again. "What's strange is the rebels are digging defensive works on the ridgeline over on the far side of the ravine."

Meade raised his field glasses and scanned the opposite heights through the thick growth. Despite his limited view, he could see gray infantry toiling feverishly to construct defensive works to match his own. *Unusual behavior for troops preparing to attack or retreat...they obviously intend to stay there for a good long time—and to oppose any move of ours toward Fredericksburg. Were the bugle calls and orders to advance a ruse? Probably, but why?* Meade shook his head. "I don't think they are going to attack us here," he said.

After a few more moments more of examining the rebel activity, Meade put away his field glasses. There weren't enough pieces of the puzzle out to make any sense of it. He still needed to check how his other two divisions were getting along. "Stay on your toes," he told Humphreys, "and let me know the minute anything happens." Meade walked back to his horse biting his lip. Something unusual was happening, and he couldn't figure out what—at least not yet.

The Parrott gun to the right fired with an ear-splitting crash. Sickles shifted his field glasses to focus on a rebel wagon in the middle of the clearing. The shell exploded in the air, first a brilliant point of light followed by a puffy white cloud. He held his breath as the smoke cleared. Through the slowly lifting smoke, Sickles could make out an increased movement in the clearing, everyone rushing to get out of view. Among the rush he saw the wagon slip into the tree line at the other side of the clearing. No effect!

Sickles glared at the battery commander. "Well, Lieutenant?"

The young officer reddened and shrugged. "We don't have enough of a view of the target, General. It's difficult to judge the range, and we can't tell if the shells are exploding at target distance. We have to guess how short to cut the fuses and then see if they are right by the effect on the target."

"Well, start guessing better!" Sickles scowled and looked back around the top of the hill. A regiment of Zouaves–infantry dressed in short open jackets and baggy trousers–lounged in the shade of the trees at the edge of the clearing, watching the artillery with only mild interest.

A small group of horsemen rode up the trail from the south. Sickles recognized the lead rider as General Birney, the commander of his lead division. Birney was short and slight, almost gaunt. A long, flowing brown beard hid his facial features, giving him an inscrutable look. It was never easy to figure out what Birney was thinking. Sickles admired him, though. Birney was a natural soldier, and even though he had no formal training, he did manage to hold his own among the clubby West Pointers. Even more to Sickles's liking was Birney's uncanny insight into the way the military mind worked. Birney was a great asset, especially at a time like this.

"Birney, I'm glad you're here," Sickles called to his subordinate. "We've been watching the rebels marching in front of us for hours, and we can't get permission from headquarters to do anything about it, except blaze away with these pop guns." He motioned derisively toward the artillery battery.

"So I've noticed," Birney replied impassively.

"Well," Sickles said, "I've been thinking that maybe we should push our pickets out a little farther forward. If they just happened to bump into the rebs and a fight started, then we would be obliged to reinforce them."

Birney blinked, inscrutable. After an uncomfortable silence, Birney finally spoke. "General Sickles, I'm not sure that is a very good idea." Birney was obviously picking his words carefully. "General Hooker has sent specific instructions for us to take no offensive actions. Suppose we did move forward without authorization and something happened, something bad. We would then be responsible for disobeying a direct order, and we both know what that would mean." Birney shot him a glance.

"Yes, of course you are right," Sickles replied, perturbed that Birney was being difficult. After some thought, he motioned to Tremain. "Major, send a message to General Hooker. Tell him I believe there is a great tactical opportunity, and I request permission to move forward to develop the situation."

Meade looked along the fieldworks snaking through the forest and nodded to Major General George Sykes, the commander of the Fifth Corps' First Division. Sykes, known universally by his fellow West Pointers as "Tardy George," was not a man of great intellect or of tremendous drive. He was undeniably a plodder, but Meade knew that he could count on Sykes to follow orders to the letter. The First Division included a brigade of regular army regiments, and the troops to Meade's front were regulars.

Meade wished his whole corps were composed of regulars. He served under Zachary Taylor in the Mexican War and had picked up some of Old Rough and Ready's dislike for volunteer soldiers. Meade had also seen firsthand the atrocities and poor battlefield performance that ill-trained volunteers were capable of.

"Who's on your right flank?" he asked Sykes.

"Hancock's division," Sykes said with a smile.

Meade smiled too. Hancock was one of the best tacticians in the Army of the Potomac and a very able officer. His division was tough and well trained, one of the best in the Army of the Potomac. There would be no worry from that part of the line.

There were other parts of the line to worry about, though. Meade thought about the tactical briefing he had received from General Hooker the night before. From Meade's left flank anchored on the south bank of the Rappahannock, the army stretched in a broad arc centered on the crossroads of Chancellorsville. Beyond the Second Corps lay the Twelfth Corps, under General Slocum, and then General Sickles's Third Corps. At the very end of the line, with its right flank dangling in the air, was the Eleventh Corps, under General Howard. Meade frowned. Now that was the part of the line to worry about. Not only was it a poor tactical position with its flank unanchored on a terrain feature, but more importantly, the Eleventh Corps was the least reliable of all the units in the Army of the Potomac. Hooker had brushed off Meade's concerns about this position. John Reynolds' First Corps was moving up to fill in the gap, Hooker breezily explained, and besides, the forest was so thick that no major attack could possibly come from that direction. Even so, Meade remained unconvinced.

From the right, far down the line, a single cannon boomed. Several more followed in rapid succession, and the entire line erupted in a heavy cannonade from the rebel lines. The group moved quickly back from the line to a more protected spot.

Sykes looked at Meade, worried. "Do you think they are preparing for an attack?"

"Either an attack or masking fire for a withdrawal." Meade hesitated. According to the book, those were the two instances for utilizing an artillery cannonade. He was ready for an attack, but a withdrawal would present different tactical requirements. "Mason"—he waved a finger at his aide—"ride up to General Humphreys. Find out if the rebels in front of him have started to move. Oh, and remind him that I want a report as soon as it happens."

Heavy rifle fire broke out on his right. *An attack…that must be it.* Meade turned to George Sykes and nodded grimly. "Get your men ready, General Sykes!"

Birney squinted toward Hooker's headquarters over at the Chancellor House. "Here comes your aide back, at the gallop. Perhaps he has some good news."

Sickles watched the aide ride up with anticipation. The aide, however, had nothing but bad news. General Hooker had reaffirmed his orders to stay in position and not to take any offensive action.

Birney shot Sickles a knowing glance. Sickles grimaced in response.

Tremain was at his elbow. "Well, sir, what do you think it would take to make General Hooker change his mind?"

Sickles smiled slyly at his aide—he got the point of the question. "I think if we convinced him that an attack was the best response," Sickles said, "then he would permit us to proceed. At this point, he is unsure what the enemy is up to."

"Would he approve an attack if he thought the enemy was retreating?" Tremain suggested.

"No doubt..." Sickles considered this scheme. "Even if the enemy is moving around to our right, then a preemptive attack could upset his timing and reduce the effectiveness of the attack." *This is worth one more try.* "Tremain, I want you to go to General Hooker. He knows you. Explain to him what we see and try to convince him to let us attack. Lay out the advantages of attacking now. We're running out of time. The enemy is possibly retreating and may slip away before we act. Tell him whatever you need to, just get permission to attack."

Tremain saluted and ran for his horse.

Some ten miles downriver, on the shore opposite Fredericksburg, the cannon fire rolled in like the rumbling of distant thunder. The sun, newly past midday, had turned the day oppressively hot. Sergeant Patrick Henry Taylor wiped a large rolling bead of sweat from his right temple and glanced around.

Known as Henry by his family, he was a trim, alert young man, just past his twenty-fifth birthday. Sandy brown hair and a neatly trimmed blondish beard framed his brilliant blue eyes. Henry had been a teacher before the war, with a mixed class of white settler and Chippewa Indian children in the frontier town of Belle Prairie, Minnesota. Just a few weeks after Fort Sumter fell, Henry resigned his teaching position and traveled 120 miles down the Mississippi River to join a newly forming regiment near Minneapolis. Now, two years later, he was a sergeant, and the regiment was still at war.

The flats on the north side of the Rappahannock River were a wasteland, stripped bare of trees and with every blade of grass trampled into dust. Across the river the shattered town of Fredericksburg, windowless and pockmarked, lay deserted and silent. Beyond the town, the hills rose up studded with rebel fieldworks. Henry's eyes narrowed at the sight of the enemy positions. The Union Army had stormed those works the previous December in wave after bloody and futile wave. The rebs were still there, as defiant as ever, daring the Union boys to try it again.

Henry's regiment, the First Minnesota, had been spared from that December blood-letting. They had stood in formation watching as the brigades in front of them were torn to pieces. Their brigade commander, Colonel Sully, refused to order the attack when he saw the insanity of continuing. Somehow the division commander didn't object too strongly, and Sully's act of insubordination was allowed to stand. Henry was under no illusions as to what an attack on that position would have cost the regiment.

Another wave of distant artillery floated downriver. Henry cocked an ear. It sounded like an artillery duel. Something was definitely happening upriver.

"Well, I guess the ball is starting without us," a voice beside him announced. "If we don't get an invitation soon, then we will just have to sit this one out."

Henry grinned and nodded. It was Isaac, his older brother and "high private" in Company E of the First Minnesota Volunteers. Isaac was a free spirit and, like Henry, a college graduate. His range of knowledge and ability to pick up new information awed Henry. Isaac certainly had the intelligence to be an officer, but his irreverent sense of humor and his devil-may-care attitude ensured that he would stay a private—at least if the army had anything to say about it.

"Yep, don't mind if we sit this one out," Henry answered. Of all the units in the army, it was his division, commanded by General Gibbon, that was out in plain view of the enemy. When the rest of the army slipped off to the west, Gibbon's division remained in place to continue the ruse and to stay between the rebels and Washington. Because of that last geographical reality, Henry was sure that they would stay where they were.

Another bit of good luck? Henry couldn't prevent the thought from slipping into his head. So far, he and his brother Isaac had experienced a streak of good luck. Captured on the peninsula during McClellan's retreat, Henry and Isaac had missed the carnage of Antietam. The First Minnesota suffered heavy losses there. After the last-minute reprieve at Fredericksburg, they now had guard duty while the rest of the army slugged it out with the Johnnies. Henry felt a twinge of guilt that they were out of danger, but he had seen too many battles to wish he were in the action upriver.

He shook his head violently to stop the thought. It was no good thinking like this—it wouldn't do him any good. He quickly looked around to see if anyone noticed his movement. Thankfully, no one seemed to be aware of what he had done. They all seemed preoccupied, lost in their own little worlds: sleeping, reading, or writing letters.

They were all good men, these veterans. Of the thousand-strong regiment that had answered Lincoln's call in May 1861, barely three hundred remained. Hardship, disease, and the winnowing of a dozen battlefields had taken the rest. The ones remaining were hard and tough—and wise to the ways of the soldier. They had also earned a reputation for being cool under fire. At Bull Run they held their ground like a regiment of regulars and then withdrew in good order while other regiments around them fled in panic.

A pattering of rifle fire drifted up from the east—from where, according to camp scuttlebutt, the Sixth Corps had forced a bridgehead across the river. Henry shook his head, trying to make sense of it. The Sixth Corps downstream, Gibbon's division in the center, and the rest of the army somewhere upriver. He hoped to God that General Hooker knew what he was doing.

Tremain arrived, breathless. "General," he gasped, "we got it!" He triumphantly thrust a paper toward Sickles.

Sickles snatched the paper and hurriedly read the message. "Advance cautiously…harass the enemy" He was disappointed. This was not the unconditional permission he had hoped for. Sickles paused to consider his options. *There must be a loophole that I can exploit.* A sly smile spread across his face. "Major, did the commanding general explain what he meant by the term 'advance cautiously'?"

Birney furrowed his brow, but Tremain caught the meaning of the question and smirked. "No sir, General Hooker did not explain it. I supposed that the meaning is clear. If one looks at the grammatical construction of the phrase, *advance* is the verb and *cautiously* is the adverb describing the verb." He winked at Sickles.

Sickles smirked as well. "So what he is actually telling us is to move forward to attack the enemy column, but to take adequate precautions in case we are counterattacked."

Tremain nodded emphatically. “That is exactly the way I interpret it, General.”

“Right!” Sickles slapped his thigh. “General Birney, you will advance your division and pierce that enemy column and take possession of that road.” Sickles read the rest of the message and then continued. “General Hooker has released General Whipple’s division for our use. We will place it in reserve here at Hazel Grove. He has also given us the Sharpshooter regiments. You will use them as a screen in front of your lead brigade. General Berry’s division will remain as army reserve near the Chancellor House.”

Birney frowned and nodded hesitantly.

Sickles raised his eyebrows. “What is the matter, General?”

Birney wore a reproachful look. “I think General Hooker’s intent is only to harass the enemy movement.”

“Oh, I disagree,” Sickles said. “He has clearly given us permission to attack the enemy column.”

Birney was silent, and Sickles continued. “I do intend to advance cautiously. That is why I am sending out the Sharpshooters as a screen.”

Birney shook his head. “But I don’t think General Hooker wants to bring on a general engagement. If we advance too far, we might be exposed in case the enemy does flank us.”

Sickles smile disappeared. “General Birney,” he snapped, “we have received permission to move forward. Why do we have to question it? If it leads to something more, then so be it!”

Birney grimaced and then nodded his acknowledgment of defeat. “As you wish, sir. I will be with my lead brigade if you need me.” He offered a stiff salute, mounted his horse, and rode down the hill toward the woods.

Sickles looked at Tremain and shrugged. Tremain smiled and pulled a silver flask from his coat pocket. "Care for a libation, General?"

"An auspicious start to a glorious day!" Sickles gulped a burning mouthful of brandy. He pulled his cigar case from the inside pocket of his jacket. There was only one cigar left. He took it and held the empty case in the air. An apologetic orderly rushed to fill it. Sickles methodically cut and lit his cigar. He took a deep draw and stared at the burning end. "So what did you tell Hooker that made him change his mind?" he exhaled.

Tremain shrugged. "If you can believe it, I actually told him the truth. I said the enemy had been moving across our front for almost four hours and was obviously a large part of Lee's army. They could even possibly be retreating. Told him we didn't know what they were up to and would not know unless we pushed forward to the road."

"That was all it took?" Sickles raised a disbelieving eyebrow.

Tremain let out a short laugh, almost a giggle. "Well, I may have said something about letting the enemy get away after such a brilliant flanking maneuver."

Sickles couldn't suppress a chuckle. "That was sure to get General Fighting Joe Hooker's blood up!"

"Even with all that, he was still worried that Lee might be trying to move around our right flank."

Sickles frowned at the thought. It remained a troubling possibility, despite his bravado. "If they were up to that, wouldn't we be getting reports from Howard that the enemy was moving across their front?" He stared again at the end of his cigar as if expecting an answer from it. "Have we received any word from Howard?"

No one on the staff had received any report from Howard of enemy movement. Sickles scowled at this mystery and receded into thought. Now that he had authority to go forward, he was going to stretch the authority just as much as he needed. But just what would he find out there?

Meade reread the message and scowled.

"Anything wrong, sir?" Colonel Webb, his chief of staff, had noticed his reaction.

Meade shook his head, unsure. "General Hooker has sent out a circular. The Third Corps has intercepted an enemy column, and headquarters believes the rebels are retreating toward Gordonsville. We are ordered to reprovision and prepare to start the pursuit early in the morning." A vague uneasiness tugged at the edge of his consciousness. He looked directly at Webb. "Has General Humphreys reported the enemy pulling out in front of him?"

"No sir," Webb said. "Nothing at all of that nature."

"I was down there less than half an hour ago," Captain Mason said. "The rebels are as thick there as ever. General Humphreys even made a comment about it."

Meade tugged uneasily at his beard. *If the rebels are retreating toward the south, why is the group in front of us still blocking the way toward Fredericksburg?*

Webb broke the silence. "Sir, do you think the rebs are up to something different?"

Meade sighed and shook his head. "It just doesn't add up. There may be something else going on, but we just don't have enough information to know for sure." He cocked his head to listen to the sounds of battle to the south. *Yes indeed. They might have a surprise before the day was out.*

Sickles and Tremain listened silently as the sporadic firing began again. To their left and right, the woods crackled as Birney's brigades moved forward.

A commotion along the road caught Sickles's attention. A long line of rebel prisoners, escorted by Third Corps soldiers, was on its way up from the fighting. Their progress was greeted by a chorus of hoots and catcalls from Birney's infantry. A Union officer led the procession. Sickles mounted and rode down to meet the column.

Sickles looked down at the officer. "Who took those Johnnies?"

"I did, sir." The provost officer was grinning. His dress uniform appeared neat and clean, with no signs of having gone through a fight.

Sickles smiled indulgently at the attempted humor—provost guards didn't fight. "The devil you did." He looked down the line of prisoners and saw several green-jacketed officers riding toward his group. "Look, there are the Sharpshooters—they captured those men."

Sickles examined the rebels as they passed by. They were well dressed and appeared well fed. Some stared dejectedly at the ground, but most were defiant and answered taunts with their own gibes. One husky farm boy was boldly answering his captor's mockery with a warning. "You think you've done a big thing just now, but you wait until Jackson gets around on your right." An old stooped rebel with white hair looked up from the ground and directly into Sickles's eyes. "Y'all catch hell before nightfall," he drawled. Sickles smiled. He was used to hearing outlandish stories from rebel prisoners. He preferred facts over anything prisoners could tell him, and this Sharpshooter lieutenant was going to provide some facts.

"Good afternoon, General. I have a report from Colonel Berdan." The lieutenant offered a casual salute—perhaps a little too casual, Sickles noted. He nodded, and the lieutenant continued. "We hit the main enemy line and managed to flank them. This forced them to pull back. Part of the Johnnies retreated to the iron furnace down to our south, and the rest pulled back to a railroad cut about a half a mile farther south. We flushed them out of the iron furnace pretty easily, and these are the prisoners we took there. Colonel Berdan pursued the other group and managed to flank them in the railroad cut. They gave up without much of a fight. Those prisoners will be along shortly. We estimate we have several hundred prisoners altogether. They say they are the Twenty-Third Georgia of Rodes's Division. That's in Jackson's corps." The lieutenant hesitated. "They are telling everyone who will listen that Jackson is moving on our right flank."

Sickles interrupted. "Yes, I've heard some of their stories, Lieutenant..."

"Lieutenant Thorp, sir."

"We all know, Lieutenant Thorp, what outlandish liars these rebels can be when they are taken prisoner. My rule has been to discount heavily anything they might say. In fact, the complete opposite is probably closer to the truth." He paused to let his words sink in. "Were you able to find out where that road goes?"

The lieutenant nodded. "We have, sir. This road we're on intersects the road the rebs were on at the iron furnace. Then a single road heads south from that point. Tracks on that road confirm the rebs went down that way. We were able to follow it for quite a ways past the railroad cut. It heads generally southwest from there for as long as we were able to go. Rebs are down there in force, and we couldn't go any farther."

Sickles thought about this information. "South and southwest, you say. No road that heads to the west?"

"No, sir. Just that one road. Well, there is a narrow path, but it was clearly not used. Oh, one other thing. When we got to the railroad cut, we found we could see through a clearing, and there was another road about a half a mile toward the east. This road runs generally north-south, and it's loaded with reb wagons."

Tremain offered a map. He had added a fresh pencil lines indicating the newly discovered road and the road leading from the iron furnace. Sickles followed the line from the iron furnace down to its end with his finger. "This road appears to intersect the Brock Road near Todd's Tavern. That's a long way around if Jackson is making a flanking movement..." He shifted his finger over to the find the other road. "And the road you saw to the east is probably this Catharpin Road. That's a parallel route to the first road."

Sickles thought for a moment. The pieces of the puzzle were beginning to come together. "This confirms my suspicion that the rebels are retreating. There are two parallel roads headed south. Both roads are loaded with rebel wagons. We have obviously encountered some rear guard action." He looked around. All of his staff were nodding in agreement.

Sickles noticed that the Sharpshooter lieutenant had a definite incredulous look on his face. "You have something else to add, Lieutenant?"

The Sharpshooter looked around at Sickles's staff. "Only an observation, General. It doesn't sound like Bobby Lee and Stonewall Jackson to run off without a fight."

Enough. Sickles held up his hand. He did not have to debate this with a lieutenant, even if he was a Sharpshooter. "Thank you for your report, Lieutenant." The Sharpshooter left after another casual salute, and Sickles turned back to stare into the woods. Perhaps there was a way he could still salvage this situation.

After a few minutes of thought, he motioned to Tremain. "Major, send word to General Hooker. Tell him we are engaged with the enemy rear guard. It is possible to capture the enemy trains, but I need reinforcements on my flanks." He hesitated a moment for effect. "I will not move forward until I am reinforced." *There. That should shake Joe Hooker into action.*

Henry Taylor shifted uneasily in the midafternoon heat. Isaac was engrossed in a book on geology. "Isaac," he said, "you didn't finish telling me about the mutiny."

Isaac looked up from the book. "I didn't?" he asked absently.

"No, you didn't." Henry waited for a reply. Isaac was back to reading his book. "Ike?"

Isaac sighed and closed the book. "Where did I leave off?"

"Why don't you start at the beginning? That way, the others will know what happened, and we can avoid all of the rumors." He jerked his head toward the rest of the group, now beginning to take notice.

"Well," Isaac said, "it started when one of the boys in the Thirty-Fourth New York inquired about his discharge. They are a two-year regiment, and he had enlisted soon after Fort Sumter. The second anniversary of his enlistment was coming up, and he wanted to know when he could expect his discharge papers."

"Seems like a reasonable question," a nearby soldier, Private Cundy, said.

"It didn't seem reasonable to the army. The poor fellow was told by his officers that his enlistment date didn't count. They said the real date was when the regiment was sworn in to US service, which is in June."

"Yes, we have the same situation," Henry said.

Isaac nodded absently at this piece of information. "Well, to make a long story short, some of the boys in the Thirty-Fourth weren't too happy about this. They say their officers told them when they enlisted that they would be discharged in two years from that date."

"Isn't that the way it works?" Private Cundy asked.

Henry shook his head. "We are in the US Army, not the Minnesota army. The army counts your service from the date you were sworn in to federal service. Besides," he said, "there's a campaign coming. The army won't start discharging people until they absolutely have to."

Isaac chuckled. "You are a bona fide cynic, Sergeant Taylor. The same idea probably occurred to those fellows in the Thirty-Fourth, and they decided they were done soldiering. They laid down their arms in protest. Said something about a false enlistment." Isaac looked around at the group with an arched eyebrow. "This didn't set very well with our generals. First off, General Sully came down to talk them out of it. That didn't do much good. Then General Gibbon came with some men from the Fifteenth Mass. He told the boys from the Thirty-Fourth that they were mutineers and that he would order the Fifteenth Mass to open fire if they didn't pick up their rifles and get back to duty."

Private Cundy whistled. "Them boys in the Fifteenth are hard. Don't doubt they would've done it."

Isaac clucked and nodded his head. "No doubt about that at all. The protesters probably considered that possibility. They picked up their weapons and gave three cheers for General Gibbon. He told them to be quiet. Wanted them to fight, not cheer."

"So that's why General Sully was relieved of command," Henry said. He shook his head sadly. "Sully was a good man. We'll be hard pressed to find someone as good as him."

"Do you want to know what else I heard, Henry?" Isaac asked.

Henry didn't answer. He was watching the E Company commander, Captain Muller, walking briskly toward the company position from the direction of Regimental Headquarters. Muller hailed Lieutenant Demarest, E Company's second-in-command, and they began a discussion. The two officers were quite different in appearance. Demarest was tall with sandy hair and a full beard, while Muller was rather short with dark hair and pork-chop sideburns. Back when the company had a full complement of one hundred men, there were two lieutenants acting as platoon leaders, but now, with fewer than forty men, Muller took control of one platoon, and Demarest was in charge of the second. In reality, most of the day-to-day supervision was in the hands of the two platoon sergeants, Henry and Sam Stites. The first sergeant, Joe Trevor, ran the company from an administrative standpoint. Demarest finished his conversation with Muller, saluted, and began to walk quickly toward Henry's group. *Perhaps we will finally do something besides lay around,* Henry mused.

Demarest hardly slowed down as he walked past. "Orders to prepare for movement. Get your people ready, Sergeant Taylor. Have them draw extra ammunition and three days' rations."

Sickles led his retinue away from the firing, moving north back along the road to Hazel Grove. He halted as they reached the iron furnace. Sickles dismounted to examine the dirt road running past the furnace, rutted and pockmarked by the passage of thousands of men, wagons, and horses. He kicked at a rut and turned away in frustration.

One of his aides found a chair in the furnace's office, and his orderlies soon had coffee brewing on the stove. Sickles knew he could do nothing but wait—wait and hope that Hooker would react quickly.

It was well over an hour later when a lone horseman rode up. Sickles recognized him as a captain on General Howard's staff. Sickles rose to hear the message from the commander of the Eleventh Corps. He had cultivated a good relationship with this one-armed West Pointer—Howard was highly regarded by the abolitionists and Radical Republicans in Washington. A friendship with him made sound political sense. "Well, Captain, what is new with the Eleventh Corps?"

The young staff officer looked put upon. "Sir, I have a message from General Howard. General Hooker has ordered him to provide you with reinforcements. He has personally brought General Barlow's brigade up to your right flank." The captain hesitated. "General Howard instructed me to inform you that he is now without any reserves. He sent me down to tell you this and to find out more about what is going on to your front. General Hooker warned General Howard about an attack to our flank, and now he has taken away our reserves."

Sickles raised his hand reassuringly. "That was based on old information, Captain. We have determined that the enemy is retreating toward the south. We are actually engaged with the rear guard right now."

The officer cocked his head quizzically. "So, sir, there is no substance to these reports that the enemy is moving around to our right?"

Sickles smiled and nodded. "Tell General Howard, that the enemy is retreating. The Eleventh Corps has nothing to worry about on its flank."

Meade started at the sound as it rolled in from the west—a strange jumble of bugle calls, roaring gunfire, trilling rebel yells, and cries of alarm from thousands of startled throats, both human and animal. All of the day's uncertainties evaporated when Meade heard the sound. He knew at once what it meant—Lee had struck the army's vulnerable right. It also meant that the unprepared army was in great jeopardy and would have to fight for its life. There were only two fords linking the Army of the Potomac with its supply bases on the northern side of the river; a flank attack could easily cut them off from these fords.

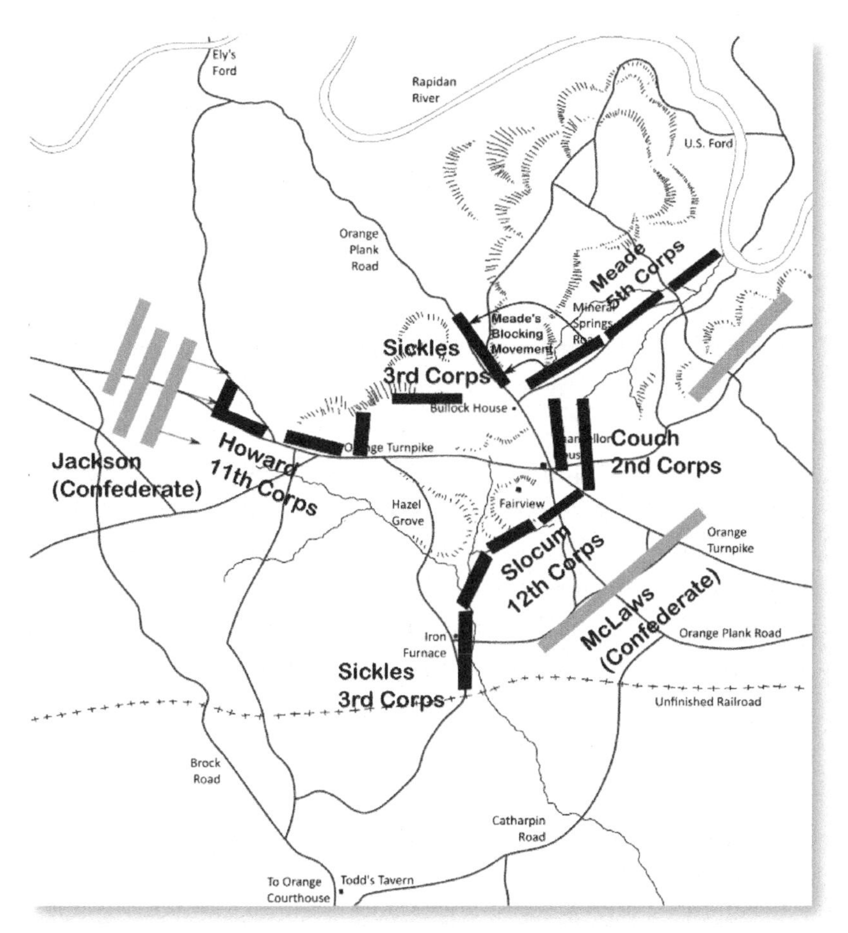

Situation—Chancellorsville 6 pm 2 May

Meade silenced the worried murmuring of his staff with an icy glare. There was not much time to react if the situation was to be saved, and there was absolutely no time for panic. He quickly scanned the map. Ely's Ford, the westernmost, was too far away to be saved, but he could hold the US Ford if he could get a blocking force in place.

"Colonel Webb," he barked, "get word to General Sykes to move his division to take up defensive positions along this road." He ran a finger along the road running at right angles to his own line and protecting the ford. "Tell him to hold this line at all hazards…tell the other division commanders to sidle to the right to fill in the gap." He looked up as aides scrambled to get the word out.

Meade shifted his gaze to Captain Weed, his chief of artillery. "Weed, Sykes's new position must be turned into a line that cannot be forced. Get every piece of artillery you can find, and place them in support of General Sykes." Weed was off with a nod and a quick salute.

Pausing to listen to the roar of battle pouring in from the west, Meade considered their chances. If they could hold on until nightfall, perhaps they could avoid being driven into the river. If not, the prospects were too grim to consider. He looked nervously toward the sun. There were still hours to go before sunset. They just had to hold on.

Chapter 2

May 3, 1863

A HAND SHOOK HENRY TAYLOR from his sleep. "You awake, Sergeant?"

Henry grunted and sat upright, rubbing his eyes. It was dark, but he could just make out the face of Lieutenant Demarest in the moonlight.

"Get your men up and ready to move, Sergeant Taylor. We have orders from Division to form for an attack." The lieutenant was already moving away to awaken the next NCO.

"What time is it, Lieutenant?" Henry called after him.

"A little past midnight" came the answer.

Henry yawned, got to his feet, and quickly moved among his sleeping men, rousing them. After collecting their gear, the men silently fell in to formation and waited for the order to move. In time-honored army tradition, the order took forever to arrive. Once on the move, the regiment followed the road down to the riverbank.

The moon was near full, hanging huge and high in the clear sky. In the pale light, Henry could make out the ripples in the fast-moving river and the black town on the far shore. Even though he could not see them, Henry knew that there were rebel pickets out there. He also knew they would be sitting ducks if they showed themselves on the riverbank in this moonlight. This was going to be another tough nut to crack.

Lieutenant Demarest came by. General Gibbon had called for a storming party, and Demarest was looking for volunteers. Henry silently thanked God that Isaac was on picket duty. Isaac was pretty unpredictable lately; no telling what he would do. Henry knew, though, that this storming party could very well be a suicide mission. He wasn't ready for suicide, not just yet.

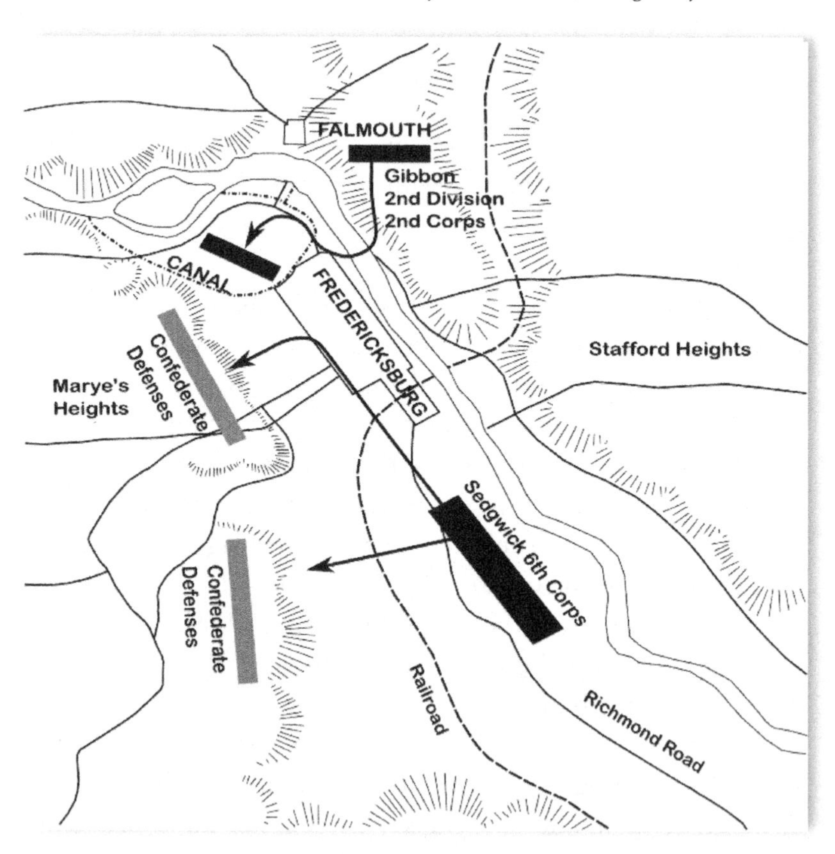

Situation—Fredericksburg, Morning 3 May

Scraping and bumping noises came from behind them as the engineers unloaded their wagons. Henry grimaced—the rebs were sure to hear the noise. If they weren't alerted before, they would be now. Henry held his breath as the storming boats and pontoons were dragged to the riverbank. It wouldn't be long now; the rebels had to know what was coming. Splashes announced the launching of the pontoons. As the pontoons slid into the water, the far shore erupted in a flurry of rifle fire. Engineers scrambled for safety behind the boats and pontoons. Some did not make it and were left dead or bleeding on the river's edge.

Federal infantry returned the fire, aiming at the flashes, and the rebel pickets soon ceased fire. *Probably conserving ammunition,* Henry guessed. After perhaps fifteen minutes of silence, the engineers ventured another try. The rebels let them get started, and as soon as they were all exposed, another blast of rifle fire knocked more engineers down and scattered the rest. Silence resumed, broken only by the gurgling of the river flowing past the pontoons and by the groaning of the wounded men.

Behind them, someone began swearing loudly and profusely. Henry guessed from the accent that it was General Gibbon. He was known to have a very bad temper and was universally considered a master of profanity. Horse-drawn limbers moved up behind them. Henry watched cannon being rolled into position and heard the order to load canister. He nodded with satisfaction at this development. That might be enough to keep the rebs' heads down.

After some prodding, the engineers resumed their work, only to be met by another volley from the other side. This time, the artillery answered, reducing somewhat, but not eliminating, the enemy firing. The engineers worked gamely in this reduced firing, but after what Henry considered an unreasonably long attempt, they finally withdrew to cover behind the pontoons.

Word came down that the division would wait until daylight, when they would begin the assault. Henry sighed and settled in for a nap. It had all the earmarks of another fiasco—just like December.

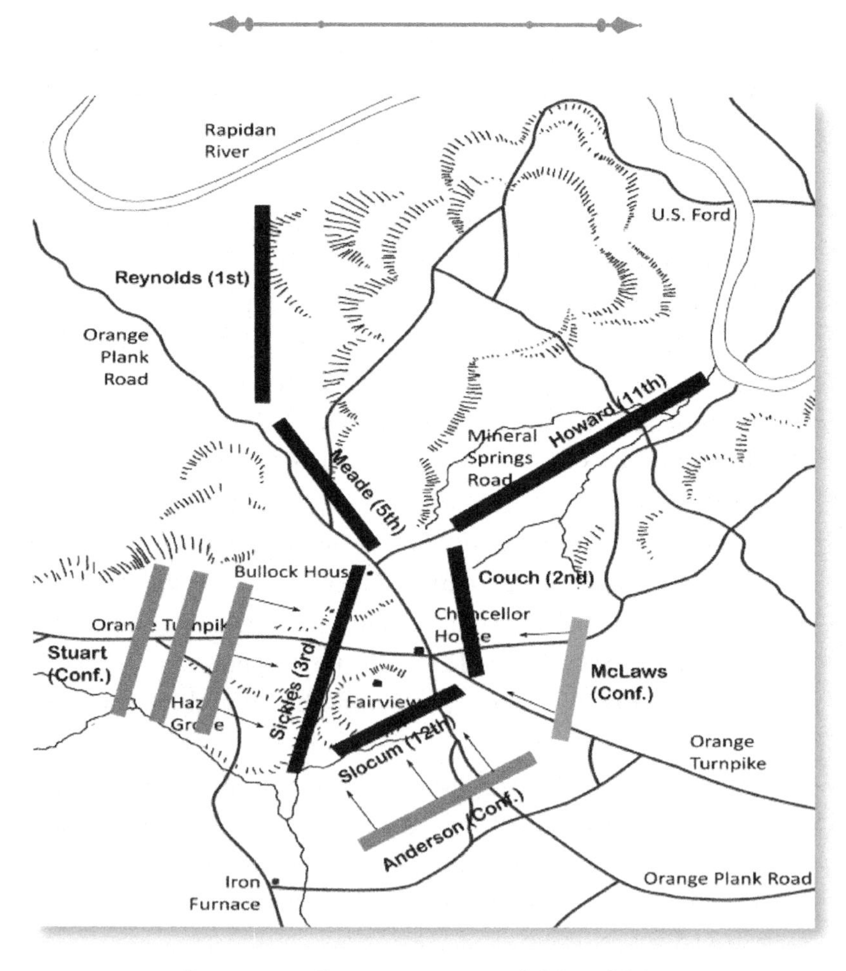

Situation—Chancellorsville 5:30 AM 3 May

The eastern sky was just beginning to turn gray, and the details of the clearing at Hazel Grove were starting to emerge from the gloom. Dan Sickles watched as Joe Hooker, eyes on the ground, paced slowly in a circle. As soon as it was light enough to see, Hooker had made his way up to Hazel Grove to evaluate the situation for himself. Sickles was glad that Fighting Joe had waited for first light. There was no telling where those lines were after the chaos of the past twelve hours.

Now Hooker was clearly wrestling with a difficult decision. He paced back and forth in front of the clump of officers. This was a Joe Hooker that Sickles had never seen and a far cry from the confident, almost brashly arrogant general who Sickles knew.

Hooker stopped abruptly and looked up. "You will have to withdraw from this position, General Sickles."

The order shocked Sickles. He had fought throughout the night to extract his corps from an extended position and bring them back to the comparative safety of this position—one that he knew had some inherent strengths. "But General," he said, "this is an excellent position for artillery. We can't just give it up."

Hooker shook his head forcefully. "It may be an excellent position, but it is outside our new lines." He stopped to look directly at Sickles. Even in the gray light of dawn, they were close enough for Sickles to see Hooker's eyes. There was a strange, uncertain, almost lost look that Sickles had never seen before in Fighting Joe. That glance unnerved Sickles, and he quickly looked away. "There is no way we can hold this position," Hooker said. "We need your corps to help form a line farther to the east that we have at least a chance of holding."

Sickles nodded glumly. He was still in shock at Hooker's apparent state of mind. There was clearly no chance of persuading him to allow the Third Corps to stay at Hazel Grove and fight it out.

Hooker nodded back and gave a forced half smile. "You will march by the most practicable route to Fairview and occupy a new line of entrenchments perpendicular to the Plank Road. General Warren and his staff will show you the exact position we have in mind." Then he was off, followed by a small group of aides down a gravel-strewn gully to the waiting horses in the field beyond.

Sickles glumly watched the party leave. Sighing, he motioned Tremain over to issue orders for the movement. *It was going to be a long day,* he decided.

The rifle pops downstream jerked Henry from a half sleep. It was light, with the opposite shore just barely visible in shades of gray and black. After a few minutes, there was more popping downriver, closer this time. Sounds of movement below prompted Henry to raise his head to get a view of the near shoreline. The pontoon bridges stretched half completed into midstream. Several dead engineers lay sprawled on the near shore where they had fallen during the night.

The storming party was already loaded into the boats, and they pushed off at the sounds of firing. Straining, they rowed hard for the far shore. There was no fire so far to greet them.

Downstream, firing came even closer. This time it was in the town. Henry squinted into the gloom. He could see flashes of rifle fire in the streets. The Sixth Corps boys were getting close.

Suddenly, a soldier appeared on the far shore, his blue tunic appearing black in the twilight. "The Johnnies have skedaddled," he shouted. "It's safe to come over."

Henry sighed with relief at the news and at the sight of the storming party scrambling up the bank on the far shore with no opposition. He realized that he had been holding his breath.

The engineers swarmed onto the pontoons—they would soon have the bridge completed. Already, officers were shouting orders to fall in. Henry stood and looked around. *Out of the frying pan and into the fire,* he thought.

Dan Sickles bit down hard on his cold cigar. Things were not going well at all. It had started off well enough—he had managed to extract his artillery and infantry along a freshly hewn road through a swamp and occupy the new positions with little interference from the enemy. Sickles was proud of his corps for that feat. He just wished the New York reporters could see his boys at work. After that, however, it was all downhill. Enemy pressure all along his line became intense, and his infantry fought off wave after wave of attacks. Here and there, the line broke, and Sickles was forced to plug the gaps with an ever-dwindling reserve. Ammunition was running out, and to make matters worse, rebel batteries now occupied Hazel Grove, pouring fire down onto the exposed Third and Twelfth Corps lines.

Sickles scowled and raised his field glasses for a look at the Hazel Grove clearing that he had only abandoned several hours before. "Must be five or six batteries up there," he snorted.

Randolph was at his side. "I count at least thirty pieces, General. It is a strong position for artillery."

"So it is," Sickles muttered. "Abandoning it to the enemy was a mistake." Sickles chewed angrily on his cigar. He should have argued more forcefully with Hooker against leaving it to the enemy, maybe even disobeyed orders.

"General Sickles," said an urgent voice.

Sickles turned as Major Tremain rode up. "Sir, terrible news! General Hooker has been wounded. I was there when it happened."

"Hooker…wounded…how?" Sickles stammered.

"He was leaning against a post on the porch of the Chancellor House when I rode up. As he leaned over to hear what I had to say, a cannonball stuck the post. Split it in two. A piece of the post struck General Hooker on the side from head to foot. We all thought he was dead, but they finally managed to revive him." Tremain paused. "I'm afraid he will not be able to remain in command."

Along with the shock of the unexpected news, a glimmer of a thought danced in his mind. "That would leave Couch in command." *There might be an opportunity here.* "Tremain, send a rider to find General Couch. Tell him it would not be difficult to regain the lost ground around Hazel Grove with the bayonet. If he approves and I am reinforced, I can move immediately."

Tremain scrambled to get a message together while Sickles contemplated the odds. It might be possible to make something out of this after all.

The roar of battle rose above the thick woods, and Meade raised his chin as if to sniff the scent of battle.

Humphreys was beside him. "What do you think, Meade?"

Meade made a motion of disgust. "Judging from the location of the noise, I'd say we are still being driven."

"We should have been able to hold on to the defensive positions we established last night," Humphreys replied.

Meade shrugged. "It's these woods. We can't use our artillery effectively, and the rebs can get right on top of us before we see them."

Humphreys shook his head. "And now we are in one hell of a mess. Hooker sure picked a great spot for a defensive battle."

Meade nodded sadly and turned to his staff waiting behind him. "Who was at Hooker's headquarters last?"

Major Biddle, another aide, stepped forward. "I was, sir."

"So what's the latest gossip?"

Biddle cleared his throat and began. "Well, General Sickles withdrew from Hazel Grove early this morning on General Hooker's orders. And now, the rebs have placed artillery on that hill and are blasting the hell out of our line. Everyone at headquarters is saying that it is the only decent position for artillery around. Our artillery can't respond effectively, and the enemy has the upper hand."

"If Henry Hunt was here, he would make sure that no rebel guns would survive on that hill," Meade growled.

"Where is Henry, anyway?" Humphreys asked.

Meade shook his head in disgust. "He had some kind of falling out with Hooker and is no longer chief of artillery. Hunt is back in the rear somewhere. Imagine—the best damn artillerist in the Army of the Potomac is left on the other side of the river!"

Meade wasn't finished with Biddle, though. "What about the rest of our lines?"

The major shook his head. "Not good. In the woods, the rebs keep outflanking and overrunning our positions. We can't set up a coherent defensive line in all this undergrowth. Out in the open, the reb artillery up on Hazel Grove is tearing everything apart. They say units are withdrawing for lack of ammunition."

"They can't be resupplied?" Meade was incredulous.

"The fire is so intense that they are not able to bring pack horses or mules across the open area behind the lines. There is some good news, though. Prisoners have reported that General Jackson was wounded last night. No one knows how severe, but he had to give up command. General Hill was wounded also, and they say JEB Stuart is now in charge of Jackson's Corps."

"Hmm," Meade replied. "Perhaps there is a little bit of hope after all. A cavalry general in command of an infantry corps... let's see what Webb has found out."

Meade motioned toward his chief of staff as Webb galloped up at the head of a group of horsemen. "General," Webb called out, "it's just as General Taylor reported. I saw it myself. The enemy has no reserves—the way is open around their flank. I can lead the way!"

Meade held up his hand. This required careful consideration. "Show me on the map what you found out."

Web dismounted and began to trace the enemy positions with his finger. "Yes, sir...General Tyler reported that he was able to break through the rebel line here and was not challenged afterward. It is clear that they have no reserves in the northern part of their line. I rode around Tyler's right flank, and there are absolutely no Johnnies there. It's the end of their line, and our corps overlaps it. The ground is generally wooded, so we can achieve total surprise if we attack."

Meade listened intently. The rebel formation had lost all its structure, and the normal three-line tactical formation had degenerated into a single mass of men pressing forward. *They smell blood,* Meade told himself, *and they have thrown caution to the wind.* What was the most startling was that the enemy was moving directly across the Fifth Corps' front with their flank exposed.

"Is the First Corps up yet?" Meade asked.

"They are just coming into position on our right," Webb said.

"Just like Lake Trasimene," Humphreys said.

There were a number of blank looks, so Meade offered an explanation. "Hannibal's ambush attack on the flank of an entire Roman legion. He annihilated them." Meade looked around at his staff. "If we are going to make this work, we need to get busy. General Humphreys, prepare your division to attack forward on my command. Send word to the other divisions to be prepared to attack forward, and send word to General Reynolds about what we are up to. Colonel Webb and Major Biddle, come with me...we are going to see General Hooker."

Meade slapped his thigh. "We've finally caught Lee making a mistake. If we attack now, we can hit him with two fresh corps and roll up his flank. Without reserves, he will be unable to stop it. We can beat Lee here and now!"

The flotsam of battle littered the narrow country dirt road. Items discarded by soldiers rushing to meet the enemy lay in the grass at the edge of the roadway—knapsacks, overcoats, and other gear that the owners judged unnecessary for immediate survival. A deck of cards, forsaken by a newly pious private, added improbable flecks of color. The wounded were there too—ashen and bloody, moving slowly back in the opposite direction of the earlier blue tide.

Meade was all too familiar with this scene. The war was entering its third year, and he had seen the same scene in far too many battles. Some of the wounded looked up and recognized him. He returned the salutes and acknowledgments and noted with satisfaction that most of the wounded still had their weapons. He saw the Maltese cross of his own Fifth Corps on many of them and nodded with satisfaction. *We helped make them into good soldiers, John Reynolds and I...the Pennsylvania Reserves...God, it seems like a lifetime ago.*

A group of soldiers lay off the road near a large bush. None had weapons or cartridge boxes. Most looked dejectedly at the ground, but one stared out with wide eyes that seemed to have frozen at the moment when Stonewall Jackson's rebels rushed screaming from the underbrush. Each man wore the corps badge of a crescent moon.

"Eleventh Corps stragglers!" Webb spat out. The army had little regard for the Eleventh Corps, with its many regiments recruited from German immigrants. "I heard from a friend in the Second Corps that some of those fellows ran straight through their lines. They couldn't even stop them. They just ran straight into the rebel lines. Maybe the rebs were able to stop them."

"Yeah, the boys are already calling them the 'flying Dutchmen.'" Major Biddle chuckled.

Meade shook his head. "They only did what their officers prepared them for. They weren't properly trained or disciplined, so they only did what came natural. I don't blame the soldiers, I blame the officers." He looked back at the major to make his point.

"Besides," he said, "what Howard did was inexcusable. Hooker issued a warning about a possible move on our right flank. We all got it, and we knew to be on the lookout. Howard had an unprotected flank with no natural anchor. He should have taken adequate measures to this threat. I would have expected a good deal more from a graduate of the military academy. Oh well, he's the darling of the abolitionists, so he won't be made to pay for his mistakes." Meade thought of poor Stone, rotting in some prison on trumped-up treason charges. His only mistake was to be in command when some well-connected congressman-turned-soldier botched up a simple reconnaissance at Ball's Bluff and got himself killed in the process. Stone was made to pay, and the Congressional Joint Committee on the Conduct of the War was formed to second-guess every decision made on the battlefield. Now it was far more important to be ideologically correct than militarily successful. "And Sickles," Meade said. "He had half the army rushing to help him finish off a retreating enemy. You suppose he would have sent out some patrols to confirm that the rebels did not turn north. He has nothing to fear either; he is Hooker's fair-haired boy..."

Webb cleared his throat. Meade looked over at him and nodded. *Better not go any further with that line of thinking,* he told himself. Words like those could get him into big trouble, especially as he was seen as a McClellan man and therefore ideologically questionable. He was tense and anxious; best to calm himself down. Worry made him irritable and turned him into a "snapping turtle"—that was what his staff called him behind his back.

They reached the crossroads near the Bullock House, where the new army headquarters was supposed to be. Everything was confusion, and the group finally found one of Hooker's staff officers after asking a number of people. "I need to speak with General Hooker. It's urgent," he told the major.

"General Hooker is indisposed, sir. He was struck by debris from a cannon shot and is resting."

"Debris? Is he wounded? Did he turn over command?"

The major sighed. "He is not wounded, sir. It's just that a reb shot split one of the columns on the porch of the Chancellor House. General Hooker was standing nearby, and part of the column struck him. He's just a little shaken up, but he is still in command."

"Well," Meade said, "if he is still in command, then I need to speak with him."

The major looked trapped. He paused. "Very well, sir. Please follow me."

Meade smiled at Webb and motioned for him to come along. They left Biddle with the horses and followed the fretting major to Hooker's tent. The pair waited outside while the major announced them to the commanding general. The major appeared at the tent flap and motioned them in.

Hooker sat on the edge of an army cot, his coat unbuttoned. Meade could see no visible signs of injury, though he did look tired. His shoulders were slouched forward, and he stared at his hands as if he was fighting some inner despair. "What did you need to see me about that was so important, Meade?"

Meade took a breath and began his report. "Well, General, I sent a brigade to aid Couch at his request. The brigade broke through the rebel lines and found nothing behind it. The rebs have no reserves left, and they have exposed their flank. Reynolds and I can move our two corps down and hit them on the flank. We will roll them up, and they can't stop it."

Hooker sighed and held his hand up. "General Meade, who authorized you to advance that brigade?"

"I did it on my own authority, General." Meade said. "Couch was in trouble, and I was not being attacked. I was easily able to spare that brigade."

"You did it without my orders, General Meade."

Meade felt a knot tighten in his stomach. He took a deep breath and tried again. "General Hooker, we have two fresh corps in reserve, full of confidence and ready to fight. Lee has presented us with an opening to crush his left flank. If we act quickly, we can hit him before he has time to correct his mistake."

Hooker shook his head. "I placed you in that position for a reason. If I wanted you to attack, I would have told you to do so. I can't have my subordinates running off and moving brigades about without permission."

Meade saw this was failing. Best try another approach. "Sir, I was wrong in moving my brigade without authority. I take full responsibility for that. But General Hooker, this is an opportunity that will not come again. We have the opportunity to finally beat Bobby Lee." He grabbed Webb by the arm. "This man can vouch for the situation. He was there and can describe it!"

Hooker's face flushed in anger. "I have heard enough of this! General Meade, you were in error to send a brigade to support Couch without receiving permission from my headquarters. Your corps must stay in position to protect the ford. There will be no more discussion."

Meade saluted and brushed past the tent flaps on his way out. Anger welled up, and his face burned. He turned to Webb, who had followed him out. "I came here with the greatest opportunity of his career, and instead I am censured and sent away."

Webb was pale and could only shake his head. "God help our poor army," he finally whispered.

The pair walked dejectedly toward the horses. Biddle saw them coming and called to them. "The boys here say Hooker has called for General Couch. They think he is going to turn over command of the army."

Meade brightened and looked up. Grim old Couch the fighter—hard as nails—he would see the tactical significance of the situation. "Let's wait for a while to see what happens," he told his companions.

He turned at the noise of approaching horsemen. At the lead was Couch—slight, frail, unimposing, but with a fierce, cold determination in his eyes. Meade smiled and called out, "Couch, what's up?"

Couch gave him a wry smile. "Hooker's sent for me. Don't know what it's about." He slid off his horse and clapped Meade on the shoulder. "Well, Meade, I guess I should go in and see what the general commanding has in mind."

There was a murmur among the group as Couch walked toward Hooker's tent. It quickly subsided as each man strained to hear any possible snatch of conversation. The thumping of cannon not a mile away drowned out all sounds.

Finally Couch came out of the tent, icy and inscrutable. A voice behind Meade cried, "We shall have some fighting now!" Meade hopefully watched Couch approach, looking for any sign that might betray the outcome of the meeting. Couch, his head bowed, kept his eyes fixed on the ground.

As Couch neared the group, he raised his head and looked Meade in the eyes. There was a certain sadness in Couch's eyes, and a sense of resignation had replaced the earlier icy determination. Couch shook his head. "I have been placed in temporary command with orders to withdraw the army to prepared positions in our rear." Couch paused while a murmur ran through the assembled officers. He held up his hand for silence. "The Second Corps will act as rear guard for this withdrawal. Detailed orders for the move will be issued shortly." He looked around at the group. "Now, we all have a good deal of work to do."

The group broke up at this not-too-subtle hint. Couch put his hand tenderly on Meade's arm. "Sorry, Meade, I did what I could. There is no use. Hooker is a beaten man."

Meade nodded and shrugged. "We have squandered a great opportunity, Couch." Then he straightened himself. "I will support you in every way I can. Please let me know what I need to do."

Couch smiled. "Thanks for that, Meade. I'll let you know."

As Couch turned away, Meade had a thought. "Couch, since you are acting commander of the army, to whom will you delegate the rear guard responsibility?"

Couch turned back, surprised. "Why, Hancock, of course."

A group of riders galloped toward the Second Corps line. In the lead was a tall figure, sitting erect in the saddle. General Winfield Scott Hancock spurred the group on. His First Division had just been given urgent orders from General Couch, commander of the Second Corps, and Hancock was racing to carry them out. He was a tall man, at least tall for his time, over six feet in height with a powerful build and an imposing presence. His booming voice was said to freeze soldiers in their tracks. McClellan had called his performance "superb" at the Battle of Williamsburg, and from then on he was universally known as "Hancock the Superb."

An officer behind the lines, his right arm in a bloody sling, smashed open the top of a cartridge box with the butt of a rifle. "Where is Cross?" Hancock called to him. The lieutenant pointed with the rifle to the right. Hancock nodded and followed the gesture toward a group of officers.

There was no mistaking Cross—a red bandanna covering his bald head, red bearded, and wiry. He was the very picture of Mars in a Union colonel's uniform. Cross wore the red bandanna so that his troops could readily spot him in the midst of the smoke of battle. The colonel was in the midst of giving order to some subordinates. When he finished giving his orders, Cross strode over to where Hancock was waiting.

"Well, General," he said, looking up, "we've certainly picked ourselves a busy spot here!"

Hancock nodded and quickly dismounted. "Cross, it's probably going to get even busier. I've just spoken to Couch. We've been given a critical assignment." Hancock crouched in the dust and began to draw a crude map with a stick. "Here's the situation, Cross. This is the Chancellorsville crossroads just behind us." He drew a cross in the dust. "Our division facing east has been able to hold without a problem. The trouble is in the west. The rebs broke our line about a half an hour ago, and they are in the process of rolling up the Twelfth Corps flank. Everything to our south and west has fallen apart. The rebs are keeping up the pressure. They know we can't organize a defense as long as they keep pushing us, and they are going to keep pushing. They've got us in a bag, Cross. If they break through north of us, they will have three corps in the bag—ours, Slocum's, and Sickles's." Hancock paused and looked up at Cross. The leathery colonel nodded.

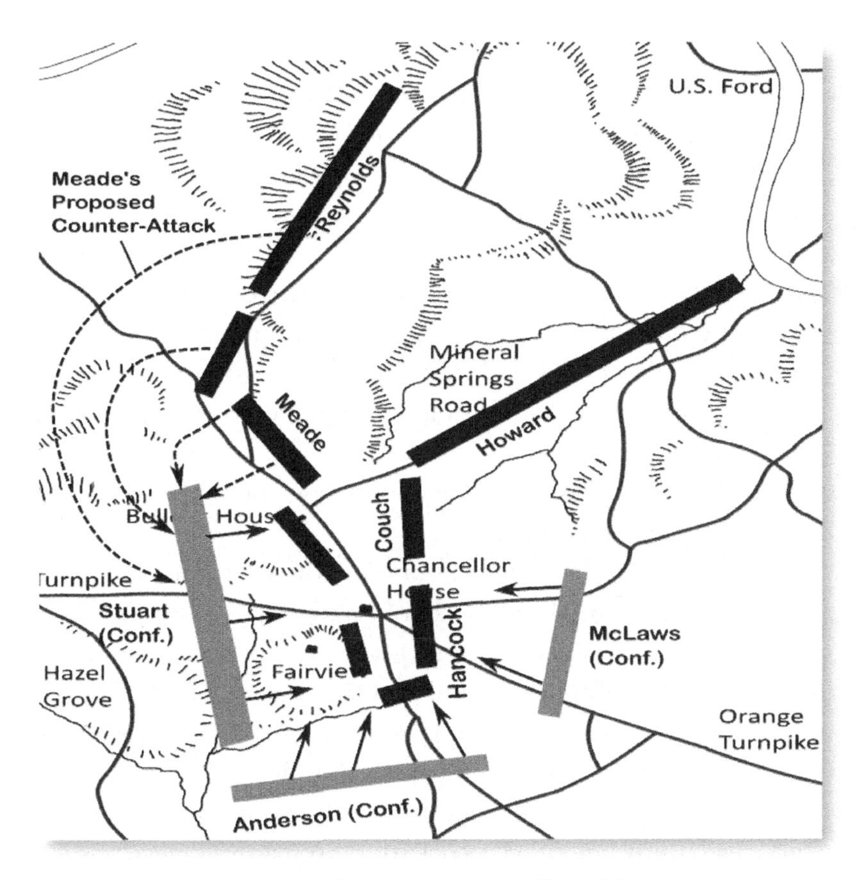

SITUATION—CHANCELLORSVILLE 10 AM 3 MAY

"The engineers have been working all night to construct defensive lines up here to our north," Hancock said. He drew a broad V at the top of the cross. "They say it's a strong position, and our plan is to withdraw the army there. But the Johnnies aren't going to let us do that unopposed, so we need time…time for the other units to get sorted out and in place. Our division has been designated to hold the enemy back until the rest of the army is ready."

Cross blew a slight whistle and looked up around the crossroads. His face contorted as he absorbed the impact of the situation. "Very well, General. What is your plan?"

Hancock broke off a piece of the stick and placed it below the left portion of the V. "French's division is up here to the north. They will stay in place to assist us." He broke off another piece of stick and placed it alongside the first. "Hooker has ordered the bulk of Caldwell's brigade from their position facing east to a position on French's left and Meagher's brigade to move from the reserve to Caldwell's left." The line of sticks extended almost to the crossroads.

Cross nodded and pointed to the open spot. "What about this space? It's pretty open."

"Couch has promised me as much artillery as I need. He will place artillery from Meagher's left flank all the way down to this crossroads. It will sweep the open ground to the south and west." Hancock broke off one more piece of stick and placed it on the right, parallel to the northern part of the cross. "We have a very strong position facing east." He placed a piece of stick showing this line. "The enemy has tried to force the position several times and have utterly failed." Hancock took a remaining piece of stick and placed it parallel to the east-facing stick. "I will take half of the units from the east-facing line and face them west."

Cross looked at the two sticks on each side of the northern road and rubbed his red beard. "So we make a corridor to hold this road open and allow everyone to move north to the new positions?"

"Right." Hancock placed the final piece of stick between the southern ends of the two sticks. "That leaves your unit, Cross. You are the linchpin of this position. I need you to hold the southern end of this corridor open. If you are forced back, both lines will be flanked, and we will be rolled up without a chance. I need you to hold on."

Cross continued to stare at the sticks on the ground. "Kind of a forlorn hope, eh, General?" He took a deep breath. "How much time do you think you will need?"

"As long as it needs. We have to gain time for the other units to clear the roads. If we get pushed back too soon, we will end up with an impassable mess, so we need to stand firm. I will come back as soon as I have the other units in place." Hancock rose and mounted his horse.

"We will be here." Cross squinted up at him. "Don't worry about us, General."

"I know you will, Cross. I can always count on you." Hancock turned his horse and rode off to the north to find his aides and collect the units he was to move to the west.

Sickles watched the line of troops make its way through his newly established defensive position. "Is that all of them, Tremain?"

"Yes, sir. That's the last of them. All we have out there is the line of skirmishers."

"It's been one hell of a day." Sickles sighed. "General Berry dead, and who knows how many others." He paused to consider the impact. "Once we gave up Hazel Grove, we never really had a chance. We just got driven from one position to another...that was our biggest mistake."

Their position was in a hellish cross fire. Artillery on the heights to their left front pelted them with long-range shells. Infantry and artillery in the woods to their front were raking them with musket and cannon fire. To their right, from Hazel Grove, not more than half a mile away, other rebel cannons were sending screaming iron at them. They had moved from their entrenched positions in the woods not ten minutes ago to this barren plain where it seemed every Johnnie in Virginia had them in their sights. This position left them exposed and naked, and they knew it; none of them wanted to stay any longer than necessary.

A shell whistled overhead and exploded in a shower of hot iron. Nearby a minie ball found its mark, striking the blue-jacketed infantryman with a hollow thunk, like an ax hitting a hollow log. The soldier crumpled and hit the ground without a sound. Smoke from their muskets hung in choking wreaths around them. Fire was all about them. Behind their position, the Chancellor House was in flames, shelled constantly by the rebel cannon. The woods to their front and right were in flames too, and the smoke rolling in from these fires carried the sickening smell of burning flesh. The dead and wounded were being consumed by this man-made hell. As the wounded around them groaned, the survivors began to look—look at their comrades to ensure they were still there—look toward their officers for an order to retreat that could not come too soon—and look to the woods beyond the Chancellor House, where they could find some respite from this rain of death.

A private looked up and wiped the stinging sweat from his eyes with his dusty sleeve. Out of the haze a rider appeared, tall and magnificent on a stately horse. The rider approached slowly, seemingly indifferent to the whine of minie balls and screech-bang of shot. The private blinked—it was suicide to remain mounted in a place like this. He squinted to make out the rider through the smoke. A smile of recognition covered his powder-smudged face. "Look, it's Hancock!"

A line of eyes looked up expectantly. Hancock looked down and felt their fear. He had always had an unerring sense of what the common soldier was thinking. Retreat from this position was unthinkable—it was the linchpin to the entire Union position. Hancock raised himself in his saddle and conjured up his loudest and firmest parade-ground voice. "Gentlemen!" He always called his soldiers gentlemen. Every eye was on him now. "We are left here to keep the enemy in check until a second line is formed." He rested his gloved hands on the pommel and looked out over the line toward the wood line where rebel infantry was forming. A minie ball buzzed past his left ear. Behind him, a rebel shell exploded with a crash. Hancock willed himself to remain motionless, a rock amid chaos. The rebel infantry was advancing now. He could hear the rattle of weapons being raised as the ragged blue line prepared to meet the charge.

The gray line edged closer. Hancock coolly judged the distance. There, that was about the right range. He looked down into the eyes of an anxious colonel and nodded. The line erupted in sheets of orange flame sheathed in billows of white smoke. Beyond the smoke, the rebel line sagged and hesitated.

Below him there was frantic rattling as the line reloaded. A second volley, and the gray line broke for the shelter of the woods. Hancock hooted his approval. "That's it, gentlemen. Pour it to them!" He rode down the line shouting his encouragement. "Take your time...pick your target...aim low...make your shot count." *They're back to concentrating on being soldiers*, he noted. *That's good.*

It was a tricky tactical situation, and Hancock was acutely aware of it. They had to let the Twelfth Corps move through their lines, form a blocking line, hold that line until ordered to withdraw, and then move slowly back while units behind Cross filed out, all under intense fire from the enemy. One misstep, one unit moving too soon, could open the doors to disaster. He would have to personally make sure that misstep did not happen.

Finally, word came that army was in position and they could withdraw. Orders were passed down the line to withdraw about a hundred yards. Hancock looked along the line—one regiment was running back. He spurred his horse toward the running troops. Running can cause panic, and panic would spread like wildfire. The last thing he needed now was panic. He came within earshot of the regiment's commander. "Why are these men running?" Hancock bellowed. Instantly, the men slowed to a brisk walk.

Hancock stayed with the line, each time walking his soldiers back a hundred yards or so and then facing them about to stand as the regiments on each side of the corridor filed out. Thankfully, the rebs did not aggressively pursue, but shells crashed in the trees around them, showering them in twigs and bark and leaves. Sometimes large branches came crashing down.

At last they reached the Bullock House clearing. Couch was waiting there to greet him. As the last of Cross's brigade filed through the lines, Couch smiled. "Very well done, Hancock."

Hancock nodded in acknowledgment. It wasn't his doing, though. It was his division. *God, how I am proud of them,* he thought.

The new Union line formed roughly three sides of a rectangle, with the fourth side formed by the looping Rappahannock to their rear. George Meade's Fifth Corps occupied the southwest corner of the rectangle, connecting with John Reynolds's First Corps on the right and the Third Corps on the left near the Bullock House.

George Meade rode slowly back and forth behind his lines, anxiously watching his soldiers improve their fieldworks in the hot afternoon sun. It would take them a few more hours to have really strong positions prepared. He glanced at his pocket watch. *Three o'clock—about three hours since we broke off contact with the enemy. Lee had us on the ropes and was sure to press his advantage, but when?*

A shout of warning gave him the answer. A mass of butternut and gray was emerging from the woods some eight hundred yards off. Meade raised his field glasses for a better look. The rebels were in column, not line of battle. The realization hit Meade that the enemy didn't know the federal lines were in front of them. *They're probably making for the US Ford Road behind us,* he reasoned. Another flanking movement meant to get between the Union army and their line of retreat. *Time to give the rebels a surprise.* Meade looked around to give the order. "General Griffin," he called out, pointing toward the advancing mass, "drive that column back into the woods."

Griffin rubbed his chin, considering the situation. This was his section of the line, and he commanded one of Meade's divisions. "Do you think, sir, that I might be able to use artillery instead of my infantry to drive them off?"

Meade hesitated. Griffin was an old artillerist, and he loved his cannons. The joke was that he would run his pieces out on the picket line if he were allowed to. “Well,” he began cautiously, “if you think gunfire alone can do the job.”

“Do the job?” Griffin snorted. “I’ll make ’em think hell isn’t half a mile off!”

Meade nodded his approval and watched Griffin quickly order the pieces into line. Captain Weed was there to help speed the action. Dismounting, Griffin strode in front of the artillery line, his face beaming. “Load double charges of canister, boys,” he ordered. “We’ll wait until the rebels are less than fifty yards away and then roll ’em along the ground like this.” He stooped and swung his arm like releasing a bowling ball.

The cannoneers quickly loaded and aimed their pieces, straining for the order to fire as the rebel column drew closer and closer. Griffin’s infantry casually checked their weapons, just in case the artillery couldn’t do the job alone.

When the enemy infantry was close enough to make out individual faces, Griffin barked the order to fire. Meade strained to peer through the smoke and debris. Was the artillery going to be enough? Through the rising haze, Meade could see the answer. The lead ranks of the rebel column had disappeared, and the column had stopped its forward motion. They hesitated for a moment, uncertain, and then began to form a line of battle.

The federal cannoneers rammed another double charge of canister home and let loose another salvo. The rebel line wavered as Captain Weed urged his artillerymen to load faster. When the smoke cleared after the third salvo, the rebel lines had receded, moving rapidly back toward the woods and safety. Griffin gave Meade a defiant grin.

Meade nodded in acknowledgment. *Yes, this is a good position. Let the rebels come on and try to take these works. They’ll be stacked up like cordwood in front of these positions if they do.*

Officers shouted orders to fall in. Henry Taylor wearily slid on his backpack and shouldered his Springfield rifle. It was afternoon, and the regiment had been marching back and forth all day. The sun had turned the day broiling hot, and they were all showing the effects of prolonged exertion.

Henry caught the eye of Lieutenant Demarest. "What's happening, Lieutenant?"

Demarest shook his head. "Don't know for sure. I think we're being moved back."

Someone groaned behind Henry, who nodded and looked after his men as they fell into formation on the dirt road. They were beyond the rebel works, on the south side of Marye's Heights.

"Wish we could just keep moving south to Richmond," Isaac muttered.

Henry just grunted and squinted toward the shimmering woods to their south. *How many Johnnies are there? Could we just keep marching? Sure would be nice—take Richmond and end the war. Still, the brass must know what they're doing. Maybe Longstreet is coming up with his corps. Wouldn't be able to march too far south with those boys in front of you!*

"Well," Henry finally said, "we have accomplished quite a bit today already."

"An uncommonly successful day," Isaac said.

It had been a successful day, all in all. They had made it across the river soon after dawn and maneuvered to participate in the Sixth Corps' attack on Marye's Heights. Gibbon marched his division to the right to attack the western side of the enemy position while the Sixth Corps came in from the left. Even Isaac was favorably impressed by the tactical approach chosen by

Generals Sedgwick and Gibbon. The only problem with the plan that Henry could see was a canal that ran between where Gibbon had marched his division and the heights they were supposed to attack. The rebels had burned the bridge over the canal, leaving Gibbon to fume and support with his artillery while the Sixth Corps boys did the dirty work.

Gibbon's division didn't get away scot-free, though. His infantry got in the way at times during the artillery duel, leaving some dead and wounded on the field. It was worth standing under that long-range artillery fire, though, to be able to see the Sixth Corps flags waving over the rebel works on Marye's Heights. How they cheered and cheered when those flags waved. If only the flags had reached there in December!

The last of the regiment fell in, and with a left-face, they began the march down toward Fredericksburg. As the column snaked its way into town, Henry could see smashed artillery caissons and dead horses. Farther up was that damned stone wall, now abandoned, the roadway behind it scattered with rifles, equipment, and lifeless butternut forms.

Beyond the wall, on the fields sloping down toward the town, hundreds of blue corpses were already starting to collect flies in the hot late spring sun. No one said a word—they didn't need to; they were veterans and had seen this same sight a hundred times before. It was a plain, inescapable reality of war. You could guard bridges for months and never even see the enemy. Then one day you are in the wrong place at the wrong time, and a single casual order leaves hundreds dead or maimed. It was simply a matter of luck, but sooner or later you were bound to get that order.

The column trudged through the town, with its vacant houses, walls pockmarked by bullets, windows missing, and doors smashed in. Henry looked around at the desolation, a coldness settling in his heart. It was a shame that these people had lost everything. Even so, they were secesh—they had brought it on themselves.

After crossing a pontoon bridge spanning the Rappahannock, the regiment halted, and companies filed off on either side of the road. Once the prescribed amount of milling around had been accomplished, E Company was ordered to take up a position near a battery of heavy artillery. Lieutenant Demarest came by with orders for the company to entrench. They were detailed to guard the artillery.

As E Company started to dig, firing began on the heights over to the west. First it was a pattering of rifle fire, then it quickly swelled to a full battle roar with the booming of cannon. Isaac, stripped to the waist, straightened to listen to the sound. He shot an impish look at Henry. "Sounds like Uncle John Sedgwick found some more Johnnies."

Henry raised his head to listen to the firing. "I think he's trying to force his way toward Hooker."

Isaac shrugged, and they both went back to work. From time to time, they would stop to rest and listen to the firing. As it began to grow dark, the firing tapered off. There was no official word as to what was going on, but rumors were rife. Henry was convinced that if a soldier didn't know what was happening, then he would have to create a rumor to fill the vacuum.

The regimental chaplain rode up as the men were cooking supper. Henry smiled—the chaplain was an excellent source of rumors. An easygoing man who loved to gossip, the chaplain had free access to regimental and brigade headquarters. Henry knew he could find out what was happening if he could get the chaplain talking.

The chaplain did not disappoint him. As they sat around the campfire, the story came out that the army had crossed the river upstream without opposition and engaged the rebels in a fierce battle. The chaplain said reports coming in from Hooker's main body claimed a great victory with over eight thousand prisoners taken.

Later, after tents had been pitched, Henry rolled himself up in his blanket and thought about what the chaplain had said. *A great victory—finally. Maybe we'll cross that damned river for good. Maybe the war will be over soon. Maybe...*Henry drifted off to sleep.

Chapter 3

May 4, 1863

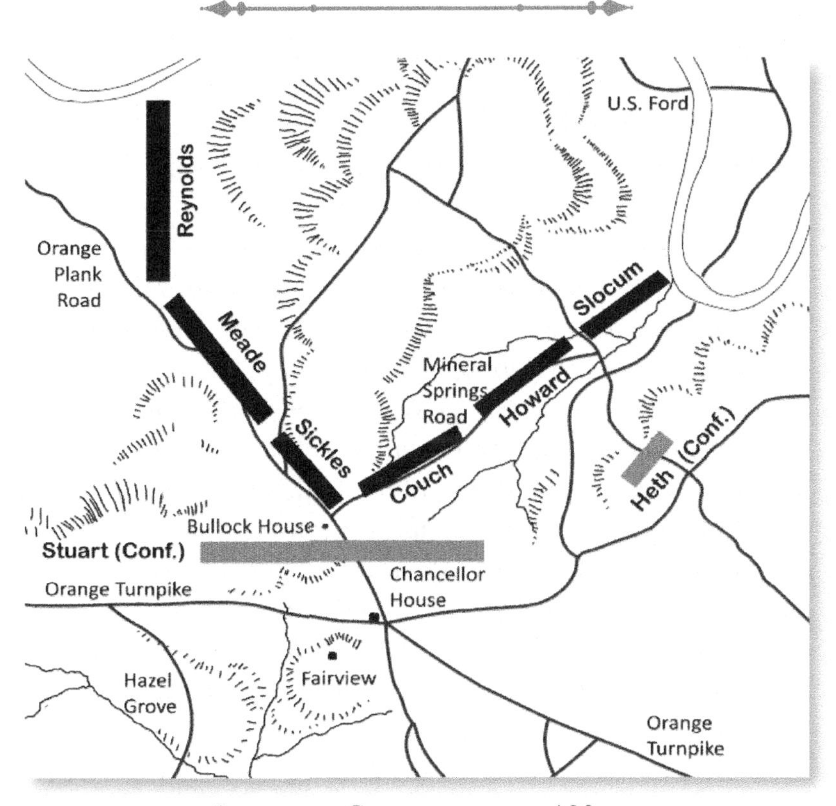

Situation—Chancellorsville 4 May

DAWN WAS JUST A FAINT glow on the eastern horizon, and the moon hung in the western sky, bathing the landscape with a pale light. George Meade rubbed his eyes and squinted out toward the black mass of trees. In this light he could see nothing. He knew that this was the best time to attack—just enough light to see where you were going and not enough light to be spotted a long way off. This gave the attacker the element of surprise and a chance to be on top of a drowsy defender before they were even aware of an attack. Meade was determined not to let this happen. "I hope those pickets are awake," he muttered. "They will be all the warning we will get."

"Yes, sir," Colonel Webb said quickly. Meade could tell he was thinking the same thing.

Meade's thoughts were interrupted by the boom of artillery off to the east.

Webb cocked his head toward the sound. "Seems like it's coming from the Twelfth Corps sector—where Humphreys was yesterday morning."

A horseman rode up the line, swearing and calling to the men. "Goddammit boys, get ready! They'll be coming soon enough." It could only be Humphreys. He pulled up close to Meade and dismounted with a little hop. Humphreys's legendary fighting blood was clearly up!

Humphreys offered Meade a quick clippie salute and motioned toward the wood line with a short upward bob of his head. "We're ready, General. Let 'em come on! We'll give them hell!"

Meade nodded. The positions had been strengthened during the night and were now much stronger than the ones the rebels had encountered yesterday. He actually hoped they would attack. "We can still win this battle if Lee makes a mistake!"

"Right, and if we don't make any more!" Humphreys snorted.

Meade grimaced. Mistakes were the only thing they had been able to do consistently since they crossed the river. The cannon booming suddenly stopped, leaving both generals looking toward the east in the eerie silence. The wood line to their front was quiet as well.

"Maybe they won't attack," Humphreys said.

"You're probably right," Meade said. "It would be foolhardy for Lee to attack these positions, even though we all wish he would." He stopped to consider the situation. "John Sedgwick is a much better target, I suppose."

Humphreys kicked at a clod of dirt with the toe of his boot. "If Lee believes he can contain Hooker with a fraction of his army and concentrate the rest on the Sixth Corps, then they are definitely a more tempting target."

Meade took a quick look around before answering. "You know Hooker will do nothing. He has been knocked senseless."

Humphreys shook his head slowly. "Then poor John Sedgwick is on his own!"

The early-morning sum illuminated the heights above Fredericksburg. Henry Taylor squinted to make out the Union signal flags "wig-wagging" on the crest of the heights. *It wasn't just a dream,* he thought. *They are still over there.*

"Coffee, Henry?" Isaac held out a tin mug of steaming brownish-black liquid.

"Hmm, thanks, Ike." Henry took the mug and sipped the hot, bitter drink, using his teeth to strain out the pieces of coffee bean.

Isaac sat down beside him and looked across the river. "We actually took those heights. Kind of hard to believe, isn't it?"

Henry took another sip. "The real trick will be to hold the position. Sedgwick's gone, and Gibbon can probably only afford to keep a brigade up there. A strong reb push will force us back off those heights!"

Isaac nodded thoughtfully. "Rumors say Longstreet may be headed up from the Carolinas."

"Yeah, that's what I mean." Henry paused to look at Isaac. "If he comes up, we will get pushed back across the river, and we'll have to fight like hell to hold Longstreet back until the rest of the army gets here."

Isaac nodded but said nothing. Henry knew what they were both thinking—that would be the end of their lucky streak. Henry reached into his knapsack for his diary. There was time for an entry.

Firing broke out on the heights, starting with a little popping but rapidly growing into a sustained roll. Henry put down his diary to watch. The rattle of weapon fire slowed to a fitful popping.

"I guess the Johnnies are looking for some breakfast," Isaac joked.

Everyone chuckled.

The firing increased in intensity again. Henry shook his head. "No, I think they want their works back!"

A sudden slackening of rifle fire was followed by a rush of bluecoats from the heights, with a ragged line of butternut close behind. Reaching the first set of lines below the hill, the blue line halted and faced about. A sharp volley from the Union line halted the rebel pursuit, dropping at least a quarter of their number.

Henry nodded with satisfaction. "That's the way to do it!"

Isaac slapped him on the back. "Yep, Henry, the Johnnies haven't learned yet not to mess with the Second Corps!"

"Clubs is Trumps!" someone exclaimed.

Henry smiled. "Clubs is Trumps"—grammatically atrocious, but quite descriptive of the *esprit de corps* in the Union Second Corps and the soldiers' pride in their three-leaved corps badge.

Behind them, the artillery began to fire, drowning out the conversation. The rebel troops on the height had drawn the attention of the Union cannoneers. Henry slid down into the rifle pit as shells whizzed over their heads. This was not a healthy place to be.

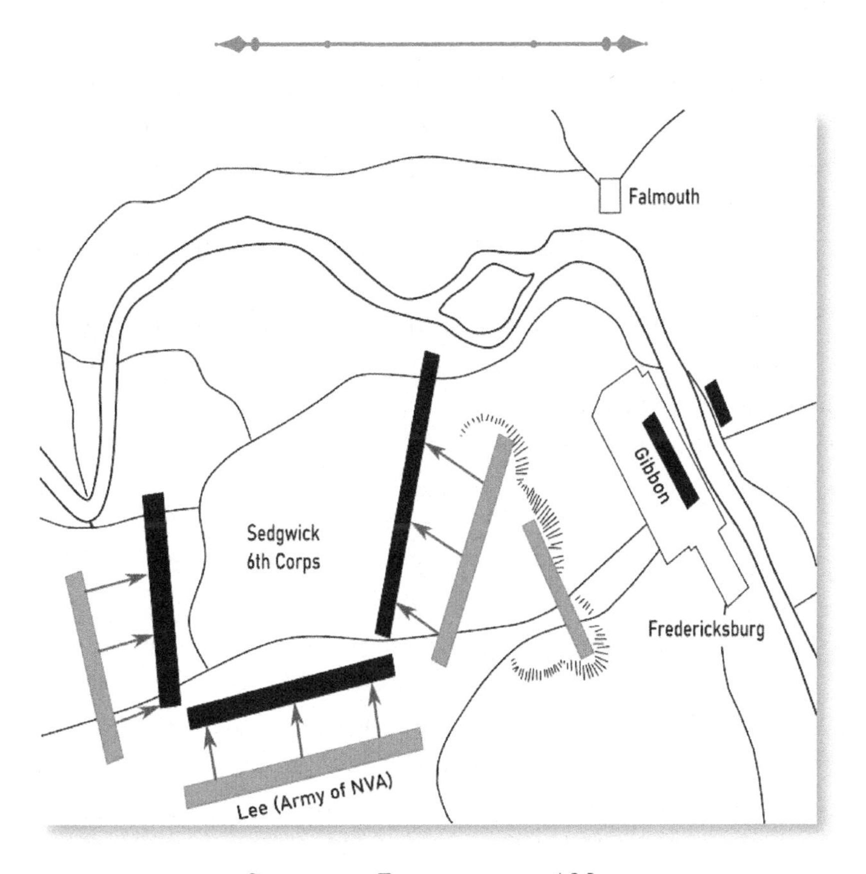

SITUATION—FREDERICKSBURG 4 MAY

Meade squinted in the midday sun as Colonel Webb rode up. He had chafed all morning with no news, so he sent Webb to headquarters to find out what was happening. He returned a quick salute. "What did you find out, Webb?"

"Well, sir, the Sixth Corps crossed the river at Fredericksburg yesterday morning with orders from General Hooker to attack the enemy's rear at Chancellorsville. They made good progress initially but were checked about halfway here. Now General Sedgwick reports he is surrounded and has asked Hooker for help if attacked."

Meade nodded. "And does Hooker intend to attack?"

Webb shook his head. "There are no plans to move from this position. I think General Hooker was expecting Sedgwick to save *him*!"

"I think by now Lee has that figured out and has shifted the bulk of his force to face the Sixth Corps," Meade said. "He knows Hooker is not going to move from this position."

"Well, that does appear to be the case, General. Headquarters has made no attempt to determine how many, if any, of the enemy we are facing here."

Meade sighed and shook his head. "Then God help John Sedgwick."

Henry watched the line of ambulance wagons inch their way toward the pontoon bridge across the Rappahannock River. Despite the best efforts of the ambulance driver, the wagons would lurch slightly when the wheels hit the ramp to the bridge, eliciting moans and cries of pain from the wounded inside.

Interspersed among the ambulances were groups of soldiers looking to get across the bridge. Henry's company had been ordered to the bridge to control the flow of these stragglers. His sentries had just stopped a group, and Henry spotted one of the stragglers trying to slip past. Signaling some of his men, Henry stepped forward to block the man from passing.

"Woah, woah, woah!" Henry held up his hand. "General Gibbon's orders. Only wounded allowed to cross the bridge." He looked the man over. "You aren't wounded, are you?"

The man's eyes darted to the sergeant stripes on Henry's sleeve and then to the three soldiers behind Henry, their weapons at port arms. He lowered his eyes and meekly shook his head.

"Right," Henry replied. "We are rallying by regiments here on this side of the bridge—First Brigade to my left, Second Brigade to my right. Find your regiment and wait for further orders." He warily watched the man move off and then signaled to his men to stand down.

Finally, the last of the ambulances crossed the pontoon bridge, and soon orders came to allow the troops assembled on the south side to cross. They moved forward in a torrent. Henry and his men struggled to maintain order in the crush. It seemed everyone was afraid of being left on the wrong side of the river.

Once all the troops were across, Henry led the last group of skirmishers back over the pontoon bridge. Their pace was slow, almost nonchalant. They all knew they were being watched from the heights above Fredericksburg, and they were determined to make the statement that their retreat was due to orders, not because the rebels had forced them to leave.

As the group reached the far shore, Henry turned to take one last look at the southern bank. To his front and right lay the ruins of the town of Fredericksburg. Above the city were Marye's

Heights. They had stormed those damned heights last December and lost thousands of men in that futile attempt.

Henry's face darkened as he spotted the red enemy battle flags in the works at the crest of the heights. This time it had been different. This time they had taken those works. Sure, maybe that was because most of Lee's army was off fighting Hooker up the river. It did feel good, though, he admitted, to see the Stars and Stripes waving above those works that had cost them so much in blood and death.

He set his jaw and turned to follow his men off the bridge. His eyes met the gaze of an engineer lieutenant for just a moment, until the officer turned away, his face showing a mix of anger and resignation. Henry shrugged. He had been in the army for nearly two years, and one thing he had learned was that nothing in the army is permanent. Sometimes you spend all day building something, only to have to tear it down the next morning.

As he stepped off the bridge, the engineers began to pull away the planking between the bridge and the shore. On the opposite side of the river, another team of engineers cut the lines holding the bridge to the shore. Henry watched as the pontoon bridge slowly caught the current and swung away from rebel territory.

"So goes the fortunes of war," a voice behind him stated.

Henry turned. It was Isaac.

"Well, it won't really matter as long as Sedgwick joins up with Hooker," Isaac said.

Henry sighed. He had seen too much failure today. "What do you think the chances of that are?"

"Oh, I wouldn't care to guess at the chances," Isaac said.

Henry turned away in disgust. "The way things are going, the odds are pretty damn slim, I would say."

The pair walked together up the corduroy road toward where E Company was assembling. As they reached their company, Henry glanced at his pocket watch—it was just five thirty in the afternoon. Shortly afterward, gunfire began beyond the hills on the other side of the river, in the direction Sedgwick had advanced. The company traded knowing glances as they listened in silence while the firing rose in tempo. They were all veterans of a dozen battles and had developed the habit of judging battle sounds. As the roar continued, they began to speculate on what it could mean.

"Sedgwick's done pitched into Bobby Lee," said one.

"Nope. Bobby Lee's done pitched into Sedgwick," said another.

Henry for his part kept quiet and listened, analyzing each change in battle tempo. The fight was not too far away, just over the hills, and they could clearly see the flashes of cannon fire through the spring foliage. Suddenly, cannon on the north side of the river opened up against the works on the rebel side, making the sounds from beyond the hills harder to hear. Sometime later, the company was ordered off the road and into a nearby field, where they were allowed to fall out.

Henry groaned softly as he found a spot on the ground. It had been a long few days of picket duty with little sleep. They were out of the habit of campaigning after spending most of the past five months in the winter encampment at Falmouth. *Not to worry,* he told himself. *We will soon be whipped back into shape!* Lying back with his head on his backpack, he listened to the gunfire from across the river.

The noise of the battle to the east rose in ever-increasing fury. Around their own position, Hancock noted, everything was quiet.

"That's Sedgwick catching hell," Couch said laconically.

Hancock looked over at Couch. His commander's lips were locked in that familiar thin line. Hancock said nothing—there was nothing to say.

After some time, Couch spoke again. "I'll wager that there isn't a division facing us right now. Lee's taken almost his whole army to pound on Sedgwick. Poor John. He doesn't have a chance."

Hancock considered this for a moment. "That's quite a gamble for Lee, leaving his rear so unprotected in the face of a superior enemy."

"Oh," Couch spat, "it's no gamble at all! Lee knows that Hooker is mentally whipped. There will be no offensive action from this army. Lee is perfectly safe from this quarter."

The two generals listened to the firing for a while longer, and then Hancock spoke first. "If I wouldn't be court-martialed for it, I would take my division right now and go to help John Sedgwick!"

Couch shook his head. "It needs the entire army. We could smash Lee in a vise right now if we would only take action—or, rather, if our commander would only allow us to take action!"

Hancock shook his head in dismay. "What has happened to the army? We never had these problems with General Scott in Mexico!"

"Well," Couch said, "we were mostly Regulars in Mexico, but the biggest difference is the leadership. As long as fellows like Hooker get high command solely on the basis of their political support instead of their generalship, then we will continue to have incompetence, disorder, and defeat."

Hancock stared off to the east in silence. There was nothing more to say.

Dan Sickles slid off his horse and tossed the reins to a waiting orderly. It was nearly midnight, but Hooker had requested to see him before the meeting with the rest of the corps commanders, so he came right away. Without waiting for an aide to announce him, he strode confidently into Joe Hooker's headquarters tent. Inside, Hooker and General Dan Butterfield, his chief of staff, were hunched over a map. Hooker looked up expectantly—his eyes showed more life than the day before. He had evidently recovered somewhat from his injury, Sickles noted.

"Sickles, thanks for coming early," Hooker said. "There are a few things we need to talk about before the meeting begins." Hooker motioned him closer and continued in a conspiratorial voice. "Butterfield and I have been reviewing the situation. We feel that our position here is risky. If the rebs attack and break through our lines, we could be trapped against the river with no chance of escape." Hooker paused and looked back at Butterfield. "The army would be destroyed, and Washington would be defenseless. We cannot allow that to happen."

Butterfield nodded vigorously in agreement.

Sickles saw where this line of thought was leading. "You must have also considered the political implications of withdrawal?"

Hooker looked again at Butterfield. The younger officer cleared his throat and smiled wryly. "Yes, we believe we can portray the engagement of the past few days as strategically insignificant. Based on the new situation and the implied threat to the army and the capital itself, we can justify the withdrawal as the only prudent action possible."

"Yes, I can see how we could sell that." Sickles paused and pursed his lips in thought. "It would hurt the argument, though, if the professional soldiers, your other corps commanders, came out publicly in opposition to the withdrawal."

"Exactly!" Hooker brightened, seemingly relieved that he didn't have to spell out the sordid truth. "That's what we need your help with. Butterfield, please tell Sickles your idea on how we can get around this."

Hooker's chief of staff moved closer to Sickles and looked him in the eye. "We have called a council of war and will vote on attacking or withdrawing. Under the circumstances, an attack would be out of the question."

"Have you counted the possible votes?" Sickles said. "These fellows are fighters, and the vote may well backfire."

Butterfield shook his head. "We don't know exactly how everyone will vote. That is where we are relying on you. We need you to convince those on the fence to vote for withdrawal." Butterfield looked at Hooker and smiled. "Of course, the commanding general will be ready to overrule any vote of the council of war that might cause undue risk to the army or to Washington. We all know what the president thinks of councils of war."

Sickles thought about this idea for a while. It was risky, but it did present some very appealing benefits if they could pull it off. Yes, the corps commanders have not had much sleep lately. They would be tired and not thinking clearly. Sickles could twist the conversation around so it could be used to his advantage, no matter what the outcome of the vote. "Fine," he said. "I think we can do it. Why don't you two plan on leaving the group for a while? I can get them to speak their minds more freely if we are alone."

Hooker nodded. Butterfield moved even closer. "There is another thing...the public will need someone to blame for what happened."

"Yes," Sickles whispered, "and you want to make it easy on the Committee for the Conduct of the War to find their friends blameless."

"Uh, exactly. Do you have any ideas?"

Sickles looked at the two officers. *Well,* he thought, *certainly not Dan Sickles!* "It seems to me that no officer with a suspect political reputation was involved in what transpired. That would be the easiest and most convenient way out. Howard is too highly considered by the radicals, so the committee would shy away from finding him at fault. I think we should blame the people everyone loves to hate—the Germans, the Dutchmen of the Eleventh Corps."

Butterfield smiled with the realization of what this idea could mean. "And the committee could find that no officer was to blame, but the public would still have someone to direct their anger at—brilliant!"

"Yes, a group with no power to defend itself and a group the public knows can't do anything right anyway." Sickles chuckled, pleased with himself for thinking of the idea. "I have some contacts with the press, as you know. We can all drop some subtle hints that the stampede of the Eleventh Corps' Dutchmen was the ultimate cause of all the troubles."

Butterfield produced a silver flask and offered him a drink. Sickles swallowed a mouthful of the whiskey and smiled contentedly as it burned its way down to his stomach. He pulled over a camp stool and lit a cigar to await the arrival of the other corps commanders. Hooker at first refused the flask, then took a hesitant drink—he had sworn off drink while he was maneuvering against Lee. Sickles noted that some of the normal color was coming back to Hooker's face and could not help wondering if the recent lack of fight in Fighting Joe Hooker was due to a sudden lack of whiskey in Fighting Joe.

Sickles watched as the other corps commanders arrived. Meade entered the tent, obviously exhausted but with eyes blazing in anger. *He is full of fight,* Sickles thought. *There is no doubt what side of the fence he is on!* Couch arrived on Meade's heels, pale and thin, with his lips pressed together into a thin line, fighting any outward display of emotion. *A swing vote,* Sickles decided. Reynolds came in too, shuffling wearily toward a seat. Beneath the fatigue, Sickles could see another emotion, a sullen rage. *Better consider him an opposing vote,* Sickles decided. Howard slid in, head down, avoiding eye contact. *No telling how he would vote.* Warren, the chief engineer, also came in. Sickles frowned at this last arrival. He would prefer that a rested professional not be in on the discussion. It could make his task more difficult.

Once they had all found a seat, Hooker looked around and began. "Thank you for coming at this late hour. We will begin without General Slocum. He did not receive notice of this meeting until quite late and will not be able to make it here in time." Hooker paused and cleared his throat. "Now, then, our situation is at a critical point. We are in prepared positions, but we do not know how long these positions can hold under renewed enemy pressure. I am, quite frankly, concerned with the want of steadiness of some of our troops." Sickles noted that Howard flinched at this remark and began to play with his coat buttons using his lone hand. "General Sedgwick reports that the Sixth Corps is under extreme pressure. We cannot hope for any support from that direction. Our mode of attack from this salient would have to be through wilderness roads against fortified positions. We have one route of withdrawal across the river. Loss of this ford would be disastrous for the army."

Hooker paused and looked around. Every corps commander was weighing the impact of these words. "My operating instructions from the president are quite simple. They consist of two basic orders. First, I am not to place the army at risk of destruction. Secondly, I am to protect Washington by keeping all or part of my army between the enemy and the capital. As I interpret these orders, I see only two courses of action. We can either begin forward movement on our front at daybreak tomorrow and renew the battle with the enemy, or we can withdraw across the US Ford and put an end to the campaign."

Hooker motioned to Butterfield. "I would like you to discuss this among yourselves and give me your decision. We will return after you have had the chance to air your opinions."

As the two generals left, Sickles looked at Warren to see if he would take the cue and leave as well. He showed no intention of moving, however. Warren noticed Sickles's gaze and offered an excuse. "I thought you might want me here to discuss the terrain. My staff and I have made thorough surveys."

Sickles grunted and looked down. *How do I get him to leave?* "Well," he said, not looking up, "Hooker's gone and laid the real tough decision on his subordinate commanders. I suppose he will blame us if things don't go right." He looked quickly in Warren's direction. A new look swept across the engineer's somewhat cross-eyed face—a combination of annoyance and revulsion. Warren quickly rose and left the tent. Sickles smiled inwardly. He knew that Warren's honor would not permit him to remain while his superior was being maligned.

So, Sickles thought, *time for some action.* "General Meade, you look like you have something to say. Would you like to start things off?" *Best to get the strongest arguments out on the table before I tip my hand.*

Meade unclenched his jaws. "Well, yes, I do. I think, however, that I should defer to General Couch, as he is the most senior here."

Couch shook his head. "No, you go ahead, Meade. I don't have all the facts, and therefore I do not feel competent to give an opinion."

"Very well," Meade said. "I believe we should advance in the direction of Fredericksburg tomorrow at daybreak. We can get Lee in between ourselves and Sedgwick. There is a chance we can crush him a vise. Besides, the issue of Washington's safety has become such a cliché that I would dismiss it from consideration."

Reynolds, who had been rubbing his eyes and fighting the urge to nod off, raised his voice. "I agree with Meade. We should attack tomorrow. I have not been seriously engaged, so therefore I will not urge my opinion. Meade has my proxy." With this, he lay back on the bed and closed his eyes.

Sickles shifted his gaze to Howard. He locked eyes with him for just a second and was overwhelmed with a sorrowful, reproachful look. Howard took a deep breath. "We all know that the army's current troubles can be laid on the doorstep of the Eleventh Corps, due to our poor performance. My men are mortified and are now ready for the work required to regain their good name. I believe we should attack also. My corps' performance does not cloud my decision. I strongly feel it is the right thing to do."

Sickles weighed his position. *Three to one, with one abstention. Not great odds, but maybe I can do something with it.* "I am not professional military, so I will have to defer to you gentlemen on the military aspects. The political aspects, however, I understand quite well, and as a former politician, I feel quite qualified to comment on them. We all know that the Peace Democrats and

Copperheads have made large gains in the last election. They are placing increasing pressure on the administration to come to some terms with the Confederacy. The public is expressing a growing peace sentiment, and the danger of European recognition of the Confederacy is growing as well. Given these conditions, the cost of defeat is so great that we must withdraw."

Couch stirred on his camp stool. "I would vote for an offensive if someone other than Hooker was in charge, but as it is..." He trailed off bitterly.

Sickles nodded to Couch. *Three to two. If I can get Howard to bend, I will have it sewn up!*

"What is so wrong with the position we are in right now?" Meade grumbled. "Why don't we just stay right here and fight it out?"

"Well," Sickles said, eyeing Howard and Couch, "what if the Johnnies break through? They have already broken through several well-prepared lines in the past several days."

Couch said nothing and looked away. Howard pulled at his beard with his one hand and spoke up. "In that case, we would have to stage a fighting withdrawal. If the river is not too high, we could probably cross the infantry at several places. The artillery and trains would require a pontoon bridge. We would probably lose a good deal of our artillery."

Meade sighed. "If the rebs catch us withdrawing, we won't be able to get the guns out anyway."

Sickles smiled at Meade and looked around at the other officers. "It seems to me that in any scenario, victory is doubtful. I really don't think that the effects of withdrawal would be fatal. If we weigh the two options objectively, I believe withdrawal is the less risky one."

Howard was nodding.

Good. Just a little more, and I might have Howard on my side.

There was a rustling of the tent flap, and Hooker entered with Butterfield behind him. *Damn,* Sickles thought. *Why couldn't you wait another five minutes?*

Hooker looked around and rubbed his hands together. "Have you had a chance to discuss the situation?" A murmur of assent rose from the group. "Well, what do you think...Couch?"

Couch shook his balding head and did not look up. "We should withdraw. No positive effort can be made in the present situation."

Meade stood and looked around at the other men. "The army will not be able to withdraw. We will lose our guns. Withdrawal is riskier than an attack." He leaned over to wake Reynolds.

Howard nodded and looked at Hooker. "I agree with Meade."

Reynolds was now awake and slightly aware of what was happening. "We should not fall back!" He collapsed backward onto the bed and fell asleep again.

Sickles watched the polling with his mind racing. The count hadn't changed; he needed to twist things around now so at least Hooker could later say that his commanders were not opposed to withdrawal. "I believe we spoke about our concern for the army's supplies and the lines of communications, which are across one ford. These we all agree are in peril if the enemy breaks through our lines. I vote for a withdrawal."

Hooker pursed his lips and nodded. "I believe we can cross the river without the loss of a single gun. General Lee would throw up his hat to have us withdraw and would not fire a gun or molest us at all. He would be only too glad to have us go back. General Butterfield, what is the count?"

Butterfield looked at his pad. "It is three to two against withdrawal, sir."

Hooker straightened and looked at his subordinates. "I will accept the responsibility for ordering a retirement. It is the only prudent thing to do."

Meade snorted with disgust and crammed his black slouch hat onto his head. "You had already made up your mind to withdraw!"

Hooker said nothing, and Meade pushed past him and out into the midnight darkness. Shouts and curses floated back into the tent as the assembled aides were told the disappointing news.

Reynolds, awake and red eyed, shook his head in disgust as he left the tent. "What is the use of calling us together at this time of night if he intended to retreat anyway?"

Sickles waited until the others had left the tent and nodded at Hooker with a sly smile. It wasn't perfect, but it would be just fine. He had everything he needed to fix things up.

Chapter 4

May 5–6, 1863

MEADE PACED NERVOUSLY IN FRONT of his open tent, waiting for his division commanders to arrive. He had bad news to give them and he did not like it one bit, but it was better to give it to them in person. As they arrived, he acknowledged each of them—Humphreys, Sykes, and Griffin. He motioned for them to gather around a map spread out on a field table. Their aides gathered in a cluster behind them. "Gentlemen," he said, "General Hooker has ordered the army to withdraw across the Rappahannock starting today."

A chorus of nos caused him to pause. "This is a very strong position. We should fight it out here," Humphreys said.

Meade held up his hand. "I argued that position to General Hooker, but it was dismissed." He looked around at the group. "Those are our orders, gentlemen!" The murmurs died down, and he continued. "The Fifth Corps has been designated as the rear guard." He drew a line with his finger on the map. "Warren's engineers have prepared a third line of fieldworks in this position. On order, we are to move to occupy these new positions and hold them until we are directed to retire." He paused briefly as his three subordinates studied the new positions. "Now for some good news: General Hunt is back in charge of the artillery, and he is positioning every available cannon on the northern bank of the river to provide covering fire for our lines. We will not be left alone without adequate artillery support."

There was a murmur of assent from the group. "Be prepared to move on my orders, and remember: the enemy must not discover our movement, so absolute noise control is essential. Detailed plans will be distributed shortly. Questions?" He looked at his generals. "All right, then, dismissed."

The group saluted and began to break up. Meade turned to his staff. "Let's get busy, gentlemen; we have a lot of work to do."

With their picket duty complete, Henry Taylor led his detail up from the rifle pits on the riverbank toward the E Company area. After hours crouched in the rifle pits, his body was cramped and sore. As he reached his company area, he spotted a rare patch of grass and lay down and pulled his cap over his eyes. Just a little rest, he told himself.

He was suddenly aware of someone shaking his arm. Pulling his cap up, he turned to see who it was. Isaac was there holding out a piece of hardtack and a tin cup of coffee. "Sorry to wake you, brother, but they were brewing some fresh coffee, and I knew you could absolutely use some."

Henry sat up and grunted as he took the thick cracker. He looked quickly at the piece before biting on a corner with his back teeth. Made of flour and water and baked until it was hard as stone, hardtack was the staple food for the army on the move. In its natural state, hardtack was difficult to chew, so much so that the soldiers universally referred to it as the "tooth duller." It didn't spoil, though, and could be easily carried in a knapsack. Best of all, it could fill a soldier's empty belly when there was nothing else available, so even though they complained about it constantly, they still carried it.

Henry took a sip of the hot coffee to help break down the hard lump in his mouth and finally swallowed with the help of another sip. "How long was I out?" he asked.

"Dunno," Isaac said. "I was gone about a half hour, or so… got some interesting information, though."

Henry looked up from his coffee. "Yeah? What is it?"

Isaac leaned toward him. "Well, I heard from an orderly who was just back from taking the morning report to brigade headquarters. There was a big battle upstream. Lee attacked Hooker on the far side of the river. Most of the generals are dead, and the army has retreated across the river."

Henry shrugged. *Camp gossip. Never know what's true.* Henry believed the first part, disregarded the second, and considered the third a possibility. "Let's wait before we share any of this with the other men."

Isaac shrugged. "OK, Henry, but the reb pickets sure were chipper this morning. Maybe they know something we don't."

Henry was distracted by a conversation near him. "Look at that!" someone exclaimed. He looked in the direction the men were pointing and saw a brownish haze rising above the green treetops to the west. A dust cloud. There was some talk about what it meant.

Henry considered the haze—thousands of pairs of feet would make that kind of cloud. "That probably means our army, or part of it, is back on this side of the river. Maybe it's the Sixth Corps," Henry said. He turned back toward Isaac who was looking up into the sky in the opposite direction. "What are *you* looking at?"

Isaac replied without looking away from the sky. "Cumulonimbus clouds. Means we're going to have a storm soon." Isaac looked away from the clouds and over at Henry. "Did you ever notice how we usually get a storm after a big battle?" He thought for a minute. "Maybe it is all of the smoke from the gunfire that triggers the storm." Isaac paused again. "Or maybe it is heaven weeping at the wickedness of man."

Henry only grunted a reply.

"Sir?"

Meade woke with a start. Squinting in the dim light, he could make out Webb standing next to his cot, holding a candle. A moment of confusion passed before Meade remembered Webb was the duty officer this evening, letting the aides have some rest.

"Uh, what is it?" Meade asked, fumbling for his watch. Just after midnight. Rain pounded on the tent panels.

Webb set the candle down on the stand next to Meade's cot and pulled a slip of paper from his pocket. "We have a report from the bridge. The river has flooded, and the water is now over the pontoon bridges. They are impassible, and the bridge commander fears we might lose the bridges entirely. We are currently cut off from the army on the north bank."

Meade blinked, trying to clear the cobwebs. "What does Hooker say about this?"

Webb shook his head. "Hooker's gone—he crossed the river earlier in the day. The bridge commander did not know who to report to, so he sent the message to the rear guard—us."

"OK," Meade said, now fully awake. "Get this message to General Couch. If Hooker is gone, then Couch is in command on this side of the river."

Webb nodded and left to send the message. Meade sighed. *Maybe we'll get to fight it out after all.*

No more than a half an hour later, Webb was back, escorting Couch, Sickles, and Reynolds into the tent.

"It's true, Meade," Couch said. "Hooker's gone, cleared out. That means I am in command of the portion of the army on the south bank." He looked at the others for emphasis. "I am suspending crossing operations immediately. We will stay where we are and fight it out."

Meade looked at the others. Reynolds was nodding his head in agreement, but Sickles was motionless with an inscrutable expression. "Very well, Couch. I will await your orders." Meade said.

As he watched the others leave the tent, Meade rubbed his beard in thought. "Something wrong, sir?" Webb asked.

"Huh?" Meade was suddenly aware that Webb had returned to the tent.

"You have a strange look on your face, sir. I was just asking if something was wrong."

"I was thinking about Sickles," Meade said. "He made no response either way when Couch announced his decision. Sickles and Hooker are thick as thieves. As much as I want to fight it out here, Couch may have overstepped his authority. If Hooker wants to bring Couch up on charges, he has a willing witness in Sickles. Hooker is still the army commander, and Couch could be guilty of insubordination or disobedience of orders."

"I see what you mean," Webb said. "What can we do?"

"Webb, who do we have who is rested and is a good horseman?"

The colonel thought for a moment. "I would say Major Biddle. He is an excellent horseman with a large, strong horse."

"Good," Meade said. "Give Biddle a copy of the note from the bridge commander. Tell him to get it to General Hooker, and let Hooker make the decision." Meade paused to look at a map on the table. "If Biddle takes the US Ford, he will have the best chance of getting across the river. He will most likely have to swim his horse across, though. Oh, and tell him to be careful."

"Yes, sir!" Webb was out of the tent in a flash.

As Webb departed, Meade fixed his gaze on the single candle flickering on the table next to his cot. *Dear God, help us to discern the right path,* he prayed. Meade shook his head. It didn't feel right asking the Deity for help in killing God's other children. Meade was a religious man, stuck in the theological no-man's-land between the mysticism of his Roman Catholic father and the rationality of his Protestant mother. As a young boy, Meade lived in Cadiz, Spain, and had witnessed the full spirituality of the Andalusian Catholic tradition. He remembered vividly the processions of the hooded penitents and *pasos,* the religious floats carried by teams of men during Semana Santa—Holy Week. After his father's death, Meade's mother had pulled her son firmly into the Episcopalian orbit, but the memories of Semana Santa and the mysteries of the Latin mass endured in a mystical and fatalistic faith. Meade sighed. *We might yet get a chance to redeem ourselves. It's all in God's hands.*

Within a few hours, Biddle was back with curt orders from General Hooker. The bridges had been repaired, and the withdrawal would proceed as ordered.

Hancock led his division along the dirt road through the steady drizzle. Dawn had just broken, and the men slogged their way through the mud in the gray twilight. As they reached the bridge, Hancock spotted General Couch on the near shore next to the road. As Hancock approached, Couch motioned him over.

The pair silently watched Hancock's division trudge toward the bridge and across it to the relative safety of the far shore. Hancock was the first to speak. "I heard last night that Amiel Whipple is near death—shot by a sniper a couple of days ago. Isn't he a classmate of yours?"

"No," Couch said, shaking his head. "He was a year ahead of me. He was a good man—I knew him well back then."

"I wasn't sure; I barely remember him. That would have made him first classman when I was a plebe." Hancock thought for a moment. "You know, I never ran into him in the old army."

"No, you wouldn't have," Couch said. "He was a topographical engineer. He led a number of surveying expeditions out west. Damn smart man!" Couch sighed and stared off into the mist. "It's a terrible loss," he said. "Whipple was the only trained professional in the entire Third Corps top leadership. The rest of them are all amateurs and political hacks, and Sickles is the worst of the lot!" With that, Couch lapsed again into silence.

Hancock decided to change the subject. "Any idea where we are going?"

"Back to Falmouth," Couch spat.

"I think the men will be outraged," Hancock replied sadly. "They are all expecting another grand flanking maneuver."

"We will get no more grand maneuvers of any kind from Hooker—he is mentally shot. What a waste. All that bloodshed for nothing..." Couch shifted his attention to the line of men marching silently across the bridge. "Excellent noise discipline in your division, Hancock!"

"Yes," Hancock said proudly. "They are very good men!"

Dan Sickles watched his men cross the pontoon bridge. *This did not turn out the way I hoped,* he thought. *If I had been allowed to attack Jackson's force earlier, it would have broken up their movement and prevented the flank attack on the Eleventh Corps. That would have been a great victory, something the newspapers would trumpet! They would have hailed me as the victor of Chancellorsville.* He exhaled in disgust. *Now, the newspapers will be howling for Joe Hooker's head. Maybe that's not such a bad thing.* He brightened to the possibilities. *Yes, I will have to play this carefully, but there is an opportunity here after all. Tremain can feed the reporters in camp selected details of the battle judiciously embellished to show how well I handled myself in the battle. It might not be a victory for the army, but it can be a victory for me.* Satisfied, Sickles turned his horse to join the column.

The men of the last two regiments of the rear guard slipped silently out of the trees and formed up into an arc covering the entrance to the pontoon bridge. Then, from the flanks, they began to file back across the bridge until the last company in the center was left to cover the movement. As the last troops crossed the bridge in the midmorning drizzle, Meade looked over toward General Barnes, the brigade commander of the rear guard, and nodded.

"That's the last of them, General," Barnes said. "We managed to get across without tipping the rebels off."

"Yes," Meade replied. "That was a bit of good luck. It would have been a disaster if they caught us with the army split between the two sides of the river."

"Indeed." Barnes paused to squint toward the trees on the far bank. "With all this rain, though, I don't know how many weapons would fire. All the powder must be damp by now."

Meade was distracted by the sight of the engineers chopping the anchor lines with axes. *They are sure in a hurry to get the bridge taken up!* "Yes, there has been a lot of rain. I bet Henry Hunt has made provisions to keep his powder dry, though!"

With the anchor lines free, the pontoons swung in the current toward the near riverbank. Meade sadly watched the engineers begin to drag the pontoons out of the water. *We just squandered a great opportunity,* he thought. *How many more will we be given?*

Henry huddled underneath his rubberized blanket, cold, wet, and miserable. The storm that Isaac predicted had arrived in the early evening with a torrential rain that had lasted most of the night. The rising river overflowed its banks, flooding the rifle pits and their company area. The deluge had let up, but not before soaking all the men and their belongings.

He looked at the ground and sighed. *Back to where we started a week ago, and nothing to show for it,* he thought. *True, the company came out of it with no casualties, but there were plenty of dead and wounded among other units.*

"Hey, boys, looks like we got company!" Isaac called out.

Henry looked up to see a long line of soldiers, heads down, slogging through the mud. He could see the red shamrock-like trefoil on their caps—First Division of the Second Corps: Hancock's men.

"Back so soon?" someone asked.

"Yeah, we was whipped!" was the reply. "Goddamn Eleventh Corps broke and ran. Get 'um next time, though!"

"Right," someone else called out. "Clubs is trumps!"

Henry shook his head sadly. The truth, he realized, was as he had feared—they were whipped again. "What is it going to take the beat these people?" he muttered.

Part Two

Encampment: Falmouth, Virginia

Chapter 5
May 12, 1863

MEADE PACED NERVOUSLY ALONG THE board sidewalk in front of his headquarters tent. Governor Curtin of Pennsylvania was in camp and had sent word he would like to meet with Meade. Such a request was impossible to ignore, given the governor's considerable power and their professional relationship. Meade had sent his aides scurrying to make the necessary preparations.

Not only was Curtin one of the most powerful governors in the North, he was also Meade's patron. It was Curtin who had taken up his case and used his considerable political pull to secure Meade's promotion from captain to brigadier general, jumping over dozens of superior officers. Curtin also had a very close relationship with Lincoln. Curtin was the first governor called to the White House by Lincoln after South Carolina seceded and provided unflinching support even in some of the republic's darkest hours.

But Meade knew it wasn't just politics that drew Pennsylvania's governor to the camp of the Army of the Potomac. From the beginning of the war, Curtin was intensely concerned with the care and well-being of his Pennsylvania volunteers. He became known as the "soldier's friend"—lobbying tirelessly to improve the common soldier's lot. Meade knew Curtin was down here to check on his boys, and that meant visiting the hospitals, inspecting the commissary stores, poking his nose into tents, and talking directly to the privates in the Pennsylvania regiments. Woe unto any officer, be he lieutenant or major general, who was found negligent during one of these visits!

Meade deeply respected Curtin for his devotion to the welfare of the soldiers. Curtin, in turn, had shown an appreciation for Meade's abilities and was one of Meade's biggest promoters. Now Curtin was on the way to see him. Meade rubbed his beard nervously—he knew this was no social call. Curtin would no doubt grill him on the recent battle and its dismal outcome. It promised to be an uncomfortable experience despite his high regard for the governor.

A carriage turned down the dirt street toward his headquarters. Meade adjusted his glasses and squinted to make out the occupant. It was a civilian—that would be Curtin. Meade looked down at his uniform and tugged nervously at his coat. He frowned at the result. *Even in my best uniform, I still manage to look rumpled,* he thought. *Well, Governor Curtin will just have to accept me the way I am.* Meade pulled himself to attention and saluted as the carriage jerked to a stop.

The governor smiled as he stepped out of the carriage and offered his hand to Meade. "It certainly is nice to see you again, Meade! How has your health been? Any problems with your old wounds?"

Meade shook the offered hand. "No, Your Excellency. My wound is fully healed, and my health, thank God, is fine. Thank you for asking. And let me say it is both a pleasure and an honor to have you visit me, sir."

Curtin raised his eyebrows. "I must say, General, you have had a remarkable recovery! You were wounded just a year ago in the arm, hip, and lung, was it?" Meade nodded. "When I heard the news, I prayed that your wounds would not be mortal. Then when I heard you were back leading your brigade at South Mountain less than three months later, I was shocked and impressed."

"I have always healed quickly," Meade said. "I still have some hip pain after being in the saddle for a long time and shortness of breath when I am fatigued, but I have to put it aside. There are much more important matters to attend to."

"Good man!" Curtin responded with an even broader smile, and his eyes twinkled. He was a handsome man with a strong, upturned, dimpled chin; lively eyes; and short, unruly hair. "General Meade, you know I have to check on all of Pennsylvania's sons in the army. How are your soldiers faring?"

"The Fifth Corps was not heavily engaged, so we are in good shape physically. I think we are more wounded in spirit at the present time."

"Yes," The governor's smile disappeared. He looked around at the gaggle of aides and the curious who were beginning to assemble. "General Meade, could we have a few words in private?"

"Of course, sir." Meade escorted the governor in to his tent and offered him a seat.

Curtin tossed his hat and gloves on to the table and scowled. "Meade, I'll come straight to the point. I've come down to see things for myself. We have been getting terrible reports up in Pennsylvania about the state of the army."

"I believe we are in as good condition as can be expected," Meade said. "The men have experienced defeat before. They are good soldiers and can bounce back—"

"No," the governor said. "I didn't mean the men. They have always responded no matter how much was asked of them. I was referring to the high command. My sources say Hooker is terribly incompetent and should be replaced immediately." Curtin's eyes narrowed in anger, and his face began to redden. "What is your professional opinion of the recent battle?"

Meade cleared his throat. The intensity shocked Meade—he had not experienced the governor's fabled temper before. *So,* he thought, *this was the reason why Curtin wanted to see me.* "Your Excellency," he said, "General Hooker is an excellent administrator. He significantly improved the operation and morale of the army after Fredericksburg. I hardly think he could be termed incompetent. He is a tough fighter and well respected by the men. Sir, I don't think it is my place to criticize my superior officer."

Curtin held up his hand. "I have spoken at length with President Lincoln after his visit, and I know what all of you corps commanders told him. Nothing you say can be a surprise to me. I value your professional opinion. That is why I asked for it." Curtin leaned forward. "If all that is true, then why did he fail so miserably at Chancellorsville?"

"Very well, Your Excellency." Meade thought for a moment. "I would say that, in general, Hooker's plan was a good one. My only criticism is that he did not keep his cavalry close to the main body of the army. If he had, we would have detected Jackson's move around our flank and would have been able to counter it. As far as execution of the plan, I do find fault there. On the first day, we were close to breaking through Lee's defensive line. A few more troops and another push, and we would be out of the woods. Instead, we withdrew to a defensive line and ceded the initiative to the enemy. Once Jackson attacked, we had the opportunity to hit him in the flank, but General Hooker refused to move. I think it is shameful that we left General Sedgwick hung out to dry and did not move to help him when he was being attacked. Just a small movement on our part would have drawn off some of the forces against him."

Curtin listened silently, and then spoke. "So what I hear you saying is that General Hooker is a good planner but cannot be trusted with operational control of the army."

Meade hesitated. *That's the question everyone in the Army of the Potomac has been asking themselves.* "I can't explain it, Your Excellency. Hooker planned an excellent campaign, and it began with excellent results. But for all his fighting spirit, he failed to show nerve and '*coup d'oeil*' that is to say, an instant appreciation of the battle situation at the critical moment."

The governor relaxed slightly. "I understand you were in favor of attacking the enemy instead of withdrawing."

"Yes, I was in favor of casting the die and letting Washington take care of itself. You know, I feel sorry for Hooker. He and I have always enjoyed a cordial relationship. I think he is a good officer with much to offer, but the fact is, he missed a golden opportunity."

"We cannot keep missing golden opportunities," Curtin said sadly. "I don't think the army's leadership understands what pressure we are under. During last fall's elections, we nearly lost political control of Philadelphia. The Copperheads and Peace Democrats are running rampant. Up in coal country, armed mobs are spreading anarchy. They have nullified the draft call in the region. Did you know that recently they stopped a train and sent all the draftees on it back to their homes?"

Meade swallowed and shook his head. "No, I had not heard that."

"Yes, well, we managed to hush that up pretty well." Curtin moved closer and grasped Meade's arm. "We're sitting on a powder keg, Meade. There isn't any time or patience left for fools or incompetents. One more defeat and we could lose it all. Either our citizens will force us to seek peace, or Great Britain will recognize the Confederacy and demand that we negotiate a settlement. Whichever, our hope of keeping the Union intact will be gone forever. The next battle could decide it all."

Meade could only nod. He had not realized things were this dire.

"So you understand, General, we need results now, and we need leaders who can give us those results. From what I hear, you are the kind of officer who can do that. In plain terms, I am prepared to go to President Lincoln and recommend that he immediately place you in command of the Army of the Potomac."

Meade's stomach tightened into a knot; this certainly was not what he had expected. "But, but, Your Excellency," he stammered. "I am not competent to command the army. And besides, there are others who are more senior to me."

Curtin grimaced at the mention of seniority. "I wish you regular army officers would forget this whole idea of seniority. It has caused us nothing but trouble. Oh, it is fine in peacetime when you are trying to decide who gets a certain assignment, or who should be introduced to the president first. This is wartime, and seniority does not count. The only thing that counts is ability and results. I would put a captain in charge of a brigade if he was the best man for the job. Now, as far as competency, you have handled every job so far with diligence and professionalism. These are not my words; they come from your peers, the other corps commanders. They have told the president that you should be given command of the army. Your record has been exemplary, and there is no reason to believe that you could not handle this job in the same manner."

"I thank you for your confidence in me, but there is a big difference between handling a corps of ten or twenty thousand men and handling an army of one hundred thousand men. I'm not sure I have the right temperament for that kind of job. It's common knowledge that I have a very short temper..." Meade paused and looked at the governor. "Besides, I have enemies in Washington. They would never allow me to be named commander."

"Oh, like Senator Chandler? I wouldn't worry about him. The word is he had reason to question your loyalty because of some incident?"

"Yes." Meade nodded. "It was just after South Carolina seceded. I was stationed in Detroit, superintending the survey of the Great Lakes and construction of lighthouses. There was a great rally organized, and word was sent for me and all my officers to attend for the purpose of renewing our oath of allegiance. Naturally, I declined the invitation. The request was unseemly and quite contrary to army regulations. I informed the organizers that I would gladly take whatever oaths my army superiors deemed necessary, but I would not renew my oath at the insistence of a mob."

Curtin cocked an eyebrow. "Um, naturally. Under the circumstances, however, the refusal might have been misinterpreted?"

"Quite so, sir. They accused me of disloyalty."

"You know, Meade, it is refreshing, in this cynical and self-serving age, to find a man of principle without a single political bone in his body." Governor Curtin smiled slightly. "I think Senator Chandler could be convinced that you have sufficiently demonstrated your loyalty...but what about this position?"

"Governor Curtin," Meade said, "please understand that I have no desire for advancement. I offered my services to the

Union as I felt duty bound to do so. Higher rank holds no attraction for me."

Curtin sighed and held up his hand. "I understand your position, Meade. No need to say any more. By the way, I read in the *New York Herald* daily praises of General Sickles with the recommendation that he be named Hooker's replacement. What is this Sickles really like?"

Meade shrugged. "Sickles is very brave and is an aggressive fighter. However, he has no formal military training and often makes errors of judgment due to this lack of training. I suppose he would make an excellent brigade or division commander, but corps or army command is beyond him. I hesitate to mention his morals. I fear he is a bad influence on General Hooker."

"Yes," Curtin said, "that was my impression as well." He rose and picked his hat and gloves up off the table. "Well, General Meade, thank you for your time. I appreciate your candid views and your insight." He held out his hand. "One more thing, though—don't be so quick to reject command out of hand. We are sometimes forced by duty to accomplish more than we ever thought we could and accept responsibilities we do not desire. Do not sell yourself short, General Meade. You are fully capable of higher command."

Meade saw the governor off and walked back to the tent, where he collapsed into a chair. His stomach was in turmoil, and he struggled to think clearly about what had just happened. *What could I have said to make it plainer to Governor Curtin that I do not want the job?*

Sickles dismounted and strode toward the headquarters tent. Dan Butterfield was outside the tent as he approached. "Hooker sent for me," Sickles said.

"He's inside." Butterfield motioned toward the tent with his head. As Sickles passed by, Butterfield grabbed his arm. "Just so you know, he is not in a good mood."

"Thanks," Sickles said as he stepped into the tent. Hooker was seated at a field table staring down at a newspaper, scowling. Sickles knew why he was unhappy. "You wanted to see me?"

Hooker looked up. The scowl did not leave his face. "Yes, I did." He looked back down at the newspaper. "What is this?"

Sickles shifted slightly. "I'm sorry?"

"These lies in the *New York Herald*." Hooker picked up the paper and thrust it toward Sickles. "Article after article with nothing but lies!" He glared at Sickles. "They lie about my performance, and they lie about everything great you did. They make you out as the hero of Chancellorsville! Now they are even calling for you to replace me as army commander."

Sickles held up his hand in defense. "I don't know anything about this," he lied.

"Really?" Hooker glared. "All these details…they could only have come from someone thoroughly familiar with what happened in the Third Corps!"

Sickles paused. *Got to think fast. He suspects the truth.* "Um, the *Herald* reporters have been all over my camp since we got back from Chancellorsville. You know how many New York regiments I have in my corps. The reporters have to know many officers personally. Soldiers like to brag and embellish stories. There's no telling where this information originated."

"Well," Hooker said, somewhat mollified.

Sickles adopted an understanding smile. *He's buying it.* "Look," he said, "I know the editor of the *Herald* personally. Let me go up to New York and meet with him face to face. I can get him to ease up on this criticism and get you some favorable comments."

Hooker shook his head. "No. We are in the middle of the campaign season. Your duty is here with your corps. I can't grant anyone leave unless it is for a medical reason." He paused for a moment. "This is not the main reason I called for you. As you are well aware, the Third Corps took some heavy casualties in the last battle. In addition to this, you are losing quite a number of two-year regiments. The fact is that I will have to reorganize your corps."

Sickles swallowed hard. "Reorganize...how?"

"We would consolidate the regiments of your three divisions into two. That would provide you with a pair of reasonably strong units for the rest of the campaign season."

"Aren't we getting any more reinforcements?"

"No." Hooker sighed. "I have been informed by General Halleck that troops are needed in other areas of operation. We are to expect a limited number of reinforcements."

"What about the draft?" Sickles could not believe this news.

"The draft has just started. It will take time for the states to collect the men and get them trained. We can't count on them arriving in the near future. At this point, we have to work with the resources we have on hand."

"Very well," Sickles said. "I will have to think about which brigade commander I will promote. Two of my division commanders were killed, as you know."

"Yes, about that." Hooker paused, obviously struggling with how to proceed. "Meade's corps is being reorganized as well.

They have a whole division being mustered out. That leaves them with an excess division commander. He is senior to any of your brigade commanders, so he has first rights to the open command."

"Who is he?" Sickles asked.

"Humphreys. General Alexander Humphreys."

Sickles heart sank. *What? That old man?* "I really don't know him, or much about him." Sickles did not dare to mention that he knew Humphreys was a West Pointer, like Hooker. A West Pointer was the last thing he wanted—he needed his subordinate commanders to have a personal loyalty to him. That way, they would always have his back in any political dispute.

"He's a good man. Regular army. Tough fighter—his division took its objective on the wall at Fredericksburg."

"But—" Sickles began.

"Look," Hooker said, "that's the way it has to be. Like it or not, he has seniority. We have to abide by army protocol."

Sickles relented. "Very well; as you command." His mind raced. *There's got to be a way around this.*

A flurry of movement caused Henry to look up from his diary. Isaac had risen and was moving toward the door of the tent with a Bible in his hand. "Where you off to, Ike?"

"The chaplain has organized a Bible study down at the Lacy House." Isaac held up his Bible as proof.

"Hmm," Henry grunted. "You sure it's not the pretty young women at the Lacy House you're interested in?"

"Well, that might provide some extra inducement," Isaac said.

"That's a hopeless cause," Henry said. "You know they are all southern sympathizers. The only reason they are nice to you is the hope that someone might spill a military secret."

Isaac shook his head. "No, they are all devout Christian women. Come with me. You'll see for yourself."

"No, I don't think so," Henry said, looking down. "You go along without me."

Isaac set his Bible down and stared at Henry. A concerned look spread across his face. "You have changed since you joined the army, brother. I mean really changed. Before the army, you used to go to prayer meetings all the time. Now, you never go. I'm worried that you have lost your love of the Lord."

"It's hard to know what to believe, Ike." Henry shifted and let out a long sigh. "All of this killing and maiming with nothing but hatred, and no seeming end to it. Each side prays fervently to God to smite the other, convinced that the Almighty favors them. None of it is very Christian at all, in my opinion."

Isaac was silent, seemingly shocked at what he just heard.

Henry looked up at him with sadness. "Just go to your Bible study. I'll be fine."

The setting sun was shrouded in rose-colored clouds, and Hancock stopped to admire the view. With the bustle of army life in encampment, he did not often have the time to pause and just admire the sunset. A group of soldiers shuffled by, cautiously hoping that the general would fail to notice them. Hancock deflated their hopes with a quick look. A squad of hands touched forage caps in salute.

"Evenin', General," a bold one said.

Hancock nodded and returned their salutes. Their caps wore the white trefoil of the Second Division of the Second Corps—Gibbon's lads. The group moved away, trailing dust and murmurs of acknowledgment: "Hancock…that's Hancock."

He was used to it and actually liked that spark of recognition from soldiers. It was a sign of respect that they did not often bestow. The soldiers knew good officers from bad and would only show respect toward those they considered worthy. Hancock considered this the highest praise.

He started on toward John Gibbon's tent. This afternoon at a review, Gibbon had invited him over for a drink and a cigar. Hancock was glad for the invitation. He had wanted to talk to Gibbon since they had returned to the encampment, but he had been too busy with his own division to do so.

Gibbon was outside his tent as Hancock walked up. "Win, welcome to my humble abode! Please come inside." Hancock warmly shook Gibbon's hand and stooped to enter the tent. "Would you care for a drink?" Gibbon held out a tin cup of whiskey.

Hancock grinned. "Don't be silly, John. Of course I would like one." After a taking a sip, he asked, "What do you hear about Hooker?"

Gibbon shrugged. "Nothing definite, but he has a lot of explaining to do, and it's not clear that Washington is buying his story."

Hancock took another sip of his drink. "He certainly does have a great deal to explain. I have heard that Hooker denies a general engagement was ever fought at Chancellorsville. He had the nerve to tell that to Lincoln. Let me tell you, if that wasn't a general engagement we were in, then I don't want to see one."

"Well, the press, for once, senses the truth and are being very hard on Hooker and Butterfield over this whole mess. Have you seen the *New York Herald* the past few days?"

Hancock set his cup down. "It's been hard to get copies before they're confiscated, but I have seen some. They are very critical, but most of what they say is true. I suppose that is why Hooker has ordered all copies of the *Herald* burned in the camp. He can't stand the truth. The *Herald* has most of the facts right. They must be getting inside information."

"Do you suppose Sickles is behind it? The *Herald* has been very complimentary of him lately."

"I wouldn't be at all surprised. That's the kind of fellow he is," Hancock said. "The way the *Herald* carries on, you would think Sickles won the battle, only to have it thrown away by Hooker's incompetence."

Gibbon shifted on his camp stool. "Well, one thing for sure: my troops have lost all confidence in Hooker. They just stare at him when he rides by. Remember when they all used to cheer him?"

"Yes, they have no further use for him," Hancock said. "Some of his subordinates feel the same way. I have heard that Couch told Abe Lincoln that he would no longer fight under Hooker. Other rumors have it that a group of the corps commanders has sent a letter to Lincoln saying they would fight under Meade. I really don't much about the man, though."

Gibbon took a sip of whiskey. "I wouldn't mind fighting under Meade. He's a good man. Let me tell you a story about him. I remember first meeting Meade in Florida, in 1849 during the Seminole War. We saw this scrawny, scraggly fellow come into camp followed by a handler leading a pack mule loaded with surveying equipment. They were back from a reconnaissance of hostile territory—just him, the mule, and an assistant. They stayed only long enough to eat and get resupplied, then they were off again. How he didn't get killed is a miracle. Meade is fearless and an excellent judge of terrain."

"I only know of him by reputation. He was with General Taylor in Mexico and then with the Topographical Bureau, so our paths never crossed."

Gibbon was silent for a while. "You know, Win, if Couch goes, then you will be in line to receive the Second Corps. You do have the seniority."

Hancock smiled at his friend. "Yes, I do have seniority, but politics would probably intervene. There are plenty of other political generals who rank me. As a Democrat and a McClellan man, I am definitely out of favor in Washington."

"Politics always seem to have a way of getting into the middle of things…another drink?" Hancock watched Gibbon pour another round. "Politics—it sure has created a mess of things," Gibbon said. "Look at enlistments. The army is losing whole regiments—two-year men and nine-month men. The politicians will not act to extend the enlistments, and we may be critically weakened this summer."

Hancock took a sip of whiskey. "I agree this is a bad time to lose people. Couch told me the army is due to lose twenty thousand men due to expiring enlistments. Coming after the losses at Chancellorsville, that means a huge cut in strength."

"That's the figure I heard as well. So now Hooker has us sitting here on our behinds waiting for Bobby Lee to make a move." Hancock scowled at the thought.

"What do you suppose Lee is going to do, Win?"

"We have surrendered the initiative to the enemy, who has reportedly been reinforced by Longstreet's Corps. The rebs have replaced their losses with Longstreet's transfer, while we are further weakened by expiring enlistments. It is clear that Lee will not squander the opportunity. For him, the strategic position in Northern Virginia is the best it's been in nearly a year. He has us on the defensive and probably close to parity in troop strength. The last time the situation was this favorable for Lee, he took the initiative and marched north. I'm afraid it's going to be a difficult summer."

Gibbon nodded thoughtfully. "That may well be. The strategic situation in the west is certainly not favorable to the Confederacy, though. It could be that Jeff Davis would want to shift forces to attack Rosecrans in Tennessee or Grant at Vicksburg. Those are the places where the Confederacy is the most vulnerable."

"This is very true, John, but my sense is that Jeff Davis believes the war can be won here in the east. If Lee moves north and wins a big battle on our own territory, then their standing in Europe is greatly improved. We could have a negotiated peace forced on us, and that would most likely mean recognition of the status quo."

Gibbon was silent for a while, staring at his hands. "If that happens, then the Union is split forever. It may be true what they say about the fate of all democracies."

Hancock looked at his companion. Gibbon was regular army—tough and uncompromising. He had given up a great deal when he stayed with the Union, and he had put up with suspicion and hostility from those who questioned his loyalty due to his North Carolina roots. "Yes, it has long been accepted that democracies are doomed to fail from within. It happened to Athens and then to Rome. Factionalism leads to anarchy, which leads to despotism and the end of democracy. We must break this cycle and preserve the Union."

Gibbon nodded sadly. "For some us, the stakes are much more personal. I could never go back to North Carolina if the Union dissolves. You know, Win, I have never regretted my decision to stay with the Union, even though my home state seceded. I felt honor bound by my oath of allegiance to defend the Union. I haven't told anyone this, but a while back I received a letter from my brother in North Carolina. He said the family wanted me to change my name. It seems they were embarrassed to have the family name associated with defense of the Union. I have been disowned by my family, and now it seems possible that we may lose the very thing we set about to protect."

Hancock moved to place his hand on Gibbon's shoulder. "It's hard for many of us to conceive of life with a dissolved Union. I for one would prefer not to live to see this happen. It would be better to take a ball in the last battle than to live on under such circumstances."

Chapter 6

June 10, 1863

Meade looked at the mound of paperwork on his desk and sighed deeply. An army in encampment invariably began to generate paperwork. *If we can't shoot bullets, they would like us to shoot paper,* he thought. It was an unavoidable reality, and he picked up a report with another sigh.

A noise at the tent door caused him to look up. It was George, his son. George had recently joined his staff as a captain after insistence from his wife. She thought he would be safer on his staff than in his position as a cavalry troop commander. Meade didn't have the heart to tell her that George was much safer with the cavalry! "Well, hello, George. Come in." He was relieved to have a distraction from this paperwork.

"Sorry to bother you, father, but I just received a letter from mother."

"Oh, is anything wrong? Is she not well? I haven't written her in a few days, as I've been buried in this paper." Meade lifted and dropped a stack of paper for emphasis.

George shook his head. "No, she's well. She is just worried about you. She has heard the rumors that you will be offered Hooker's job, and she doesn't think you should take it."

Meade chuckled. "Your mother's mood swings daily between elation that her husband is to be named commander of the Army of the Potomac and dread for what it might mean to me personally."

George brightened. "You mean you are going to accept it?"

"Hold on. In the first place, I have not been offered the position. In the second place, I have no powerful political friends to press my case in Washington, so I am highly unlikely ever to receive such an offer. And in the third place, I have no desire for the position and would turn it down if it was offered to me."

George received this with an incredulous look. "Why wouldn't you want the job? Isn't it a great honor?"

Meade nodded. "Oh, it is a great honor, all right. Tell me, George, how many commanders has the Army of the Potomac had?"

His son counted on his fingers. "Let's see, there was McDowell, and McClellan, and Burnside, and Hooker. That's four, in all."

"And I would be the fifth in two years," Meade said gently. "It is a precarious position. The politicians meddle in every decision, and the Committee on the Conduct of the War stands ready to cashier the unfortunate or unwitting general who crosses them or who fails to display the proper radical zeal. I have no following in Washington. The sharks there would eat me up in a minute and destroy me completely. No, I have no ambition in this regard. Why would any sane person want that job?"

George nodded and looked up from his boots where he had been staring. "Some of the junior officers are saying nobody wants Hooker's job because they would have to face Bobby Lee."

Meade paused. Someone had finally said the question he had been avoiding asking himself ever since he was first mentioned as a possible replacement. *Is that really it? Down deep, is it really my fear of Lee that keeps me from wanting the job? No, not fear—respect,* he told himself. George was looking at him, waiting for an answer. "Lee is a superb general. Extremely intelligent, aggressive, and well skilled in the military art. He has the support of excellent officers and tough, well-trained soldiers. They are a formidable enemy, and to lead an army against them is the ultimate test for any general." Meade looked at George, who had a disappointed look. "Look at what it did to Fighting Joe Hooker," he said. "There was no general more bellicose or sure of himself than Hooker. When he finally had to face Lee, match him move for move, Hooker lost every bit of confidence he had. I'm not sure what I would do, if I could measure up." There, he had finally admitted it.

George smiled weakly. "Well, like you say, it is unlikely that you will be selected. I'll write mother and tell her not to worry."

"Give her my love, son. Tell her I will write as soon as I am able." He watched George leave and sighed. Meade turned back to his paperwork. *It's not about Lee at all,* he told himself. *I really do not want the job.* Sighing again, he went back to the paperwork.

A few papers later, there was noise outside the tent. A familiar voice called in. "George, mind if I disturb you?" It was John Reynolds.

"John, yes, yes, come in. You're not disturbing me at all." He looked at the tall patrician stooping to enter the tent.

"George, it's been a long time, and I'm sorry that I haven't come by sooner. My duties as a corps commander always seem to get in the way of socializing."

Meade motioned away the apology. "I have been delinquent as well, John. So tell me, what's new?"

"Well," Reynolds said, "there is a lot of talk about Hooker's replacement, and the different factions are all busy pushing their own candidates. You know that Governor Curtin came to see me?"

"Yes, he visited me also. I think his primary concern is to have a Pennsylvanian in charge of the army."

"Well," Reynolds said, "I told him that I did not want the job and he had better look elsewhere. He told me that he was going to see you, Meade." Reynolds arched an eye. "Did he tell you that he was going to see the president about you?"

Meade shook his head. "Well, he did mention that, but I told him that I was not suited for the job and did not want it. I did meet with President Lincoln when he was down here recently. It was a very strange meeting. We talked about everything except the war. I don't know what to make of it."

"I think he was trying to judge what kind of man you are. He's like that—always looking beneath the surface, trying to see the inner man. I think he likes you, George."

Meade shrugged and said nothing. Reynolds continued. "I saw Lincoln, too, a few days ago. A friend in the War Department slipped me word that I was being considered as Hooker's replacement, so I went to the White House and asked to speak with the president. I told him that I would not accept the job if he was not prepared to give me a free hand. Both you and I know that there is no way he could accept those terms, so I'm off the hook. He did indicate to me that he was going to keep Hooker on, at least for a while. I think you're off the hook, too, at least until the next time Hooker blunders."

"You schemer!" Meade chuckled. "I should have thought of that myself."

"Well, it's too late, George! I thought of it first, and it won't work a second time. You should get yourself prepared for the inevitable—you will be named Joe Hooker's replacement at some time, probably at the worst possible moment."

"John, doesn't the president know I'm not qualified? I'm an engineer, for God's sake, not a professional soldier. Three years ago I was superintending the construction of lighthouses. The only thing I know about maneuvering large bodies of troops is what Professor Mahan taught us at West Point, and that was twenty-eight years ago."

"George," Reynolds said, "don't sell yourself short. You are a fighter; everyone knows that. We all saw what you were made of at Marye's Heights. You were the only one to capture your objective in the rebel defenses. Besides, I happen to think that you have one thing on Bobby Lee that the rest of us don't have."

Meade cocked his head. "What's that?"

"You are a damned good engineer, George, like Lee is, and you think like he does. Lee has constantly run circles around us because he has outthought us. Now, it's true that McClellan was an engineer, but he was too wrapped up in himself to really outthink Bobby Lee. But you can, George. You are the right man for the job, no doubt about it."

Meade could only stare at his hands. "But John, I don't want the job!"

Hancock followed General Couch's orderly to the door of the tent and waited to be announced. He looked around and sniffed the air. Night was falling, and in the twilight the army was settling into its evening routine. Campfires were started, and soldiers gathered around them smoking their pipes. The pungent blend of wood and tobacco smoke hung in the still and humid June night. Music started up at a nearby fire. It was a sentimental tune called "The Vacant Chair." Hancock sighed as he thought of the many vacant chairs this war had created. *There will be many more before this is all over,* he thought.

Hancock shook his head. *Can't think of that. Have to stay focused on the things that matter. Why did Couch send for me?*

"General Hancock, General Couch will see you now." The orderly held back the tent flap, and Hancock stooped to enter the tent. As he straightened, he saw Couch in a dress uniform.

"General Couch, you sent for me?"

Couch smiled broadly.

Not a common sight lately, Hancock thought.

"Yes, Win, I did. I have a big announcement. Uncle Abe has finally come through for me."

"A transfer?" Hancock guessed.

"Exactly, I just received it. Lincoln approved my request to-day. I leave tomorrow for Harrisburg. I am finally rid of that idiot Hooker!"

"Harrisburg?" Hancock couldn't think of a military com-mand there.

"Yes, the War Department has created a new military district, and I have been named commander. It's based in Harrisburg."

"Well, that's great news for you." Hancock knew his tone was less than enthusiastic. He hated to see Couch, or any other good man, leave. They needed every competent commander they could find.

"There is even better news, for you Hancock. The president has appointed you as the new commander of the Second Corps. Congratulations, Win. You deserve it." Couch held out his hand.

Hancock shook his head in disbelief—he had not expected this. He knew Couch detested Hooker, but he never thought the War Department would let such a valuable officer go. And yet, the Second Corps—this was quite an honor. He took Couch's hand. *Must stay focused and pay attention to the details.* "So, Couch, what can you tell me about the rest of the corps?"

"I have asked the staff to prepare reports on the status. They are working on these reports now and should have them completed for your review in the morning. The president has indicated that Hooker will remain in command of the army. I am glad he has seen fit to grant my request for reassignment. I could not bring myself to serve under Hooker for another campaign. It would only mean leading my troops to purposeless slaughter."

Hancock nodded. *Does this mean that I will have to lead them to slaughter? Not if I can help it!*

Couch continued. "Well, it seems Lee is on the move—we have some confirmation now. You are aware of Hooker's cavalry foray yesterday?"

"No. Only that something was going on. No hard information."

"Well, Hooker had been receiving reports from spies and deserters that Lee might be shifting toward the west and decided to conduct a reconnaissance in force to find out if it was true. He sent three cavalry divisions backed up by two infantry brigades from the Fifth Corps across the Rappahannock. Yesterday morning, at first light, the cavalry attacked. The main fighting was around Brandy Station, up northeast of Culpepper Court House. It seems our boys did pretty well for themselves—pushed JEB Stuart's cavalry back and held their own. They finally withdrew in the afternoon after rebel infantry came up. Details are still sketchy, but it seems we have confirmed that the rebs are moving north."

"Hmm. Another Antietam?"

"Possibly. Or perhaps farther north, to Pennsylvania."

"Perhaps your new job in Harrisburg won't be as quiet as you thought."

"Perhaps not; whatever the destination, we will have to march long and hard to catch up. They do have a head start on us. You will need to get the corps ready to march. Hooker is bound to give you very little notice, so be prepared."

"Yes, of course." Hancock's mind was racing with the thoughts of everything that needed to be done.

Couch was talking again. "I will miss them, the boys of the Second Corps. They have always done everything I have asked them to do and more."

"Yes, they have always done their duty."

"Yes, this is true." Couch paused and looked at Hancock. "You know, Win, most men struggle to do their duty. They have to be reminded and shown what their duty is. But you don't seem to have that problem. You always seem to know instinctively what your duty is, and you carry it out superbly. I admire you for that. One word of caution, though. Duty can be a harsh master: it can demand of you more than you are able to give. Sometimes it will demand everything of you. Win, you have the habit of trying to do too much yourself. Don't try to do it all. Let others so some of the work as well."

Hancock nodded; he did have that habit. "I'll try."

"Well, you have a lot to do, and I need to finish packing. I'll see you tomorrow before I leave."

Hancock muttered a farewell and slipped out of the tent. He was already thinking of the many things he had to do. *Focus on the details,* he told himself, *and indulge in pride later on.*

The doors to Delmonico's Restaurant opened before Dan Sickles, and he stepped into the dining room, wearing his full dress uniform for the occasion. The clatter of dinnerware and the murmur of scores of conversations collapsed into silence as the diners recognized him and craned to get a view. Sickles swallowed at the silence; he had hoped it would be different this time. A single handclap started an avalanche of applause, and instantly all were on their feet. Hands reached out to touch him, and voices called out his name. Some were the very same faces that had turned away from him in his darkest hours, but now they were smiling as he passed. *This is more like it,* he thought. *Like the old days!* He grinned broadly at the warmth of the reception. *What better place to make my appearance than at the swankiest restaurant in New York City!*

At the table, he busied himself with the menu while straining to overhear nearby conversations. They were talking about him, but now the comments were all favorable.

"General Sickles?" He looked up; it was Bennett, the editor of the *New York Herald.* "It looks like the people of New York have a new hero."

"Much of it is your doing, Mr. Bennett. Please have a seat."

"General, thank you for the invitation to dine with you this evening. I do appreciate this opportunity to speak with you at length."

"No, Mr. Bennett, it is I who must thank you for the very kind words you have to say about me in your paper. This invitation is my way of saying thanks." It was also his chance to get Bennett to reduce the amount of criticism the *Herald* was heaping on top of Hooker. And it was also a chance to butter up someone who could continue to do his career a great amount of good. Sickles gave him his very best smile.

"Based on reports I receive from my correspondents with the army and from the reports your aide was kind enough to supply, I believe everything we have said is richly deserved. You are the toast of the town. By the way, how is your wound?"

"Oh." Sickles waved his hand. "It's nothing serious, just a flesh wound. A spent shot struck me in the belt. The surgeons felt it was best if I had it looked after here in New York, where I could recuperate away from the distractions of a corps headquarters." Sickles smiled smugly at his successful scheme to pry a medical leave out of Hooker.

"Yes, indeed. I understand things are quite busy down at Falmouth. Hooker has had a stream of visitors—the president, the members of the joint committee, various governors, senators, and congressmen, everyone wanting to know what went wrong. If all that was not enough, he has busied himself with burning my newspapers."

Sickles grimaced. "General Hooker felt the articles in the *Herald* were untrue and detrimental to the good order and discipline of the army. He actually is mad at me. He thinks I put you up to it."

"Oh, really?" Bennett arched his eyebrows in mock surprise. "I only printed what everyone in the Army of the Potomac was saying."

"Even so, you should not overdo the criticism of Hooker. It seems likely now that Lincoln will keep him on, and further attacks will only weaken Hooker's position with the army." Sickles shot the editor a glance to make his point. He needed Hooker right now, especially if Hooker was going to stay on. He couldn't afford any bad blood between the army commander and himself. Despite the plan, Bennett had proved not to be as controllable as Sickles had thought. He instinctively dug deeper and saw the truth of any situation. The blame was laid squarely on Hooker, and Sickles could not stop it. The best he could do was to get up to New York as quickly as possible and try to smooth things over. He had finally persuaded Hooker to approve his leave request so that he could meet with Bennett face to face. The supposed flesh wound was just an excuse to allow for his long absence from his corps. "Besides," he said, "I think General Hooker was not as much to blame as you may think."

Bennett shrugged. "Public anger has run its course. There is little more that can be said that will sell more newspapers. Tell me, General, what do you really think caused the defeat?"

Sickles paused to consider the question. While the answer was full of hidden dangers, it was a question that had nagged him ever since the army had crossed back over the Rappahannock. This was a time when he needed to craft a clever answer. He was likely to see in print whatever he said tonight, and Bennett was too good a newspaperman to fall for a flimsy story. "As I have said before," Sickles said, "the fundamental cause of the defeat was the failure of the Eleventh Corps to stand and fight when attacked. It is true that they were surprised, but there was some warning. Yet no reasonable preparations were made. Some regiments simply turned and ran at the first sign of the enemy." *No reason not to throw Howard to the wolves at this point,* he thought.

"That was the first evening," Bennett said. "I understand that lines were stabilized during the night, and the army was entrenched and ready for the enemy in the morning."

"That is true up to a point, Mr. Bennett. The attack, however, left my corps exposed, and we had to fight to withdraw back to Hazel Grove. That is the high ground on the south side of the battlefield. Once at Hazel Grove, I was attacked from three sides, and I found that I could not hold that position with the troops I had available. Since no reinforcements were forthcoming, I was compelled to give up Hazel Grove. In retrospect, that was the key to the battle."

Bennett, who had been listening attentively, took a drink and considered this last statement. "Why do you say that?"

"Hazel Grove commanded essentially the entire battlefield. Once we lost those heights, we were under Confederate artillery the entire time. Every line we formed was blasted apart by rebel artillery. The outcome of the battle was fixed once we were forced off the Hazel Grove heights."

"Hmm. I understand that the losses in your corps were very high."

"Yes." Sickles nodded sadly. "I lost two division commanders killed on the battlefield, Generals Whipple and Berry. Both were very good men. I also lost many good regimental officers and soldiers. The Third Corps did a splendid job in the face of great adversity, and I must say that I am very proud of all of them. They fought like tigers in the face of overwhelming odds."

Bennett nodded and pursed his lips, forming a question. "Umm, it's our impression, several hundred miles away from the front, that General Hooker should have been more aware of the situation and taken more vigorous action."

Ah, here it comes, Sickle thought. "Yes, it is unfortunate that General Hooker was rendered hors de combat at the critical moment and was not able to direct the army as ably as I am sure he would have. He is a fighter, and who knows how the battle would have turned out if he had been able to direct the fighting."

A waiter interrupted the conversation as he slid two large steaks in front of the men. The pair cut hungrily into the meat. After a few bites, Bennett put down his fork. "I must say, General, you are really standing up for Hooker. Most generals, given this opportunity, would use it to promote themselves at Hooker's expense."

"Well, Mr. Bennett, I believe that General Hooker is a good man who has been unfairly maligned. The army can use his skills right now. Besides, I am happy where I am as a corps commander." *The truth is,* Sickles thought, *I don't have the political support to be named Hooker's replacement and cannot risk antagonizing the man who placed me in command of the Third Corps.* Besides, he had to admit that he was not excited about the idea of having to face Robert E. Lee. At this point, he had everything to lose by going after Hooker's job. Why risk it? *Better to bide my time,* he thought, *and wait for the opportunity which would certainly come.*

"Well, Hooker may get the chance to redeem himself soon," Bennett said. "Have you heard the latest news?"

Sickles shook his head. He had not seen the evening paper. "What news?"

"There has been a big cavalry fight in Virginia, west of the army. The rumors have it Lee may be on the move. Details are still coming in, so we should know more in the next day or two."

Sickles stroked his mustache at this news. "I am sure I will be notified if it's anything important." He wondered what this might mean but decided to dismiss it for the evening. They could engage in small talk for the rest of the dinner now that his main objective in meeting with the *Herald*'s editor had seemingly been achieved. Besides, he was planning a visit to his favorite bordello later, and nothing could be allowed to spoil this perfect evening.

Part Three

The March North

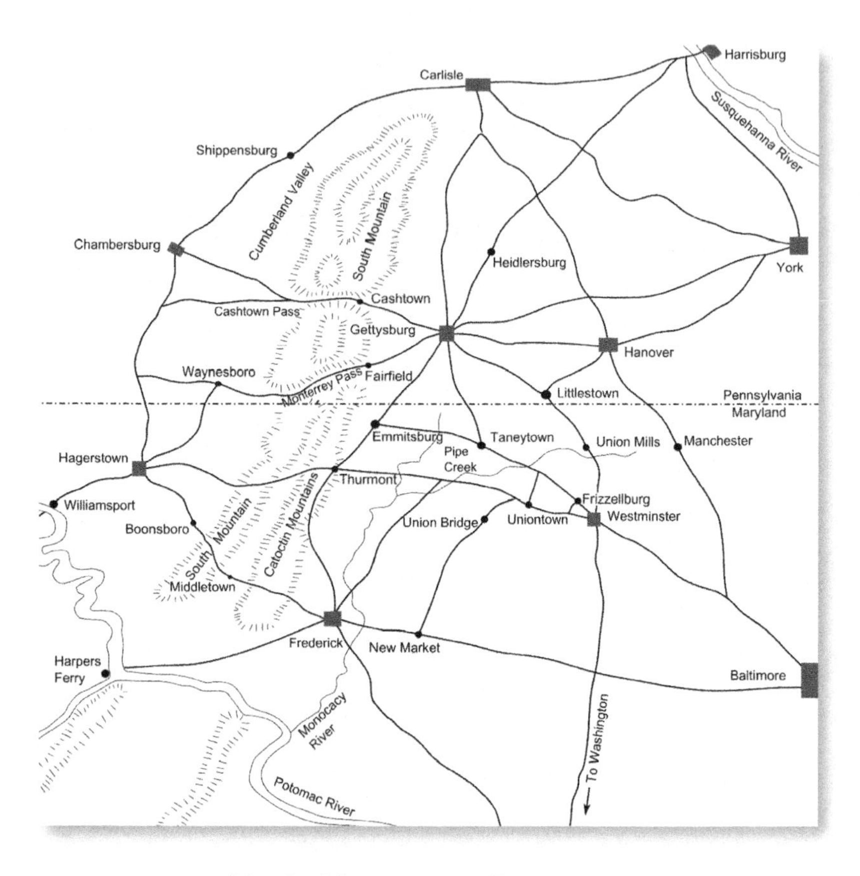

MAP 3—MARYLAND AND PENNSYLVANIA

Chapter 7

Centreville, Virginia

JUNE 19–20, 1863

THE MEN MOVED ALONG THE dusty road at the route step, stooped over from the weight of their packs. It had not been a bad march this day—just over six miles and three hours on the road. A cloudy day had made the temperature tolerable, but the weight of carrying fifty pounds of regulation gear plus all their personal items on their backs was still tiring.

Captain Muller moved off the road and stopped. "Kompanieee, halt!"

The men of E Company shuffled to a halt.

Henry managed a tired smile. Captain Muller was Swiss, and he sometimes mixed German and English, especially when he was excited or tired. In this case, they couldn't really tell—the words sounded the same.

"Right, face!" Muller commanded. The company turned to the right in unison. "First Sergeant!" Muller called out. First Sergeant Trevor moved to face Captain Muller and saluted, then did an about-face toward the company. "Eee Company, fall out!"

he shouted. As the tired troops moved out of formation, he added, “Platoon sergeants, see me.”

Henry nodded to Corporal Jock McKenzie, one of his squad leaders. He was a little Scotsman and a natural leader. Jock would keep things organized while he met with the first sergeant. The work of the NCOs (noncommissioned officers) was just starting—details to organize, a guard mount to arrange; all the admin tasks of an army on the move. As he walked toward First Sergeant Trevor, Henry heard a military band off in the distance. Artillery pieces and caissons pulled by teams of horses began to rattle by on the road.

Sometime later, finally finished with all his admin tasks, Henry could relax. He walked back toward his platoon area and pulled his tin mess cup out of his pack. Jock was ready with the communal coffeepot and poured him a cup. Henry nodded and sat down. Normally, Jock would make a snide comment about the lack of tea, but this time he was silent. *Must be tired like the rest of us,* Henry thought.

As he sat blowing on his coffee to cool it down, Henry thought about what was happening. News was nonexistent, and all they got was camp rumors. He discounted all that. He just wished he could get his hands on a newspaper.

“Hello, brother,” a voice said, interrupting his thoughts. Looking up, he saw it was Isaac standing above him.

“Where you been?” Henry asked.

Isaac grinned. “Went down to see the ‘sogers’ on ‘p-rade.’ They were all prettied up with dress uniforms and white gloves.”

Henry grunted. “Who are those guys?”

“Twenty-Second Corps—General Heintzelman’s valiant defenders of Washington,” Isaac mockingly said. “I did talk to a couple of them. They’re a brigade of New York regiments. The guys I spoke with are with the One Hundred Eleventh New York, from up in the middle part of the state. Those two fellows were from a little town called Cato."

"The ancient Roman senator?"

"That's the one, and those boys are itching to get into battle. I think they need to be careful what they wish for." Isaac chuckled.

Henry nodded. "Well, if they do, I hope they fight like ancient Romans."

Isaac sat down next to Henry. "Yeah, I hope so too. Got some news."

"Yeah, what?" Henry turned toward Isaac.

"Rebs took Winchester, Virginia, a few days ago. Looks like they are on their way north."

Henry stared into his coffee. *Another Antietam,* he thought. *Let's hope it's not as bloody as the last time!*

Hancock stood over a map spread out on a field table. Next to him, Colonel Morgan held the recently received orders for their next day's movement. Just as Morgan began to read the orders, a commotion interrupted him.

Hancock heard an assertive voice shouting "I demand to speak with your commanding officer!"

The group parted, and a burly, red-bearded brigadier general in dress uniform, sash, and sword barged through. Hancock recognized him immediately. It was his classmate and old friend Alexander Hays.

Hays straightened himself and looked Hancock in the eyes. "General Hancock, I am in command of this post. Your artillery is parked on my parade ground. They will have to find another place. In addition, your troops are out of control. You must enforce discipline in your corps! I have doubled my guard, with orders to shoot the first man who interferes with them."

Hancock was a bit taken back by Alexander's forceful and almost insubordinate tone. Still, he knew his classmate very well, and that outburst was pure Alexander Hays. "You are right, General," he said. Turning to Colonel Morgan, he began to give orders. "Morgan, get word to Captain Hazard. Tell him that he will have to move his artillery. Have him coordinate with the post provost for a suitable place. Oh, and get word to each division commander—they must get their people under control. Have them make contact with the provost as well, to ensure order is maintained." He looked at Hays, who smiled and nodded. "And now, gentlemen, General Hays and I have other matters to discuss. If you will excuse us?" He motioned to the inside of his tent and followed Hays in as the group broke up.

Once inside the tent, Hancock spread his arms wide. "Sandy, it's great to see you."

Alexander moved in, and the two hugged in a back-slapping embrace. "It's good to see you too, Win."

Alexander stepped back and looked at Hancock. "Major general and corps commander. Not bad, Win. You look good. It's quite a difference from that skinny sixteen-year-old I met on the first day at West Point!"

"Yes, I was pretty small and scrawny…hadn't finished growing." Hancock chuckled. "It was a good thing I had you around to protect me!"

"That upperclassman who used to torment you—what was his name?"

"Crittenden," Hancock said.

"Yeah, Crittenden." Hays paused to recall a memory. "I had to challenge him to a fight to get him to stop bullying you."

"That was one hell of a fight, Sandy. You both beat the hell out of each other. I remember Crittenden's classmates carrying him off after the fight. He was in bed for days afterward!"

"Yup, and he didn't bother you any more, did he?"

"No, he didn't." Hancock chuckled. "Crittenden's bullying did teach me a couple of things, though. Never back down, and never show fear."

The pair paused for a few moments remembering that time.

"So, you're not doing so bad yourself, Sandy—brigadier general and brigade commander," Hancock said, changing the subject. "Tell me about your brigade." He motioned to a seat.

Hays sat down and gave a deep sigh. "Well, you remember last September when Miles surrendered Harpers Ferry without a fight?" Hancock nodded. "These fellows were part of the garrison that was surrendered. Since that time they have been called 'the Harpers Ferry Cowards,' which was very unfair, as they had no part in the decision to surrender or fight."

"Must have been pretty tough on morale," Hancock said.

"Yeah, it has been. The biggest challenge was to get them to feel that they are good soldiers. We've been drilling and holding dress parades—things we would do in the regular army. Slowly they have come around, and I think we have some good, solid regiments. There were a few problems on the way, though."

Hancock raised one eyebrow. "Like what?"

"The Thirty-Ninth New York—the Garibaldi Guards—they claimed that they were not properly exchanged and refused duty. Well, I had to knock that out of their heads! Their colonel, D'Utassy, encouraged this claim. He had a large entourage with servants and caterers—living like a European prince. As you might imagine, discipline in his regiment was nonexistent. We finally got rid of D'Utassy by court-martialing him. Once he was gone, I cleaned house by mustering out NCOs and officers who weren't up to snuff. Then I put Hildebrandt in command; he's a good officer, ex-Prussian military, tough and strict. Most of the soldiers in his regiment have served in European armies, so they know what to do. They just needed the right kind of leadership."

"Sounds like you handled the situation with subtlety and sensitivity! That's the Sandy Hays I know," Hancock said.

"Yes, I have never believed in beating around the bush." Hays paused. "The rest of the regiments have been no real trouble. They are mostly farm boys from upstate New York, used to hard work. They make good soldiers."

Hancock held up a whiskey bottle, and Hays nodded. He was silent while Hancock poured a glass. "I heard some Washington scuttlebutt that you might be interested in..."

"Oh?" Hancock replied, pouring himself a glass.

"Do you know Alex Webb?"

"Meade's chief of staff?"

"Yes. He's been recalled to Washington—due for promotion to brigadier general. As I understand it, he is currently unassigned. He's got a good reputation, Win. If you need a brigade commander, you might be able to snap him up."

"Hmm...I am definitely interested. I have a couple of ideas where he might be used." Hancock took a sip of whiskey.

Hays set down his glass. ays

"Oh, and I have some good news for you. I received notice that after you leave, I am to send all unnecessary equipment back to Washington, prepare my brigade for movement, and then march to join the Second Corps."

Hancock sat up in his chair. "That is great news! Our Third Division is short a brigade, and you would be the senior officer, making you the division commander. Wonderful! So who is your brigade's senior colonel?"

"Colonel Willard. He's a good man, regular army—was a sergeant in the Mexican War, cited at Chapultepec and given a battlefield commission. He'd make a great brigade commander!"

Hancock, suddenly serious, leaned toward Hays. "I'm glad to hear that, Sandy. We need every unit at maximum fighting condition. It looks like we are headed north to a big battle that we cannot afford to lose!"

Early the next morning, Henry Taylor was called to a meeting with the company command team. At the end of the meeting, after saluting Captain Muller, Henry walked back to his platoon area with their orders for the day. The night had been uneventful, for which Henry was thankful. Around him, men were engaged in the activities that filled a soldier's free time. Some were reading, others writing letters, a few were napping, and a group was playing cards. Henry shot a quick look toward the sky—overcast. The weather might cooperate today with cooler temperatures for the march. *Not like two days ago,* he thought. The combination of high temperature and high humidity took a real toll on the troops. Large numbers fell out due to heat exhaustion. The lack of clean water was also a big factor. Fortunately, Henry noted, General Hancock sent his ambulance corps to pick up those who had fallen out of ranks. Who knew what would happen to them with bushwhackers and reb cavalry on the loose?

When he reached the platoon area, Henry found his three corporal squad leaders grouped together waiting to receive the day's orders. They were a good lot, Henry thought, looking them over. Jock McKenzie was his little Scotsman. Edwin Austin and Ben Staples were his other two squad leaders.

Henry nodded to them and began. "Looks like we will have a leisurely march today. We will break camp and form up on the road at noon. May have to wait a bit there. We have been assigned as the rear brigade and will follow the trains, so expect it to be slow."

"Ayuh," Corporal Staples said. "And we'll be kicking road ahpples all day!"

Henry chuckled. Staples grew up in Maine and had not lost his "down east" accent one bit. Still, a long stream of horse- and mule-drawn artillery and supply trains was bound to leave the road littered with prodigious amounts of dung. "Well," he replied, "we'll just have to watch where we step!"

The group chuckled, and Henry continued. "Take this opportunity to check everyone out. Make sure their gear is in good shape, especially their shoes. Looks like the rebs are moving north, and we will have a good deal of marching to do in the next couple of weeks to catch up with them, which will probably be up somewhere in Maryland." His squad leaders nodded in acknowledgment and moved off to attend to their squads.

At noon, the company formed up on the road and, after a bit of standing around, was allowed to fall out to the side of the road. Henry stood next to his platoon, thinking about what waited for them in Maryland.

"Sergeant Taylor?" A familiar voice interrupted his thoughts. He turned to face Jock McKenzie. "I canna find Isaac—he's gone."

"Shit!" Henry swore under his breath. He had assigned Isaac to Jock's squad because he knew Jock could keep him under control. "He's wandered off somewhere—can't have gone too far. When he gets back, send him to me."

Jock nodded and walked away.

A while later, Isaac ambled up to Henry. "Jock said you wanted to see me."

"Isaac, where the hell have you been? You know you can't just be wandering off from formation like that!"

"Well," Isaac said, "it was not technically a formation. We were ordered to fall out. Besides, I wasn't all that far away. There was a cemetery across the road and down a ways. I was looking at the epitaphs. Not much there, though; kind of disappointing. I think a man's epitaph says a lot about their life, don't you?"

Henry just rolled his eyes in disgust. "Isaac," he said, checking his anger, "I am responsible for the discipline in this platoon. If I let you wander off without permission, all the others will think it is OK for them to do it too. From now on, if you want to leave the platoon, you get permission from either Jock or me. Is that clear?"

Isaac looked down and nodded.

"Fine," Henry said. "Now get back to your squad."

Chapter 8

June 27–28, 1863

FREDERICK, MARYLAND

THE LAST DIVISION COMMANDER REPORTED closing on the camp, and George Meade had one less thing to worry about. He still had quite enough to keep him fretting, the most important of which was the situation. There were no orders waiting for him when he arrived at this campsite just south of Frederick in Central Maryland. Lack of orders made him nervous, and he received so little information from army headquarters that he had to rely mainly on the newspapers and word of mouth from the civilian population. At least up here they supported the Union and he could rely on most of the information, but still, why couldn't he get the information he needed from his own commander?

Around him, his Fifth Corps made camp for the night, with a murmur of voices and the banging of tent pegs being driven into the ground. They hadn't had a bad march today—only about sixteen miles, and they had arrived with enough light to make camp properly. Meade liked that; he wanted his men to be well rested and in good spirits. The time would come very soon, he knew, when they would have to meet Lee's army, and then he would have to ask them to perform the seemingly near impossible—save the Union.

Meade scowled at this last thought and looked around. To his north, the church steeples of Frederick rose above the trees. The ragged blue-green wall of the Catoctin Mountains loomed to his west. *Somewhere beyond that ridgeline,* Meade thought, *Lee's army is on the prowl.* The only trouble was, he had no idea where Lee might be. Hooker might know, but he hadn't seen Hooker in two weeks, and Hooker had the disagreeable habit of not keeping his subordinates informed. Meade's stomach knotted a little more.

A lone horseman pounded down the dirt road—it was the aide he had sent to find Hooker. "Did you find General Hooker?" he called out hopefully.

The aide reined in his horse a dozen paces from Meade. "No, sir, but I found his headquarters. I reported that the lead elements had closed on Frederick, and I asked for orders as you directed. There is no one at headquarters who knows anything about our orders for tomorrow, sir."

"Butterfield couldn't tell you?" Meade was incredulous.

"General Butterfield wasn't around either, sir. They couldn't tell me when either general was expected back. It's pretty much chaos up there, sir." The aide shook his head.

Meade's eyes narrowed. "Well, that's goddamn ridiculous. What kind of way is that to run an army?"

The aide shrank back a little—the snapping turtle was making its presence known. Meade hesitated. *No need to take it out on him; it's not his fault.* He looked over to an orderly. "Bring my horse. I'm going up there to find Hooker myself." Meade mounted the horse and galloped off toward Frederick, trailing a pack of nervous aides.

He wasn't any more successful than his aide. The headquarters tent was empty except for a few orderlies and the duty officer, a young captain. "Do you know where General Hooker is?" Meade asked.

The young officer hesitated, then answered sheepishly. "No, sir. He rode off this morning, and we haven't seen him since."

"He didn't leave any word on where he was going or when he would be back?"

"No, General, he did not. There was some talk last night about visiting the garrison at Harper's Ferry, but they didn't say that was where they were going."

"And General Butterfield?" Meade snapped.

"He went with General Hooker, sir." The captain's voice quavered just a little.

Meade slapped his hat on the pommel in disgust. "I don't suppose either of those fine officers left word as to what I am expected to do with my corps tomorrow?" He was fighting to keep his anger in check.

"No, sir. The only thing I could suggest is to wait until General Hooker gets back—"

"And you have no goddamn idea when that would be." Meade had had quite enough of this. He reined his horse around. "Tell General Hooker that I came by. If he has orders for me or wishes to speak to me, I will be with my corps!" With that, he spurred his horse to a gallop and headed back to his camp.

It was starting to get dark when they returned to the camp. Dinner was being prepared, and an orderly brought Meade a plate of food. He had no hunger and could only pick at the contents of his plate. Finally, he put the plate down and stared into the campfire. Tired and disgusted, he sat silently, lost in his thoughts. Governor Curtin's words came to him: "no time left for fools or incompetents." Now Lee was in Pennsylvania—he could even be at the outskirts of Harrisburg. *How can the army possibly beat Lee if they are so disorganized? Fools and incompetents?* Meade shook his head to clear these thoughts. He was tired, and it had been a long day. Maybe it was time he turned in. Hooker's orders would no doubt arrive long before dawn, and it would be another long, tiring, and no doubt frustrating day tomorrow.

In his tent, Meade pulled off his boots and placed his dusty jacket on the table. He would sleep in his clothes in case he needed to get moving in a hurry. As sleep surrounded him, he thought once more of Governor Curtin's warning.

The voices outside his tent woke him. He cracked open one eye and looked around. It was still dark; no telling what time it was. Hooker had finally sent his orders, Meade decided. *Just deliver the damn orders and shut up!* He wanted some more sleep. Meade was suddenly aware of someone in his tent.

A hand touched his shoulder. "General Meade?" It was a voice he did not recognize—not one of his own staff.

"Yes…" Meade fought the grogginess. *Who is this person?*

"Sir, I'm Colonel Hardie of the War Department."

"War Department? What are you doing here?" This did not make any sense to Meade. He fought to make his brain work. *The War Department should be talking to General Hooker.*

"I'm afraid, sir, that I've come to bring you trouble," Hardie said.

Trouble? What could that mean? Meade rubbed his face. *Trouble—he has come to arrest me. It must be Hooker's doing.* He pulled himself up straight. "If you've come to arrest me, my conscience is clear."

"Oh no, sir." Sounds of hands fumbling with a matchbox and the rasp of a match being struck. Meade turned away from the sudden flare of light. Colonel Hardie lit a candle on the bed stand and reached into his pocket and pulled out a letter of several sheets sealed with wax. "Here is an order from President Lincoln appointing you commander of the Army of the Potomac. General Halleck has included a detailed set of instructions you are to follow."

Meade took the packet reluctantly and did not open it. He was now fully awake, and the enormity of what was happening became clearer. "No, this will not do!" He shook his head forcefully. "I have made it quite plain that I do not want this job. Why was Reynolds not chosen?"

Hardie managed a pained smile. "Sir, the president and General Halleck have considered all these factors and have nonetheless decided to appoint you to the command. I am directed to accompany you to General Hooker and witness the transfer of command."

Meade was not ready to accept any of this. "I wish to wire General Halleck immediately and ask to be excused."

Hardie's smile disappeared. "General Meade, with all due respect, sir, this is an order, not a request."

Meade sighed at Hardie's response. *Yes, of course he's right.* Meade was too old a soldier to argue any more. It was an order, and he would have to carry it out, even if he did detest it. He sighed and nodded. "Well, I have been tried and condemned without a hearing, and I suppose I shall have to go to execution." Meade broke open the orders and looked at the first sheet. It was there in black and white; President Lincoln had even signed it. He looked at the instructions from General Halleck and scanned the details. Old Brains had detailed everything in his typical pedantic style. Meade was sure there was much of value in these instructions; he respected Halleck's great intelligence and military knowledge. *There's probably everything in here except how to beat Lee,* he thought. Meade folded the papers and put them in his pocket.

He pulled on his mud-spattered boots and, buttoning his jacket, stepped outside the tent. His whole staff was awake and gathered around expectantly. *They must have heard I had a special guest,* he thought. He looked for his son. "George, could you have a horse saddled for me and for Colonel Hardie? Oh, and have the cook make us some coffee and a little breakfast." He walked away from the fire. "I will be right back. I need to speak with General Warren."

Warren's tent was not far away, and Meade had no trouble finding it. If the past few weeks had taught him anything, it was that he needed a chief of staff with military training and a temperament to match his own. Butterfield had neither, and Meade did not really get along with him—or trust him, for that matter. Now, Warren would make a good chief of staff. He was a West Point graduate and an engineer, and he was good friends with Meade. Meade rubbed his beard. If he was going to have any chance of success, he would need a competent chief of staff. Meade stepped into Warren's tent and gently shook his friend. "Warren, can you wake up? It's George Meade."

Warren woke with a start. He threw off his blanket and sat up. "George? What's wrong?"

"Nothing's wrong. I just need to talk to you about something very important. You awake?" Warren blinked several times and nodded. Meade continued. "I've just received word that I am to replace Hooker, and I'm going over to headquarters with a colonel from the War Department to make it official."

Warren squinted. "They've chosen the worst time possible to make a change in command. We will most likely be engaged in battle within the next several weeks."

"I am painfully aware of that," Meade said. "But the decision is out of my hands. Look, the reason I'm here is that I need a good chief of staff. I need someone I can rely on, and I would like you to take the job."

Warren was quiet for a moment. "George, I don't think I would make a good chief of staff. If we are going to have a battle soon, then you need an experienced man who is acquainted with how the army runs. It would take me several weeks to get everything figured out, and by then it would be too late. Besides, I could be of greater use to you in the capacity of chief engineer."

"Well," Meade said, "I just don't have much confidence in Butterfield. He is clearly Hooker's man."

"He's not that bad, George. I've seen him at work, and he does a good job. Why don't you give him a chance?"

"Yes, well, I'll think about it. If you change your mind, let me know."

Warren nodded. "I will. Oh, and George, congratulations."

"Thanks, I think." *I don't really feel like celebrating,* he thought. *The others get a choice, but I get orders.* Meade shook the thought away. *Must not brood on the negatives. There is so much to do, and I don't know anything about what is happening outside of the Fifth Corps.* He pulled aside the tent flaps, left Warren's tent, and walked slowly back toward his own headquarters.

They ate breakfast in silence. Meade's head was swimming with hundreds of questions that no one could answer. Dawn was beginning to lighten the eastern sky as they mounted and started off toward Hooker's headquarters.

As they rode up, Hooker appeared outside his tent in full uniform. Meade guessed that he had received word that a War Department visitor was in camp. Hooker shifted his cold blue eyes between Meade and Hardie. *He knows,* Meade thought. *He is prepared for this—I wonder how I will take it when they replace me.*

Colonel Hardie broke the awkward silence. "General Hooker, I am Colonel Hardie of the War Department. I have business of a critical and confidential nature. May we speak to you in private, sir?"

Hooker nodded glumly and motioned for the men to follow him. Once inside the tent, Colonel Hardie wasted no time. "General Hooker, I have orders here from the War Department relieving you of command and assigning you to command the Baltimore garrison." He handed Hooker a letter as he spoke.

Hooker sadly broke the letter open and scanned the contents. "It was very kind of the president to accept my resignation so quickly." A blend of sarcasm, relief, and sadness.

Colonel Hardie cleared his throat nervously and pressed on. "General Halleck has directed me to be present for the transfer of command. Perhaps we should brief General Meade on the general situation?"

"Of course. Let me send for General Butterfield. He can help with the briefing."

Hooker left to find his chief of staff. He soon returned with Butterfield, who appeared hurriedly dressed and flushed. *He must not be taking the news very well,* Meade thought. *All the more reason to find a replacement as soon as possible.*

Butterfield spread the map out on the table, and Hooker began the briefing, pointing out the position of each corps. Meade grew uneasy as the army's disposition became clear. Hooker had four corps on the west side of the Catoctin Mountains and three on the east side. Lee could easily block the two mountain passes, cut the army in half, and crush one part before turning on the next. *They are certainly out of supporting distance from each other!*

"I am afraid our forces might be a bit scattered," he said.

Butterfield and Hooker both looked up, glaring. Hooker's face turned red. "You have no idea of the overall tactical situation!" he snapped.

Meade held up his hand. "I didn't mean anything by that," he said soothingly. Hooker nodded and looked back down at the map. *Change the subject,* Meade told himself. "How about this garrison at Harper's Ferry?" he asked, "It seems like a good position to threaten Lee's lines of communication in the Cumberland Valley."

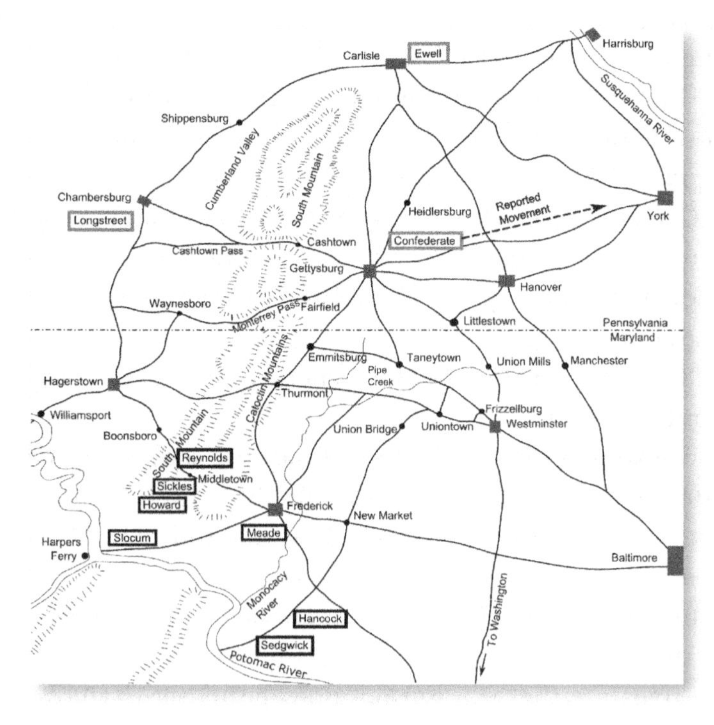

SITUATION—28 JUNE

Hooker shook his head, and Butterfield chimed in. "The post lacks sufficient provisions. A small enemy force could cut it off and prevent it from being resupplied."

"The garrison is in danger and could be used much more effectively elsewhere," Hooker added, his face turning red. "I have been trying to convince Halleck to let me withdraw them, but he would hear none of it!"

Meade shot a quick glance at an impassive Colonel Hardie—no reaction. *Best to move on.* "OK, what do we know about the enemy?"

"We have a report from General Couch in Harrisburg that the rebs are in possession of Gettysburg, five thousand strong, moving eastward toward York." Butterfield moved his pointer to the two southern Pennsylvania cities. "Other reports have Ewell's corps up here in Carlisle." The pointer moved to a city about fifty miles north of Gettysburg. "Longstreet's corps is reported to be in Chambersburg." Butterfield pointed to the city to the west of Gettysburg.

The news of the enemy left Meade chilled. This meant the enemy was north and northeast of the Army of the Potomac with the Union army facing west. Meade shuddered as he realized this was like Napoleon's Ulm campaign—where the French surprised and enveloped an Austrian army facing the wrong way.

Looking at the map, he considered the reported enemy locations. "Any ideas on Lee's intentions?" he asked.

"Well," Hooker said, "we know that Lee doesn't have any bridging equipment in his trains, so he will not be able to cross the Susquehanna. He most probably will follow the river down toward Baltimore or Washington."

"Umm, the Susquehanna is neither deep nor swift in that section," Meade carefully said. "It would be possible for them to cross at a low-water point."

Butterfield and Hooker stared at Meade, silent. *Is that it?* Meade asked himself. *No briefing on what you were going to do? If you expect Lee to head south along the Susquehanna, why face your army to the west?* Meade rubbed his beard. Hooker didn't seem to have any plan; he was transfixed, unable or unwilling to act in a decisive manner.

After a long uncomfortable silence, Meade concluded that they were done with the briefing. He stood and thanked the pair. Stepping outside to where his son George was waiting, Meade sighed and said, "Well, George, I am in command of the Army of the Potomac."

His son smiled wryly—he already knew.

Meade nodded and sighed again. "George, go back to camp and pick up my belongings. Bring them and the rest of my staff here to my new headquarters."

"General Meade," Hardie said, "General Halleck has instructed me to remain in camp until the announcements of change of command have been made. I know you have a great deal of things to do. If there is anything I can do to clarify General Halleck's instructions, please let me know." He ended with a salute.

Meade returned the salute and turned toward the staff tent to look for an empty desk where he could work. An orderly directed him to a desk, where Meade began to write his telegraphic response to General Halleck. "The order placing me in command of this army is received. As a soldier I obey it and to the utmost of my ability will execute it."[1] He paused, suddenly overcome by the enormity of the task before him.

Meade pulled Halleck's instruction letter from his pocket and read it again. Key phrases jumped out: "act as the covering army of Washington as well as the army of operation against the invading forces of the rebels...maneuver and fight in such a manner as to cover the capital and also Baltimore." For a moment, he felt overwhelmed and helpless.

Shaking this off, he concentrated on the facts, building a logical structure to the situation. It was his engineer training, and he felt comfortable using this approach. He had solved hundreds of complex problems in his career, and this could just be another one. Doubt and despair melted away as he fell into the practiced rhythm of the engineer: start with the facts, link facts together, build a logical model, and design a solution.

It all was becoming clearer now, logical and precise. First off, he had to assemble the army to remove it from the danger of defeat in detail. Then he would change the direction in which the army was facing. Practiced eyes traced the best routes on his map. It would mean some very hard marching, but it could be done within two days.

In the larger strategic picture, he knew that he needed to distract Lee from trying to cross the Susquehanna and capture Harrisburg. He thought fleetingly of Curtin and Couch in Harrisburg—he was their only hope. *Forget that,* he caught himself. *Concentrate on the problem at hand.* The logical solution was to advance carefully north. If Lee was spread out and separated from his supply lines in the Cumberland Valley, he would be compelled to pull back and concentrate to meet the threat. Once concentrated, Lee would either defend or attack, and the army must be ready for either. If Lee ignored this threat and moved toward Washington, Meade would need a blocking force to hold Lee up until the rest of the Army of the Potomac could join it. The logical choice, he concluded, was John Sedgwick's Sixth Corps. They were in Poolesville, Maryland, and could move unimpeded toward the northeast. He put his finger on the map near Westminster, Maryland. There was a ridgeline there that would offer some defensive position, and he knew John Sedgwick would pick the best one and hold on until relieved.

Satisfied with his plan, Meade turned back to his message to Halleck. "I can only say that it appears to me," he wrote, "that I must move towards the Susquehanna, keeping Washington and Baltimore well covered, and if the enemy is checked in his attempt to cross the Susquehanna or if he turns towards Baltimore, to give him battle."[2] When he finished writing, Meade read it over, and satisfied with the contents, he handed it to a waiting orderly.

Meade scratched out rough orders for the corps commanders to assemble on Frederick, Maryland. His staff could clean them up, but he would need to get all his army corps marching right away.

The train lurched to a stop, and Dan Sickles braced himself, ready to hop up as soon as the train stopped moving. He was tired from the long trip but anxious to be back with his corps after thirty days away. During this convalescence leave, the Third Corps had marched up from Falmouth, Virginia, to Middletown over the mountain west of Frederick, Maryland.

As he stepped out onto the platform, Major Tremain stepped forward to greet him, and nearby, other aides waited with his horse. Sickles smiled; his aides sure new how to treat him right. After a few formalities, Tremain moved closer. "General, I have some distressing news. We were informed this morning that General Hooker has been relieved of command and General Meade installed in his place."

Sickles's smile disappeared. "Are you sure of this?"

His aide nodded sadly. "Yes, sir. We received an order to move early this morning, by orders of General Meade. One of the boys rode down to army headquarters and confirmed it."

"And General Hooker—where is he now?"

Tremain shrugged. "Still at headquarters, as far as we know, General."

Sickles stood quite still for a few moments. "I need to go to army headquarters immediately. Please show me where it is."

On arriving at the headquarters, Sickles found that the report was all too true. Meade was in Hooker's tent, busy sending out orders. He found Hooker in Butterfield's tent. Hooker was despondent, as low as he had been at Chancellorsville. Butterfield was flushed and angry. A sickly feeling spread over Sickles. All his plans, once so well constructed, were now in danger of falling apart. There had to be a way to save at least some of it.

Taking a deep breath and conjuring up his most charming smile, Sickles pulled up a chair and sat next to Hooker. "Cheer up, Joe. Lincoln has made a bad political move. No one supports Meade. This won't last long."

Hooker shook his head. "The damage has already been done. My career is finished."

Sickles shook his head. "The damage can just as easily be undone. Meade is a political innocent and not very highly regarded among the Radical Republicans. He will soon commit enough political blunders to have the entire radical wing of the Congress demanding his removal. Lincoln then will have no choice but to comply, and you, General Hooker, will be first on the list of Meade's replacements. I will see to that."

Hooker brightened slightly and nodded. "Yes, I can see that. I must remain optimistic."

"Of course you must," Sickles said. "And you must continue to show that you are the one most fit for command. Put up a good show. Be as gracious and stoic as possible, even if your heart is breaking. The call will once more come to you."

Hooker thought for a while and nodded. Sickles grinned back. He could turn things around yet; he just needed a little time. Hooker had no idea that the president would never have him back. If Meade was forced out, then the door would be open for Dan Sickles.

"Perhaps I had better offer my resignation," Butterfield said. "I have heard that Meade has been asking other officers if they would consent to be chief of staff. My days in this position are clearly numbered. Besides, I have never really liked Meade, especially after he bumped me out of command at the Fifth Corps on account of seniority."

Sickles was quick to squash that idea. "No, Dan. It is important that you stay on as long as Meade will have you. During this time, you should serve him as best you can."

"Why? What is so important that I stay on working for someone I do not like and, in return, does not want me around?"

Sickles lit a cigar and smiled. "Because you have a very important task during this period, Dan. I want you to keep a record of every questionable move that Meade makes, any disloyal statements, or any hint of defeatism. If I am right about Meade, we will soon have plenty of evidence to use against him when the time is right. And don't you worry. I know just the right people in Congress to feed this evidence to."

"Very well," Butterfield said. "I will stay on. However, you need to be careful yourself."

Sickles arched an eyebrow. "Why do you say that?"

Butterfield moved closer. "I understand that General Meade has received authority from Halleck and Lincoln to replace anyone at his discretion without prior approval from the War Department, and he can promote people without any regard to seniority."

Sickles stewed over the meaning of this last bit of information all the way over the mountain to his Third Corps encampment. He had not expected the War Department to give Meade so much power. What he had thought would be very easy was now turning out to be much harder and more dangerous to him personally.

"Sir?"

Meade looked up; it was one of the orderlies.

"General Reynolds has arrived, sir."

Meade got up from his desk and stepped outside the tent. John Reynolds was striding toward him in full dress uniform. He stopped and saluted. "General Reynolds reporting to the commanding general. I wish to extend my congratulations!"

Instead of returning the salute, Meade extended his hand. "John, thank you for coming." He motioned with his head toward the tent. "Let's go inside, and I can fill you in on what's going on."

Once they entered the tent, Reynolds put his hand on Meade's shoulder. "Well, George, the army finally has a real commander!"

Meade shook his head. "John, I never asked for this job, and I tried to turn it down, but I was ordered to take it. I had to choice but to obey."

"If it's any consolation, George, had it come to me in the same way, I would have been obliged to take it as well." Reynolds paused for a moment. "I am glad, though, that it did not." Meade was silent. "Look, George, I am convinced that President Lincoln made the right choice. You are the only general in the army with the training and intellectual ability to match Lee, and you have my unconditional support in whatever you decide to do."

Meade brightened a bit. "Thank you for that, John. I appreciate you saying that. Now, why don't we look at the map?" He spread his arm out toward the map table.

"Now here's the general situation. Lee's army appears to be spread out, with reported positions out here in the Cumberland Valley around Chambersburg and with units advancing toward Harrisburg and York. We don't know if Lee intends to ford the Susquehanna and make toward Harrisburg and on to Philadelphia or move down the Susquehanna toward Baltimore and, ultimately, Washington. Either way, we need to turn his attention back toward the west by moving against his rear." Meade looked up at Reynolds.

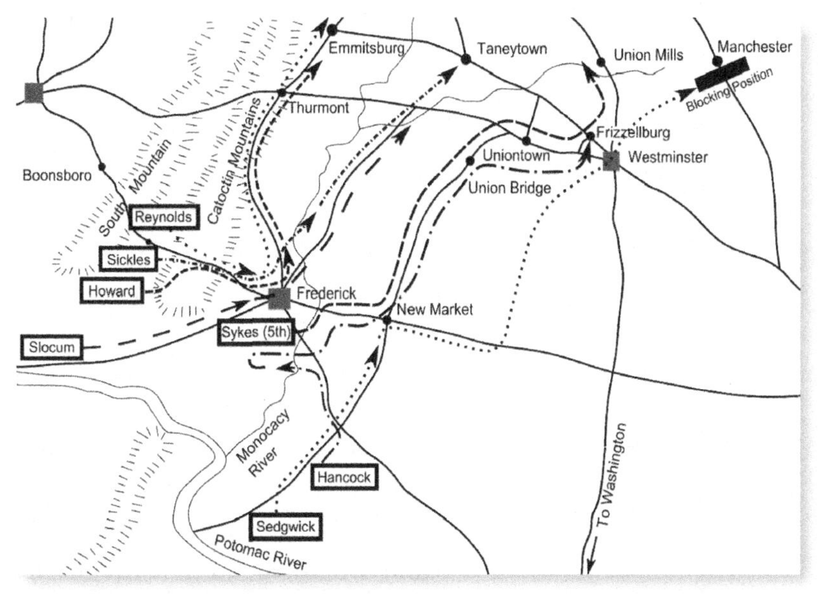

Meade's Plan

Reynolds considered the map and nodded. "Yes, I agree. We must take the initiative and make him react to our moves."

"So the first step, which is going on right now, is to assemble all the corps in the general vicinity of Frederick so that they are in supporting distance of each other." Meade made a circle around Frederick on the map with his finger. "The next step, which will take place tomorrow, is to position the army on a line from Emmitsburg here in the west over to around Westminster in the east. Once there, we will be in a position to respond to whatever Lee decides to do. By that time we will, hopefully, have a clearer picture of enemy positions and movements. We can then act accordingly. My intent is to move forward into Pennsylvania on a broad front."

Reynolds considered the map. “I think that’s a good plan. What do you need me to do?”

“I intend to send a left wing north, with you in command, hugging the eastern side of the Catoctin Mountains and South Mountain up into Pennsylvania along the axis of Emmitsburg-Gettysburg-Carlisle. If the bulk of Lee’s forces are truly in the Cumberland Valley, they may try to attack through one of the passes and hit us in the flank. I am not very familiar with this terrain, though.”

“Well, I am,” Reynolds said. “I grew up in Lancaster, and I did a fair amount of hunting in those mountains as a boy. They are heavily forested, with few decent roads that would support major troop movements. The only two feasible routes of attack are this pass from Waynesboro through the Monterey Pass to Fairfield and over South Mountain from Chambersburg through the Cashtown Pass in the direction of Gettysburg.” Reynolds looked up from the map at Meade. “You know, George, we are going to need some top-notch support from the cavalry if we are going to pull this off.”

“Yes, I am well aware of that. The cavalry’s performance at Chancellorsville was quite disappointing. I spoke to Pleasanton earlier today about this. He believes more aggressive leadership is needed, and he recommended the promotion of three outstanding captains to brigadier general.”

“Whew!” Reynolds said. “That is one hell of a jump—four grades. Bet that will ruffle a lot of feathers. How are you going to pull that one off?”

“Well, Halleck has given me authority to promote anyone, irrespective of seniority. I have wired for formal permission, and I expect to get it soon, hopefully yet today.”

"I didn't think they would ever allow that." Reynolds shook his head. "Looks like they are finally ready to let us run things. It's about time!"

"Yes, and Halleck has also assigned an additional cavalry division to us. We will finally have the cavalry manpower to match up with the rebs. I am assigning General Buford's cavalry division to your left wing, John. He will have responsibility for screening your left flank and front as you move forward."

Reynolds nodded enthusiastically. "Excellent. He is the best cavalry commander we've got!"

Meade leaned closer to Reynolds and lowered his voice. "Halleck also gave me authority to relieve, at my sole discretion, any officer I see fit. I need your opinion on the corps commanders."

"Well, let's see," Reynolds said. "We don't need to worry about Hancock. He is fearless and is a tactical genius. John Sedgwick is rock steady. He will accomplish whatever order you give him. You know George Sykes much better that I do: slow but steady. Howard is a smart fellow, but a little inexperienced. His great misfortune was inheriting a corps with serious discipline and morale problems. Slocum and the Twelfth Corps are steady. He won't stick his neck out, but he will do whatever you tell him to do. The only one I have doubts about is Sickles. He is fearless and would make a great brigade commander, maybe a division commander, but he doesn't have the experience, temperament, or training to be a corps commander. What he did at Chancellorsville makes me question his judgment—pushing out unsupported like that. He almost got his whole corps cut off."

Meade was silent for a while. "Yes, that was my impression as well. If I had to replace General Sickles, who do you think would make a good replacement corps commander?"

"Hmm…none of my division commanders. I would say the first person who comes to mind is John Newton, Sixth Corps. He is an engineer, like you, so he is very detail oriented. An excellent leader, and absolutely fearless. He personally led a bayonet charge at Marye's Heights last May and took the position. Class of '42—he was a year behind me at the academy. Even though he is a Virginian, he remained loyal. Yes, John Newton would be an excellent choice."

"Well, let's hope it doesn't come to that. Thanks for the advice; I will certainly keep it in mind."

Chapter 9

June 29, 1863

NORTHERN MARYLAND

MEADE LOOKED AT HIS STAFF gathered around the map table, illuminated by candlelight in the predawn darkness. "So, what new information do we have about the enemy?"

General Butterfield stepped forward toward the map. "General Buford reports signs of a large cavalry force having moved north through the Cumberland Valley in Maryland from Boonsboro here in the direction of Hagerstown. The enemy cavalry in our rear continues to work around toward our right flank."

"Hmm," Meade said, "they may be trying to distract us from our movement north—we can't let them do that. What new information do we have about the forces in Pennsylvania?"

"Nothing new at this time," Butterfield said. "The reb cavalry in or rear have cut our telegraph line, so there is no communication with Washington and Harrisburg. Captain Norton has his signal crews out to find and repair the breaks, but it will take some time to get them operational. In the meantime, we will have to depend on dispatch riders."

Meade considered the situation. *No change to the basic situation, so we stay the course.* "OK, we keep on as planned. I want you all to realize that this movement we are making today is complex and will require great exertions on the part of our men. I have selected routes for each corps to maximize movement. I want all corps commanders to report their progress on a regular basis and to immediately report any delays." He looked around at the group. "Everyone understand that?" Heads nodded in response. "Well, then, let's get that information out to the commanders." The group saluted and broke up.

Meade caught General Warren on the way out of the tent. "What do we know about the terrain up in front of us?"

Warren shook his head. "The available maps are quite poor and lacking detail, so we don't have a clear picture of what's up there. In general, the ridgelines around here tend to run north to south."

"I have a mission for you and your engineers, then. Have them scout out the terrain between here and the Pennsylvania line for a suitable defensive position. If we are going to have a battle, I want it to be on ground of our own choosing."

Warren nodded and put his hand on Meade's shoulder. "Don't worry. If there's suitable ground out there, my boys will find it."

"God DAMN the man!" Hancock was in a towering rage. Meade's orders for the Second Corps movement had arrived early in the morning, but a clerk had neglected to pass them on, instead filing them and going to breakfast. Once the orders were discovered and the troops underway, nearly three hours had been lost. Hancock checked his pocket watch and swore again.

"Sir?" It was Colonel Morgan. "We just received a reply from General Meade. He says that he regrets the delay and suggests that we punish the clerk responsible."

"You bet we punished him," Hancock snorted. "Sent him back to his regiment—he's marching with them now, and by nightfall his tender clerk feet will be rubbed raw." He paused. "Reply to General Meade that we have punished the individual and that we will try to make up the time."

"Is it feasible to make up three hours, General?" Morgan asked.

"Well, by my estimation, Colonel, we have some thirty to thirty-five miles to march today to reach our objective. At two and a half miles per hour, that would normally take twelve to fourteen hours. If we do not try to make up the time, we will end up marching a good part of the way in the dark. Cutting ten to fifteen minutes off breaks and unnecessary halts each hour would make up the lost time. Celerity, Colonel Morgan. We must always practice celerity. General Meade is depending on us to be in position on time, and by God, sir, we shall."

Hancock glanced at his chief of staff, who nodded in response. Celerity, swiftness of action, had been the cardinal military virtue that Professor Mahan had preached to them at West Point. Hancock knew he did not need to say any more: Morgan was a West Pointer, and he understood exactly what this meant. Wars are won by the army that moves swiftly and makes its own luck in the bargain.

"Besides," Hancock said, "we are in a race with time to complete our strategic change of direction without the enemy discovering how vulnerable we are right now."

"Vulnerable, sir?" Morgan replied, concerned.

"Yes. The enemy and the threat are to the north, and we have been facing west. Now we must move rapidly to occupy key terrain facing north before the enemy notices our blunder. For once, Bobby Lee has not pounced instantly on one of our mistakes."

Morgan was silent for a while as they rode together. "It seems strange to me that General Hooker did not see this danger."

Hancock snorted in derision. "General Hooker's actions have confounded us all. But Meade has grasped the situation perfectly and is moving in the correct direction to meet the enemy. He also takes great pains to keep us informed of the situation. It is a wonderful change from Hooker's lack of direction."

Morgan was respectfully silent at this criticism of a superior officer.

"Besides," Hancock said. "Meade's plan is very well conceived—a textbook approach to contact."

"With three columns of *corps d'armeé,* marching in parallel—*le bataillon carré.*" Morgan was quick to hop in.

Hancock smiled; his chief of staff clearly had not slept through Professor Mahan's recitations. Yes, Napoleon's bataillon carré: a square formation of army corps, able to move rapidly in any direction, once contact was established. "That is why we must push on and make up time. I expect Meade to move forward as soon as all of his corps are in position, and we must not hold him back."

Morgan nodded. "Once we make contact, I suspect everyone will have to move rapidly again—march to the sound of the guns."

Hancock swatted a fly off his horse; the day was getting muggier. "Yes, exactly, and the army that concentrates first stands a good chance of winning the battle." He paused for emphasis. "That is why we must always practice celerity."

The group approached a ford where the road disappeared into a stream. It was a shallow ford, no more than six inches deep. To the side of the ford, two logs covered with planking acted as a footbridge, with room enough for only one man at a time. On the other side of the stream, a regiment was halted beside the road, putting their shoes back on.

Hancock's anger was reignited. "There's no time for this delay, Morgan. They stop this side to take their shoes off and then stop on the other side to put them back on. That's no damn good. You stay here and make sure the other brigades don't stop. Make them go through the stream with their shoes on. I will go forward and get those brigades moving faster." He splashed across the stream toward the stationary troops.

The line of mounted men followed George Meade down a country dirt lane. Ahead of him, the cavalry escort moved forward through the fields on each side of the road, sweeping the route as they advanced. Meade glanced around at the rolling countryside. *Beautiful country, but no obvious defensible position, so far.* Pulling his hat off, he wiped his forehead with his sleeve. *Not yet noon and stifling hot already. It will be tough on the troops.* He wondered if the day's march was too aggressive, given the heat.

He scowled at the thought. The plan was already beginning to develop some kinks. Hancock had already reported a three-hour delay in movement. This would back up the Fifth Corps, which needed to march along some of the same route. *The soldiers will have to pay for this, especially the Second Corps. They have one of the longest marches to make. If Lee will give us one more day, we can get this sorted out.*

Major Ludlow rode up beside him. “Message from General Slocum, sir.”

“Yes, what is it?” Meade turned toward his aide.

“He reports the Twelfth Corps movement has been delayed by the Third Corps supply trains, which are blocking the route of march. He adds that these wagons should not even be on that route.”

“Dammit!” Meade exploded. “Get a message to General Sickles. Tell him this situation is totally unacceptable. He is to look into this matter personally and sort it out immediately!”

Meade returned Ludlow’s salute and turned back toward the road ahead. *Maybe Lee needs to give us two days to sort this all out.*

Henry Taylor was feeling the heat. It was warm and humid when they started the march, but it grew hotter and hotter as the sun climbed in the sky. The start of the marching was delayed, and the boys thought that maybe they wouldn’t have to march today, but they were wrong, and now they were marching hard. Word had filtered down that a mistake had been made at headquarters. Henry smiled wryly at the thought. *A mistake was made at headquarters, and now the soldiers are going to have to pay for it. Well, that’s a soldier’s lot!* He rubbed the sweat from his eyes with his free hand. They had all stripped down and were mostly marching in their undershirts, with handkerchiefs tied around their heads. From the look of it, the day was really going to be a hot one. He glanced around at his men; they were all holding on, but he kept his eye on a few he knew were sick or weak and might fall out soon.

As they came over a rise, Henry could see the column stretched out before him, curving along the country road, up and down over hills like a giant blue millipede. For an instant, Henry thought of calculating how many feet this millipede actually had. He quickly rejected the notion as just too much effort in this heat.

The column trudged around a bend, and Henry could see a ford up ahead with a mounted officer waiting beside the road. As they came closer, the officer motioned Colonel Colvill, their regimental commander, over. It was too far away for Henry to hear the brief conversation, but murmuring arose from the front of the regiment.

Colonel Colvill rode down the line. "Sorry, boys, we have to bulge this stream. General Hancock's orders—there isn't time to stop to take your shoes off."

Henry knew what that meant, for sure. Crossing the stream with their shoes on meant walking in wet shoes and socks for miles, which would rub their feet raw. The men grumbled softly, resigned to the inevitable pain.

The regiment behind them, the Fifteenth Mass., was less stoic than the First Minnesota. They greeted the orders with loud hissing. Henry could see that this made the mounted officer, a colonel, very upset. "They are likely to pay for that," he told Isaac, who was walking beside him.

Henry's shoes quickly filled with water as they marched across the stream. They initially squished as he walked, but the excess water soon ran out, and the wet socks chafed across his feet. By the time the next rest stop was called, Henry's feet were on fire. When the order to fall out finally came, the entire regiment collapsed on the sides of the road.

"Get your shoes off right away, boys, and take those wet socks off," Henry called out. "You need to have dry feet when we start marching again. I'll come around to take a look at your feet."

A wave of groans rippled toward him from the back of the brigade. He looked up to see the officer from the stream riding toward him. *He still looks angry,* Henry thought. The colonel rode past him, jaws clenched, and stopped to speak to Colonel Colvill. The two spoke for a few moments, and then Colonel Colvill nodded and turned away as the other officer rode off. Colvill stared at the ground with shoulders slumped and then spoke to his adjutant.

Henry was working his way along the line of his platoon, checking feet, when Lieutenant Demarest called for him. "Captain Muller needs to see us right away."

Muller was pacing back and forth when Henry arrived, clearly upset. "Colonel Colvill has been placed under arrest for failure to maintain discipline."

Demarest spoke up. "But Captain, that wasn't even our regiment!"

Muller shook his head. "Yes, this is totally unjust. Pass word to all of your men zhat, in the future, zhey are to keep silent and maintain proper discipline!"

Henry rejoined his platoon just as the order to fall in came. He looked down at his feet, his shoes and socks still wet. He knew he was going to pay for this.

Dan Sickles reined his horse away from a giant pothole in the center of the road. "This goddamned road...who chose this route?"

Tremain was a horse length behind him and heard his comment. "Well, sir, my understanding from headquarters is that General Meade personally chose all the routes."

"Pah," Sickles snorted. "And he's supposed to be such a great engineer! This road is terrible. I could have chosen a better one myself." He shifted uncomfortably in the saddle. A month of wining and dining in New York had added a few pounds. It was surprising how quickly one fell out of shape for long days in the saddle. Yesterday had been a long march, and today promised to be more of the same. He sighed at the thought.

Hoofbeats behind him caused Sickles to turn; an orderly was galloping toward him. Tremain moved to intercept the orderly. After a salute and an exchange of a note, the orderly galloped back down the road in the direction he had come from.

Sickles looked at Tremain. "What is it?"

"A message from General Meade, sir." Tremain scanned the note. "It says the Third Corps supply trains are blocking the road, preventing Twelfth Corps from advancing." He cleared his throat dramatically. "General Meade directs you to go down there and see to the matter personally."

"See to the matter personally?" Sickled was incredulous. "I have a corps to command. I don't have time for that! Send somebody down to get it sorted out."

Sickles scowled at this development. *This fellow Meade is turning out to be very difficult to deal with! What is the big hurry?* Meade had sent out a long-winded circular about a change of direction. Sickles had scanned it but didn't see much relevance. *Hooker would never have bothered me with trivia like this!*

Henry grimaced in pain. *Misery* was too tepid a word to describe their march this day. The rolling countryside outside Frederick had changed as they marched northeast toward the Pennsylvania border. Gone were the gentle hills and open fields. In their place were narrow winding roads and frequent steep hills. If the terrain before could be compared to a gently rolling ocean, they were now in an angry sea, with high wave crests and deep troughs. They were forced to follow the road up, over, and down these crests in a seemingly unending succession. To make matters worse, a series of towering black-bottomed clouds had passed overhead, drenching the Second Corps column in a string of heavy downbursts. Water from these downbursts ran down the narrow dirt road in rivers and collected in pools at the base of the hills. The rain turned dirt to mud and soaked everyone's shoes. At first, they welcomed the cooling rain, but the sun soon came back out. As the moisture evaporated, the heat and humidity became even more oppressive. The exertion of climbing the steep hills was bad enough, but the trip back down the hill forced them to use their feet to act as brakes. The rubbing of wet socks on already-raw feet was excruciating. To make matters worse, Henry stepped on a loose stone, which caused him to turn an ankle. This added a limp to his problem of burning feet.

First Sergeant Trevor moved up beside him. "You all right, Henry?"

Henry managed a feeble nod. "I'll make it."

"Well, I have an assignment for you."

"What's that?" Henry asked.

"We have a few men who are in serious distress. I need someone to be in charge when they fall out and keep them together."

Henry shook his head. "Find another NCO. I can't fall out."

Trevor moved in closer. "Listen, Henry," he said sternly. "There is a big fight up ahead, maybe the biggest we've ever seen. I need every man ready for action, and you are no good to me with heatstroke or with feet too raw to walk. I need these other fellows in ranks as well when the fight comes."

"The men..." Henry began.

"The men won't think any less of you," Trevor said. "Now, do I have to get Captain Muller to order you?"

Henry sighed and shook his head. Reluctantly, he followed the first sergeant to collect the men who needed to fall out.

A large oak tree offered a convenient place to rest. The spreading branches would provide shelter from any additional rain, and a nearby creek would provide drinking water and the opportunity to cool off. They all collapsed around the trunk of the tree, too exhausted to move. Finally, Henry stirred; the light was failing fast, and they needed to get prepared before it grew too dark to see. Reaching the creek, he stripped to the waist and splashed the water over his head and torso. The cool water soothed his sweaty skin, and he let out a soft sigh. Straightening up, Henry wiped his face and looked over toward the oak tree. The men were beginning to stir. He filled his canteen and stepped gingerly back to the group.

"Get your canteens filled, boys. We all need to drink plenty of water. And let's see if we can get a fire started before it gets too dark." Henry sat down on his pack and pulled off his shoes and socks. His hands ran over his feet, heavily callused from many marches. Some of the calluses were red and irritated, but there were no signs of blisters. That was good news. Blisters could easily hobble you for days.

Henry looked over the men moving slowly about. They all seemed to be doing OK, or at least better than when they had stopped. He was most concerned about Private Berry, who had been shot through the torso at Antietam. He had recovered and returned to the regiment. Today's exertion had left him weak and gasping for air, but Berry was showing signs of improvement. The other member of his platoon in the group, Private Cundy, was moving about and looking much better. A lumberjack before the war, Cundy was strong and resilient, but recently he had been suffering from an intermittent fever, which sapped his strength. The other two members of the group were from the other platoon, and Henry did not know them well. They looked to be recovering also.

As he watched the group build a fire, movement on the road caught his attention. It was hard to make out in the growing darkness, but a form was moving slowly down the road toward them. As the form came near, it paused and called out in a German accent, "Hallo. Vat regiment?"

"First Minnesota," Henry said.

"Me also," the form called back. "Can I join you?"

As the form moved in toward the growing firelight, Henry could make out a burly man in a private's uniform. "I am Augustus Koenig, B Company," the man announced. "Zey call me Beer Keg." Someone in the group snickered. Private Koenig patted his ample stomach and chuckled. "Yes, as you can see. But I am also a brewer."

Henry smiled at that—a double reason for the name. "Well, Koenig, we are all from E Company, but you are certainly welcome. Join us…find a space near the fire."

"Danke." Koenig dropped his pack near the fire and sat down on the ground with a loud sigh. The group introduced themselves and began to eat their hardtack in silence. They were all too tired for much conversation.

Sometime later, a twig snap outside the ring of firelight startled the group. They all instinctively reached for their rifles. An old man with gray hair and a bushy white beard stepped into the firelight. Noticing the group's hands on their rifles, he put his hand up. "Sorry, boys. Didn't mean to startle you!" A nervous laugh. "I noticed the fire from my house up the road, and I figured you might want something to eat besides hardtack." He pulled two loaves of bread from a sack and held them out. "My wife just baked them. They're still warm."

"Thank you, sir. That's very kind," Henry said. He motioned for the men to take the loaves. "Can we offer you something for the bread?"

The old man shook his head. "No, no, it's the least I can do for you boys." He paused, his face growing sad. "You know," he said, "they say the rebs are up in Pennsylvania. There's bound to be a terrible fight. You boys take care of yourselves, now. We will all be praying for you here." With that he raised his hand in farewell and walked slowly away from the fire. Calls of thanks from the group followed him.

They were all silent for a while, chewing on the bread. Finally, Cundy looked up and asked, "Sergeant Taylor, is it true what the old man said? Are we bound to have a big fight?"

"I'm afraid so," Henry said. "The rebs are up there in force and won't leave without a fight."

"Oh." Cundy looked at his feet. "Some of the boys were saying that the rebs are too far north and would skedaddle back home if we came after them..."

Henry shook his head. "When have you ever heard of Bobby Lee running away from a fight? I'm afraid we will have to drive them out, and they won't leave without a big fight." Henry paused to let that sink in. "The thought is that the South needs one more big victory. If we lose another battle, then the Peace Democrats and Copperheads will force President Lincoln to negotiate a peace treaty. That will mean independence for the Confederacy and an end of the Union—everything we've fought for." He paused again, choosing his words. "Every one of us will have to do everything he can possibly do to make sure we win the next battle. We cannot afford to lose." He looked around at the group; they were all nodding gravely. *They already know the truth,* he told himself, *but saying it makes the truth even starker.*

Private Berry was the first to respond. "I joined up right after Fort Sumter. I seen some hard campaigning. Don't regret one bit of it, though. I did it because the president said he needed us to help save the Union." Berry paused for a moment and then continued. "My family thinks I've paid enough with my wound and all, but I'm ready to pay even more if it means saving the Union." He looked over at Henry. "You enlisted right away too, didn't you, Sergeant Taylor?"

Henry nodded. "I was teaching children at a mission school up in Belle Prairie. When I read President Lincoln's call for troops, I knew that I had to enlist to protect the Union. Can't say it's been easy, but I know everything has been necessary..." He grew silent, unsure of what else to say.

Private Koenig, Beer Keg, had something to say as well. "In '48, ven the rebellion started, I vas a young man—a *Lehrling*... how you say it...an apprentice, just learning to become a brewer. Vee all joined the rebellion. Zhey promised liberty and better conditions, but zhe government crushed us. Zhings were very bad. Ven I leave Chermany and come to Amerika, I find all the liberty vee vere promised in '48. Zo I fight for zhis country now and for my liberty."

The others murmured in agreement. Henry looked them over approvingly. "If we stick together and follow our officers, we will do well."

Hancock looked up into the night sky. The moon hung high in the eastern sky, with just a sliver missing. *It will be full moon in a day or two,* he thought. *Enough light for the men to see where they are stepping.*

He pulled a map from its case and a stub of a candle from his pocket. "Can someone strike a match for me?"

A short pause, and then the rasp of a match being struck. Hancock held his candle out to be lit. Once the flame stabilized, he pulled the candle back and held it close to the map.

Hancock scowled as he studied the map. This had been a very frustrating day. It was bad enough to get a very late start, but the map was woefully inaccurate. The distance they had to travel was longer than that shown on the map, and the terrain made it even worse, not to mention the weather. His march objective for today, Frizzelburg, was at least four miles away, or so the map had it. That would be another two to three hours at the pace they could make in the dark across this rough terrain. His troops were worn out, and he knew it. Meade had sent a message earlier cautioning his commanders not to exhaust the troops—they would have to march again tomorrow. *It's better to call a halt and get a fresh start in the morning. Let the men rest,* he told himself.

According to the map, the road they were on intersected with the road running between Westminster and Taneytown at

Frizzelburg. The hamlet of Uniontown lay along their current route somewhat west of this junction. Hancock considered the situation. Uniontown seemed to be a good location to stop. A bivouac near the town would allow them to move quickly in any direction.

"Gentlemen," he said, blowing out his candle, "we are going to call a halt at Uniontown, the next village up the road, maybe a mile or so. Colonel Morgan, take a couple of your officers and ride ahead into town. Find the mayor. Wake him up if necessary. We need help finding a suitable place for our entire corps to bed down."

Morgan saluted, motioned to a couple of aides, and galloped down the road to the town up ahead.

"We need to get a message to General Meade," Hancock said. "Tell him that we are stopping for the night in the vicinity of Uniontown and will resume the march first thing in the morning. I await further orders."

George Meade looked down at the map and rubbed his beard. Markers on the map showed the positions of his army corps; most of them had not reached their day's objective. *It was a very aggressive plan after all,* he admitted. Even so, they had achieved a large part of his overall objective. While not in their anticipated positions at the end of the day, they had achieved the strategic change of direction the plan envisioned. All his commanders had pushed their units to achieve their assigned objectives. *All except the Third Corps,* he noted sadly.

Meade continued to study the map. His gaze returned to the Third Corps marker. Shaking his head, he turned to his senior aide. "Major Ludlow, do you have the latest report from the Third Corps handy?"

Papers rustled. "Right here, sir."

Meade removed his glasses and rubbed his tired eyes. "Could you read it for me, please?"

Ludlow held the message up to the candlelight. "It says, 'Lead elements closed on Taneytown approximately five fifteen p.m. Poor road conditions and heavy rain squalls impeded progress.' That's all they reported."

Meade was silent, considering the message. "Well, if they left at four a.m. like they were supposed to, it took them over thirteen hours to march thirteen miles. That is one mile per hour—totally unacceptable!"

Ludlow nodded. "Yes, sir. The Second Corps marched over twice that distance in the same amount of time!"

"Well, we can't let this continue," Meade replied. "Send a message to General Sickles. Tell him that poor roads and bad weather cannot excuse the poor performance of his corps. In the future, they must move much faster." He looked up to see Butterfield scowling and then quickly turn away.

As Ludlow wrote the message and left to find an orderly, Meade considered his options. *Now that we have successfully changed direction, what should the next move be? We still need to take the pressure off Harrisburg, so we need to continue to move forward. But where is Lee?*

"General Meade?" Warren interrupted his thoughts. "I have a report from my engineers; it looks like we have found the perfect spot for a defensive line." Warren held out a map for Meade to examine. It was the same type of map Meade had, except that it was marked up with blue and brown pencil. "My lads have added some detail, based on their reconnaissance work today," he explained. "The blue line you see is what the locals call the Big Pipe Creek. It flows roughly toward the west from near Manchester to almost Taneytown." Warren traced the creek's path on the map with his finger. "As a barrier, it's not much—no more than ten to twenty feet wide with steep banks. The real barrier is the line of hills just south of the creek. These hills start here in the east just north of Manchester and stretch some twenty miles to south of Taneytown. In the east, the hills are quite impressive—one hundred to two hundred feet in elevation. Down around Taneytown, they are more rolling, but still quite defensible." Warren pointed to the hill line marked in brown pencil on the map. "My engineers tell me that these positions are better than the ones the rebels had at Fredericksburg."

Meade studied Warren's map. "It looks like there may be usable roads behind these hills."

"Yes," Warren said. "I've been on some of them today, and the sections I was on would support rapid troop movement from one position to another along the line."

Meade smiled; this was good. "I see all three of the main routes down to Baltimore go through this hill line. I like it, Warren! Have your engineers draw up a defensive plan."

"We will get started on it right away," Warren said, straightening up. "What shall we call this plan?"

Meade looked up at his chief engineer. "Let's just call it the Pipe Creek Line."

Warren departed, and Meade returned to the new map. *Yes, it is a good defensive position. No matter what happens up in Pennsylvania, we will have a solid defensive position to fall back on!*

Meade yawned and looked at his pocket watch; it was almost midnight, and they would start again very early in the morning. He still had time, though, for a quick note to Margaret. Taking pen and paper, he began to write. "We are marching as fast as we can to relieve Harrisburg, but have to keep a sharp lookout the Rebels don't turn around us and get at Washington and Baltimore in our rear. They have a cavalry force in our rear, destroying railroads, etc., with a view of getting us to turn back; but I shall not do it. I am going straight at them, and will settle this thing one way or the other. The men are in good spirits; we have been reinforced so as to have equal strength with the enemy and with God's blessing, I hope to be successful. Goodbye."[3]

Chapter 10

June 30, 1863

NORTHERN MARYLAND

HANCOCK PULLED THE TENT FLY open and stepped out into the cool night air. Around him, the camp was silent. *Let them sleep a while longer,* he thought. *They certainly earned a rest after yesterday.* In the west, the waxing full moon was low near the horizon, while the eastern sky was just beginning to lighten. Hancock liked this time of the morning before the camp began to stir. The quiet time let him consider the day ahead without constant interruption.

A dozen steps or so brought him to the headquarters tent. The duty officer, a young lieutenant, spotted him entering and called the tent to attention. Hancock nodded to the group. *After what happened yesterday, they are all on their toes,* he told himself. *That's good; we certainly will need extra diligence in the next few days!* "Carry on," he called out, and the group resumed its work.

"Lieutenant," he said to the duty officer, "any messages arrive during the night?"

"Yes sir, we've had a couple." The young officer moved over to a field table. "I left them here on Colonel Morgan's desk. I scanned them, though, when they came in. There is nothing urgent."

"Good. What do we have?" Hancock moved closer to the desk.

The lieutenant picked a several papers from under a paperweight. "Well, sir, the first one is an acknowledgment of our report of reb cavalry in Westminster."

Hancock cocked his head. "That's it? Just an acknowledgment? No order to check it out?"

"No, sir. Not in any of the other messages either."

"I guess they didn't believe us. I hope we didn't miss the opportunity to give JEB Stuart a bloody nose!" They had reported word from local civilians that Stuart's cavalry was in Westminster. A brigade of infantry against cavalry would be like a fox in a henhouse. *Just as well. The men were all fagged out last night.* "OK, what else do we have?"

"Movement orders for today, sir. It looks like we are to remain in position. Otherwise, I would have informed Colonel Morgan…" He handed the paper to Hancock.

"OK, let's take a look at this." Hancock scanned the order. Yes, it was true—they were to remain in place at Uniontown today. That was good news. He thought for a moment and then motioned to an orderly. "Send a message to all my division commanders. Tell them we are to remain in position today. Let the men rest up. I expect additional hard marching in the coming days."

Henry woke early as well. The predawn air was chilly on his bare skin, almost uncomfortable. He lay there for a moment, listening to the others snore softly. *Best get yourself moving,* he thought. Sitting up, he tried to stretch the stiffness from his back, the result of sleeping all night on the ground. His feet were the first concern. Feeling his bare feet, he could tell that the soreness, while still there, was not as severe as the night before. The ankle, while still tender, did not hurt as much. His shoes, which he had left near the fire to dry out, were stiff but dry. Henry started to knead the leather and bend the soles to make the shoes more supple. After a few minutes, he was satisfied with the result. *With dry socks and no rain today, it'll be OK,* he thought.

His movements roused some of the group, who were starting to move and stretch. "Good morning," Henry said. "We should try to get on the road soon so we can catch up with the regiment before it gets too late. Don't want to be trying to catch up in the middle of the day."

After a short breakfast, the group prepared to get underway. With a communal groan, the men lifted their heavy packs onto their backs and stepped out onto the road. Henry took a deep breath. "OK, let's go!" They plodded along the road, which sloped up to the next hill crest.

As they marched along, Henry looked over the group. The evening rest had revived them, and they looked capable of making the march. He decided that slow and steady was the best approach, keeping an eye on them and taking rest breaks as necessary. His own feet still hurt, but that was less important.

Another soldier was sitting by the side of the road perhaps a quarter mile after they began. The man was looking away, perhaps pretending not to see them or maybe just ignoring them. Henry looked at the soldier. "Hey, fall in!" he shouted at the man.

The soldier looked up. "What regiment?"

Henry shook his head. "Doesn't matter which regiment. Fall in! Your regiment needs you!"

The man shrugged, lifted his pack, and joined the back of the group.

Along their route they encountered other soldiers. Some joined the group without a sign from Henry, while others needed Henry to beckon with his head or signal to come on with his hand. The sergeant stripes on Henry's sleeves were enough inducement. Eventually, he had some two dozen men following him.

After trudging up and over a series of steep hills, they crested a rise to find the road running along the crest. *Some flat marching for a while, at least,* Henry thought. Up ahead, Henry spotted a provost guard standing at the intersection of the road.

The guard looked the group over as it shuffled up. "Let's see your passes," he ordered.

Henry handed over his pass and waited while the guard checked the others. Satisfied, the guard nodded to Henry. "OK, Sergeant, turn right here and go straight down the hill and all the way through the town. We are camped about a mile outside of town. You can't miss it."

Henry cocked his head. "They haven't started marching yet?"

"Nah," the guard replied. "General Hancock has given us a day of rest. We certainly need it after yesterday!"

Henry nodded and led his group down the steep hill into the village of Uniontown. It was a neat place, with trees lining the streets and whitewashed buildings in the town center. Already, shops were open, and townspeople were setting up stalls on the side of the street. *Must know the soldiers are in town for the day,* he told himself.

Once through town, they began to encounter soldiers heading the opposite way into town. One of them was Isaac. He looked Henry's group over. "Well, brother, you have certainly become a Pied Piper!"

"Very funny," Henry said. "Where are you off to?"

"I'm going into town. Today's payday, and I'm tired of hardtack and pork. I want to buy some real food, and I have a handful of cash to do it. Oh, and I did get permission from Jock before I left."

Henry grunted and continued to walk. *What a gift—payday, plus a day to rest and recuperate. It's almost too much to ask.*

Meade turned to look over his shoulder. His headquarters group was stretched out behind him, moving slowly along the dirt road. In the distance were the rolling hills that formed the western end of the hill line that Warren had told him about. They had come through these hills on the way up to Taneytown from Middleburg, and Meade was impressed with the potential. This was reported to be the less formidable end of the line, and Meade could only imagine what the eastern end looked like.

As they reached the village of Taneytown, a guide met them to direct the column toward the designated bivouac area to the north of the town. On reaching the farmer's field designated for the headquarters area, they were hailed by General Butterfield, who had moved forward earlier to set up an operating headquarters. This would enable more rapid resumption of headquarters operation.

"General Meade," Butterfield called out, "we've received several important messages."

Meade dismounted his horse, Old Baldy, and handed the reins to an orderly. "Yes, go ahead. What are they?"

"The first one is from General Kilpatrick," Butterfield said. "He reports a cavalry battle at Hannover, Pennsylvania. His cavalry division engaged Stuart's cavalry and drove them off. He reports that the general movement of the rebs in the area appears to be toward the west."

"Hmm," Meade said, pulling out his map. "What else?"

"A dispatch courier arrived just as we were leaving. I took the message with me so that we could get them decrypted." He looked to Meade for a nod. "They contain messages from General Couch in Harrisburg and General Haupt—he's in Harrisburg too, I think. Couch reports the rebels have fallen back toward Chambersburg, passing Shippensburg last night in great haste. His latest information is that Early, with eight thousand men, went toward Gettysburg or Hannover. The rebs are saying they expect to fight a great battle there and didn't want to be outflanked by Hooker."

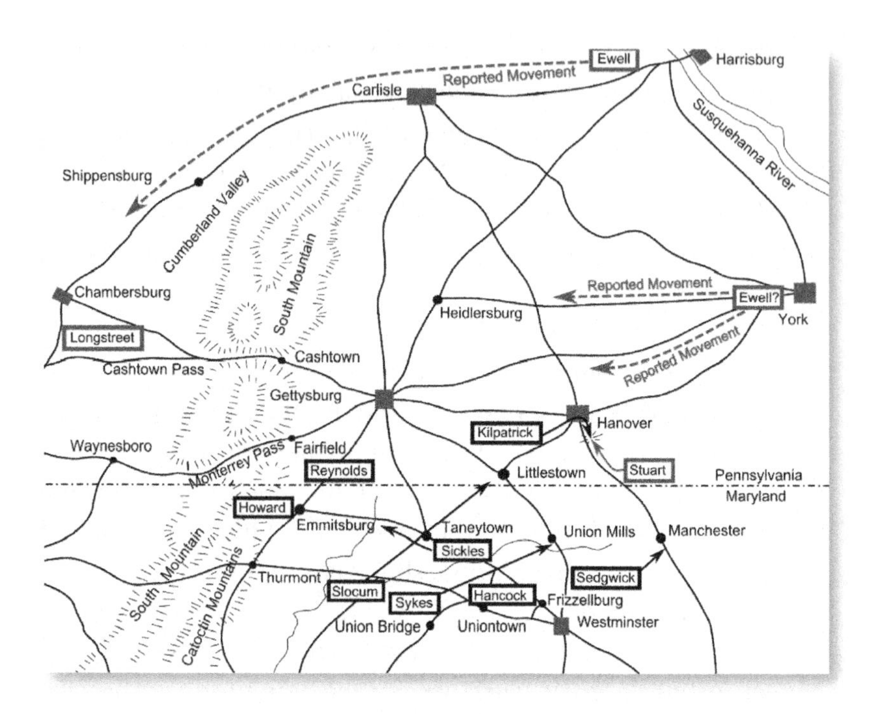

Situation—30 June

Meade held up his map and put his finger on each of the cities as they were mentioned. "Well, it is interesting that they think Hooker is still in charge. That may be an advantage for us. What did Haupt say?"

"His report is similar. Lee has fallen back suddenly from the vicinity of Harrisburg and concentrating his all his forces. York has been evacuated. Carlisle is the process of being evacuated. The concentration seems to be at or near Chambersburg. Their object, he believes, is a sudden move against us."

Meade was silent for a moment, considering the news. "Well, I suppose our movement in the past several days has achieved its goal of relieving Harrisburg."

"Oh," Butterfield said, "we have more information as well on enemy dispositions. These reports are from civilians. I have checked out the stories, and they are all from highly respected members of their communities. They report both Longstreet and Hill are in Chambersburg, and Early is in Carlisle and York."

"*Was* in Carlisle and York," Meade replied. "Yes, I saw those reports before I left Middleburg. It appears Early is on the move. Kilpatrick reported only cavalry involved in his fight, so it's unlikely Hannover is their objective...it's most likely Gettysburg."

An orderly quickly brought a field table to them, and Meade spread his map out. Meade studied it, absorbing the new information. *Two-thirds of Lee's army is west of the mountains. That's where the danger is.* After some more consideration, Meade addressed his staff. "If Lee intends to fall on us, it would have to be through either of the two passes. That's either through the Monterey pass down here closer to Maryland or the Cashtown pass up here in Pennsylvania. Right now, the Monterey pass is unprotected. We just had the First and Eleventh Corps move north away from Emmitsburg." He turned to Butterfield. "Send orders to General Sickles. Have him move his corps to Emmitsburg and place his divisions across the road to Fairfield west of the town of Emmitsburg. He is to defend the line at all hazards. Oh, and send word to General Pleasanton—he is to maintain at least a brigade of cavalry in the pass. That should give us sufficient warning of any enemy movement through the pass."

As aides scrambled to prepare the orders, Meade turned back to the map. *Dangers and opportunities. Must chart a way through all this. A battle is certainly imminent. I must get my key commanders informed of the possibilities and how we would react to each one.* Looking up from the map, he spoke to Butterfield. "Get word to Generals Reynolds, Hancock, and Sedgwick. Tell them that I would like to meet with them here as soon as possible." Turning back to the map, he began to formulate his plans.

Time seemed to stand still for Meade when he was engrossed in a problem. His staff knew better than to disturb him when he was in the problem-solving state. An interruption could result in some very cross words directed toward the unfortunate interrupter. So Meade worked on undisturbed, studying the map, rereading the dispatches, measuring distances on the map, and weighing probabilities in his head. Eventually, a picture began to emerge, becoming clearer as he worked. Finally, he sighed and placed his hands on the table. He had a plan.

Looking up, he noticed Warren and Hunt standing nearby, obviously waiting for him to finish. "Ah, good afternoon, gentlemen. I didn't notice you standing there."

Warren raised his hand and smiled. "No problem at all. We saw you were busy and didn't want to disturb you." He motioned toward Hunt with his head. "Henry and I have a report on the defensive line we were considering to the south of Pipe Creek."

"Oh, pull up a chair and let me know what you found out."

Warren laid a map out on the table and smoothed it with his hand. "I had my cartography section work up a proper map, based on the surveys my engineers made."

Meade leaned over to study the map. From his experience as a topographical engineer, he could tell that it was quite detailed and had taken a significant effort to create. "Well done," he said.

"Yes," Warren replied, "I thought so too. Anyway, Henry here has inspected the entire line. I will let him tell you his impressions."

Hunt moved closer to the map. "In general terms, the terrain is steeper in the east and becomes more rolling in the vicinity of Taneytown. There are over a dozen natural promontories that provide excellent fields of fire for our artillery. With a little spade and ax work, Warren's pioneers could make this into an impregnable position. I think it is a better position than the rebs had at Marye's Heights. What do you think, Warren?"

"You are absolutely right, Henry. It's one of the best positions I have seen in a long time. Not only do we have excellent fields of fire, we also have steep slopes and high elevations. This would make an infantry assault tougher, and enemy artillery would have a harder time elevating to reach our artillery on the heights." Warren leaned over the map and ran his finger along the road from Middleburg through Uniontown to Westminster. "As we hoped, this road behind the heights is in very good condition and would allow rapid movement of reinforcements across most of the line. Other roads east of Westminster toward Hampstead and Manchester are in even better shape to handle rapid movement. To answer your question, Henry, I agree that it is an excellent position."

Meade sat silent, studying the map for a while. Finally, he cleared his throat. "Thank you, gentlemen. That is very good news. We may be compelled to use this position in the very near future. It's good to have a strong defensive option in our back pocket as we move forward."

"Sir, Generals Reynolds, Hancock, and Sedgwick are here," Major Ludlow said as Meade finished speaking.

"Ah, gentlemen, please join us." Meade beckoned. "We were just discussing the terrain for a possible defensive line." He rose to greet the trio as they walked to the map table. "Thank you for coming. I know you are all very busy with the movement of your commands, so I won't take much of your time. The reason I called you here today is that a battle is imminent, and I am relying on you as key subordinates. Each of you will have an important role." They all nodded gravely.

"Let's start with the overall situation," he said as he spread the regional map on the table. "Reports have the bulk of Lee's army located in Chambersburg, on the western side of the South Mountain. Early is said to have abandoned York and is moving west." Meade pointed out the locations as he spoke. "I believe Lee has ordered a concentration of his army around Chambersburg or farther east in the Cashtown Pass area. If this is so, then Early will have to move through Gettysburg here." He pointed to a spiderweb of intersecting roads on the map where the town of Gettysburg was located. "I believe we need to move up to this area to prevent Early from rejoining Lee's army, if we can get there in time."

Reynolds looked up from the map. "We are not that far away. We can be there tomorrow."

Meade nodded. "That's what I thought. If we do get there first, Early may fight to get past us, or he may try to bypass Gettysburg entirely. We need to be prepared for either possibility. In either case, we have the opportunity to outnumber Early and defeat him before Lee can send reinforcements."

The group murmured in approval. Meade continued. "Here is what I propose. I will assign the Third Corps to the left wing, under your command, John." He nodded to Reynolds. "I have already ordered Sickles to move to Emmitsburg. Additionally, I will move the Twelfth Corps up to Two Taverns, which is about seven miles south of Gettysburg. If Early tries to move south to bypass the town, Slocum will be there to block him. You will move your corps to Gettysburg, John. In either event, we can have four corps available, the First, Eleventh, Third, and Twelfth, to concentrate on Early—odds of at least four to one in our favor."

"That should be more than sufficient," Reynolds said. "What if they manage to get past us before we arrive in Gettysburg?"

"Then," Meade said solemnly, "we will have a much more dangerous situation on our hands. With his army concentrated, Lee will have a free hand to move as he pleases."

The group was silent for a moment, and then Meade continued. "So let's consider that situation. What is Lee likely to do? He will obviously block the passes over South Mountain and dare us to attack. The situation would be similar to what it was before the battle of Antietam. I would have to carefully consider our plan if that were to happen. We all remember the hard fight we had in getting through the blocked passes on the way to Antietam. It ate up our manpower and gave Lee an extra day to prepare. In any event, I can't imagine Lee sitting still for long. He will look for an opportunity to attack. So I can see three possibilities. The first one is an attack down from the Cashtown Pass toward Gettysburg. In that event, the blow will fall on you, John. Try to hold out until we get reinforcements up to you. If you cannot hold your position, fall back to Emmitsburg, and I will get reinforcements to you there."

"Understood," Reynolds replied.

"The second possibility," Meade said, "is an attack through the Monterey pass west of Emmitsburg. Buford's cavalry encountered a brigade of enemy infantry to the west of the pass, so that route is a possibility. I have Sickles stationed in the pass to block that route of advance with a cavalry screen to the west. We would detect any movement there and have some time to react by bringing reinforcements from the east of Emmitsburg. That is where you come in, Hancock."

"Oh?" Hancock asked.

"Your corps will be my fire brigade, Hancock. I will position you here at Taneytown so that you can support any of the defensive positions we have designated. It is a central position with good roads to all of the possible battle sites."

Meade turned toward Sedgwick. "And John, I haven't forgotten you. Your corps will play an important role as well. My instructions from General Halleck are to keep Baltimore and Washington covered while I maneuver against the enemy. I am moving the Sixth Corps to Manchester to take up a blocking position along the main road that runs from Hanover to Baltimore. In the event that Lee slips around us and tries to move on Baltimore, you will hold him off until we can reinforce you."

"Understood," Sedgwick said.

"Your position will play another important role, John. In the event that we are forced back from our forward position, we will take up a defensive line just south of the Pipe Creek." Meade pulled the map of the Pipe Creek line out and placed it on top. "The terrain has been judged an excellent defensive position by my experts here." He nodded toward Warren and Hunt. "The Sixth Corps will anchor the right of the line, which would stretch from Manchester down to near Middleburg. I hope we do not have to use this line, but we must be prepared. Everyone clear on their roles?"

The group nodded. "Good," Meade said. "It is imperative that we have rapid movement of all units to any of the designated potential battle areas. That means we strip down for hard marching. Only ambulances and ammunition trains are to move with your corps. We will designate a central position where the supply trains will be held. Issue sixty rounds of ammunition and three days' rations to your men. Make sure you are familiar with the routes between your position and all the battle areas. There is some hard fighting up ahead, and we must be as prepared as humanly possible. Any questions?"

Meade looked at his three corps commanders. They were all shaking their heads. "Fine. I will let you get back to your commands. Formal orders will be issued later today. I thank you for your time, gentlemen."

As the group broke up, Meade turned back to the map and rubbed his chin nervously. *What have I missed? Lee certainly knows we are here; have I anticipated his moves correctly?*

Dan Sickles watched his troops slog past in the afternoon heat. He kept going over in his mind the message received from Meade late the night before. *"Unacceptable performance." Is he looking for a reason to relieve me?* His thoughts were interrupted by a group of horsemen riding up. Birney was in the lead.

"Good afternoon, General," Birney said with a salute.

"Nothing good about it," Sickles snarled. "Why did we start out so late, marching in the heat of the day? I thought Meade wanted us to go easy on the men and not wear them out."

Birney frowned and stroked his beard in discomfort. "Well, perhaps they have new information that necessitates a rapid repositioning," he said.

"More like a sign of pure incompetence," Sickles muttered.

Birney paused, clearly uneasy about this insubordinate talk. Sickles did not care at this point. Finally, Birney cleared his throat. "I understand we are now under the command of General Reynolds. Are there any changes to our orders?" Sickles shook his head. Birney hesitated. "In that case, General Sickles, I will see to my command." With a salute, Birney and his aides rode off.

Sickles watched Birney disappear behind a stand of trees. *He's not a regular. What does he care about military protocol?* Sickles returned to stewing about Meade's rebuke.

Tremain interrupted his dark thoughts. "Sir, we have a dispatch from General Reynolds."

"Yes? What is it?"

Tremain read the message silently. "Um, he has ordered us to Emmitsburg, but…"

"We knew that already," Sickles snapped.

"Yes, well, he orders a different disposition at Emmitsburg than what General Meade ordered."

"Why am I not surprised?" Sickles exploded. "This is just more goddamn incompetence! We wouldn't have this mess if Hooker were still in charge!"

Tremain hesitated. "So what should we do, General?"

Sickles thought for a moment. "Send a copy of both orders to Meade and Reynolds. Ask them for clarification. In the meantime, we continue on to Emmitsburg."

Hancock spread the map out on the field table and looked up at his division commanders, Generals Caldwell, Gibbon, and Hays. Behind them, their aides crowded in. Hancock's own aides stood close behind him. "OK, gentlemen, here is the situation," he began. "The enemy is currently dispersed, with the bulk of their army to the west of the mountains. A smaller force is moving west from York, we believe with the intent of linking up. General Meade is moving the army north to Gettysburg, a location between the two enemy forces."

"Central position—very good," Gibbon said.

Caldwell interrupted. "What's central position?"

Hancock looked at Caldwell. An innocent question. He was the only nonacademy graduate among his division commanders. He had clearly never heard of the term. "Central position," Hancock said, "is a strategy Napoleon used. It involves finding a position between a dispersed enemy so that you can concentrate your forces against part of the enemy and so defeat your opponent in detail."

Caldwell nodded in understanding, and Hancock resumed his briefing. "Enemy intentions at this point are unclear, so we must be prepared for a number of eventualities. General Meade has identified the most probable battle areas and is moving units to these areas. Our corps has been designated as a strategic reserve. Tomorrow morning we will move to Taneytown and take up position as this reserve. Once the army makes contact, we will have to march hard to reinforce the unit engaged. The situation is extremely fluid, and we must be ready to move with little notice. I want all commanders to prepare for rapid movement. We must be able to march fast and be ready to fight instantly on arrival at the battleground. Pare down all unessential gear. No extraneous animals, and only ambulances and ammunition wagons are allowed with the column. Detailed orders will be forthcoming. Now, go see to it!"

As the group moved off, Morgan stood beside him. "So, a fight is imminent?"

"Yes." Hancock nodded. "It appears so. We must be ready for whatever happens, and we *must* have a victory. There is too much on the line. Now, let's get busy. We have a great deal of planning to do. Let me show you the battle areas Meade has identified so we can develop a plan to move to each one of them."

Meade worked through a stack of orders and dispatches, holding each one toward the lamplight so he could read it better. "General Butterfield," he called out, "where is the circular for the Pipe Creek defensive line?"

Butterfield looked up from his paperwork. "We haven't started on it yet. The staff has been very busy getting orders out for tomorrow's movement."

"General," Meade replied coldly, "it is absolutely critical that we have this plan distributed to the corps commanders."

"I didn't think it was relevant anymore," Butterfield said. "We have issued orders to move north toward Gettysburg and prepare for battle there."

"That is true," Meade replied, barely holding his temper in check. "However, we do not know what will happen in the next few days. In the event that we are forced back from Gettysburg, we must have a prepared position to fall back to. If we publish the circular now, the subordinate commands will have time to prepare for their part in the defensive plan. Waiting until we are forced back would be inviting disaster." Meade looked over his glasses at Butterfield. "Now, get it finished!"

"Very well, General," Butterfield replied meekly.

Major Ludlow was waiting in the shadows for this interchange to end, and he stepped forward as Butterfield turned back to his work. "Sir, we have just received a report from General Buford."

Meade removed his glasses and rubbed his burning eyes. "Could you read it to me, please, Major?"

"Certainly, sir...General Buford reports arriving at Gettysburg in the afternoon and finding enemy infantry preparing to enter the town. Upon his arrival, the enemy retreated in the direction of Cashtown, leaving pickets about four and a half miles west of Gettysburg."

Meade pondered this information. "West toward Cashtown, you say? No indication of any enemy force to the east?"

Ludlow shook his head. "No, sir. Just the one enemy force."

Meade stood and moved over to the map table. *Is it possible Early marched the forty-plus miles from York to Gettysburg in a single day? Not likely. So that means there are more enemy forces near Gettysburg than we originally believed.* "OK, Ludlow. Make sure we get this information to General Reynolds. He may already have the report, but let's make sure."

Ludlow moved off, and Meade sat back down at his desk. After watching his staff work for a few minutes, he pulled out a sheet of paper and began to write a letter to Margaret. "All is going on well. I think I have relieved Harrisburg and Philadelphia, and that Lee has now come to the conclusion that he must attend to other matters. I continue well, but much oppressed with a sense of responsibility and the magnitude of the great interests entrusted to me. Of course, in time I will become accustomed to this. Love, blessings and kisses to all. Pray for me and beseech our Heavenly Father to permit me to be an instrument to save my country and advance a just cause."[4]

Chapter 11

Morning of July 1, 1863

NORTHERN MARYLAND

MEADE SIGHED AND THREW OFF his blanket. Sleep was impossible, he realized after a few fitful hours of attempting it. His mind was racing with countless questions and possible scenarios. Sitting up on his cot, he pulled on his boots and sighed again. *Best get at it,* he told himself.

After lighting a candle, he moved to his field table. A map was spread out along with the dispatches of the previous evening. Buford's report still troubled him, and he picked it up from the pile. *Enemy withdrawing to the west? What could that mean? Early was too far away to have already marched past Gettysburg...wasn't he?* Meade rubbed his eyes and considered the map.

"Still at work, General?" A voice startled him.

He looked up to see Major Ludlow holding open the flap of the tent. "Oh, Ludlow, come in. No, I just got up; couldn't sleep. Too much going on to be able to sleep."

Ludlow nodded, moving into the tent. "To tell you the truth, sir, I was having trouble sleeping as well. I saw the light on in your tent and thought I'd check to see if you needed anything."

"Well"—Meade shrugged—"I suspect there is a great deal of that going on tonight." He paused for a moment and then held up the dispatch from Buford. "I am having trouble with this report from John Buford. The implications are troubling." He handed it to Ludlow to examine.

Ludlow scanned the document. "You mean the part about the rebs retreating without a fight?"

"No." Meade shook his head. "The part about them withdrawing to the west…it just doesn't make sense. The reports we have place the bulk of the enemy out near Chambersburg. Early was reported to be in York, and it is hard to imagine that he could march his whole division past Gettysburg in a day and then turn back to enter Gettysburg. Buford reported that the enemy was just entering the town when they arrived and then retreated back west toward Cashtown. That implies they initially came from the west."

"So that's not Early's division?"

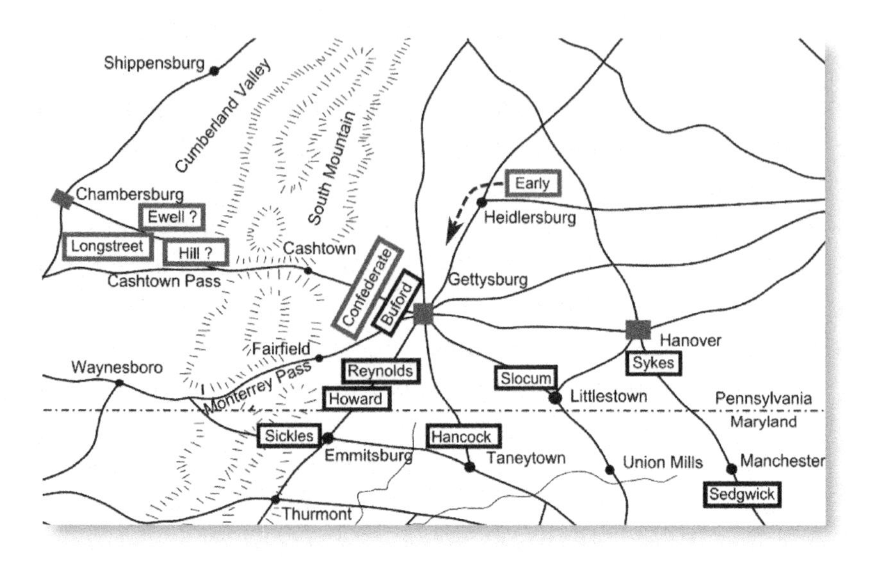

Situation—Early Morning 1 July

"Precisely," Meade replied. He turned to look at the map. "It means that some of the enemy force at Chambersburg has moved east through the Cashtown pass."

"So what do we do, then, sir?"

"We need to prepare for the eventuality that the rebels might get to Gettysburg before Reynolds does. They are only a few miles to the west of the town, closer than Reynolds. I have already instructed General Reynolds to withdraw slowly if he encounters a superior force. If so, then we will withdraw to the Pipe Creek defensive line. I expect Reynolds to retreat slowly, checking the enemy advance while the rest of the army moves to occupy the Pipe Creek line." Meade paused for a moment to consider that eventuality. "In that case," he said, "I expect Lee would sense blood and try to envelop Reynolds's command to destroy it. In that event, we have to be ready to fall on the enemy's enveloping force."

Ludlow cocked his head, looking at the map. "What should we do then, sir?"

Meade rubbed his beard in thought. "I think we are well positioned in that event. If Lee tries to envelop from the west, we have Sickles at Emmitsburg and Hancock north of Taneytown. For an envelopment from the east, we have Slocum at Two Taverns and Sykes at Hanover..." He paused to consider this. *What if Lee swings wide? Can't do it in the west; Sickles has the mountain pass there. In the east—that's the danger. There's a ten-mile gap between Slocum and Sykes. It's possible to slip through there. What if they reach the Pipe Creek positions before we do?* Meade looked up at Ludlow. "I think we need to alert General Sedgwick of the situation and let him know he needs to be prepared to move to provide support at a moment's notice."

Ludlow nodded. "Very good, sir. I will go and get a pad and pencil. We can work up a draft message to send out."

As Ludlow moved toward the door, Meade spoke up. "Oh, Ludlow?"

"Sir?"

"Thank you."

"Sir?"

"For helping me to clarify my thoughts on this situation."

Captain Muller looked over his command team as he finished his briefing. "Und zo, ze enemy is ahead of us, and vee are moving to meet zhem. Vee must be ready to march and fight at a moment's notice. Now, go and prepare your soldiers!"

Henry and the rest of the group saluted and moved off toward their men. "All right, gentlemen," Henry called out. "Prepare for movement! Light marching order. Take all extraneous items to the quartermaster's wagon. We are traveling light, so no extra weight. I *will* be checking! Corporals, check your squads. Each man is to have sixty rounds of ammunition. They are to draw three days' rations from the quartermaster as well as any extra ammunition needed. Let's get moving!"

As the men moved to collect their gear, Henry turned to Lieutenant Demarest, who was standing nearby. Demarest nodded in approval. "That's good, Sergeant Taylor. We need to keep them on their toes. The situation is very uncertain up ahead, and we need to be ready for anything."

Henry nodded and moved toward his own gear. They did need to be ready for anything—that was for sure.

When Henry returned, he found a group huddled around Isaac. "What's going on, Isaac?" he asked.

Isaac looked up. "Newspaper—first one I've seen in over a month. Not since Hooker banned newspapers from the camp in Falmouth. There was a fellow coming through selling them."

"Anything of importance?" Henry asked.

"Well, it says here that the Army of the Potomac, commanded by Major General Meade, is moving north from Frederick to meet Lee's army in Pennsylvania. I guess that confirms the rumors of where we are going."

"We were hoping that it would be Little Mac who would come back," Cundy muttered.

Henry nodded understandingly. Most of the men had a great respect for General McClellan. He was their commander early on and had been instrumental in training and equipping the Army of the Potomac. He had made them into soldiers, and they all respected him for that. Henry cleared his throat. "Ahem. I don't think that was ever likely to happen.

Reports are that the president was very unhappy with General McClellan's performance."

"And insubordination," Isaac added.

"Yes, that too," Henry replied. "Still, it should not be a surprise that Hooker was replaced. His performance at Chancellorsville was universally condemned in the press."

"That's why newspapers were banished from the camp in Falmouth," Isaac said. "I understand the reason Hooker was replaced. I just don't like the idea of replacing him so close to a battle."

"Well," Henry said, "Meade does have a good reputation. I guess we will just have to hope for the best."

At that moment, the long roll on the drums began. "Let's fall in, men!" Henry called out.

Meade paced nervously outside his headquarters tent. For over an hour, rumbles of artillery, like distant thunder, rolled in from the north. There was a fight going on up there, and he had no reports at all. Waiting was nearly unbearable. Meade picked nervously at the lint on his jacket. If Reynolds got in over his head, he would have to get him help right away. He hoped Reynolds would remember his instructions to withdraw if things got too tough. Meade took a deep breath. *Stop worrying,* he told himself. *Reynolds is the best man you have. He will do the right thing.* Still, he had to admit, it would be less nerve racking if he had some news.

He kept glancing up the road toward Gettysburg, hoping that a messenger would appear. Finally, he spotted a rider galloping toward him at a breakneck speed. As the rider came closer, Meade recognized him as Captain Weld, one of Reynolds's junior aides. He was gasping for air, and his lather-spattered horse seemed ready to collapse. An orderly grasped the horse's bridle as Weld dismounted. He was a short, slight man—more like a jockey, Meade noted. Must be why Reynolds had chosen him to bring the message.

The aide quickly saluted Meade. "I've brought a report from General Reynolds, sir," the young captain said. "He told me to get here as quickly as I could—even if it meant killing my horse."

Meade glanced at the condition of the horse. "It looks like you came close to doing that, Captain." He motioned to the orderly holding the horse. "See if you can get this poor animal some water."

Meade motioned for Weld to continue. "General Reynolds reports the following: 'The enemy are advancing in strong force. I fear they will get to the heights beyond town before I can. I will fight them inch by inch, and if driven into the town, I will barricade the streets and hold them back as long as possible.' That's all, sir"

Get to the heights before I can? "Good God," Meade blurted. "If the enemy get Gettysburg, we are lost!"

Meade paused to calm himself down. "Could you repeat the report, Captain?" Weld repeated the report and at the end, Meade slapped his hands together. "Good. That is just like Reynolds. He will hold on to the bitter end."

Meade considered the information. One very important thing was missing from the report. "These heights beyond the town you mentioned—did General Reynolds say if they were suitable for a defense?" Meade asked.

"No, sir, he did not mention that. I did not really look at the heights, as I was rushing to get down here."

Meade nodded and thanked Weld for his report. *We are to have a battle today—that is for sure. But is Gettysburg the right place to assemble the army for a defensive battle? How can I know? Reynolds is clearly engaged in fighting the battle, and there is no one else up there I would trust with that decision. I need a separate set of eyes on the problem and not bother Reynolds with it.* He called out toward his aides, "Can someone find General Warren for me and tell him that I need him to go up to Gettysburg to inspect the terrain and report on its suitability?"

Meade scowled at the map. He would have preferred it if Reynolds had been more specific in his report. *Is the ground good? In the absence of specific information on the terrain, is it wise to move any more of the army toward Gettysburg?*

"General?" Meade's thoughts were interrupted by Butterfield. "We have just received a report from General Buford."

Meade looked up from the map. "Can you read it to me, please?"

"Dated July 1, 10:10 a.m.," Butterfield said. "The enemy's forces"—A.P. Hill's—"are advancing on me at this point and driving my pickets and skirmishers very rapidly. There is also a large force at Heidlersburg that is driving my pickets at that point from that direction. General Reynolds is advancing and is within three miles of this point, with his leading division. I am positive that the whole of A.P. Hill's force is advancing."

A knot formed in Meade's stomach. *A.P. Hill? Where did he come from? So the reports were wrong. Hill is not behind the mountains at Chambersburg—he's on the east side, moving toward Gettysburg! What am I going to do? There isn't enough data to make an informed decision!*

"So," Meade began, "with A.P. Hill coming in from the west and north and Early from the east, Reynolds could possibly be outnumbered two to one. He will have to fight like hell to survive and will have no other option but to retreat!" He looked over at Butterfield. "When did the Pipe Creek circular go out last night?"

Butterfield looked down toward the floor. "It was only issued this morning."

"Goddamn it!" Meade exploded. "We discussed this last evening, General Butterfield. You know how important these orders are. Now we are in contact with the enemy, and my corps commanders do not have the crucial instructions in the event we have to withdraw to our chosen defensive positions."

Butterfield glared back with clenched jaws.

Meade turned back to his map. "We need to be prepared to react to whatever happens." He looked back at Butterfield. "Send word out to all the corps commanders. Hurry up Hancock and all the other commands."

A booming voice outside the tent caused him to look up. It was an unmistakable voice—Hancock. Meade smiled and hurried to the door of the tent to welcome the commander of the Second Corps.

Meade left the tent and greeted Hancock warmly. At this time of uncertainty, it was comforting to have Hancock here. Hancock was his usual radiant self, with a simple officer's jacket buttoned at the top over a clean white shirt. Meade always wondered where Hancock managed to get those clean shirts in the field. Hancock was quick to get down to business. "I've brought my corps up as ordered, General Meade. Do you have any further orders?"

Meade motioned Hancock into the tent, where they stood at the map table. "Our latest reports on the enemy are quite a bit different from what we discussed yesterday. It appears that the enemy is actually east of the mountains. General Reynolds has run into strong rebel forces just outside Gettysburg, probably all of A.P. Hill's corps. We are waiting for more information."

Hancock looked at the map and nodded.

Meade continued. "We do have several options. One is to assemble at Gettysburg and fight a battle there. We do not have an adequate report on the terrain around Gettysburg, nor do we know if John Reynolds can hold off whatever rebel force he has encountered.

"The other option is to withdraw to a defensive position where we can concentrate our forces. There we can either defend or resume the offensive."

Taking a pointer, Meade traced the road from Gettysburg to Emmitsburg. "If Reynolds is forced back, one option is to withdraw to Emmitsburg. The Third Corps is already there, and John should be able to hold there with three corps until we can bring the rest of the army up. If that route of retreat is blocked, we can withdraw to the defensive line along the Pipe Creek. I have John Sedgwick over there with his corps anchoring the line. If Lee tries to slide farther to the east, then John will pitch into him and slow him down until we can assemble the rest of the army. Those are all the possibilities. Hopefully we will know more soon."

Hancock nodded slowly, evaluating the situation. "Do you think that Reynolds has been attacked to keep him away from the pass at Cashtown? That would seem to be a pretty important strategic point for the rebs."

"I hadn't considered that. Perhaps it is the reason. I had thought that Hill might be trying to reach an assembly point east of Gettysburg. Nothing is clear right now."

"Well," Hancock said, "this contact changes everyone's plans. I suspect Lee is calling on all his forces right now."

Meade nodded. "If I was sure of the situation, I would order up the entire army right now, but I must be cautious until we are certain of Lee's intentions."

"Yes," Hancock said. "But we must not wait too long."

The pair talked for a while longer, trading impressions of the campaign so far and possible meanings for some of what had happened in the past several days. When Hancock finally left, Meade was sorry that the visit was over. He went back to his maps with a sigh.

Dan Sickles looked out over the fields from the farmhouse porch just east of Emmitsburg. The golden wheat gleamed in the midday sun. He had made this farmhouse his headquarters upon his arrival a short time ago.

He looked at Major Tremain incredulously. "Tell me what he said again?" Tremain had just returned from meeting with General Reynolds up the road near Gettysburg.

Tremain cleared his throat. "General Reynolds's exact words were, 'Tell General Sickles I think he better come up. The cavalry has run into rebs north of Gettysburg and they expect a fight today.'"

"He *thinks* I better come up? What the hell does that mean? Is it an order or not?" Sickles scowled and took another pull on his cigar. He couldn't figure out what was going on here. Meade had ordered his corps to Emmitsburg with clear instructions to stay there, but he had also assigned Sickles to Reynolds's left wing. This, on paper at least, should mean that Sickles would take his orders from Reynolds.

His aide shrugged. Sickles paced along the porch; his hand found the folded paper in his pocket. A formal rebuke—Meade had given him a written reprimand for moving his corps too slowly for the "old snapping turtle's" liking. Contempt had begun to be tempered with concern. *Is Meade trying to build up a case for relieving me of command? If so, then disobeying a direct order from Meade would certainly be enough reason. Reynolds is my superior, however, and I should obey his order and move my corps up to Gettysburg.*

If Joe Hooker were still in charge, Dan Sickles knew exactly what he would do—tear up road and pitch into the rebs. He knew Hooker would forgive any mistakes taken in the name of aggressive action. The problem was Joe Hooker wasn't in command anymore. It was that bookish engineer George Meade. Sickles knew Meade well enough to know that the new commander expected his orders to be obeyed.

The right thing would be to take his corps up to Gettysburg. If they were going to have a battle up there today, Reynolds could use all the troops he could get his hands on. No telling how many rebs were up there, and all Reynolds had was his cavalry and the First and Eleventh Corps—not very much if Lee had the whole Army of Northern Virginia nearby.

Dan Sickles had never shrunk from a fight—that was his nature and what had gotten him promoted. *There might even be some more fame waiting for me up there in Gettysburg,* he mused. *Still, you have too much to lose right now. You're a corps commander. You've come so far—don't do anything stupid and lose it all.*

That was it. I have to take the conservative course; there was no other choice. The safe thing to do was to sit right here in Emmitsburg as I've been ordered. And Reynolds's order? Well, I'll go back to Reynolds and get clarification. A direct order from Reynolds to come up should cover me. He turned to Tremain. "How is your horse? I need to send you back up to Gettysburg right away."

Tremain shook his head. "I rode him hard, General. I don't think that he has another trip left in him."

"The quartermaster will issue you a replacement, then. Have one of the orderlies get it for you."

Tremain moved off to find an orderly, and Sickles began to pace along the porch. *Must phrase this message perfectly, think it through.*

His concentration was broken by the noise of a horse and rider galloping up to the farmhouse. It was a cavalry trooper, soaked from a recent shower, with a horse flecked with foam. The trooper looked around and spotted Sickles. "I have a message from General Howard, sir. He says that General Reynolds has been killed and asks for you to come up."

Sickles looked the trooper over. *He seems to be reliable; no reason to discount his report. Reynolds dead? That changes the situation. Howard is in command of the left wing now, and he has asked me to come up. I think that would hold up under scrutiny.*

Tremain was back. "I have a horse, General. What are your orders?"

Sickles paused for a moment before replying. "Go find Howard and tell him where we are. Inform him that we will come up at once."

Tremain saluted and moved off the porch toward his waiting horse. He stopped before mounting to watch another cavalry trooper gallop toward the farmhouse.

"Urgent message for General Sickles," the trooper called out.

"I'll take it," Tremain said. He opened the scrap of paper and scanned the note. "It's a very brief message. It says 'General

Reynolds is killed. For God's sake, come up. Howard.' That's all, sir."

It must be serious, Sickles thought, *for the pious Howard to invoke God like that. We definitely need to come up.* An idea popped into his head. *If I leave a detachment here in Emmitsburg and move up to Gettysburg with the rest of the corps, I can obey both Howard and Meade.* He looked toward Tremain. "Tell General Howard that I will reach him as quickly as possible with all my corps except for a detachment to hold the post of Emmitsburg as previously ordered by General Meade." *There, that should do it.*

As Tremain mounted and turned his horse toward Gettysburg, Sickles called out to the rest of his aides. "OK, get word out to the division commanders. We march for Gettysburg immediately. Tell General Birney to leave two brigades here at Emmitsburg. Get moving!"

Meade looked up as a major shouldered his way toward him through the hubbub of the busy headquarters. He recognized this man as another one of Reynolds's staff. The officer appeared grief stricken, his face ashen. "General Meade," the officer said, "I have some tragic news to report. General Reynolds was killed about ten fifteen this morning, at the beginning of the battle."

A collective gasp filled the tent, and all conversation ceased. Meade sank heavily onto the camp chair, his head spinning. *Reynolds, dead? Is this possible?* "Please tell me the details," he said softly, not looking up.

"The first troops had just arrived, part of Wadsworth's division," the major said, "they came in alongside Buford's cavalry, who were fighting dismounted. General Reynolds was directing the placement of these troops when he was struck in the neck by a ball. He never regained consciousness and died about fifteen minutes later."

Meade was numb. He could barely think. "Who is in command now?" he whispered.

"General Howard is in command, sir. The Eleventh Corps was coming up when I left to bring the message to you."

This was truly shocking news. Meade left the tent and walked some distance away to be alone for a few minutes. He had relied on Reynolds a great deal—perhaps too much. John's support was one of the major reasons he had been able to make it through the past few days, and now he was gone. It had never seemed possible that Reynolds could be killed, yet he was, taken from them at the worst possible moment. Meade felt so very much alone and helpless.

Out of the corner of his eye, Meade caught some movement, and he looked up. It was a cavalryman from New York. Meade had walked to the edge of the headquarters perimeter and encountered a guard standing his post. The man stood a respectful distance away, but Meade knew he was being watched. *They are all counting on me,* he thought. *Can't let them down now.*

Meade rubbed his grizzled beard. *What am I going to do?* The difficult part of it was that he didn't have enough information to make any kind of a decision. Others might make decisions on gut feelings, but Meade always liked to make decisions based on hard facts. It was his engineering training, he guessed. Perhaps he should go to Gettysburg himself, see the situation firsthand, and make decisions on the spot. Meade shook his head. *No, that's too risky.* He would be out of contact with the rest of the army for hours. If Gettysburg was only a diversion, he could be out of touch with the army when it needed him the most. *Lee is too wily an opponent. Better not risk that.*

Well, if not me, who? He had little confidence in Howard after Chancellorsville, and there wasn't anyone else on the field at Gettysburg who had the necessary experience and rank. Among the other corps commanders, only Hancock possessed all the traits he was looking for. He had just discussed his plans with Hancock, so there was no other corps commander who was as well informed. Hancock also had a well-deserved reputation for being able to size up terrain and make appropriate tactical dispositions. Finally, with Reynolds gone, there was no one more inspiring than Hancock. Meade walked back to the tent and called for his aides. He was going to ride over to see Hancock right away.

Hancock was outside his tent when Meade and his aides arrived. They all wore expressions of profound grief, and Hancock knew that it wasn't good news they were bringing.

The news, when Meade delivered it, shocked even Hancock. He knew and respected John Reynolds; there weren't many in the army who could come close to Reynolds as a soldier. Hancock recognized this as a severe blow.

The second bit of news came as even more of a shock. Meade placed a rolled-up map in his hands and looked him in the eyes. "Hancock, I want you to turn command of the Second Corps over to General Gibbon and immediately go forward to Gettysburg to take command over all forces on the field. This is the best topographical map I have. It just arrived today."

Hancock looked at the map dumbly, not knowing what to say.

"I need you up there, Win," Meade said. "I don't know what's up there. I sent Warren up there, but I have heard nothing from him. Reynolds may have been killed before he had a chance to make any tactical arrangements, and there is no one up there in whom I can place any trust."

Hancock nodded; that was the harsh reality. "What are your instructions, General Meade?"

"I must know if Gettysburg is a good place to fight, considering the terrain," Meade said. "If so, I will order all commanders to march on Gettysburg immediately, and I ask you to hold on until you are reinforced. If the terrain does not favor the defensive, or if you cannot hold, then you should order an immediate withdrawal. Find the nearest place where an army can concentrate, or if need be, withdraw all the way to the Pipe Creek line, where I will have the rest of the army assembled and ready to receive the enemy."

Hancock considered Meade's instructions. It was not going to be easy dealing with the personalities involved. A lot of feathers would be ruffled. Hancock would have to broach this subject tactfully. "Ah, I understand your request, General Meade, and I will willingly carry it out. There is, however, a problem. I am junior in rank to both General Howard and General Sickles. In addition, General Gibbon is not the senior division commander in the Second Corps."

Meade shook his head violently. "Seniority does not count now. What is most important is to have the best man in the position of authority. Secretary Stanton has authorized me to make whatever changes I see fit among my commanders, regardless of seniority. There is no time for fools or incompetents, Hancock! The fate of our country is at stake. Here. I will write orders to this effect, which you can show to anyone who questions you." Meade took a pad from one of his aides and began to write furiously.

There was no arguing with this logic. Hancock saluted in acknowledgment. "Very well, General Meade. I will leave for Gettysburg immediately." He watched Meade ride off and then turned to send his aides scurrying.

It took a few minutes to get his horse prepared and his aides ready to leave. Hancock dictated an order to Gibbon and saw to a few last-minute details. When all was ready, Hancock climbed into a waiting ambulance, where he could spread the maps out and study them while on the way.

The map was not detailed, but Hancock knew it was the best available at the time. He traced the spiderweb of roads spreading out from Gettysburg. It seemed that every road in the area passed through that small Pennsylvania town. It looked preordained for a battle, Hancock mused, and that was either good or bad, depending on who was the fastest.

As for terrain, the map showed very little. There was, of course, the long north-south line of South Mountain lying to the west of Gettysburg. No other real terrain features were noted on the map. *For a topographical engineer, this must be a nightmare,* Hancock thought. *No wonder Meade is in such a state.* He sighed and scanned through the orders he had received over the past few days, looking for any more information or guidance. Finally he reached the order Meade had just written for him. *This is perfectly legal,* he thought, *but it will not go over very well.* He would need to show a great deal of tact, and Hancock knew that tact was not his strong suit.

He leaned over and tapped the driver to stop so that he could mount his horse. Once mounted, the group made faster time. There wasn't much conversation as the group rode quickly past fields of ripening wheat and fruit orchards. Hancock didn't notice any of the countryside's beauty; he was too busy weighing the imponderables. How well would Howard's troops hold up, and what shape would they be in when he got to Gettysburg? The First Corps was one of the best, and even without Reynolds, they would give as good as they got. The Eleventh Corps—now there was another matter. Its troops were of uneven discipline and had shown the inclination to bolt rather than dig in and fight it out. *Their commander,* Hancock mused. *What of him? Howard will be the ranking officer and naturally be in command. Does he have the presence to hold things together?*

A lone ambulance appeared on the road traveling towards them. The driver called out to them when they were within hailing distance. "It's General Reynolds. We're taking his body to Lancaster—to his family."

Hancock nodded grimly and reined his horse to the side of the road. The group removed their hats and solemnly watched the ambulance pass by. *Goodbye, friend,* Hancock thought. *We will all miss you. Well,* he realized, *there is no denying reality now.* He closed his eyes. *Forget about that. Focus on the work at hand.*

With a hand gesture from Hancock, the group resumed their ride in total silence.

Part Four

Gettysburg, Pennsylvania

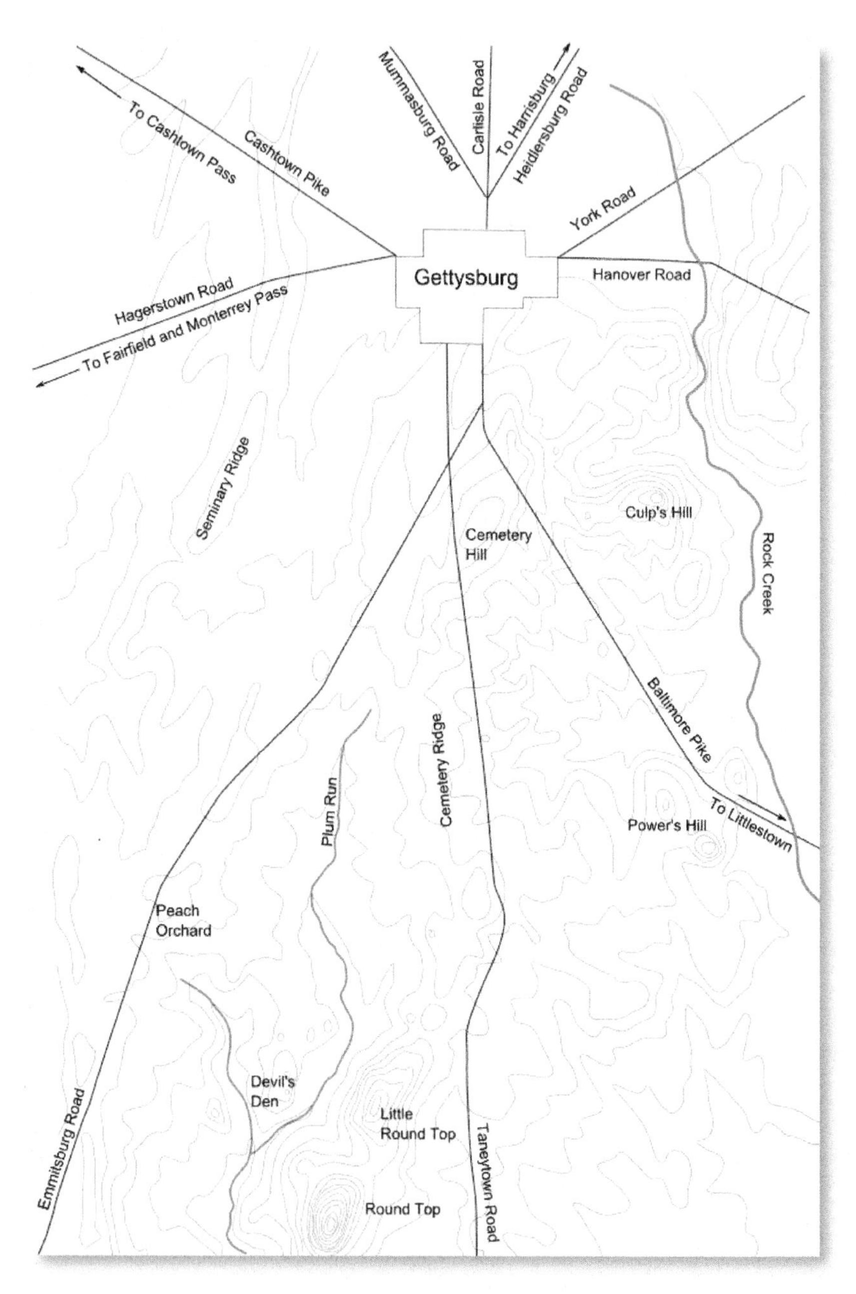

Map 4—Gettysburg Battlefield

Chapter 12

Late Afternoon: July 1, 1863

THE HEIGHTS ABOVE THE TOWN of Gettysburg, which the locals knew as Cemetery Hill, were a site of total pandemonium. The Union defensive lines north and west of the town had been broken, and now the remnants of the fight were streaming up the hill from the town below. Some regiments trudged back in battered and bloodied order or doggedly skirmished with their pursuers. Others had disintegrated into small groups or individuals who fled in single-minded panic toward the rear and some measure of safety.

Some of them continued their flight down the Taneytown Road, past the Widow Leister's small white cottage and farther down behind the brow of Cemetery Ridge. Most milled about in confusion near the crest, unsure of what to do but unwilling to retreat any farther without orders. The rout and subsequent flight through town had stripped the two corps of their command structure. Commanders lay dead and wounded on the battlefield or caught up in the crush of thousands of men desperately trying to find their way through the narrow streets and blind alleys of this little Pennsylvania farm town.

Firing in the town heightened the sense of panic; the rebs were still after them, and in a few minutes, they might come storming up the hill. Men looked about in desperation for a direction in which to flee should this position break. The left wing of the Army of the Potomac teetered on disaster. A quick gray-clad push would cause it to topple, and with it, perhaps, the fate of the Union.

From the south, a group of horsemen rode up the Taneytown Road toward Cemetery Hill. Leading the group, mounted on a magnificent sorrel, was a tall and well-built officer: calm and self-assured.

Confused, desperate men squinted to make out the rider. Grins of recognition and relief flashed white teeth in powder-blackened faces, and the word spread like electricity. "Hancock… it's Hancock…Hancock's here." Eyes turned to watch his progress. Everyone in the Army of the Potomac knew of Hancock.

Hancock took the situation in as he approached. It was not good; he could see that from the condition of the fleeing troops he had met in the past mile. Up here on this hill, it looked even worse. The day's line of battle had evidently been broken, and the survivors had fled to this hill, or beyond it, he noted wryly. Still, he remained impassive. Now was the time to show strength and inspire confidence. The first order of business was to find Howard and get some control over this rabble.

"Find me General Howard," he snapped over his shoulder.

An aide galloped up the road in response. As the road reached the crest, Hancock paused to look around. To his left, in a small grove of trees, groups of men were beginning to form. He noted the circle badge of the First Corps on their caps. *The*

First Corps is trying to get formed up. That is what I would expect of them. To his right a brigade-sized group of men lolled near the crest of the hill, in and around a cemetery. They appeared not to have seen action this day. Hancock scowled—they were wearing the crescent moon of the Eleventh Corps.

His aide reappeared and led him over the hill to the right. Howard, surrounded by aides, sat on his horse near the cemetery gate, a large red brick arch. He clearly was not happy—the aide had evidently told him the purpose of Hancock's presence. *Well,* he thought, *best to get this over with as quickly as possible.*

Howard scowled at Hancock's approach. Hancock tried his best friendly smile and opened the conversation. "Good day, General Howard. I have been sent up here by General Meade to take command of all troops on the field."

Howard's scowl turned into a sneer. "Why, Hancock, you cannot give orders here. I am in command, and I rank you."

Howard's aides looked away, embarrassed.

Hancock clenched his jaws. *This is exactly the reaction I expected.* He tried again. "General Meade has given me written orders to take command on this field. If you would care to see them..." He reached into his pocket for the orders.

"NO," Howard snapped. "I do not care to see them!"

Hancock held his temper and coldly looked the group over. It was clear that no one would move a muscle at his orders unless Howard acquiesced—and the one-armed general showed no signs of backing down. Meanwhile, things around them were slipping out of their control. There certainly wasn't time to waste arguing about who was in command. The rebels could be on them soon, and this position needed to be ready. *OK,* he thought, *try another approach.*

Hancock turned slowly in his saddle for emphasis as he looked over the terrain. *This is a good position,* he thought. *Good enough to make a stand here.* "You know," he said, "General Meade has been considering a defensive line farther south along the Pipe Creek. He says there is excellent defensive terrain there, and I have seen some of it myself."

He looked at Howard and got a nod in agreement. The younger man had softened a bit. "But I think," Hancock said, "that this is the strongest position by nature on which to fight a battle that I ever saw. If it meets with your approbation, I will select this as the battlefield."

Howard blinked and looked around uncertainly. "Yes, I think it is a very strong position."

Hancock snapped his head. "Very well, sir. I select this as the battlefield." No objections from Howard. A few of his aides smiled with relief.

So far, so good, Hancock thought. *Now, let's try something else.* "It seems to me that we might discourage an attack if we could make the enemy believe we have been heavily reinforced."

Howard nodded, this time with more animation. He seemed relieved to have someone suggesting what to do. "I agree," he said. "But how do we do that?"

Hancock pointed to the troops lounging nearby. "Those men look fresh."

"Yes," Howard said. "They are part of Steinwehr's division. I left them in reserve here on Cemetery Hill."

That was a wise move, Hancock thought. *And it might well be what saves the day.* "May I suggest, General, that you have Steinwehr's division push forward to the stone wall farther down this slope? Oh, and it would be helpful if they made as much of a show of it as possible. You know, fly every flag. Wave them in defiance. Make the rebs know they have arrived."

Howard nodded and turned to send an aide racing off with the order to make it happen.

Hancock watched another battery rattle up the Baltimore Pike from the center of town. "Another thing we can do is to get this artillery into position and start firing back at the rebs from this height. They won't be able to tell if they are fresh batteries from that distance." He paused. "One thing is certain, Howard: if we are to hold on until reinforcements arrive, we must make the absolute best use of every man and every artillery piece."

Howard gave a determined nod. "Yes, there is no question about that."

"Very well," Hancock said. "Then may I propose that we consolidate all our artillery under one chief of artillery? Colonel Wainwright, the First Corps chief of artillery, is the best artillerist on the field. I suggest we give him the job of siting each battery and developing a coordinated plan of coverage for the entire position."

A nod from Howard.

Hancock turned to an aide. "Find Colonel Wainwright and tell him to come see me."

The aide raced off, and Hancock returned to his business with Howard.

"The next thing we must do, in my opinion, is get our infantry straightened out." He pointed for emphasis at the lines of sweating, begrimed soldiers trudging wearily along the sides of Baltimore Pike up toward the hill. "Since Steinwehr's division is already pointed toward the west, we can best meet the threat of the enemy to the north if you place the remainder of the Eleventh Corps at right angles, facing in that direction. Stretch them out as long as you can. That stone wall down the slope a bit would be a good position, don't you think?"

Howard actually smiled. "Yes, that is a good position. I don't think we can reach all the way to that hill, though." He pointed off to the east.

The hill—Hancock looked at it again. It was a good anchor for the right of the line. Covered with trees, it might not be a good artillery position, but Hancock knew that in a few hours, experienced infantry could make it very hard to take. The trouble was, he couldn't be sure there was any capable infantry available in the Eleventh Corps. "Well, don't worry about that, Howard. I'll speak to General Doubleday. Perhaps he can find some troops to spare."

"That's fine. We could use the help." Howard was mollified now.

"Since both corps seem to be pretty well mixed up, may I suggest that we get personally involved in sorting them out? I can take the First Corps—they've lost their corps commander, and I know Doubleday could use some help. If you wouldn't mind, why don't you work with the Eleventh Corps? I am sure they would respond well to your personal leadership."

With a nod, Howard turned and rode down the hill toward his milling corps. Hancock smiled as he rode off. *My wife should have seen this act, he thought. She insists that it's impossible for me to hold my temper.*

He was starting to turn his horse toward the First Corps when he was halted by a call. "General Hancock!" It was General Buford, the cavalry general, riding up the Baltimore Pike.

"General Hancock! By God, I'm glad to see you!" Buford's frock coat was dust covered; a clean bullet rip across the right sleeve exposed the lining. His horse looked even worse, with flecks of lather and blood spotting its flanks. "I told them, Pleasonton and Meade, to send Hancock up. Everything was coming apart. We needed someone to take charge of this mess."

Hancock extended his hand as Buford drew alongside. "Hello, John, and I am damn glad to see you too! What's the situation?"

Buford frowned, cracking the layer of dust and smoke on his face. "They were flanked and routed, Win...simple as that. As you can see, both corps are trying to find their way through town." He jabbed his finger toward the center of Gettysburg. "It's a real mess in there, and I suspect we will lose a good number of men as prisoners. Can't be helped, though." Buford paused for a deep sigh. "I've got one of my brigades off to the east of that hill to our right, and the other brigade was on the left flank of the First Corps. I was on my way over to check on them when I ran into you."

Hancock nodded. "What shape are your brigades in?"

"They are pretty shot up. We had to hold out against Heth's division for two hours before the First Corps came up. They're still full of fight, though."

"Good. I need to ask them to hold on a little longer, John. We expect reinforcements up in the next several hours. When they get here, we will be in a much better position. The enemy may try to work around our flanks, so you need to spread your boys out on either flank in a screen. Just have them hold on if the enemy does come at them. I will get whatever help I can and bring it over personally."

"I'll do that, Win. I know that I can count on you, no matter what happens."

Hancock's face softened a bit. "I know it's been a hard day, John. Meade tells me that John Reynolds was killed at the beginning of the battle."

"Yes, and the command devolved onto incompetents!" Buford's eyes flashed. "I kept telling them, it's a meeting engagement, don't get decisively engaged, find out what the enemy has, trade space for time until reinforcements come up. Instead, they stood and slugged it out—just let the enemy bring up more troops until they had us just where they wanted us. Outnumbered us and rolled up our flanks. Perhaps if John Reynolds..." He trailed off.

"Yes," Hancock said gently, "perhaps, but we must soldier on with what we have, John. The next two hours will decide if we will have a chance to hold on to this position. If we do, then perhaps tomorrow we will be given the chance to redeem ourselves." He looked around, breathing in. "This is very good terrain, John, a very favorable place for a battle."

"It is that," Buford said. "Some of the best I've seen." He pulled his gloves back on. "Now let me get over to Gamble on the left and get him deployed. Devin is on the right, and he is already in a screening position. You just let me know what else I can do for you, Win." Buford moved his horse forward with a barely imperceptible motion of his legs. "And I am *damn* glad they sent you up here!"

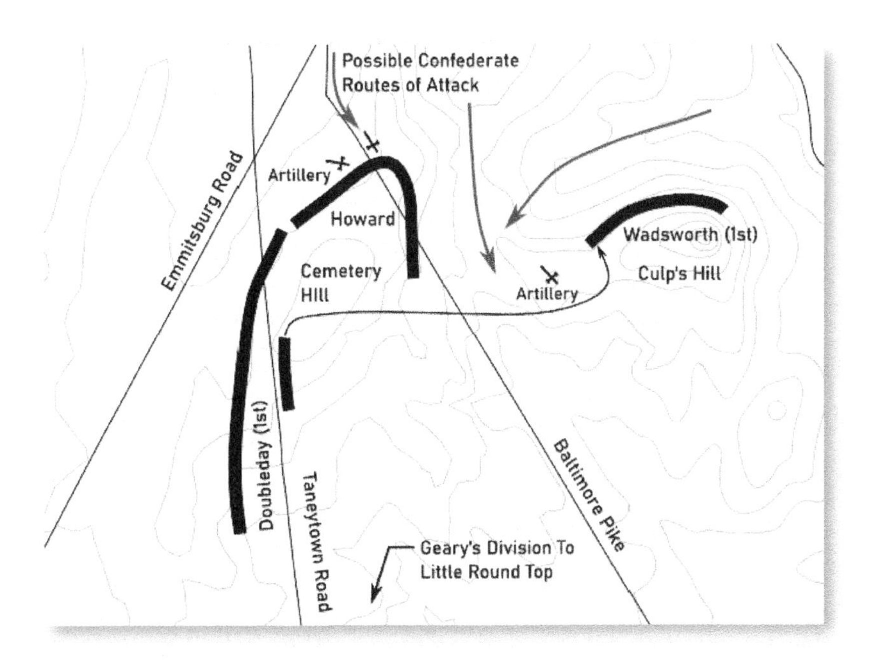

HANCOCK'S PLAN FOR DEFENSE—1 JULY 4 PM

Hancock briefly watched his friend ride off. *I wish we had ten more just like him.* Hancock dismissed the thought. There was too much to do. He looked around to evaluate the tactical position. The hill line they were on resembled an inverted J. Here next to the cemetery, the hill mass towered over the town. From there, the hill ran roughly to the south, slowly deceasing in height. At the southern end, two mound-shaped hills punctuated the end of the hill mass. The ground to the west of this line sloped gently for about a mile with open farm fields. *Excellent fields of fire,* he thought. From the cemetery the hill mass curved gently toward the east in an arc, ending in another hill. His practiced eye searched the position for flaws. *Every position has flaws,* he told himself. *If you don't compensate for the flaws, even the best position can be broken.* The biggest flaw was just to his right, where Cemetery Hill dipped into a low saddle before rising to a wooded hill beyond. "That saddle is a direct route into our rear. We need to plug it." He eyed his aides. "Anyone seen Wainwright?"

The artillery chief was nowhere to be found. Hancock cursed impatiently. He would have to take care of this himself. A battery was resting near the cemetery gate, horses snorting after dragging the heavy pieces through the town and up the hill. The men were sweaty and covered with powder soot and dust. Still, Hancock noted, they were in fairly good shape. "Lieutenant," he called to the officer in command, "I have an important job for you."

The younger officer straightened and saluted.

Hancock moved close so that he could see the young man's eyes. *Good,* he thought. *No sign of fear. A little defiance—that's good.* He returned the salute and pointed to the east. "You see that saddle over there, between this hill and the wooded one a little farther to the east?"

The lieutenant nodded.

"I want you to take your battery over there and find a position where you can prevent the enemy from coming up that saddle. It's important that you hold on. I will get reinforcements over there as soon as I can, but you must hold on. Can you do that for me?"

The young man clenched his jaws and nodded. Hancock nodded back. This fellow would hold on. With an order from its commander, the battery rolled forward.

Hancock turned to his next problem. The Baltimore Pike coming up from the town was wide and provided an excellent attack route to his position. Hancock visualized several rebel brigades in column storming up this street. He looked at the single small brigade stretched along the stone fence about fifty yards down the hill. *That's not enough to stop a determined attack,* he thought. The popping of rifle fire was growing closer, and the flood of blue troops had slackened. Rebel skirmishers might only be a few blocks inside the town. There was no telling when that street could be filled with thousands of howling rebs, pushing up the street and over the thin line of troops holding the wall.

Canister—that's what we need. A battery firing canister would tear apart that charge before it got within a hundred yards of the stone wall. There was another battery limbered up nearby, and Hancock rode to find its commanding officer. He found the captain in charge in a group with the other officers. They had no orders and were waiting to be told where to go. Hancock motioned the captain over and received a stiff salute as the battery commander rode up to him. His eyes were different from the other artillery officer. Hancock looked in and saw uncertainty and fear. *This one will pull out if pressed,* Hancock thought. *He needs to be told to stay here in no uncertain terms.*

"Captain," he began, "I want you to place three guns covering this pike and the others at right angles. Remain in this position until I relieve you in person. Is that understood?"

The junior officer blinked and nodded uncertainly.

He wonders who the hell this general is giving him orders, Hancock reasoned. *Will he stay here? Does he know how critical this position is? Better make it more critical to him personally. That way, he'll think hard about pulling out.* Hancock motioned an aide over. "I want you to witness this order in case there is any question later." He turned back to the battery commander. "I am of the opinion that the enemy will mass in town and make an effort to take this position. We need to sweep the street with canister if they attempt an assault. I want you to remain here until you are relieved by me or by my written order and take orders from no one else. Is that quite clear?"

The captain gulped and looked from Hancock to the aide and back. The orders were clear—given by a major general with an officer as a witness. *He knows if he moves now without an order from me,* Hancock thought, *it will mean a court-martial.* "Yes, sir," the battery commander replied.

Hancock kept an eye on the battery as he rode down to the stone wall. This was his only hope until reinforcements arrived. He rode along the wall, speaking to the soldiers of Steinwehr's division. "I have placed a battery to support you...we need to hold on until nightfall...reinforcements will be here within the hour...we must hold on until that time." The men nodded grimly and took positions behind the stone wall as he rode by.

The trip west along the stone wall led Hancock to the end of the Eleventh Corps line. Beyond that, the remnants of the First Corps were grimly constructing defensive positions. Hancock rode toward the First Corps flag to find General Doubleday. He knew Doubleday from West Point, where he had been two years Hancock's senior. He was competent but not brilliant; the First Corps was certainly less capably led now than under John Reynolds.

Hancock found Doubleday on the hill trying to bring order to his scattered brigades. From the look of things, they were having some measure of success. Doubleday appeared harried and looked up with some relief when Hancock called him. "General Doubleday, good afternoon."

"Win," Doubleday said, "thank God you're here. Is the Second Corps up?"

"No, General Meade has sent me forward to take command of the field and to determine if we should fight a battle here."

Doubleday showed no surprise. "You will want a situation report, then. We were forced out of our position on the ridgeline to your front. This was due to the collapse of the Eleventh Corps on our right flank combined with the overwhelming strength of the enemy to our front. Some of the corps was forced to retreat through the town. Of these, many are missing and may be captured by the enemy. The rest came across the fields." Doubleday sighed. "The corps has suffered heavy casualties and is short on ammunition."

Hancock looked around at the tired soldiers doggedly constructing defensive positions. "What dispositions have you made on this ridge?"

"I have ordered the corps to connect with the Eleventh Corps on the right flank and then form a position facing to the west."

Hancock quickly scanned the positions. *They're too narrow,* he thought. He could see that standard procedures were being followed and the defensive line would be hopelessly short. "What I would like you to do, Abner, is to extend your line as far as possible to the south. Put all your people in one line; don't assign a reserve. We need everyone on the front line."

Doubleday scowled and shook his head. "That is highly irregular. We wouldn't have a reserve to react to any enemy attacks."

Hancock held his temper. "Yes, I understand that, but we must convince the enemy that we have been heavily reinforced if we are to forestall an attack against this position tonight. The way to do that is to spread our forces out. The enemy will not be able to tell that we are one line thin."

Doubleday shook his head again. "I can't take the chance with no reserves. It's too dangerous."

"I will take the responsibility. There are no reserves anywhere on this field. If you are attacked, I will find reinforcements somewhere and personally bring them to you."

"Very well," Doubleday said. He spoke a few words to an aide, who galloped off to spread the word.

"One other thing, General," Hancock said. "Our right flank is unsecured. We must occupy and hold at all costs the hill that anchors our right flank. This is a job for your best division, the one with the Iron Brigade."

"That would be the first, General Wadsworth's division. But that's not practical—"

"General Doubleday, we must occupy that hill, or we will most certainly be flanked out of this position. There are no other troops available."

Doubleday would not yield. "My men have been fighting since early this morning. Wadsworth's division in particular has taken very heavy casualties and is in no condition to do any more marching."

Hancock's temper snapped. He drew himself up in his stirrups, his face reddening. "General Doubleday," he roared, "I am in command on this field. Send every man you have!"

Doubleday appeared shocked at the outburst and stared open mouthed at Hancock, as if ready to say something more. Instead, he nodded and looked away. "I understand your orders, General Hancock. If there is nothing else, I will excuse myself and personally see to these movement preparations."

Hancock nodded, and the First Corps commander rode off. This was no time for courtly behavior. The rebs could be on them at any minute. Around him, the men of the First Corps were moving to respond to his orders. He noted their actions with satisfaction and rode off toward the crest of the hill.

Wainwright met him near the cemetery with a report on the artillery. "General, we found a knoll in that saddle to the right that gives us excellent fields of fire. We are able to fire across the front of the Eleventh Corps' position as well as down the saddle. This helps to cover a weakness in their position. The ground falls off steeply in front of their position, allowing an attacking force to approach under cover. I am siting each battery personally as you requested." With a nod from Hancock, the artillery officer rode off to continue his work.

Hancock rode to where he could see the right side of the line. *Yes,* he thought, *Wainwright has done a good job there.* Below him, Howard had succeeded in placing the remnants of the Eleventh Corps along the stone wall. As he turned to look behind him, he could see Wadsworth's division forming to move to the right.

Hancock allowed himself a slight smile. *Things are beginning to come together.* He could now take a longer, more critical look at the terrain. *It's a good position,* he thought. *Almost too good to ask for.* He visualized the entire Army of the Potomac up, with an unbroken line of blue running from the wooded hill on the right around the hill he was on and then down along the ridge to the two hills in the south. *Yes, it's an excellent position.* "You know," he said to Colonel Morgan, "if we can hold these hills, here is the place to fight a battle."

"Those hills to the south are unoccupied, General," Morgan said.

"Yes," Hancock said. "I have no troops to put on them at this time. We can only hope that the enemy doesn't discover this before reinforcements come up. What do we hear of the Twelfth and Third Corps, by the way?"

"The Twelfth Corps is very nearly up, sir. The last report put them about two miles to the south. One of General

Sickles's aides is here to give you a report." He motioned for Tremain to approach.

Hancock looked Tremain over. "Let's have your report, Major."

"Sir, General Sickles is moving up to join us here with his entire corps, less two brigades he left in Emmitsburg to guard the approach from the Cumberland Valley."

"What time did he depart, Major?"

"I'm not sure, General," Tremain replied. "General Sickles sent me up to report to General Howard as soon as he received the request to come up. The units had not yet started to march when I left."

"And what time was that?"

"I think a little after two p.m., sir. I did not check my watch." Tremain shifted nervously in his saddle.

"So how far is it from Emmitsburg to here, do you think, Major?"

"I would guess about twelve miles, sir."

"All right. Thank you for your report, Major. I will let you know if I have any more questions."

As they watched Tremain ride away, Morgan said, "You sure had to pull information out of him, sir!"

"Yes, I did," Hancock replied. "So," he thought aloud, "that puts Slocum here in about an hour's time. The Third Corps is en route from Emmitsburg. At about twelve miles away, and a departure time of, say two thirty, we can't expect Sickles until eight or nine this evening. Send a rider down to find the lead division of the Twelfth Corps. Have the commander come up and find me as quickly as possible. With a little luck, we may be able to hold on to this position."

With the immediate problems dealt with and preparations underway, Hancock was satisfied that he was as ready as possible to meet an enemy attack. It was now up to the rebels. A stone wall offered a convenient spot where he could watch what Bobby Lee's boys were up to. Hancock dismounted and pulled out his field glasses.

From the west to the north, out beyond the ridge past the town, through the haze of powder and smoke, he could see the signs of the day's battle. Rebel columns moved past long, dark lines stretched across the fields—Union dead and wounded. Hancock could not grieve; he had seen too much death in the past two years. They had done their duty and paid the price.

"May I join you, General Hancock?" A German accent.

Hancock looked up to see General Schurz approaching. He knew Schurz, one of Howard's division commanders, by reputation. Schurz had been a newspaper reporter before the war, and before that a Prussian officer and veteran of the German Revolution, forced to flee when the revolutionaries were crushed. Hancock respected Schurz's European military experience and keen reporter's eye.

"Of course, General. Please make yourself comfortable." Hancock waved to the flat rocks of the stone wall and raised his field glasses to his eyes. "I'm trying to figure out what the rebels are up to. I can't see very much, though. They are masked by the town and the ridge behind it."

"Yes, I see what you mean," Schurz said. "It is impossible to tell if the enemy is massing for an attack."

"Right, and if they are, we will get very little warning." Hancock scowled.

Schurz cleared his throat. "You know, General, I am more than a little nervous. This has been a very hard day on us, and our lines are very thin. Even though we have a very strong position, I fear we may not be strong enough to withstand a determined assault."

Hancock lowered his field glasses. "I must confess that I am nervous as well, and for the very same reason. I do think, though, that we can hold until the Twelfth Corps is up. They are very close and should arrive soon. Once they arrive, we will be in much better shape."

Schurz nodded pensively, and both men resumed their watch of the enemy.

Hancock finally spoke. "I cannot tell what they are up to down there. There is a great deal of movement, but they don't appear to be massing for an attack."

"It is difficult to tell, but I think they are making merry after their victory. If that is so, they will not attack soon." Schurz paused to consider what he had said. "Is it possible they are so confident that they celebrate their victory before they have finished winning it?"

Hancock shook his head. "I can't say, but if they let us have this evening undisturbed, we will be ready to give them a real surprise tomorrow. It won't be so easy with the entire army up."

"Yes." Schurz rubbed his chin. "Let us hope that they will allow us at least this evening."

"It's better to go this way, General. Less chance of running into the rebs over here."

Sickles nodded, and Tremain led the way as they turned off the Emmitsburg Road onto a narrow country lane. His aide was waiting for them as they approached Gettysburg. As soon as he decided to move most of his command up to Gettysburg, Sickles had left General Birney in charge and rode forward with his aides. The rumble of artillery, so constant for most of the ride up from Emmitsburg, was now silent. Toward the north, tall pillars of smoke rose above the countryside.

The dirt lane led toward the east, winding past some large hills. It ended at a wider and much more well-used road. Tremain was at his side. "General Howard's headquarters is only a couple of miles up this road, sir."

Sickles spurred his horse to a gallop. The group raced up the road, past brick farmhouses and tidy red-sided barns, past a little white cottage and up to the crest of the hill. The sight caused him to pull up. This hill had a spectacular view of the day's battlefield. Before him, at the base of the hill, lay the little town of Gettysburg. Beyond the town, the fields still smoked from the day's battle.

"General Howard's headquarters are over here, General Sickles." Tremain again.

They trotted past a cemetery rutted with cannon tracks and with gravestones knocked flat. Cannoneers worked feverishly to throw up some earthwork protection in front of their pieces. A few of the soldiers looked up at his passing and, curiosity satisfied, returned to the backbreaking work.

Aides and orderlies swarmed around the cemetery lodge. Howard met Sickles at the door with a warm greeting. "Ah, General Sickles, you are here. I knew I could count on you."

Sickles smiled hesitantly. It was a much warmer greeting than he had expected, given the problems at Chancellorsville. He had heard that General Howard blamed him for the Eleventh Corps' misfortunes there. "Yes, General Howard, I came as soon as I got your message."

A horseman galloped up the Baltimore Pike from the south and clattered to a halt outside the lodge. The rider, a slight, sallow corporal, raised himself up in his stirrups and looked around at the throng of officers. "Hancock—where is General Hancock?" he called out.

"He's gone down toward the two hills to the south," someone shouted back.

The corporal nodded and spurred his horse off.

Sickles glanced at Howard. "Hancock is here?"

Howard reddened at the mention of the Second Corps commander's name. "Yes, General Meade sent him up after he learned of General Reynolds's death. Can you believe the cheek of that fellow Hancock? He thought he was going to just ride in and take over even though I outrank him. General Slocum is coming up. He has seniority and will take command." Howard worked his mouth silently for a moment as if struggling to say something more.

Strange, Sickles thought. *Don't all West Pointers adhere religiously to seniority?* He let the silence drag on for a minute or so and then changed the subject. "Do you know when General Slocum is expected?"

Howard shook his head. "Hard to say. Could be a while. By the way, have you had dinner? My cook is making some excellent pancakes. If you're hungry, I can have him make you up a batch."

Sickles brightened. His stomach was reminding him of how long ago he had eaten. Besides, there wasn't much to do until Slocum arrived. "Yes, Howard," he said. "That would be very nice."

The noise of approaching horsemen caused Hancock to turn. In the lead was General Geary of the Twelfth Corps. There was no mistaking him; he was a tall man, near 6½ feet in height, towering over his aides. Hancock rose to greet the group.

Geary acknowledged him with a salute. "My division is less than a mile down the road, General Hancock. Your aide tells me you have command of the field. As far as I know, General Slocum is not yet up. What do you want me to do?"

Hancock nodded and pointed toward the south. "Do you see that knoll on the left, the rocky one, just there?"

Geary squinted in the direction Hancock was pointing and nodded.

"That knoll is a commanding position, and we must take possession of it," Hancock said. "If we can hold on to it, then our line is secure and we can fight a battle here. If we fail to fight here, we must fall back at least ten miles to find a suitable defensive position." He paused for Geary to consider what he had said. Geary nodded. "In the absence of General Slocum, I order you to place your troops on that knoll."

With no hesitation, Geary turned to an aide. "Veale, ride back and order General Greene to double-quick his troops diagonally across the fields and take possession of the knoll."

Geary's aide saluted and galloped off. Hancock raised his field glasses and scanned the fields and wood line to the west of the priceless knoll. There were no signs of the enemy approaching the area. He breathed a sigh of relief.

As he watched Geary ride toward the hill, Hancock began planning his next move. *If the Twelfth Corps is almost up, we can use the rest of the corps to shore up our right flank. The First Corps men could certainly use the help.* He turned toward Morgan, who was waiting nearby. "Colonel, ride down in the direction that General Geary came from. See if you can find the other Twelfth Corps divisions and hustle them up here. Have them take up position on our right flank, extending General Wadsworth's line."

As Morgan rode off, Hancock scanned the western landscape again with his field glasses. *Good—no sign of any enemy movement. It's almost too late to make any move tonight. Just a little bit longer, please.*

"General Hancock?" His thoughts were interrupted by a strange voice. Hancock had seen the man with General Howard; the officer was one of Howard's aides. "Sir, Generals Slocum and Sickles have arrived at General Howard's headquarters."

"Good. I'll be right there." Hancock slid his field glasses back into their case. *All the players are here. This is the opportunity to solidify our plan for this evening. I just need to send my report to General Meade.* He pulled a message pad out and began to write his report. Once done, he tore the page off and handed it to his aide. "Captain Parker, take this message to General Meade. Deliver it as rapidly as possible."

Howard's headquarters was surrounded by a gaggle of aides, orderlies, and their horses. The multitude parted as Hancock arrived, allowing him to enter the lodge. Inside, Howard, Slocum, and Sickles were enjoying a pancake meal.

Howard looked up. "Ah, Hancock. Would you care for some pancakes?"

"Not right now, thanks. It's important that we discuss our plans for the evening first." Hancock waited for everyone's attention. "After learning of General Reynolds's death, General Meade sent me up here to assess the situation and to report on the suitability of this position." He paused, looking at Howard, who had his head down. *Best to leave the part about being in charge out of this discussion.* "I have reported back to General Meade that I believe we can hold out until nightfall. The enemy has given us a huge gift by not following up on their success of today. We have one division of the Twelfth Corps up, and the rest are expected to arrive soon. The Third Corps is on their way. By later this evening, we will have half the army concentrated here."

The group nodded in agreement.

"So in regard to the position, I believe that it is very strong. The wooded hills on each flank present some danger of being turned, but I think that can be compensated for. I have communicated this opinion to General Meade along with my recommendation that he order the army to concentrate here." More nods. "The decision, of course, is up to General Meade, as is whatever unit disposition is to be made once the army is up."

"General Slocum." Hancock turned to face the Twelfth Corps commander. "You are the ranking officer on the field, and the command is now yours. I am returning to the Second Corps to await further orders from General Meade."

The humid late-afternoon air was still. Meade got up from his chair and walked to the door of the tent. It had been hours since he sent Hancock up, with no report forthcoming. Warren had been sent up even earlier, and he hadn't heard from Warren either. Sighing, he looked up the road to Gettysburg. *Where could they possibly be? I should have heard something from them by now!*

"Anything I can help you with, General?" Major Ludlow asked, standing behind him.

"Uh, no, Ludlow, thanks. I was just thinking that I should have received a report by now from someone. Not knowing is the worst part of waiting." Meade looked again toward the north.

"Wait. You can help me with something. Find for me all the reports we have received today."

Ludlow was back in a few minutes with a stack of papers. "I've got them all here, sir."

"Find me Buford's report from this morning."

"It's right here, sir."

"Tell me what is says, Major."

"Buford reports a strong force from the direction of Cashtown pass driving in his pickets and also another strong force coming in from the direction of Heidlersburg. He says he is positive that all of A.P. Hill's corps is advancing."

"Do you recall any mention of Longstreet's corps in any of the dispatches?"

"No, sir, I do not."

"So," Meade said, bending over the map, "Heidlersburg is on a direct route from York to the Cashtown pass. Early was reported to be at York yesterday, so the force Buford is seeing coming from Heidlersburg most likely belongs to Early. Hill's corps was previously reported in Chambersburg, but they have obviously moved east through the Cashtown pass." He paused to consider the implications. "With no reports on Longstreet, it is likely they are still in Chambersburg. If we concentrate the army now at Gettysburg, we have the opportunity to attack tomorrow morning and defeat part of Lee's army before they can assemble."

Meade walked outside and strained to spot a rider coming south with the information he desperately needed, but there was no one to be seen. *If, if, if,* he told himself. *How can I make a decision with no information? If I make the wrong decision, it could mean disaster—for the army and for the Union.* Frustrated, he began to pace back and forth in front of the tent.

He interrupted his pacing to peer up the road again and then noticed that everyone was watching him. *This is not solving the problem,* he admitted to himself. *Even if I got a dispatch right now, it probably would not have sufficient information to make a proper decision. Without information, I can only make a decision from the gut. Best to follow Napoleon's maxim: "March toward the sound of the guns."*

With that, Meade turned back into the tent. "Attention, everyone!" he called out. "We will concentrate the army at Gettysburg. Orders need to be sent out to all commanders. Now, let's get to work."

The Second Corps was on the march again. After a few hours of rest at Taneytown, the long roll had started, and they were called back into formation to resume their march. The rumbles that had come from the north in long, deep waves earlier in the afternoon had ceased, leaving an ominous silence.

"Anybody know where we're heading?" someone asked.

Henry looked over his left shoulder toward the afternoon sun. "North," he said. "North toward the fighting...Pennsylvania."

Henry shrugged to adjust his backpack. They all hoped it was the rebs getting the worst of things, but they knew it probably wasn't true. It had been a long time since the rebs had gotten the worst of any battle. *Well, we'll be marching straight to the battle,* Henry told himself, *even if it takes all night. Hancock will see to that.*

Henry glanced toward his platoon. "I want everyone to check your weapons and ammunition at the next rest stop. If there are problems, let me know. We may be going directly into battle from the march, so there won't be time to fix things or get more ammunition when we get there. Squad leaders, do a check at the next halt."

The column shuffled on in silence, with the earlier artillery a reminder of what was waiting for them up the road. The day was hot and sultry, like many of the days since they had left Falmouth. Henry thought back to when they had left their winter camp. It seemed like so long ago, and the days in between were a blur of marching and collapsing at the side of the road only to wake up the next morning and do it all over again. *Up the road, though,* Henry thought, *there is an end to this. Maybe an end to our luck, too.* He quickly shook the thought from his head.

Beside the road, a farmer had parked his wagon and was holding up a bucket to the column as it passed by. "Here's some cool Maryland water for you boys." A dipper passed down the line. Henry got a swallow as it went by him. "God bless you, sir," he called out.

The farmer looked up. "No, God bless you, all of you. Good luck up there. We are praying for you and for our country." Murmurs of appreciation fluttered down the line, and the regiment moved inexorably on.

Cheering from up in front of the column caused the men to look up. "What's going on?" No one knew, but their curiosity was satisfied a few minutes later as they passed the stone marker for the Maryland-Pennsylvania state line.

Isaac caught the significance first. "That must have been Webb's brigade. They're all Pennsylvania regiments. Glad to be home, I imagine."

Home. That's a strange concept—fighting a battle in one's home state. Henry tried to imagine what it would be like to fight a battle in Minnesota. *Well, we fought the Indians during the Sioux uprising, but this is different. Pennsylvania is like home in a way. It's the North.*

"The last time we fought a battle in the North, we beat the rebs," Isaac said.

"That was Antietam," someone said behind him. "One hell of a bloody fight. Wouldn't want another one of them."

A chorus of agreement.

Maybe that's the only way to beat Bobby Lee, Henry thought. He opened his mouth to answer but closed it. *Better to let it be. They'll see what's in store for them when they arrive. No sense getting everyone upset and even more worried.*

The first real sign of a battle was the teamsters. Forced to the side of the road at gunpoint by the officers of the Second Corps, they could still run their mouths even if they couldn't escape any farther south. "Don't go up there, boys," one fat teamster told the infantrymen. "The Johnnies are whipping the hell out t'us. They done killed Ginral Reynolds, and I s'pect they will capture the whole First and Eleventh Corps."

The men would have nothing of this. "Shut up, you fat windbag."

"The rebs better watch out. They don't know the Second Corps is on its way."

"The Johnnies must have forgotten that clubs is trumps. Guess we will have to go up there and teach them again."

Henry smiled at this last jeer and he glanced at the dirty white trefoil patches on the top of their caps. *In this next fight,* he thought, *let's hope that clubs are truly trump!*

Farther on, the column encountered stragglers, infantrymen headed south or milling about on the side of the road. The men were quick to notice the crescent moon of the Eleventh Corps and the absence of weapons on many of the stragglers. "Just like Chancellorsville, damn Dutchmen," someone up front muttered.

"Where the hell's your weapon?" a man near Henry asked.

"We were routed. The whole corps is destroyed," a straggler bleated.

"Well, fall in," came the answer. "We're going up there to whip hell out of the rebs, and you can come and watch it if you're too scared to fight."

The men hooted at this and taunted the stragglers as they tramped toward the battle. It came as no surprise to the men of the First Minnesota that none of the stragglers joined them.

It was dusk when the regiment filed off the road and into a field just south of a tall wooded hill. Lieutenant Demarest found Henry. "We are camped a couple of miles south of the battlefield. It's beyond that big hill. Brigade has ordered us to construct barricades to fight behind in case the rebs try to move around south of that hill. Take a fatigue detail, Sergeant Taylor, and report to regimental headquarters. They will show you where to construct the barricades."

Henry responded with a casual salute and went through the company picking his detail. *Enough to do the job, but not too many,* he told himself as he moved along. Silently and automatically, the tired soldiers constructed hasty firing positions and stumbled back to their regiment. Henry found Isaac making coffee. He collapsed near the fire and took the hot cup of coffee that Isaac offered. As the brew brought back some energy, Henry found some hardtack in his haversack and slowly gnawed on the thick biscuit.

The rising moon gave them enough light to improvise beds on the ground. Henry and Isaac lay side by side and looked up at the sky. "You awake, Henry?" Isaac asked.

"Uh-huh. Too keyed up to sleep. There's bound to be one hell of a battle tomorrow." Henry looked over at his brother.

Isaac nodded. "I just hope we fight well tomorrow. Can you believe the Eleventh Corps? Damn them, running like that in two battles."

Henry thought for a while. "Yeah, I can't disagree. Maybe we can make it up tomorrow. We just have to."

"I just don't know, Henry." Isaac sighed. "Maybe we just can't do it, can't lick them."

"Sure we can, Isaac. Just as long as our forces are well handled and our troops fight. We can do it; I know we can." The pair was silent for a while. All at once, the thought was back in Henry's head. *We have been too lucky.* He felt like shouting it out and getting rid of it, once and for all. "Isaac?"

"Yeah?"

Henry stopped. *No, I won't say it. Maybe we haven't been too lucky. Maybe saying it would make it go wrong.* "Nothing. Just good night."

Chapter 13

Morning of July 2, 1863

It was past midnight, and George Meade had not yet reached Gettysburg. Traveling at night, he told himself, was always much slower, even with this bright full moon. Compounding the problem was the Second Corps' trains, which clogged the roads, forcing them to ride cross-country. Fortunately, they had Captain Paine as a guide, one of Warren's best engineers.

The field narrowed, and the group skirted a tree line close to the road. Meade heard a quick swish and yelped in pain as a branch smashed across his face. He grabbed the pommel to keep from falling from the saddle as he doubled over.

Concerned voices called a halt, and hands helped him from his horse and onto his feet. Meade put his hands to his smarting face and pulled them away. In the faint moonlight, he could see that there was no blood. He relaxed a bit, then realized in horror: his glasses, they were gone. Meade dropped to the ground and felt around for them. The other members of the group joined him. He would not be much use as a commander if he could not see. Several fruitless minutes later, he called a halt to the search.

How could he function? Headlines raced through his head: *"Blind General Loses Battle." Calm down; there must be a way out. Did*

I pack an extra pair? "Wait," he said to the group. "I might have another pair in my saddlebags." He carefully felt around inside the bag and pulled out a leather case containing a spare pair of glasses. He held them up, and the group sighed in unison. "George," he told his son, "we need to write home to your mother and have her send more spare glasses." Everyone chuckled with relief as Meade put his new glasses on. "OK," he barked. "Let's get back on the road."

They kept mainly to the fields after that, with Meade careful to avoid any trees. When they reached the point where the Second Corps was filing off the road, they were able to make better time.

"We are up to the battlefield, General," Captain Paine finally announced. "That large hill over there is the left of our line."

Meade strained to make out the details. All he could see was a large black hill with a smaller hill off to the right. He grunted. Even with the full moon, it was hard to make much out.

The group clattered to a stop in front of a small building, and Meade climbed wearily from the saddle. The ride had taken three hours, and his face still smarted from his encounter with the branch. Inside the building, alerted in advance of his arrival, were all his corps commanders with troops on the field. He looked around and acknowledged the group: Howard, Slocum, Sickles, and Warren.

Meade was quick to get to the point. He was very tired and in no mood to engage in needless conversation. "Well, Howard, is this the place to fight a battle?"

Howard nodded vigorously. "Oh, yes, General. This is excellent ground."

Meade looked at the others, who also nodded in agreement.

"I'm glad you say that, General," Meade said. "I have called up the entire army, and it is too late to change it. Everyone except the Sixth Corps should be up by tomorrow morning, and they should be up by tomorrow afternoon." He considered the situation for a moment. After waiting for information all day, this was his opportunity to finally get as much information as he needed. "And now, gentlemen, I would like to have your reports. Let's start with you, Howard. I would like to know what happened today."

Howard's report was more than grim. As he reported it, the Eleventh Corps had come up to the battlefield in time to check the enemy's forces coming in from the north and northeast. Together with the First Corps, they held off the growing enemy numbers until General Doubleday withdrew his First Corps, leaving Howard's corps in an impossible position. The subsequent withdrawal through the town had cost the Eleventh Corps many men lost as prisoners. The First Corps was luckier, and most of their troops were able to avoid the town. Meade shot a glance toward Warren, who was looking toward the floor, jaws clenched. *There's more to this than I am being told,* Meade thought. *Clearly, though, both the First and Eleventh Corps are shells of what they were before the fight.*

The other officers offered routine reports, since none of them were on the field when the battle took place. They all reported a hard march to reach Gettysburg and tired, footsore troops.

Meade looked around anxiously. "I would like to see the field as soon as possible. With the full moon, it is light enough, I think. Would you care to join me, General Warren?"

"Of course, General. Please excuse me for a moment while I get ready."

Warren scurried off, and Meade looked around the room. He did not see a map. *Damn,* he thought, *I need to know what the ground looks like!* "I'll be waiting outside," he told the group as he turned for the door.

The moonlight allowed a limited view of the hill he was on. Batteries had been dug in on the forward slope, and their exhausted crews slept around the artillery pieces. In the pale moonlight, Meade thought, they looked like corpses. He shuddered at the thought and looked away. Out beyond the hill, toward what Meade guessed was the north and west, he could see a broad arc of campfires several miles away.

The rebels, he thought. *Looks like they have a good part of their army up.* Suddenly he remembered John Reynolds. "Oh, John," he whispered, "why did it have to be you?" Meade looked around to see if anyone had heard him. His staff was a respectful distance away. If they heard him, they showed no sign of it. Meade sighed. *Keep your mind on the problem. It is going to be hell this day. Either I will attack first, or Lee will. By this time tomorrow, the fate of the Union could well be determined.*

The fate of the Union, in his hands—it was almost too much to bear. Meade took his hat off and looked up into the washed-out sky. A few of the brighter stars were able to shine through the moonlight. It was all in God's hands now.

In this quiet time before the armies clashed, he could allow himself a brief prayer. "Dear God," he whispered, "I don't ask anything for myself. You have designed a role for me, and I will accept it without complaint. I don't ask anything for my country either. You have decided its fate before the world was formed. What I do ask, Lord, is for these boys, these men, asleep around me. They have endured so much and have lived with so much shame and ridicule. These are good soldiers, Lord. Whatever happens in the next few days, Lord, victory or defeat, please let these soldiers fight their best so that they can at least have that memory to hold on to."

"General Meade?" A familiar voice behind him disturbed his prayer.

Meade turned. "Ah, Warren. Thank you for joining me. I suspect you may have something to add to Howard's report?"

"Yes, I do. Things did not happen exactly as Howard reported. I was not there in person, but I have heard from people who were. The Eleventh Corps broke first, which forced the First Corps to retreat. I can't say how well Doubleday handled the First Corps after Reynolds's death, but we can't blame the First Corps for this defeat."

Meade thought for a moment before responding. "Yes. At any rate, I have sent for General Newton of the Sixth Corps to come up immediately and take command of the First Corps. Do you know Newton?"

"No, never really crossed paths with him before the war. He's an engineer like us, for what it's worth. He was a number of years ahead of me at the academy. I think he's a classmate of Doubleday...and Longstreet."

"Hmm, just wondering...he came highly recommended. Didn't think I would ever need him as the First Corps commander..." Meade trailed off. They were both silent for a few minutes, then Meade said, "You know, Warren, I did not get your report on the suitability of this terrain until quite late."

"Um, yes, General. I arrived on the battlefield when the lines were beginning to collapse. General Howard asked me to help sort things out. It was not until Hancock arrived that I had time to begin my survey."

"We delayed a movement decision for hours waiting on a report. Even a quick yes or no message would have been sufficient to make a decision. Now we have troops marching in the dark to make up for this delay. In the future, please remember this." Meade paused to let this sink in. "Now," he continued, "let's go back inside, and you can brief me on the details of the terrain."

Morning came early for the Second Corps. The buglers blew reveille just as dawn began to lighten the eastern sky. Henry rolled over and sat up, stretching his aching muscles. He thought longingly about a night's sleep in a proper bed. Beside him, Isaac was already starting to pack his gear. "Morning, Isaac," Henry muttered.

"Mornin' to you," Isaac replied. "You ready for this, brother?"

Henry nodded. "Suppose so." Looking up at the sky, he added absentmindedly, "Looks like it will be another hot one."

"Yes," Isaac said. "In more ways than one, most likely." Isaac turned to look at him. "You OK, Henry?"

"Uh? Oh, yeah. Just a little groggy, I guess. Didn't sleep much last night. Maybe some coffee will perk me up." He turned away from Isaac. The thought of the potential consequences of the imminent fight kept running through his head. He had confidence in his men and his regiment—they were all solid soldiers. But would the rest of the army perform as they should? What if they were to break and run like the Eleventh Corps? Henry shook his head to get it out of his mind. *Concentrate on the task at hand,* he told himself. "I'm going to check on the platoon," he told Isaac as he walked away.

Henry walked slowly through his platoon bivouac, exchanging small talk with his soldiers. Yesterday's march had been another long one, and he wanted to judge the physical condition of his people. They were all seasoned soldiers and were preparing to march just as they had done some many times before during this war. Private Cundy was bent over his haversack, pulling out some hardtack.

"How are you this morning, Cundy?"

Cundy looked up and smiled. "I'm well, Sergeant Taylor."

Henry looked Cundy over. He looked fine. "No problem with the fever?"

"No, Sergeant. Not at all." Cundy hesitated a moment. "Is it true that we are up to the battlefield?"

"Yes. As I understand from Lieutenant Demarest, we are about two miles south. That's why we built barricades last evening."

Cundy slowly nodded his head. "So we will have a fight today."

"Sure looks that way," Henry replied.

"Then we shall have a fight. I am ready!"

Private Berry was nearby and said, "I'm ready too, Sergeant Taylor!"

"You breathin' all right?" Henry asked.

"That doesn't matter," Berry said. "I'm ready to fight!"

"Good!" Henry nodded in acceptance. "Let's finish up breakfast. They will probably call assembly soon."

Henry had just finished a cup of coffee and some hardtack when the long roll started for assembly. Once the regiment had fallen in, Lieutenant Peller, the adjutant, stepped forward. "Attention to orders! From General Gibbon, division commander, Second Division, Second US Army Corps. We are on the eve of a battle, which is to be the greatest battle of the war..."

The greatest battle of the war, Henry thought. The greatest sacrifice of the war as well?

Peller continued, and his final sentence caught Henry's attention. "Any soldier leaving the ranks without leave will be instantly put to death."

Henry locked eyes with Isaac, who smiled. Henry nodded. He had never heard this tone before in an order. If any soldier doubted the seriousness of the situation, this order would drive it home.

With the order read, the regiment formed up in marching order and began to march toward the north and the battlefield.

Meade stood outside and looked toward the eastern sky. Dawn was fast approaching, finally providing sufficient light to see the terrain. Anxious to get started on his review of the defensive positions, Meade turned to his aides. "Please summon General Howard. I would like him to join us when we ride along the lines. He is the only one who can provide context on what transpired yesterday. General Hunt, would you accompany us as well? I would like your input on the suitability of the ground for artillery."

An aide moved off to find Howard.

Hoofbeats announced Howard approaching on his horse. Meade adjusted his hat and moved to take the reins from an aide. He turned toward his engineer guide. "Captain Paine, could you come with us and make a sketch of the position as we go?"

The group rode along the crest of the hill, carefully picking their way around the sleeping troops. Meade looked at the moon to his right, hanging low in the west—they were headed south. The hill dropped in elevation and flattened out as they went.

"May I suggest we stop by the headquarters of the field officer?" Howard asked. "He will be able to give an update of the situation to our front." The army routinely appointed a field officer after duty hours to see to security and to monitor the situation.

"That's a good idea," Meade said. "Who is the field officer?"

"It's General Stannard. He just arrived this evening with his brigade."

"Stannard," Meade said. "I don't know that name. Is he regular army?"

"Ahem." Howard hesitated. "He was a militia officer before the war. He is not a regular. As I remember, General Stannard fought on the peninsula in command of a Vermont regiment."

Great, Meade thought. *Another amateur with political connections.* "His brigade—what about them?"

"They are all from Vermont, General, nine month enlistments."

"Nine month enlistments." Meade shook his head sadly. "We just get them trained to be a soldier and then their enlistment is up." The group murmured an agreement. "I do appreciate reinforcements," he added, "I just hope these ones are ready to fight."

General Stannard was outside his tent when they arrived. "I heard horses riding up, and I thought it might be you, General Meade," he said. "I heard that you had arrived."

"General Stannard, perhaps you could give General Meade a report on the situation," Howard said.

Stannard led them up to the crest of the hill. "The hill we are on slopes down toward the west," he said. "You see that dark object out in front of us?" They squinted to see in the feeble dawn light. "That's a large barn, a good stone-and-wood barn at that. Locals call it the Codori farm. It's on the Emmitsburg Road. We have pickets out there along that road." Stannard stopped and looked at Meade.

After a nod from Meade, Stannard continued. "Beyond the road, the ground starts to rise, and it continues up to another ridgeline about a mile to our west. That one is wooded, and the rebs are there in force. You can see some of their campfires from here."

Meade looked out toward the fleck of light in the distance. "Any contact with them?"

"No, sir," Stannard replied. "It's been very quiet. They're probably every bit as tired as we are."

Meade nodded. "What about our disposition?"

"The First Corps is at the northern end of this ridge, and Birney's division of the Third Corps and Geary's division of the Twelfth Corps are spread out between the First Corps and the hills to the south. Geary's division has occupied those hills. Humphrey's division is behind the ridge in reserve. On Cemetery Hill, General Howard's corps has the northern side of the line, and General Wadsworth of the First Corps occupies the hill to the east of Cemetery Hill. I think it's called Culp's Hill. Did I forget anything, General Howard?"

"Well," Howard said, "only that Williams's division of the Twelfth Corps is along the Baltimore Pike, about a mile to our rear, and Buford's cavalry forms a screen south and west of the hills to our south."

Meade thought for a moment and nodded. "Good. We have four corps on the field, with the Second and Fifth nearby. They will be here early in the morning. When John Sedgwick arrives with the Sixth Corps, probably late this afternoon, we will be all up. That should be sufficient." He paused again to think about what he would do if Lee did not attack. Would he attack Lee?

Should he attack Lee? Meade realized that the group was waiting for him to say something. "Thank you, General Stannard. That was a very professional report." He meant that. It was more than he had expected, certainly, from a militia officer.

The sky was continuing to lighten in the east as Meade and the others rode off toward the south. In the gray twilight, they could see the forms of the smaller hill and the larger one behind it. "These hills have names?" he asked Captain Paine.

"The locals call the big hill, the sugarloaf, 'Round Top,' and the smaller hill they call 'Little Round Top.'"

"Little Round Top," Meade said. "Not very lyrical, but I suppose it will do."

The group rode up the gradually rising northern slope of Little Round Top until they reached an outcropping of boulders rising to the top of the hill. "Let's spare the horses and not go any farther," Meade said.

Henry Hunt spoke up. "General, Round Top, to our left, is heavily wooded and is not suitable for artillery without extensive preparation. This hill, Little Round Top, is naturally clear on top and toward the west. It offers excellent fields of fire once we get artillery up here, which may require some effort." Hunt scanned the view from the west toward the north. "This position also provides the possibility of enfilading fire on our position to the north if the enemy were to occupy it."

Meade looked in the direction Hunt was looking. "Yes, you are quite right. This is the key to our entire position. We must occupy and hold this hill in strength." He looked to the west, where the hill dropped steeply to a narrow, fog-shrouded valley and rose up in a rocky ridge much lower than Little Round Top. "The way that ridge falls off in front of us will prevent the enemy from advancing directly on this hill from the west, acting like a moat. He will be forced to attack from the south or the north up the valley below us and then will have to wheel to attack the hill. All that time, our troops will be taking them in the flank. Yes, this is a very good position."

"There is a flaw in the position, though, sir," Paine said. "The low ground to the north prevents long fields of fire in that area. The infantry occupying that part of the line would be vulnerable."

Meade looked at the low ground to the north. *Paine was right,* he thought. "What do you think, General Hunt? Can we cover this gap with artillery from this hill and from the ridgeline to the north?"

Hunt squinted toward the gap. "Yes, that is quite possible. It will take us a little time to get set up, but it can be done."

"Good." Meade nodded. "With overlapping artillery and good entrenchments, that low ground can be easily defended." He needed to select a corps to occupy this sector. Meade looked north toward the rebel campfires several miles to the north. This position was well out of harm's way. Of his two problem corps, the Eleventh was already in position, and the Third was just a little to the north of Little Round Top. *This would be a good place for Sickles,* he thought. *Someplace where he can't get into trouble.* "Captain Paine, designate the Third Corps to occupy this part of the line."

The group clambered back down the boulders and rode off toward the north and on to the hill on the right of the line, the one the locals called Culp's Hill. Once there, Meade considered the heavily wooded hill. *Not much for artillery fields of fire,* he thought, *but the steep slopes could make for an excellent infantry defensive position, once properly prepared.* "This is a good terrain feature on which to anchor our right," Meade said.

Dawn arrived, with an angry red sun blazing through a slit between the clouds on the eastern horizon. The group finished their ride along the lines just as the sun began to rise, turning the eastern sky red. "Red sky of Austerlitz," someone said. Meade glanced toward the east—Austerlitz was one of Napoleon's greatest victories. *An omen? If so, who is to be Napoleon this day?* Meade turned away without a comment. There was too much to do to worry about superstitions.

They ended up back at Cemetery Hill, where Captain Paine spread his map out in front of Meade. Paine had drawn the map as they rode, resting his drawing board on the pommel. Meade considered the work. It was very well done, but then Paine was considered the best there was at this kind of work.

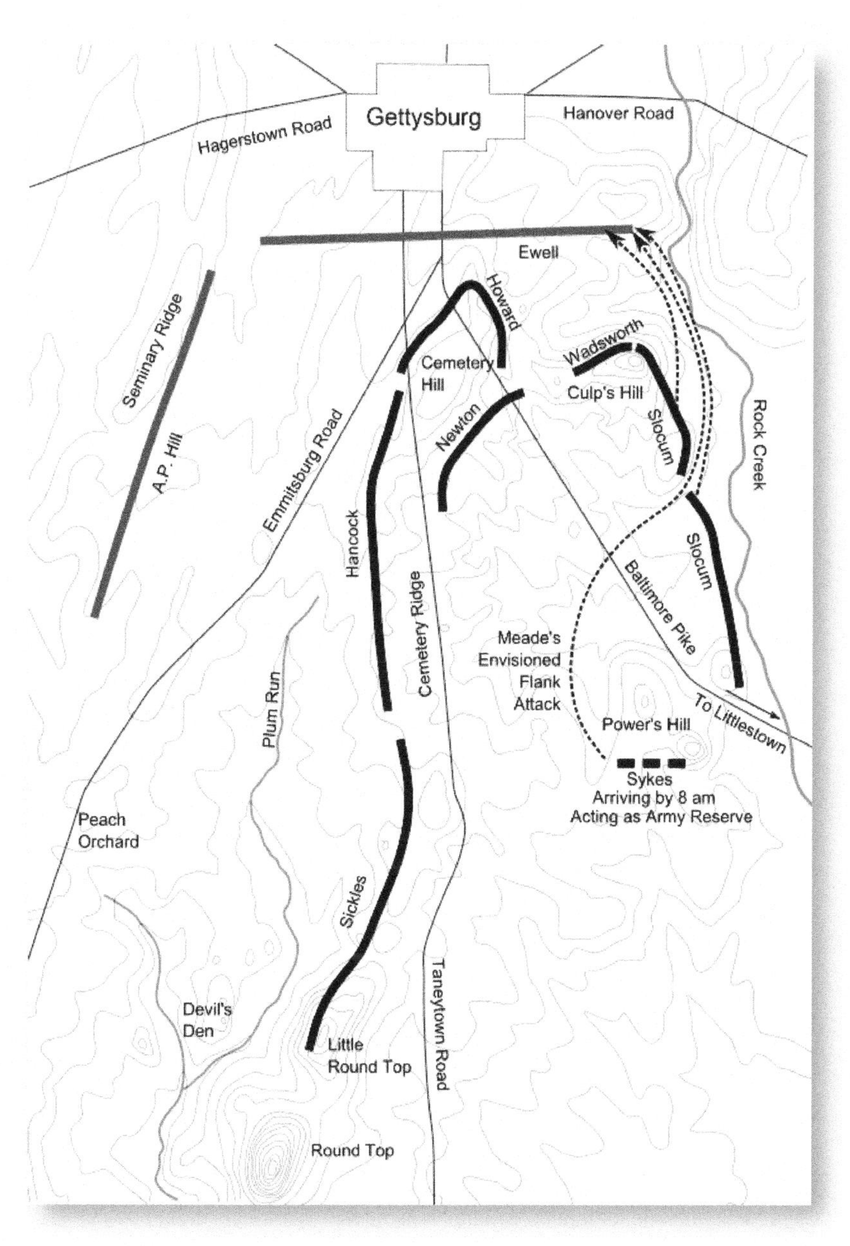

MEADE'S PLAN—6 AM 2 JULY

The defensive line as drawn on the map resembled a fish hook, with the eye of the hook on Little Round Top and the barb of the hook on the southern slope of Culp's Hill. Meade looked the map over carefully. T*he position is good,* he thought, *but Hancock is right—it can be turned on either flank. Still, the convex line allows for rapid reinforcement of any point. Well, the Fifth Corps is not up yet; they can be my reserve.* Meade looked up from the map. "The enemy can easily overlap our line on Culp's Hill. If they do this, they can threaten or even cut off Baltimore Pike, our line of communication. I believe the right is the area of the most danger. When the Fifth Corps comes up, I want them placed in reserve where they can guard against that."

He would have Hancock occupy the line between the First Corps and the Third Corps while Slocum's Twelfth corps would occupy Culp's Hill. Meade drew his finger along the outside of the line where the enemy would most likely place his line. The left of the enemy's line hung in the air, with the Twelth corps position overlapping the enemy's flank. He pointed to the spot. "This may be an opportunity for us. If Lee does not attack, then we should consider an attack at this spot. We could roll up the enemy flank. Please have Generals Slocum and Warren reconnoiter the ground for this possible attack. We would attack after the Sixth Corps is up."

Meade watched his aides ride off to notify Hancock, Slocum, and Sickles where they were to move their corps, and then he went back to studying the map.

"General Meade," Major Ludlow said, interrupting his thoughts. "General Newton has just arrived."

"Ah, Newton," Meade said as he rose to greet him. "Thank you for coming."

"I got here as quickly as I could, General Meade. I rode all night to get here."

"Well, it's good you're here," Meade said. "I have an important assignment for you. Let's step outside. I want to show you the position I have in mind for you." Meade led him toward the Cemetery Gate House, a large redbrick arch built in the Italianate style, and out onto the brow of Cemetery Hill.

"I'm not sure if you've heard," Meade said, "but General Reynolds was killed yesterday morning, early in the battle." Newton nodded gravely. "I am quite dissatisfied with the way the First Corps was handled," Meade said, "and I believe we need to make a change. I am placing you in command, Newton."

"Thank you for your confidence in me, General Meade. I will perform my duty to the utmost of my ability."

"I believe you will, General Newton. You were highly recommended by a person in whom I had absolute confidence."

"Yes, sir," Newton said. "What are your orders?"

Meade motioned to his front with his arm. "The positions to our immediate front are manned by the Eleventh Corps. To their right is one division of your corps, Wadsworth's. Your other two divisions are to the left of Howard's men. I'll be quite frank with you, Newton. I don't trust the Eleventh Corps. They broke again yesterday, and they might break again if they are pushed hard."

Newton made a face. "I concur with your assessment, General Meade."

"Yes," Meade said. "The First Corps sustained heavy casualties yesterday, so we must take that into consideration in any assignment. Wadsworth is fully entrenched, and I don't think we should move him. Your other two divisions are available, I think. Once the Second Corps is up, I will move your two divisions to a position behind the Eleventh Corps to act as a reserve. If they show any sign of wavering, we will commit you to shore up the line..."

The whiz of a minie ball interrupted Meade. He quickly looked around to see a puff of dirt rising from the ground. The ball had gone between them, Meade realized. Just a chance shot?

"Look, General!" a nearby civilian cried out.

Meade looked in the direction the man was pointing and saw gun smoke around the steeple of a church in town. "Sniper," he spat. "General Newton, let's continue our discussion in a less exposed location."

Once behind the Cemetery Gate House, Meade continued his instructions. "My intent is to have your two divisions available as a rapid reaction force for this part of the line. Being in reserve will give your officers the opportunity to regroup." Meade paused to find the right words. "Umm...General Doubleday is currently in command of the corps. He will not be happy to learn that he has been relieved. I understand he is a classmate of yours?"

"Yes, General, he is my classmate and I know him personally, but there could be a problem. He does outrank me."

"Don't worry about that, Newton. I have authorization from Washington to make any personnel changes I see fit, irrespective of rank or seniority."

Newton nodded. "Very well, General Meade. I know Doubleday. Let me smooth things over with him. We will be fine."

"Good, Newton. I'll leave you to it."

On his way back to the Cemetery lodge, Meade met up with Major Ludlow. "Sir, we've found a possible headquarters location. It's a little small, but it is very well located."

Meade mounted up and followed Ludlow a brief distance down the Taneytown Road to a small white clapboard house surrounded by a white picket fence. Meade looked the location over. *Good access, right off the road that runs behind our position, close to the front but protected by the hill from enemy fire.* Stepping onto the porch, he glanced inside. There was a main room and another room off to the side—probably a bedroom, he guessed. "Yes, this will do," he said.

As his aides and orderlies scurried to make the farmhouse into an army headquarters, Meade stood on the porch and considered the situation. *What is Lee planning? Will he attack before I have all my people up? I need to attack first, if I can, but I need Sykes here, and I need that report from Slocum and Warren. If Lee will just hold off.*

His thoughts were interrupted by horsemen approaching. General Hunt was leading a group of aides. Hunt dismounted, strode toward Meade, and gave a quick salute. "I have a brief report for you, General." Meade nodded, and Hunt continued. "I have been to check with all artillery units, including the artillery reserve. Everything is fine, except for the Third Corps. They have left their artillery trains in Emmitsburg."

"Goddamn them!" Meade swore. "What kind of incompetent sons of bitches does Sickles have around him?"

"It's not that a great a disaster," Hunt said. "The trains are already on their way up here, guarded by two brigades of infantry. Besides, I brought extra ammunition in my trains. I have more than enough to supply the Third Corps if they run out."

"All right," Meade said. "Will you please let me know when their trains arrive?"

Hunt nodded, and Meade went back to his thoughts. *Are we ready for an attack? Are the units in position?* "George," he said, catching his son as he walked up the steps to the porch, "can you please bring me the latest reports from my corps commanders?"

George went inside the house and brought out a stack of papers. Meade took the stack and began to study them. *Twelfth Corps—Geary has joined them and now all in position. Eleventh Corps in position; Fifth Corps up with two divisions; Third Division expected by noon; Second Corps in position, has relieved First Corps divisions, which are now in their reserve position; Sixth Corps on their way. All good.* Meade scowled. *There is no report from the Third Corps.* "George," he growled, "ride down to General Sickles's headquarters. Let him know where my headquarters is located and ask him to report if he is in position and on anything else I need to know."

"General Sickles, are you awake?" It was Tremain.

Sickles groaned and opened one eye. "What is it?" he snapped.

"Sorry to bother you, General, but we have just received orders from General Meade to take up new positions."

"Tell me what the orders say." Sickles looked around his tent. There was daylight, but no telling what time it was.

Tremain held the paper the paper to the light. "It says we are to take up a position on the left of the Second Corps and extend the line down to the hill on the left called Little Round Top."

"Hmm…" Sickles thought. "Any time given that we are to be in position?"

Tremain referred to the paper. "No, sir. It just says to move as soon as possible."

"Well, then, they can wait until I get a little more sleep. Meade kept us up most of the night! Send notice to Birney and Humphreys that we will move soon." Sickles paused. "How long have I been asleep?" He rubbed his aching forehead.

"Only about twenty minutes, General."

"The courier hasn't returned from Emmitsburg yet, has he?"

"No, sir, not yet."

Sickles shook his head. "I can't believe we left the ammunition train in Emmitsburg."

"Yes," Tremain said, "but at least we know they were still there at last report. I had fears last night that they were lost on the road somewhere and would make the wrong turn and end up surrounded by rebs."

"So did I," Sickles growled. "That's why I was up all night. If we lose that ammunition train to the rebs, Meade will have my head on a platter."

"I think it's under control now, General. The courier should confirm when they left so that we will know when to expect them."

"If those wagons weren't so slow, our infantry should escort it up. That would be the safest."

"The two brigades will precede the wagon train, so he will make sure the road is clear all the up from Emmitsburg. I'm sure it will be all right," Tremain said.

"I suppose you're right. Now, let me get a few minutes' sleep. Please make sure I am not disturbed." He pulled his blanket up and covered his eyes with his cap. He just needed a few more minutes of sleep, and he would be fine.

There was a rustling at the door of the tent. "Uh, General Sickles." The noise caused Sickles to wake with a start. "General Sickles?" It was Captain Randolph. "There is an aide here from General Meade. He wants to know how we are getting along."

Sickles sat up and rubbed his eyes. "What time is it?"

"It's about eight o'clock, sir."

"Eight o'clock? Damn!" He had been asleep over two hours. Sickles blinked, trying to think. He slept much longer than he had intended to. "Charm him, Randolph. Tell him…tell him we are not yet posted. There is, uh, some question as to where we should go."

"Right, sir." Randolph was off.

I'd better get moving, he told himself. Sickles pulled on his boots and buttoned his coat. He stuck his head out of the tent and called for an orderly to bring his horse.

Meade's aide was back in only a few minutes. In that time, though, a transformation had taken place in the Third Corps headquarters. Tents were struck and wagons were being packed. Sickles watched the aide ride up. He recognized him—it was Captain Meade, the general's son. "Well, Captain," he said. "Back so soon?"

The younger Meade saluted but did not dismount. "General Meade says you are to extend the line along the ridge already formed by the Second Corps, with your left on Little Round Top."

Sickles managed a charming smile. "Thank you, Captain, I understand now. Tell the commanding general that we will comply with his orders."

Another salute, and Captain Meade was off. As they prepared to move, Tremain brought another interruption. "Sir," he whispered, "there's an aide here from General Geary. He says Geary sent him down with orders to point out the positions they occupied last night. I sent him away earlier, while you were asleep."

"I don't think that will be necessary. We can pick out our own positions," Sickles snapped. "Wait…tell him that we are busy right now, and we will attend to it later."

Tremain nodded, and with a sly smile, he left to deal with Geary's aide.

An orderly brought up his horse, and Sickles called for Tremain and Randolph to accompany him. He wanted to see this ground firsthand, before his corps was placed.

The group galloped up the lane toward the crest of the ridge. At this point, the ridge was flat and low. *Not very appealing,* Sickles noted. To the north, the Second Corps was already in position. Their lines ran up the ridge toward Cemetery Hill. Sickles frowned. *Now, that is a good position, a strong position—much better than the one I have.* Sickles looked to the south, and his heart sank. The ridge disappeared into low, wooded ground before rising to the hill that was his designated left flank.

At this moment, General Birney rode up with an aide. "Good morning, General Sickles. I understand we are to move to a different position."

Sickles smiled at his division commander. His regard for Birney had continued to grow after Chancellorsville. Not only was he a good officer, almost a natural, he was not a haughty West Pointer like Humphreys, his other division commander. "Yes, General Birney. Why don't you join me? I was just going to take a look at the new position." *Birney can give me some good advice,* he thought. *Especially with this problem of the ammunition train.*

Sickles moved off toward the south, and the group followed him. When he reached the point where the ridge ended, he pulled his horse up short. Stands of trees blocked the view to the west. There was no more than a few hundred yards of visibility. "There are no fields of fire down here," he said.

"A terrible position for artillery," Randolph said.

They continued on toward the south, picking their way through the woods. Just north of Little Round Top, they reached a tree line, and the ground opened up a bit. To the southwest, a low valley ended in a ridge not more than five hundred yards away. "Pah," Sickles spat. "This is hopeless." He scanned the rocky crest of Little Round Top. *Maybe that will be better.* "Well, let's get up there and see what that's like."

They found the last twenty feet or so of elevation too steep for the horses. Birney's aide held the reins while the rest of the group scrambled to the top.

The view is excellent, Sickles thought, *but the position leaves much to be desired.* The crest was long and narrow, broken by large boulders. "What do you think of this as an artillery position, Randolph?"

His chief of artillery looked around critically. "There is only room up here for one battery. From the steep slope, probably all you would be able to get up here would be three-inch rifles. Good long-range fields of fire, but you probably wouldn't be able to depress the guns enough to support the infantry in a close in assault. All in all, a pretty mediocre position."

"Yes, hmm..." Sickles considered the crest. It dropped ten feet to a ledge, ran level for ten to twenty yards, and then dropped steeply to the valley floor below. "This place is as bald as a billiard ball. No place for infantry—they'd be perfect targets."

Birney moved closer and pointed to the west. "Ah, General, there is the terrain mask out there. You see where the Emmitsburg Road disappears into the woods as it reaches that ridgeline? Now look and see how the road is masked for a while by the ridge. The enemy could march south, masked by the trees and the ridge, then cross over and come up on our left. Round Top to our south would mask their approach, and they could use the woods to get right up on our position before we knew they were there."

Sickles nodded. *Birney's right. This position is quite vulnerable.* "We would be better off facing more southwest, wouldn't we?" He pulled out his field glasses and scanned the terrain to his front. "You see that orchard up there on the Emmitsburg Road? Now, that's high ground." He panned to the south. "It controls the road for miles to the south. We would be able to see the artillery trains on the way up if they don't make the turn as ordered. Plus, it would make us less vulnerable to a flank attack. We need to occupy that high ground."

"It is rather far out," Birney said. "Perhaps we could find something a little closer in."

Sickles looked toward the lower ridge to his front. It was less masked than Little Round Top. "Let's take a look at that ridge down there." They turned to go, and Sickles glanced for a moment to the north. The Second Corps lines ran straight toward him. Sickles turned away and followed the rest of the group to the horses.

To get to the next ridge, the group descended the north slope of Little Round Top, crossed the valley, splashed through the meandering stream in its middle, and rode up the slope from the north. A field of wheat lay off to the northwest of their position, and the center of the ridge was wooded. The southern end was more to Sickles's liking. It ended in a jumble of huge boulders, and the bare rocky ground was wide, with a clear view toward the southwest. "This is a much better position for artillery, don't you think, Randolph?"

Randolph looked around and nodded. "Yes, sir. It's flat with good fields of fire. We would have no problem getting artillery in here. It's a better position than up there." He jerked a thumb toward the tall hill to the east.

"Good. General Birney, place your left flank here. Captain Randolph, place artillery in this position. Point them to the southwest. Birney's infantry will provide support. Now, let's see what the ground looks like toward our front."

They retraced their path north along the ridge and then turned to the left and crossed the wheat field. On the far side, the ground turned rocky and rose some twenty feet or so. A country lane was on the top of the rise. The group turned left on the lane and headed west. They rode several hundred yards and stopped, in awe of the view to the south. "Look at that," Sickles said. "It must be at least a mile of open ground. They sure wouldn't be able to get around on this flank."

"Look to the west, General," Randolph said. "The hill there masks this position from the enemy. We could place a line of batteries along this lane pointing south, and the enemy couldn't touch us."

"I like this line even better!" Sickles exclaimed, and he turned his horse west along the lane toward the rise with the orchard on top. As they approached, Sickles noted the half-ripened peaches hanging from the branches. The Emmitsburg Road ran just west of the crest of the hill. Sickles stopped in the middle of the road and turned around in his saddle. Toward the north, the west, and the south, this position provided excellent fields of fire. Better even than the Second Corps!

Sickles smiled broadly. This was the position he was looking for. *Just let Bobby Lee try a flanking movement on the Third Corps!* "General Birney," he commanded, "place your right flank on this hill. Captain Randolph, provide General Birney with several batteries to support this position. Oh, and place as many batteries as you can along the lane behind us to provide protection from a flanking movement."

Birney cleared his throat. "General, if I may, there are a couple of technical details we should attend to."

"Like what?" Sickles turned to confront his subordinate.

"Well, please remember that I have only one brigade up. Colonels Burling and de Trobriand are still on their way from Emmitsburg. I need to place a brigade here and two brigades on the ridge on our left flank. Even with the batteries along the lane, there is still a huge gap that I cannot cover."

"Your point is well taken. What else is troubling you?"

"This position faces to the southwest, but the enemy is to the west. I would not be able to face many of my troops toward the west, and I would therefore be vulnerable to a flank attack from that direction."

"We can solve that by bringing up Humphreys's division on the right. He will provide all the support that is needed."

"There is one other thing, General. This disposition of your corps…while it may be much better than your original directive, it is clearly not within the scope of those orders. It, ah, would be, ah, prudent to obtain General Meade's approval before making such a move."

Sickles considered these arguments. "OK, I accept your position," he said, "but we must make preparations to assume this disposition once approval has been granted. I believe we can safely stretch my orders to enable us to take up a position with our left on the ridge as I indicated and the right of your division to the north of the lane, generally in a north-south orientation. Do you agree?"

"Yes." Birney nodded. "I do agree that we can do that."

"Now," Sickles said, "this hill must be occupied and held. We need a strong presence here, at least a regiment. Reinforce it if we need to, just don't let the rebs have it. Our people may possibly be coming north along this road, and we need to protect their approach. Randolph, be prepared to bring up artillery in support, if needed."

Both subordinates nodded.

"As for approval of this plan, let's try the direct approach. Major Tremain, please accompany me to see General Meade. We will tell him that we are moving into position as he directed and, ah, remind him that there are no troops to the left of the Third Corps. When he shows some concern, we will try to steer him toward giving us permission to make the appropriate dispositions. If we get that, we will have room to make whatever changes we desire. Do you concur, General Birney?"

Birney nodded. "I believe that would be sufficient, General."

Sickles slapped his hands together. "Good. Let's get started. Major, come with me."

Voices on the porch caused Meade to look up. Warren and Hunt were walking into his office together. "Ah, gentlemen." Meade sighed. "I have been waiting for you both. What do you have to report?"

Warren began. "We've just come from Culp's Hill. I met Hunt there when I was reconnoitering the ground on our right flank with Slocum. It's not good news, I'm afraid. There is a stream that runs just to the east of our line, and the ground is low and waterlogged there. In addition to that, the terrain has a number of large boulders, which would seriously hinder large troop movement. All in all, it's not a very favorable place for an attack. Hunt has some reservations from an artillery perspective as well." He nodded toward Hunt.

"As you know, General," Hunt said, "the area around Culp's Hill is heavily wooded. Artillery fields of fire are limited, so our support of an infantry attack would be limited as well. Not only that, but there is an open area to the east of Culp's Hill behind the enemy lines. This area is covered by rebel artillery on a hill to the north. Any attack of ours would break out into that open area only to be subjected to concentrated enemy artillery."

"I see," Meade said. "That's too bad—it does seem the logical place to attack. For Lee as well, I would imagine. Still, Lee would perceive the same disadvantages you two have pointed out. We will just have to remain on the defensive and wait for the situation to develop more."

"What about our left flank?" Warren asked.

"The Round Tops?" Meade said. "Far less likely, I would think. Sickles has our line well anchored with fortified positions on those hills. Lee would have to extend his line quite a bit to attack our left and conduct a long march to get there. Not a very appealing objective, all in all."

Several cannon booms sounded from the direction of Cemetery Hill. Meade raised a questioning eyebrow toward Hunt. "What is going on up there, Henry?"

Hunt smiled. "Colonel Wainwright is having the batteries in the Eleventh and First Corps conduct ranging shots. By this afternoon, we will be able to hit any point in front of that part of our line with absolute precision. The rebs will have a difficult time getting anywhere near our position with that kind of accuracy!"

"Very good! Wainwright is a good man," Meade said, satisfied. *I wish I had a hundred more like him.*

Not long after, Butterfield bustled into the room. Meade looked up from his papers. "Ah, Butterfield, you're here. I am glad you made it. There's a lot to do."

"What can I do to help?" Butterfield asked.

"First off, we need to get a firm grasp on our defensive alignment here. Send an order out to all corps commanders. They are to submit to headquarters without delay a sketch of their positions. This should include information on the roads to their front and rear as well as their estimation of the apparent strength of the enemy to their front. I would like you to assign a staff officer to each corps to learn the location of the corps headquarters and the positions of their artillery, infantry, and trains. They should pay close attention to the nearby roads that could be used for rapid movement in any direction."

"We should be able to do that rather quickly. Anything else I can do?"

Meade paused to consider the question. "Yes. I would like you to become thoroughly familiar with the position of the army and the complex of roads leading up to our positions. In the event of any contingency, you would be ready to meet it without any additional orders from me."

"Very well, General. I will get started right away."

Meade watched Butterfield walk out the door. *With these reports from my corps commanders, perhaps I can see an opportunity to take some kind of action.*

Sickles and Tremain rode up the Taneytown Road to the white cottage that Meade had made his headquarters. The ride was only a few minutes, but Sickles used it as a chance to rehearse his pitch to Meade. *Put it in precise terms,* he told himself. *Meade is an engineer and likes to deal with facts.*

Meade was inside the cottage, sitting at a table studying a map. Sickles wasted no time getting to the point. "General, I have placed my troops in position as you directed. I must say, however, that I am very concerned about my left flank." Meade frowned. *Facts,* Sickles told himself. *Deal with facts.* "There is no other infantry to my left, and the ground offers a concealed route to my left and rear."

Meade pulled his glasses off and pondered the information. After several minutes of silence, he responded. "That presupposes the enemy will move several miles to the south in an attempt to attack a flank anchored by a strong natural obstacle. Given the availability of other, more attractive targets, I think that is unlikely."

Sickles smiled weakly. "General Meade, the wooded country to my front and left will allow the enemy to move south and around my flank undetected. I am convinced that the enemy will attack there."

Meade dismissed this with a wave of his hand. "Oh, generals are all apt to look for the attack to be made where they are. Besides, your flank is covered by a cavalry screen."

Sickles hesitated. *Was that an insult or just a joke? No matter; this is too important not to try again.* "I have found positions that provide much better fields of fire toward the southwest. They also would prevent the enemy from moving to my left undetected. Perhaps if you rode with me to the position, I could show you the basis for my concerns."

Meade shook his head. "I'm sorry, General Sickles. There is too much happening here at headquarters. We are trying to position the troops as they arrive while keeping an eye on the enemy. I must be here at headquarters if they attack." Meade sighed, his eyes tired and dull. "Look, what I want you to do is to extend from Hancock's left down to Little Round Top. Take up the positions Geary's division occupied. I saw those positions this morning, and I believe they are acceptable."

"Well," Sickles said, "Geary really didn't have positions as far as I know. He was massed for the most part." *Another idea—try it.* "General, may I post my corps as I see fit?"

Meade cocked an eye. "Certainly," he said warily, "within the limits of the general instructions I have given you. Any ground within those limits you choose to occupy, I leave to you."

Sickles clenched his jaws. This conversation was going around in circles. Perhaps he could find someone more flexible to deal with. "Since you are unable to leave your headquarters, General Meade, perhaps one of your staff, say General Warren or General Hunt, could accompany me to examine the position?"

"Yes, all right." Meade slowly rubbed his eyes. "General Warren, though, is off on another task. I believe General Hunt is available." He motioned to an aide. "Please see if General Hunt is outside."

The artillery chief soon joined them. "General Hunt," Meade said, "I have been speaking with General Sickles concerning the positions we have assigned to his corps. He is dissatisfied with the area assigned because he cannot use his artillery effectively from it. Would you accompany him to his positions, see what his concerns are, and help him properly site his artillery?"

Hunt and Sickles took their leave and rode quickly along the crest of Cemetery Ridge and then out across the fields toward the Peach Orchard hill. Sickles brought the group to a halt at the crest. Across the road, a battery was set up and was firing ranging shots in a slow, deliberate manner. Hunt looked them over with a practiced eye. "Three-inch ordinance rifles—Calef's battery, from Buford's cavalry division."

Sickles nodded and swept his arm in an arc from south to north. "This is the position I have in mind. Look at the fields of fire. You can sweep the Emmitsburg Road and its approaches to the north and the south. It will be impossible for the enemy to get around our left undetected if we take up this position."

Hunt carefully examined the position before he responded. "Yes, the fields of fire are quite good. How would you deploy your corps to occupy this position, though?"

This is better, Sickles thought. *I have someone reasonable to deal with!* He cleared his throat. "I would place a brigade here at this peach orchard to anchor the flank and then run General Humphreys' division north up the Emmitsburg Road so that his right flank overlaps the left flank of the Second Corps. From this peach orchard, I would bend the line ninety degrees and follow the high ground back toward the Little Round Top. My artillery can cover the gap along the lane, and Birney's infantry will cover the woods."

Hunt rubbed his neck and considered Sickles's proposal. "There are some difficulties with the position you have suggested. The most obvious one is the gap between your right and the Second Corps' left. That leaves your right flank in the air and vulnerable to a flank attack. To close this gap, the Second Corps would have to advance. If they do this, they will give up the excellent position they have on that ridgeline."

Sickles nodded. "I will grant you that, but I have learned it is sometimes necessary for one unit to take up an inferior position so that the entire army may have a superior one. At any rate, I think it is only a slight deficiency compared to the strength it provides against a flank attack, and we all know how Bobby Lee likes flank attacks. Besides, this position would control the Emmitsburg Road. I have two brigades and trains coming up this road, and I need to keep it covered until they arrive."

"Hmm," Hunt said. "It does have good fields of fire for that."

"Yes, it does have excellent fields of fire."

"You know," Hunt said, "this position would form a salient. The troops occupying it would be open to attack from three sides. They would have to be a strong enough force to resist that kind of attack. Your corps is probably too small for that." Hunt looked out at the lower ground toward the west. "On the other hand, our occupation also prevents the enemy from turning it into an artillery position to be used against our line."

"Like Hazel Grove," Sickles said, quick to agree.

"Exactly. Plus, it would provide an excellent springboard for an attack should General Meade decide to launch one."

"I didn't know he was planning one," Sickles said innocently.

"He is not sure at this time. Once the Sixth Corps is up, Meade will make the decision. We certainly shouldn't move out to this position until that time."

Suddenly, artillery boomed from Cemetery Hill. Hunt turned toward the heights, concerned. "I better go see what is going on over there."

Sickles felt his opportunity slipping away. "So do I have permission to move to this position?"

Hunt shook his head. "Not on my authority. I will report my findings to General Meade for his instructions." He turned his horse and paused. "If you are concerned about having your flank turned, you should send out some pickets to see what is out there in those woods." With that, he galloped off toward Cemetery Hill.

Sickles watched Hunt leave. His gambit had failed. "DAMN!" he swore. Looking out on the terrain surrounding him, his eyes rested on the woods to his west. "Tremain, get word to General Birney. Have him send some Sharpshooters out to see what is in those woods."

Meade was on the porch speaking with George and Ludlow when Hunt rode up from the south. "Ah, General Hunt, did you get Sickles's concerns resolved?"

Hunt shook his head. "I don't know what he was thinking. The position he showed me was at least a half mile in front of the positions he is currently occupying. It has great fields of fire, but there is no way he could hold it, given the strength of his corps and its exposed position."

"Yes, hard to tell with him what he is thinking. I hope you disabused him of that idea."

"I certainly did! He wanted my permission to move out to that location. I told him I could not give it to him, but I would pass on my observations to you. By the way, if you do plan an attack in that area, the spot would be excellent for supporting artillery."

"I'll keep that in mind." A series of rapid cannon shots interrupted Meade. He cocked his head toward the cemetery. "What's going on up there?"

"I need to go up and find out. If you will excuse me, General?"

Meade raised his hand in assent and watched Hunt gallop off. *I should have relieved Sickles when I had the chance,* he thought. *It's too late now, though. I'll just have to make the best of it.*

Major Ludlow interrupted his thoughts. "Sir, I have some good news. General Sykes reports that his last division has closed."

"Good," Meade replied, looking wistfully down the Taneytown Road. "Now all we need is for the Sixth Corps to get here. If Lee will wait until then, we will be in good shape."

General Birney looked toward the ground and kicked a clump of dirt with the toe of his boot. "Just what don't you like about this position, General Sickles?"

Sickles waved his arm toward the south and Round Top. "Just look at this forest. It's so wooded we have no fields of fire and observation. The enemy could sneak up on us, and we wouldn't know they were there until they were on top of us! And we couldn't see them to fire a shot either."

Birney hesitated, considering his reply. "We did send the Sharpshooters out as skirmishers, and Buford's cavalry is out there as well. Certainly between them, they would detect any enemy movement!"

Sickles shook his head violently. "NO! I just don't like it! It's too risky. That's what happened to Howard at Chancellorsville. He got no warning at all even though there was supposed to be cavalry out in front of him. Why can't Meade see this? Is he that incompetent?"

Birney was respectfully silent at this insubordination. He looked around and motioned toward a rider racing toward them. "Looks like one of General Ward's lads." When the rider pulled up in front of them, Birney called out, "What do you have for us, Lieutenant?"

The young officer rendered a quick salute. "Sir, General Ward reports a body of troops marching north on the Emmitsburg Road."

Sickles looked at Birney, then back at the lieutenant. "Troops? Ours or the enemy's?"

"We could not make them out at the time, sir. General Ward wanted to get this information to you as soon as possible."

"Hmm. Let's get down there, Birney, and see what's happening!"

The group rode quickly down the low ridge to the end, where a battery of artillery was placed. To their left was the jumble of huge boulders that would later become famous as Devil's Den. Ward was waiting as they arrived.

"General, they are down there to the southwest." Ward pointed in the direction everyone was looking.

"Can you make out who they are?" Sickles asked.

"We can see them better now. They are our men—probably the rest of the troops from Emmitsburg. And look down farther to the south. Behind the line of troops, you can see wagons."

Sickles raised his field glasses and looked in the direction Ward was pointing. *Yes,* he thought, *there are wagons in the column!* Relief swept over him. "They brought the ammunition train with them!"

"I'm sure they would," Birney said. "Both Burling and de Trobriand are pretty level-headed officers."

Sickles nodded. Both of those brigade commanders were good, reliable men. A panicky thought hit him. "Are they going to know where to turn? If they go too far, they will run into the rebs."

"No," Birney replied, shaking his head. "I sent General Graham down to meet them and guide them up here. Besides, we have several regiments out near the Peach Orchard as skirmishers. They wouldn't let the column go past the turn."

"OK." Sickles was relieved. "Let's go up and meet the column. We will want to place the brigades as they arrive."

Sickles waited impatiently as the first brigade turned at the Peach Orchard lane and marched east toward his position. A group of riders broke away from the head of the column and galloped toward him. At the head of the group, Sickles recognized General Graham.

As he reached Sickles, Graham pulled up and flashed a quick salute. "I've brought your lost sheep, General!"

"I see you've brought the ammunition train as well," Sickles said, returning the salute.

Graham nodded. "Burling and de Trobriand thought it best if they escorted the ammunition train. It was probably was a wise decision, as we did not run into any cavalry pickets on the way up. Who knows what could have happened to an unescorted line of wagons."

"Wait," Sickles said. "What, no cavalry? We are supposed to have a division of cavalry down there. Tremain, send some people down on horseback to check it out."

Chapter 14

Afternoon, July 2, 1863

"THEY'RE GONE? ARE YOU SURE?" Sickles shifted his gaze from Birney to Tremain. They were both nodding their heads.

"Yes," Birney said. "Colonel Berdan had his Sharpshooters out as skirmishers this morning on our left flank. They made contact with the cavalry pickets at that time. About an hour ago, they lost contact. He doesn't know what happened to them."

"We also sent out mounted orderlies to look for the cavalry, as you ordered," Tremain added. "They reported finding the cavalry's campfires and plentiful horse droppings, but absolutely no troopers. They've cleared out, I'm afraid, sir."

"GODDAMN!" Sickles exploded. "This is such incompetence! They have left my flank totally unguarded!" He paused to consider his next move. *It may be possible that Meade is unaware of this situation,* he thought. *Perhaps I can use it to help justify a move out to the forward position near the Peach Orchard.* "Tremain, send a message to General Meade. Inform him that the cavalry screen on our left flank is gone."

Tremain nodded and the group broke up, leaving Sickles to consider his possible options.

Sickles paced nervously, considering the situation. *Should we just move out to the forward position? If I do this without some justification or authorization, I open myself up to being relieved of my command or even court-martialed. Meade hates me, so he would do his worst. Even my friends in Congress might not be able to help me!*

A quick popping arose from the other side of the Peach Orchard hill. "They've made contact," Sickles said to himself. "Let's just see what they find." Walking in the direction the noise was coming from, he found Birney also looking in that direction.

The popping increased in tempo. Suddenly it erupted into a constant rattle. "Sounds like they've hit at least a regiment in line," Birney said.

Sickles nodded and bit his lip. *Is this confirmation of my fears?* He stared up at the empty lane leading up to the peach orchard. "Where is Berdan's report?" he asked impatiently.

Birney cleared his throat. "Colonel Berdan is very good about sending reports, General Sickles. I know we will get word from him as soon as he is able to send it."

The group trained their field glasses on the peach orchard. Soon, a lone rider emerged over the rise and pounded down the lane toward them. "That looks like a messenger now," Birney said.

As the rider came closer, they could see that he wore a green jacket—he was a Sharpshooter. "That's Captain Briscoe of the Sharpshooters," an aide announced.

Briscoe pulled up in front of the group and gave Sickles a hurried salute. "Report from Colonel Berdan, sir. We entered the woods to our front as ordered and encountered a line of skirmishers. Behind the skirmishers we saw a line of rebel infantry drawn up, at least two regiments, maybe as much as a brigade. Colonel Berdan sent me off to report and said he would pitch into them as soon as I was well enough away. From the sound of things, he has engaged the main rebel line."

"A brigade, you say," Sickles said. "I knew it, Birney! I knew the Johnnies would come around our flank." Birney was silent. Sickles kicked at a clod of dirt. *It's time to try again to get Meade to approve the move,* he thought. Turning to Tremain, he said, "OK, Major, let's work out a script for a report you are going to make to General Meade."

Hancock leaned against his horse and shook his head. "I can't understand it, Gibbon. Lee should have attacked long ago." The day had turned hot and sultry. Hancock wiped the sweat from his eyes with his sleeve.

"Yeah," Gibbon said. "He must know that the longer he waits, the stronger we get."

"He must be up to something. Otherwise, he would have attacked at dawn, right up the streets and over the top of the Eleventh Corps."

Gibbon nodded. "Our weak link." He paused and looked out toward the Seminary Ridge to the west. "If he's up to something, what could that be?"

"Hard to say. Bobby Lee is a resourceful fellow. One thing, though. If I were George Meade, I'd watch my rear and flanks."

Gibbon looked toward the south and the Round Tops. "Lee does like flank attacks, that's for sure. I'm not sure about attacking those hills, though."

Hancock looked south as well. "We have our flank anchored on those hills. They are very strong natural barriers. It's unlikely that Lee would try to crack a position that strong."

"Yes," Gibbon said. "But if he found a way around the end or a gap?"

"Well, that's possible, I suppose, but Buford's cavalry is down there on that flank. They would detect any move around our left and would hold the rebs off long enough for us to get our reserves down there to block them. I talked with General Meade this morning about that possibility. Meade believes Lee will not move south, as it will stretch his line too much and leave his left vulnerable to an attack from east of Culp's Hill."

"I haven't seen the ground around Culp's Hill."

"I've seen a little of it. The problem is it's very close to Baltimore Pike. Lee could easily move against our only line of communication and flank us out of this position. The right—yes, that's the flank we have to keep an eye on."

"I have an administrative matter to discuss with you," Gibbons said, changing the subject. "General Harrow reports that one of his regimental commanders, a Colonel Colvill, was placed under arrest by your Colonel Morgan for failure to maintain control of his regiment."

"Yes," Hancock said, "I remember that. Had something to do with lack of discipline when crossing a stream a few days ago. What about it?"

"Well, General Harrow maintains that Colvill is a fine leader and a dependable commander. He requests that Colvill be released from arrest and allowed to command his regiment, at least for as long as the battle lasts."

Hancock looked over at Gibbons. "And we've had no other issues with Colonel Colvill?"

"None whatsoever."

"OK, then, I agree. There is no reason we should keep a good officer away from his regiment on the eve of battle. I will have

Colvill released from arrest and given back his sword to return to his regiment right away."

Sustained firing began down to the south and front, in the direction of the low hill with the orchard. They couldn't see any puffs of smoke—it was too far away. "Third Corps skirmishers," Gibbon said. "I wonder what they've run into?"

Meade wiped the sweat from his face with a handkerchief. The air inside the cramped cottage they had made into their headquarters was stiflingly hot and humid. His face stung from the branch strike, and his torso ached where he had been wounded the year before. No sleep the previous night conspired with the heat and humidity to impose an almost irresistible drowsiness. *Have to stay busy,* he chided himself. *Can't fall asleep!*

The jolt of the message from Sickles over a half an hour earlier announcing the departure of the cavalry on the left flank had roused him and catapulted him into a towering rage, but that rage had dissipated. *When I gave Pleasanton permission to relieve Buford's cavalry,* he told himself, *I fully expected them to be replaced.* He had ordered Pleasanton to recall or replace Buford immediately, but the left flank still drew his attention. Looking at the map of the army's positions, he tapped his finger on the Round Tops. *Maybe I should hedge my bets on the left flank,* he mused. *I'll have Sykes move the Fifth Corps more toward the center of the line so that he can reinforce the left if needed.* Calling for an aide, he recited his order for the Fifth Corps to move.

Sighing as the aide left the room, he rolled out a map of Adams County, Pennsylvania, that showed the roads in the vicinity of Gettysburg. Rubbing his forehead, he tried to make his sleep-deprived brain focus. *What if Lee does not attack? Will he move around my position? If he moves to my south, I will be forced to abandon this position to keep between the enemy and Washington.*

Meade was suddenly aware of a change in the noise coming from outside. Looking up, he noticed a figure standing in the doorway. Meade squinted to make out the motionless figure. *It's Sickles aide,* he realized. "Well, sir?" he asked.

"Sir," Tremain began, "I have a message from General Sickles in three parts. The first part is to report that his last two brigades and the artillery trains have closed on his position." Meade nodded, and Tremain continued. "The second part is to report that our skirmishers have made contact with a brigade-size enemy force in the woods to the west of the Emmitsburg Road." He paused to look at Meade, who gave no response.

Tremain gave a nervous cough and continued. "The third part concerns whether you have any instructions for protecting the Emmitsburg Road."

Meade stared at the aide, moderately irritated. *Why did Sickles send his senior aide to bother me with such trivia? This could all be contained in a written report! Everyone has enemy out in front of them, and the Emmitsburg Road is almost a mile out in front of Sickles's designated position. What the hell is Sickles thinking?*

After a long silence, Tremain repeated his report.

Meade, now highly irritated, cut the conversation short. "Thank you, Major." He watched Tremain leave and then went back to his map.

Henry Taylor shifted on the ground uncomfortably. The regiment had moved a few hours ago to this new position. They were in a slight depression beyond the crest of the ridge and sheltered from the enemy's direct fire. Even so, stray artillery rounds flew overhead, exploding here and there. The men lay in the depression, somewhat oblivious of the artillery bursts, all the while attempting to find some degree of comfort in the hot midday sun.

"Do you reckon that's General Meade's headquarters?" Cundy asked out of the blue.

Henry shifted to look at the small white cottage behind him and to the right. A number of horses were tied to the white picket fence that surrounded the house with groups of men around the porch. "Suppose so," Henry said. "There's sure a beehive of activity over there."

"Then we are in a good position." Isaac laughed. "You know generals like to select a safe place for their headquarters!"

Henry grunted and rolled back to a more comfortable position. It was too hot for idle conversation.

"Look at that. Colonel Colvill is back!" someone exclaimed. Behind their position, Colvill was surrounded by regimental officers, shaking hands and smiling.

"Well," Isaac said, "at least someone had the good sense to give us our commander back!"

The men lay silent under the beating sun, some dozing, others absorbed in other activities to counteract the boredom of waiting. A sudden nearby explosion down to their left startled the group. Cries and shouts of alarm caused them to look toward the point of explosion to see what was happening. Word was quickly passed up the line—an exploding shell had killed one man and wounded another.

"Did you ever notice how random death is during war?" Isaac asked, lying on his back, looking up into the sky.

"I had noticed that," Henry said.

"I mean, during peacetime, there are accidents, sure, but usually death is anticipated. You get sick and die, or you grow old and die. During war, even when you think you are safe, death can snatch you up in an instant."

"I suppose it does come down to luck in a way, doesn't it?" Henry said.

"Well, we've been pretty lucky so far," Isaac said.

Henry grimaced. *Don't say it. Don't jinx us,* he thought. "Yeah" was all he could say.

The pair lay silent for a while amid the booming of cannon, the exploding shells, and the popping of skirmishers in the distance. Finally, Isaac spoke out. "It can provide comfort to a person to know that they will have a proper epitaph on their tombstone." He rolled to look directly at Henry. "Don't you think?"

Henry turned to look Isaac in the eyes. He was deadly serious. Henry had never heard his happy-go-lucky brother speak so morbidly before. Henry could only nod in response.

The group of horsemen galloped toward his position, and Sickles strained to make them out. One of the two men in the lead wore the green uniform of a Sharpshooter. The other was definitely Birney. He could tell by the long beard and the First Division headquarters flag held by an orderly trailing behind. As they came closer, Sickles could tell that the Sharpshooter was Colonel Berdan.

The group pulled up before Sickles and both Birney and Berdan dismounted, trading quick salutes with Sickles. "We've come to give a detailed report on Colonel Berdan's reconnaissance," Birney said. He motioned toward Berdan. "Go ahead, Colonel."

"Well, General, we advanced across the Emmitsburg Road into the woods to our south. I sent Captain Briscoe with a preliminary report that we spotted what appeared to be up to a brigade of enemy infantry." Sickles nodded, and Berdan continued. "We engaged their skirmishers and drove them back onto the enemy's first line. Our heavy fire forced their lines back, but another enemy regiment moved up on our flank, and their flanking fire ultimately forced us to fall back. During this engagement, we spotted three columns of rebel infantry moving toward the south."

Sickles raised an eyebrow. "South, you say? So they could be attempting to move around our left flank."

Berdan nodded. "That is certainly a possibility, sir."

Sickles considered this for a moment. "So Meade promised to immediately replace the missing cavalry on our flank. Any sign of them?"

"No," Birney said. "I gave my skirmishers explicit orders to notify me the minute any cavalry showed up. So far, there has been nothing."

Sickles paused to consider this information. *Meade will be no help with this. He rejected Tremain's report. "Frosted him" was the term Tremain used. Is Meade deliberately trying to set me up?* He was getting madder the longer he thought about it. "DAMMIT," he finally exploded. "This is just like Chancellorsville! We have enemy moving on our flank through the woods with no screen on our flank to protect us. I can't wait any longer! I am not going to be caught with my pants down! General Birney, you will move your division to the positions I identified earlier."

Birney nodded. "Of course, General. Right away."

Meade waited on the porch of the Leister house for news. He had given up on working in his makeshift office. It was too hot inside the one-room house, and the traffic of staff officers in and out made his aching head hurt even more. Outside it was still hot, but not as stuffy as inside. Besides, he was having trouble staying awake in there. He watched a lone rider gallop up the Taneytown Road from the south. The rider pulled up beside a group of his aides gathered by the picket fence and spoke to them. Major Ludlow moved away from the group toward Meade.

"Look, General, toward the southeast. Do you see that dust?"

Meade squinted in the direction Ludlow was pointing. Yes, he saw it. He hoped it was the Sixth Corps, not a rebel force.

"That rider is a courier from General Sedgwick. He is less than two miles down the road and requests instructions as to where to position his corps."

Meade cracked a smile—the first, he reckoned, in several days. "Hurrah for the Sixth Corps! We are all up now." *Have we won the race to assemble? In time we'll know for sure.*

"Send word to all corps commanders. The Sixth Corps will arrive within the hour. I will have a meeting of all corps commanders at this headquarters immediately." Aides flew off to deliver the word. "Oh, and Ludlow, send an aide down with the courier to meet General Sedgwick. Ask him to meet me here. I want the Sixth Corps to occupy the position on the right that the Fifth Corps previously occupied. Have the aide escort the lead element to that position."

Ludlow nodded and moved off to carry out the orders.

It's now down to waiting, Meade told himself. *Waiting in these defensive positions for Lee to make the next move.* He would have liked to take the initiative and launch an attack, but he knew there was no clear decisive point to launch that attack and, besides, Sedgwick had marched all night to arrive. His troops were in no shape to join in any assault. Hopefully, Lee would give them a chance to rest.

As his corps commanders began to filter in, Meade took the opportunity to chat with them about their impressions of the ground to their front and the condition of their men. He enjoyed the interchange—it was good to speak to his subordinates directly and not through couriers. Finally, all his commanders had arrived except two: Sedgwick, who was due to arrive soon, and Sickles who was nowhere to be found.

Meade scowled—no Sickles! "Ludlow," he called out. "Send another messenger down to find Sickles and tell him to get up here." He was suddenly aware of some firing down toward the southwest.

The messenger returned quickly. "Sir," he said, "General Sickles says he is too busy right now, and he asks to be excused."

Meade swore under his breath. "Go back down there and tell him to get up here *now.* That's an order!"

The rest of his commanders were standing around, waiting for the meeting to start. *No need to keep them all waiting,* Meade told himself. *I can fill Sickles in on anything he missed.* "Gentlemen," he said, "I would like to discuss our current status and plans going forward." As he was speaking, one of Warren's aides arrived, hurried to Warren, and whispered in his ear. Warren had a shocked look on his face and asked the aide something. The aide shook his head in response. Warren nodded and moved toward Meade.

"Ah, General Meade, pardon me for interrupting, but something has come up that you need to know about. It's Sickles. He's moved his corps forward, about three-quarters of a mile out from Little Round Top. We don't know if there are any troops on Little Round Top at this time."

Good God, Meade thought. *That damn Sickles will ruin everything! We need reinforcements out there right away. The Fifth Corps is in reserve. They can get there quickly.* He turned to General Sykes. "George, move your corps as fast as possible to fill the gap and hold that hill at all hazards."

Sykes mounted quickly and galloped off toward his corps.

Sickles finally arrived, trailed by a number of aides.

Meade scowled. "General Sickles, don't dismount. You are needed at your front. Please return to your command, and I will join you there."

Sickles gave an exasperated look, saluted, and rode off.

Meade turned to his orderlies. "Bring my horse up."

"Sir, he's not ready. His saddle is not on," an orderly said sheepishly.

"Damn," Meade said. "I can't wait."

"Why don't you use my horse?" Pleasonton suggested. "He's saddled and ready to do."

Meade gratefully took the reins to Pleasonton's horse and rode down toward the left of his line, followed by Warren and a group of aides. As they reached the point where the ridge dipped toward the woods, Warren made a movement of his arm in the direction of the Round Tops. "This is where the line should be."

Meade looked and grunted. *Yes,* he thought. *That is exactly where I told Sickles he was to be!* He could tell that Little Round top was devoid of any troops. Only the flag of a Signal Corps station could be seen.

They could perceive some firing beyond the round tops to the southwest. *If those hills are not occupied, that firing could indicate some real danger,* Meade told himself. *They are the key to our position here on the left.* "Warren," he said, "I hear a little peppering going on in the direction of that little hill over there. I wish that you would ride over, and if anything serious is going on, attend to it."

Warren nodded and rode off with two of his aides and a group of orderlies.

Meade's remaining group turned west on a farm lane. To his left, south, there was wheat field, and beyond that Meade could see some of Sickles's troops stretched out facing southwest. As they continued on up over a low forested stony hill, their view extended out to an orchard at the end of the lane on an even higher hill. Meade's heart dropped to his stomach as he took in the view. There were no troops visible along the lane. He could see more units in formation stretching from just north of the orchard back toward Cemetery Ridge. "What the hell is Sickles thinking?" Meade muttered. "There is no way he can hold this advanced position!"

They found Sickles along the lane just before they reached the peach orchard. "General Sickles," Meade called out, "I am afraid you are too far out." He turned and pointed over toward Little Round Top. "Back there is where I wanted your line."

Sickles made a face. *Annoyance or disgust?* Meade wondered.

"I was seeking a more elevated position with better fields of fire. This hill is much higher than the one I just left." Sickles swept his arm around the hill to his front.

Hold your temper, Meade told himself. *This is no time to dive into an argument. We need to get this problem fixed right away.* "General Sickles," Meade said icily, "this is in some respects higher ground than the one in the rear, but there is still higher ground in front of you. If you keep on advancing, you will find constantly higher ground all the way to the mountains."

Sickles clenched his jaws and then replied. "General, this position in particular is important. I felt that I had to occupy it to prevent the enemy from placing artillery positions here and dominating the lower ground to our rear."

Meade shook his head. Sickles didn't understand; this position was untenable. "General Sickles," he replied with a softer tone, "this is neutral ground. Our guns command it as well as the enemy's. The very reason you cannot hold it applies to them as well."

Sickles suddenly appeared shocked. "If you think it prudent, I will order my troops to withdraw," he said meekly.

There was an artillery burst near the group. Meade's horse began to rear and plunge. *I don't know this horse, how to control him.* He managed to steady the horse a bit. Meade looked toward the tree line to his west. Rebel artillery batteries were lined up in front of the woods, and more were unlimbering. He pointed toward the artillery. "I wish to God you could withdraw, but those people will not permit it without a fight." This would end the waiting, make Lee react to him. Not perfect, but it might upset Lee's plans. "Well, it may as well begin now as at any time. If you need more artillery, call up the reserve."

Another nearby artillery burst caused his horse to resume rearing. The shells were bursting continuously now. *I can't control this horse.* A shell exploded in the earth, this time very close, showering them with dirt. Meade's horse bolted. "Just try to hold on. I'll send you reinforcements," Meade shouted over his shoulder. He held on to the pommel, trying to remain mounted as the terrified horse galloped back toward Little Round Top.

Sickles watched Meade race off, fighting for control of his mount. A sick feeling settled on him. *What have I done? Stay calm,* he told himself. *There is a way out of this.* To his front, the peach orchard was shrouded in smoke and exploding shells. *They are really getting pounded up there. Maybe Meade was right—the position cannot be held. At any rate, they are going to need support up there and soon.* He looked to Tremain. "Major, order General Humphreys to move his division forward to the Emmitsburg Road, extending north from General Graham's right flank."

Tremain rode off, and Sickles swung to Captain Randolph. "Captain, find General Hunt. Tell him General Meade authorized support from the Artillery Reserve. I want to line this lane filled with batteries firing south. When the rebs come, we will give them a wall of canister."

"General?" It was Birney.

"Birney, I'm glad you're here. I was just going to call for you. It looks like the enemy is going to attack any minute now. We need to prepare."

"There is a real problem, General Sickles. We have stretched my division across three-quarters of a mile. My brigades are stretched thin. I have no reserves to support the front line if they get into trouble."

Sickles looked to the east along Birney's line. *The line is a little long. If only I had another division. Well, Meade offered infantry support.* He motioned to the remainder of his staff to come close. "Gentlemen," he said, "we are in a desperate situation. We have taken the only possible position, and now the enemy will attack us for it. I expect some very hard fighting, and we need all the help we can find. I want each one of you to go out and round up every regiment, every battery you can find. Tell them General

Meade has authorized their transfer to our support. I don't care what corps they belong to; just get them here."

The aides mounted and raced off.

"General, look to the south!" General Birney shouted.

Sickles swung around. "Where?"

"Toward the ridgeline. It's the rebs!"

He raised his field glasses and scanned the ridgeline. A long line of gray infantry had emerged from the woods on the ridge and were advancing from the Emmitsburg Road toward the Round Tops beyond. Already, Birney's artillery on the left was engaging the advancing rebels. Sickles lowered his field glasses. "It's started."

"Tremain," Sickles added, turning to his aide, "send word to General Humphreys that he is to move his division to connect with the right of General Birney's division near the peach orchard."

Tremain saluted and mounted his horse to deliver the message.

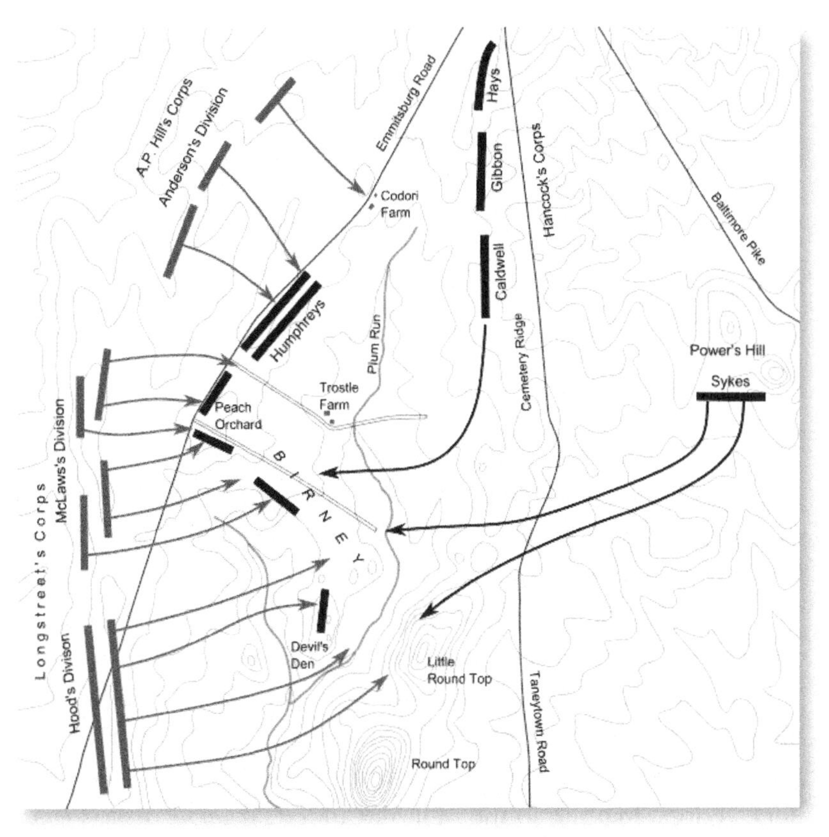

SITUATION—LATE AFTERNOON 2 JULY

Humphreys rode up not long afterward. "General Sickles," he called out, "I have received orders to move my division forward, but I have a problem executing those orders."

"Why's that?" Sickles asked.

"I cannot cover the distance between General Birney's right flank and the Second Corps left. If I maintain proper unit spacing, that would leave almost a quarter-mile gap between my right and the Second Corps' left. We would both be quite vulnerable."

Sickles waved his hand dismissively. "The Second Corps will just have to cover that gap."

"But General Sickles," Humphreys said.

"General Humphreys," Sickles snapped, "those are my orders. If you are unable to carry them out, I will find someone who can."

Humphreys straightened in the saddle. "Very well, General. I will carry out your orders."

Hancock lowered his field glasses and scowled. "We can't see a thing through all those trees. From the sound, though, it's getting pretty hot down there."

He had come down to Caldwell's division on his left to get a better look at what was happening. The action to his south was completely blocked by trees, and he hoped Caldwell's position had a better view; unfortunately, it did not. The heavy rifle fire that had died off earlier had now erupted into sustained artillery. "I don't like the sound of it," he added. *What on earth* is *going on down there? It sounds too far out—it couldn't be contact with our line, could it?*

"General, look at Humphreys' division!"

Hancock looked to his left front toward the wooded position where Humphreys had previously placed his troops. Beyond the woods, toward the Emmitsburg Road, three lines of blue infantry moved through the fields. *That's his whole division. What is he doing? Humphreys knows better than that. It must be Sickles's doing. He is going to get them all killed!*

It was an impressive sight. The lines moved as if on a parade ground. A chill raced through Hancock's spine. *So beautiful,* he thought.

"What a magnificent sight!" someone said.

Hancock shook his head. *Magnificent, but insane. They cannot be supported.* "Wait a moment. You will soon see them tumbling back," he replied.

Onward the line advanced until the rightmost unit reached the Emmitsburg Road. When the move was completed, a line of blue stretched along the road from the peach orchard on the left up nearly as far as the large barn to Hancock's front.

A messenger rode up, looking for Hancock. "Orders from General Meade, sir," the aide said. "You are to send a division to the left to support General Sykes."

Well, this is it! Hancock nodded. "Caldwell, get your division ready."

The division became a place of hectic activity. Hancock rode off a ways to study the ground in front of him, his aides trailing behind. He trained his field glasses on Humphreys's line. *That right flank is hanging and dangerously exposed. Need to do something about that!* "Take a message to General Gibbon. Tell him to detail a regiment for forward duty. I will place the regiment personally." *There will be a gap in the line once Caldwell's division marches off. Better take care of that too.* "Oh, and tell Gibbon to spread out his division as far as possible to cover some of this gap."

An aide rode off with the message.

Caldwell's division was falling in and was preparing to march off. Hancock rode back toward the division and passed the Irish Brigade. They were on one knee, facing toward a chaplain, a Catholic priest. Hancock recognized him. It was Father Corby.

"I am about to give you general absolution," Father Corby began. "This is pardon for all your sins. If you die in battle today, you will meet the Lord free of sin. I must add, however, that the Catholic Church refuses Christian burial to the soldier who turns his back upon the foe or deserts his flag. Now, please uncover."

The brigade removed their hats. Hancock did as well. "Dominus noster Jesus Christus vos absolvat," Corby intoned, making the sign of the cross. "Now, go with God."

The men rose and straightened into lines. Hancock looked over the meager ranks, thinned by so many bloody battles. *God, protect them this day.* He put his hat back on and rode toward Cross's brigade, the first one in line and ready to move out.

He found Cross at the head of his brigade, as usual. Instead of the red bandanna Cross usually wore, though, he had a black piece of silk tied around his head. Hancock raised an eyebrow. *That's odd. Wonder what that is all about.* Cross appeared preoccupied and did not see Hancock ride up. "Well, Cross," Hancock said, "this is the last time you'll fight without a star!" The papers promoting Cross to brigadier general were expected any day.

Cross looked up at him with an expression that Hancock could not fathom—a mixture of sadness and resignation. Cross shook his head. "It's too late, General. This is my last battle."

Last battle...what does he mean? He must think he is going to die! Hancock was shocked at the thought of losing Cross, his best fighter. Shaken, he saluted Cross and rode off toward the north to find the regiment coming from General Gibbon.

His left, Birney's division, was in trouble, and Dan Sickles knew it. Ward's brigade on the ridge next to Devil's Den, the left flank,

held against the first wave but was crushed and swept aside by subsequent waves of determined rebels. Some Fifth Corps units had occupied Little Round Top and were now fighting to hold their position. From his position near farmer Trostle's barn, Sickles could see Little Round Top smoking like a volcano.

Nearer to him, De Trobriand's brigade had fought like wild men but were forced back after they ran out of ammunition. Luckily, Caldwell's division from the Second Corps arrived in time to prevent a breakthrough. The battle line seesawed across the wheat field as each side sent in new brigades. Now Caldwell was out of new brigades, and the enemy continued to pile on fresh troops. Without some help, Caldwell would soon be pushed completely out of the wheat field.

Sickles shook his head. *I have nothing to send, and besides, Caldwell is taking orders from Sykes. There is certainly enough on my plate without worrying about General Sykes's problems!*

Sickles spurred his horse up the lane toward the peach orchard. To his right, Humphreys's division wasn't seeing much action. He had been able to take regiments from Humphreys to help shore up Birney's beleaguered units, over Humphreys's objections. Sickles shrugged. *They weren't seeing any action, so what was the problem?*

The conditions at the peach orchard were worse than they had looked on the way up. Graham's brigade in the peach orchard was being pounded unmercifully. Sickles looked around at the carnage. The infantry, forced to lie waiting around the cannons, was taking a frightful beating from the shells aimed at the Union batteries in the peach orchard. Scores of men lay dead or wounded in the back of the infantry lines, struck by shell fragments. Sickles frowned. *These lines are very thin, too thin. Can they hold up against an infantry assault?* He turned to an aide.

"Tell General Humphreys to send a couple of regiments to help General Graham immediately!"

"Sir, the last time we told him to send some help over, he complained that we took away his third line, his reserves. He is bound to argue that he will be unable to withstand an assault when it comes."

"I don't care," Sickles growled. "Tell him to send three regiments. That's an order!"

Sickles looked to his left, toward the south. The batteries along the wheat field road were blazing furiously away at rebel infantry closing in on them from the southwest. He didn't know how long they could hold on.

"General, look!" an orderly shouted.

Sickles looked in the direction the orderly was pointing. Gray-jacketed infantry were filing out of the woods, forming up behind the artillery. He could see that an attack was imminent. "Damn!" he swore. They couldn't hold without reinforcements. He spurred his horse toward General Graham, who was frantically directing his troops to get into line. "Hold this position, Graham," he shouted. "I am going to get you reinforcements!"

By the time he returned to the Trostle farm, Sickles could tell the peach orchard position was doomed. The noise from the other side of the hill rose to a crescendo, and the trickle of refugees from the front line was joined by the artillery batteries, rolling back toward Cemetery Ridge at full gallop.

"Hey, where are you going?" he shouted to a passing officer.

"Orders from General Hunt. We are to reform on the ridge to the east and set up firing positions there."

"You can't leave. We need you here!" Sickles shouted frantically.

"You'll have to take that up with General Hunt. We take orders from him." With that, the captain and his battery rolled away.

Sickles swore in desperation. *The infantry will be retreating soon. They can't hold up against an assault without artillery support.*

In a short while, the infantry did follow, some running, others slowly walking to the rear, loading their weapons as they walked. Sickles rode up to a group of twenty or so soldiers. Their leader, a colonel, was carrying the regimental colors on his shoulder. "Colonel," Sickles called out, "for God's sake, can't you hold on?"

The colonel paused and looked up at Sickles, tears streaming down his powder-smudged face. "Where are my men?" he asked plaintively.

Sickles let the group move past. *Is that all that's left of his regiment?*

Shell and shot began to fall around them, and Sickles motioned to his dwindling staff to follow him to the far side of the Trostle barn, where they could find some shelter. This was not what he had bargained for. Sickles rubbed his face, trying to get his brain to work. *There must be some way out of this. If Graham's position goes, then Humphreys will be forced to retreat. Maybe I can make a stand farther back.* Sickles moved out from behind the barn to look.

A white-hot pain flashed from his right leg to his entire body. Sickles, lightheaded, teetered in the saddle. *Need to get down.* He swung his leg over to dismount and lost his strength, falling toward the ground.

Sickles was barely aware of his aides catching him and easing him to the ground. He tried to move, but his arms and legs wouldn't obey. A terrible nausea welled up in his stomach. Hands gently rolled him over onto his back.

"My God, General, your leg!"

Sickles raised himself up and caught a glimpse of his right leg. It lay at an obscene angle from his body. Bright red blood spurted from below his knee. Sickles collapsed back to the ground, his head swimming. *Don't pass out! The leg—it's cut in two. Do something, or you'll be dead in minutes!* Sickles gritted his teeth and rasped, "Quick! Quick! Get something and tie it up before I bleed to death!"

There was a flurry of conversation. *Great,* Sickles thought. *No one knows how to apply a tourniquet.* His aides made bandages from handkerchiefs and managed to slow the flow of blood. Another aide returned, leading a stretcher bearer. The private pushed the aides away and quickly fashioned a tourniquet using a saddle strap.

"Drink this, General. You need water—all the wounded develop a terrible thirst."

Sickles drank from the offered canteen as the private held his head up.

Hands lifted him onto the stretcher and carried him off. "Put him behind this boulder. He will be safe here until the ambulance comes," the private directed.

Sickles looked around as the stretcher was set upon the ground. Soldiers streamed by, headed back toward Cemetery Ridge. *The line must have broken. The rebs will be here soon. They will take me prisoner and let me die out of spite.* "Please," he told his aides, "don't let them take me prisoner."

"Don't worry, sir. We won't let them do that. There's no sign of the rebels yet."

Sickles relaxed a bit. The nausea had subsided, but the pain was intense. *Don't pass out. Need to stay alert.*

"General Sickles, you're wounded!"

Sickles opened his eyes. It was Tremain.

"Yes, it's serious, I'm afraid. Go find General Birney. Tell him that he must take command." Sickles felt in his coat pocket for his flask. He always kept a flask handy. He pulled off the top and filled his mouth with brandy. The effects were rapid, and Sickles could think more clearly over the pain.

Birney rode up, and Sickles turned his head to see him dismount. *Need to show strength,* he told himself. Sickles summoned his energy. "General Birney, you will take command, sir."

Birney strode quickly to him, eyes darting to Sickles's right leg and then back toward his eyes. "What are your orders, General?"

Sickles squeezed his eyes together, trying to concentrate. "Graham is finished up there. Humphreys can't hold with Graham gone. Order him to withdraw to Cemetery Ridge."

Birney nodded. "I'll do that, sir."

The pain shot up his leg again; Sickles clenched his teeth until the worst was over. "Birney, take good care of these men. If I don't survive, make sure people know how hard they fought here today." He extended his hand.

Birney took his hand and shook it gently. "You'll survive, General; I have no doubt of that." He rose and saluted before walking away toward his horse.

Sickles was suddenly aware of the groups of soldiers pausing to look at him and speaking among themselves in hushed tones. "What are they saying, Private?"

"They think you're dead, sir," the stretcher bearer said.

"Dead? I'm not dead." He paused to think. "Private, reach inside my coat. The inside pocket has a cigar holder. Pull a cigar out and light it for me."

The private did as he was told and placed a lit cigar between Sickles's teeth.

"Now," Sickles asked him, "can a dead man smoke a cigar?"

There was a murmur from the group of soldiers. Sickles raised himself up on his elbows, cigar clenched between his teeth. "I'm OK, boys. You stand firm, and we'll lick the rebs yet!"

Henry looked around, trying to get his bearings. General Hancock was in the lead, taking them God knew where.

To the south, in the direction of the Round Tops, the battle roared and smoke rose in giant plumes. "There's hell to pay down there!" someone near him exclaimed.

"Looks like Bobby Lee is trying one of his flanking moves again," Isaac added.

Henry shifted his Springfield rifle and craned his neck to see where they were headed. The head of the regiment was pointing toward the Round Top. Henry blew out a breath. *They say Caldwell's division* was *sent down there,* he thought. *Maybe it's our turn now. Is this it? Is this when our luck runs out?*

To the universal relief of the regiment, Hancock halted them about fifty yards south of a battery of artillery. The cannoneers were busy trading counter battery fire with rebel artillery on the far ridge. A cannonball struck the earth in front of one of the pieces and sent an enormous geyser of earth and sod into the air.

"Solid shot," said Isaac. "The ammunition of choice for counter battery fire."

Henry smiled at that. His brother was an inexhaustible font of trivia.

"I sure wouldn't choose to have that fired against me," another man joked. It was answered by a round of nervous laughter.

Hancock spoke to Colonel Colvill briefly and then continued on toward the south. Colvill moved the regiment forward of the battery and ordered it to lie down. No one complained; the battery was drawing way too much fire to be standing nearby.

Henry looked out to their front, where the ridge fell off gradually for some six hundred yards to a creek bed bordered with scrub bushes and boulders. Beyond that, the ground rose gradually for about the same distance until it met the Emmitsburg Road. Beyond that lay the wooded ridgeline known as Seminary Ridge, where the rebels had their guns. They could see flashes and puffs of smoke as the rebel batteries fired.

Along the Emmitsburg Road, a line of blue soldiers awaited the enemy advance. To the left of the line, the ground rose up in a hill covered at the crest by an orchard. The orchard and land around it were swathed in smoke. Black and orange flashes marked the exploding rebel shells. "Looks like the boys over in that orchard are catching it," Isaac muttered.

Henry nodded in agreement. Behind the hill, a lane ran down to a patch of woods to their left front. Beyond that patch of woods, another battle raged. Artillery batteries were placed nearly hub to hub along the lane and were firing constantly toward the south.

"The rebs are after the orchard!" a voice called out.

Henry could see the line of gray come out of the wood line, heading toward the orchard. The orchard erupted in more smoke and flame and the rebel line did as well, obliterating their view of the action. The men watched speechlessly as the smoke rose up in billows. A trickle of blue figures started to leak out of the back of the orchard, rapidly growing to a torrent. "Looks like they're breaking," Henry said disgustedly.

Artillery batteries rattled out of the orchard and down the lane toward them. Retreating infantry scrambled to avoid being trampled. Henry hung his head. *Yes, they're breaking.*

The regiment watched in horror as the left of the advanced Third Corps line crumbled. Batteries along the lane limbered up and pulled out. A line of gray broke out of the peach orchard and began firing at the retreating batteries. Henry felt sick.

He felt a nudge. Isaac was beside him, pointing toward the Union troops on the right. Rebel infantry in long lines had emerged from the woods on Seminary Ridge. In an instant, both lines were blazing at each other. Henry could see that the rebel line was longer than the Union line. The enemy would eventually overlap the blue-coat line and force them back. It was a simple matter of geometry.

The line held firm, then wavered and fell back to a second position.

The rebel advance slowed and halted. Henry felt a brief moment of elation.

They're holding! The feeling crashed when he saw another brigade emerge from the wood line slightly farther to the north. The Union line had no chance of success, it was clear. The second rebel brigade pressed on, and the Union line was forced to give way, slowly retreating back toward the creek bed and Cemetery Ridge beyond.

Henry felt a tremendous sadness. *Is this it? Is the battle lost? I can't stand another whipping and the humiliation.*

The gray line continued its inexorable movement toward them. "Well, boys," Henry said, "it may well be up to us."

Hancock was like a caged tiger, roaming up and down the limits of his line, forced to watch the battle but unable to take part in it. His anxiety was heightened by the lack of information on

Caldwell's division. Dense woods blocked his view of Caldwell's fighting, but the roar of battle from that area was ferocious. The roar was punctuated every so often by the crash of an entire line firing its rifles in unison. Deep-throated hurrahs and high-pitched yipping wails marked temporary Union or Confederate advantages. Smoke roiled up above the trees, testifying to the severity of the conflict in the wheat field beyond.

In the sector of the battlefield where Hancock could observe, things were not going well at all. Confederate infantry had swept over the peach orchard hill and down into the woods to Hancock's left front. Rebel artillery had taken position in the peach orchard and was now hammering the positions on Cemetery Ridge with shot and shell. To his front, Hancock watched Humphreys's division being pushed back by overwhelming numbers. The swale lay directly behind Humphreys's position. Hancock scanned the rocky area with his field glasses. *With a little luck, Humphreys can use the cover to rally. If not, it will only break up his formation.*

In Hancock's own sector, the enemy had finally emerged from the wood line on Seminary Ridge and was driving his pickets in. Hancock ordered limited counterattacks to restore his advance line, but he knew it was inevitable that the massed rebel brigades would eventually drive them back. He recognized the enemy tactical formation—an attack in echelon. The textbooks taught that an echelon attack would cause the defender to shift forces to the point of initial contact, thereby weakening the other part of the line to subsequent attacks. Hancock looked north along the bare stretch of Cemetery Ridge. *So far, your echelon attack formation seems to be working, General Lee. Let's just see what we can do to spoil your plans.*

Batteries were frantically setting up on the ridge about two hundred yards to his south. Hancock made a face. *Strange—there's no infantry nearby...better investigate.* He spurred his horse to a gallop.

As he came closer, Hancock could see from the different types of cannons that these were fragments of batteries—two guns from one, three from another. He also recognized the man giving orders, Colonel McGilvery—commander of one of the brigades in the Artillery Reserve.

"Where's your infantry support, Colonel?" Hancock asked. He already thought he knew the answer.

"Don't have any, General," McGilvery said. "The rebs are down in those woods, coming at us. If we don't stop them with these guns, they will split the line in two. I can hold on for a little while, General, but I need infantry. Can you get me some help?"

A loud booming to his front caused Hancock to raise his glasses for a better look. In the farmyard to his front, a Union battery was deployed in a semicircle, blowing canister at the rebel infantry circling around it. "Who's that?" he asked.

"Captain Bigelow, Ninth Massachusetts. I told him to hold that position as long as possible at all hazards."

Hancock nodded. "He'll probably lose all his pieces."

"Can't be helped, sir. I need time to get set up."

Hancock slid his field glasses back into the case. "I will bring you help, Colonel. You just hold on." He turned his horse back toward the north and spurred it to a gallop.

While he rode, a plan formed in his head. An echelon attack presupposed that the defender would be unable to react to strengthen the weakened areas in time. This attack had developed slowly, and the delay might give him enough time to plug the gap.

Gibbon waved to him as he rode up. "There's a messenger here for you from General Meade. You are requested to send a brigade to help General Birney. Want me to send one?"

Hancock shook his head. "No, I need you for other things." He turned to an aide. "Go tell General Hayes to send me his best brigade. Have them report to me. I will lead it to the correct position."

The aide was off.

Hancock turned back to Gibbon. "The enemy is attacking us in echelon. We need time to correct the weakening in the center of our line. I propose to use our reserves to hit each successive brigade hard as they come up and drive them back as possible. This should give us time to bring up reinforcements." He motioned to an aide. "Take a message to General Meade. Tell him our center is bare and we need all the support up here that he can send."

The sun had set, and the shadows were getting longer. Hancock strained to make out details along Seminary Ridge. He could just barely see another brigade emerging from the gloom. "That brigade will probably strike your position, Gibbon. Keep a strong reserve, and be ready to strike him when he is repulsed. If he overlaps your left, I will find troops to attack him on that side."

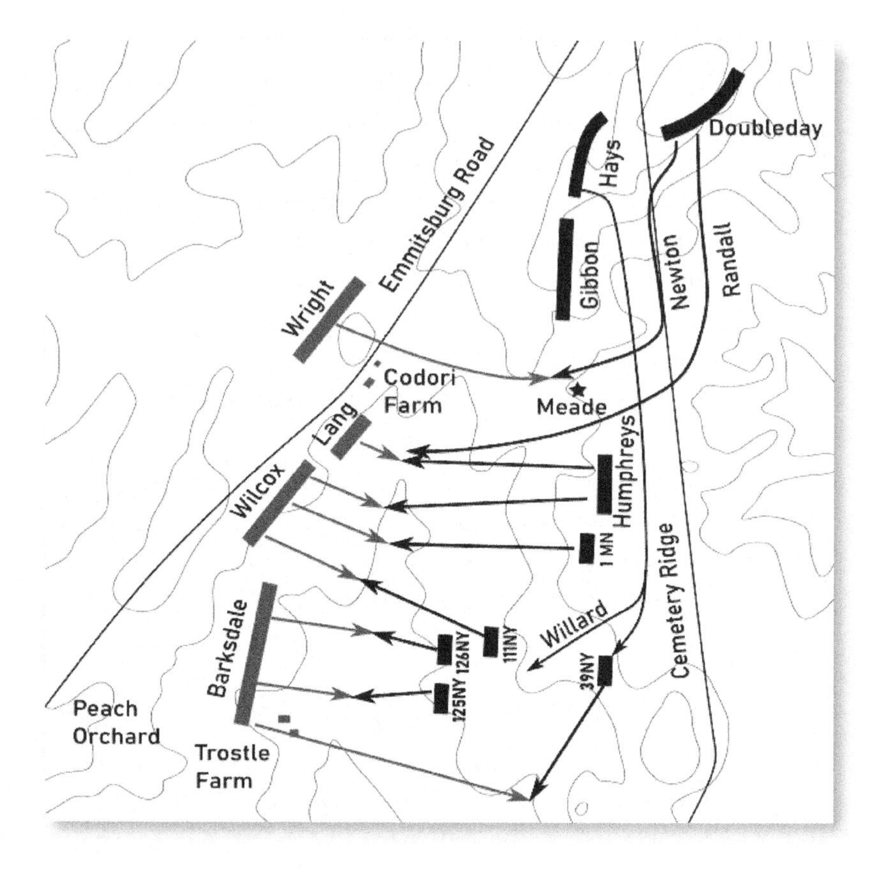

Hancock Counter Attacks—Early Evening 2 July

A messenger galloped toward him and pulled up with a shout. "General Hancock! Urgent message from General Meade. He reports General Sickles is wounded and out of action. General Meade requests that you take command of the Third Corps in addition to the Second Corps."

Hancock made a face and nodded. He watched the messenger ride away and turned to Gibbon. "It looks like I got the bad end of the bargain, giving up a perfectly good corps for one that has been misused and shot to hell!" Then, with a sigh, "Well,

Gibbon, take command of the Second Corps. I will see what we can do with what is left of the Third Corps!"

A column of troops clattered at the double-quick toward him. Hancock searched for the brigade pennant. There wasn't one. Realization hit him. *It's Willard's brigade. They're so new, they don't even have a brigade pennant. Great, I asked Hayes for his best brigade, and he sends me these people. Are they cowards? It's time to see!*

Hancock rode toward Willard. "Colonel," he called out, "have your brigade follow me at the double-quick time!" He turned and trotted toward McGilvery's cannons. A column of troops moving along the ridge was a target that no rebel artilleryman could resist, and soon shell and long-range rifle fire was whistling around the running column. Hancock turned several times to check; the column kept up with him, though it trailed dead and wounded.

As the head of the column moved in behind McGilvery's guns, Hancock called a halt. He turned to Willard and pointed toward the swale where a rebel brigade was pushing its way through the shrubs and boulders. "You see that brigade down there? Drive it back!"

Willard saluted and ordered his lines to dress. Flocks of soldiers wearing the Third Corps diamond patch ran up the hill and broke through the ranks, increasing the confusion. The advancing rebel line began firing in their direction. One regiment began to fire back. "Goddamn it, Willard," Hancock growled, "get them aligned and attack!"

Willard managed to stop the firing and get the brigade aligned. Then he ordered the advance, and the regiments stepped off.

Hancock watched them move forward. *Just a bit ragged, though not bad for green troops.* The march was slow and deliberate, with the line firing on the move. Rebel fire raked the brigade, and gaps appeared and the line staggered. Hancock held his breath. *Close it up, close it up, don't fall apart!*

From the ranks, someone shouted, "Remember Harpers Ferry!" The whole brigade replied in kind. "Remember Harpers Ferry!" The lines straightened, and the pace increased. At ten yards' distance, the rebel line unleashed a final volley, but Willard's line did not falter. In an instant, they were on the rebel's first line. The mass of blue and gray hesitated for what seemed an eternity, and then the rebels broke.

Hancock grinned. "That's right! drive 'em, Goddamn it!"

The blue line chased the rebels back toward the woods. Hancock was suddenly aware of firing on his right. He could see that another rebel brigade was taking Willard's brigade under fire from the flank. If they kept it up, they could break up the counterattack. Hancock rode to the reserve regiment trailing behind Willard's first line. "What regiment is this, Colonel?"

"Hundred eleventh New York, sir" was the reply.

"Well, Colonel, you take your regiment and hit that brigade over to the right in the flank!" Hancock watched with satisfaction as the regiment executed several difficult maneuvers faultlessly while the enemy raked it with fire. *Hays, you were right. This is your best brigade!*

Hancock couldn't afford to enjoy the glow of this one little success for long. There was a huge gap to his north, and several rebel brigades headed for it. He gave Willard's brigade one last look and spurred up the slope.

At the crest, Hancock found Humphreys shouting orders. He called to the division commander, "Humphreys, General Meade has placed me in command of the Third Corps. Reform your division in the space where General Caldwell's division was this morning!"

Humphreys looked at him with clenched jaws. "They are already formed, General. There they are, or what's left of them." He pointed toward a line of men.

The line was formed up slightly behind the crest. Even though the small number of troops in line made it look like a small brigade, Hancock could tell from the many flags that this was all that was left of Humphreys's division. He nodded. "Hold them in readiness. I will let you know when I need you."

Hancock looked around. *Good—Humphreys can plug at least part of the gap. Must be some other Third Corps remnants we can rally.* In the gun smoke and gloom of the gathering darkness, a line stumbled out of the swale below him. Hancock squinted to make out the line. *The jackets—are they blue? I think so, yes, they are.* He looked around for his aides. Only one, Captain Miller, was still with him. He had sent all the others off on errands. "Come on, Miller, let's get them formed up." He spurred off toward the line. As they came closer, Hancock was not so sure the jackets were blue. Suddenly, bullets were zipping around his head.

"They're Rebs!" Miller exclaimed.

"Get out of here, Miller!" Hancock shouted and dug his spurs into his horse. He reined his horse to a halt at a safer spot and turned to look at the situation. There was a gap between Willard and Humphreys. The rebel brigade was headed straight for that gap. He needed to plug it before the enemy split his line in two. Miller rode up beside him, bent over. "You OK, Miller?"

"I'm hit, sir," he gasped.

Hancock looked him over. "Can you still ride?" Miller nodded. "OK," Hancock said, "let's go." He rode up to the center of the gap, looking for a unit to fill the void. As he came to the crest, he could see a small group of several hundred infantry near a battery. There were no other troops around.

Hancock reined in his horse and looked at his meager reserve. "My God! Are these all of the men we have here? What regiment is this?"

A colonel stepped forward. "First Minnesota, General."

Hancock looked down at the officer and pointed toward the advancing rebel line. "Colonel, do you see those colors?"

The colonel looked in the direction Hancock was pointing and nodded.

"Then take them!" Hancock barked.

Henry Taylor's eyes darted from General Hancock to Colonel Colvill, to the approaching enemy line, and back to Colonel Colvill. His stomach tightened into a knot. He knew what the order meant. They all knew what it meant. The regiment was being sacrificed to gain time. No one could expect to come out of this unscathed. Henry closed his eyes. *Our luck has finally run out.*

Colonel Colvill drew his sword and saluted General Hancock, then turned to glance again at the advancing rebel line as his shoulders slumped. Straightening, he turned again to face the regiment. "Who's going with me?" he asked quietly.

"I am!" Henry shouted. The whole regiment shouted the same in unison.

Colonel Colvill nodded and gave the order: "Fix, bayonets… forward, double quick."

In the front of the line, a pink plume sprayed from Captain Muller's head. He collapsed without a sound. Henry had seen enough battle casualties to know that Muller was dead before he hit the ground.

The regiment lurched forward at Colvill's command and moved down the slope, gathering speed as it went. Henry was aware of little except the yelling and the zipping of bullets past his ears. Men fell around him, cut down by concentrated rifle from the brigade to their front. Shells exploded overhead as rebel artillery got their range. The gap separating them from the rebel line rapidly shrank as the howling mass ran down the hill. They were going so fast now that Henry knew he couldn't stop even if he wanted to. The rebel line to their front hesitated, then turned and crashed back through the swale to the safety of the second line. Screaming in triumph, the First Minnesota pushed through the brush to face the second line about thirty yards away. Both sides discharged their rifles in an awful crash, and those in Henry's regiment still standing retreated to the comparative safety of the brush and boulders.

Henry looked around quickly. This had all happened so quickly, he needed to regain his bearings. Beyond the swale, the enemy line had stopped, unable to move forward. His own men were very few in number. A soldier near him stood up to take aim and was instantly shot, falling next to Henry with a thud. "Take cover, men," Henry shouted. "They can't come in and get us, but they can shoot us if we show ourselves." He glanced quickly around the terrain, fading in the dusk. *There can't be more than a quarter of an hour left before it's completely dark. If we're lucky, we will be able to hold on until then.*

A bullet whined off a boulder next to him. Henry looked to his left to see flashes coming from the Union side of the swale. He suddenly realized that the rebs were working their way around their line, surrounding them. Maybe darkness wouldn't come soon enough.

Hancock briefly watched the First Minnesota charge. When he saw the enemy's first line hesitate, he knew the charge would succeed in at least slowing down the advance. They had bought him some time, but he was not out of the woods. He quickly looked around for more reinforcements.

Humphreys's division was there, drawn up in a thin line, companies where regiments should have been. They would be enough, Hancock judged. *There are only a few minutes of light left. If the First Minnesota fails and the enemy still comes on, then Humphreys has enough strength to stop them. If need be, we will counterattack in the dark to drive them off this ridge.*

His eyes followed Humphreys's line toward the north. Between the end of Humphreys's line and Gibbon's left flank, there was a gap of about three hundred yards. Hancock stared through the smoke and gloom toward the west. There was another rebel brigade advancing past the large white barn of the Codori farm. It was headed straight toward the gap.

Hancock spurred toward the gap, looking for any possible troops he could use to plug it. There were none. As he reached the gap, one of his aides rode up, trailed by another officer.

"General," called the aide, "I've brought you a regiment from the First Corps! This is Colonel Randall."

Hancock looked the colonel over. *He looks ready. He will have to do.* "Colonel, the enemy are pressing me hard and have captured that battery yonder," he shouted, pointing toward the Codori farm. "They are dragging it from the field. Can you retake it?"

The colonel set his jaw. "I can, and damn quick, too, if you will let me!"

Hancock smiled. That was the attitude he wanted to hear. "Well, Colonel, you can try, but you will have to get through that brigade coming at us."

The colonel grinned and rode back toward his advancing column to bring them into line.

Hancock looked toward his aide. "Any more reinforcements?"

"Yes, sir," the aide replied. "General Doubleday said he would follow with the rest of Standard's brigade. They should be here any minute."

Hancock nodded and looked back toward the advancing Confederate line. *It will be very tight. They had better get here soon, or we are finished!*

George Meade pulled his horse up short and scanned the ridge-line. *There is a gap here. This is why Hancock asked for reinforcements.* He looked down to the far side of the ridge. There was no sign of any reinforcements. Meade had been shuffling troops around for hours, trying to hold on after Sickles's move created a huge gap in his previously strong defensive line. *They were holding, though. These boys were fighting their best battle ever.* Meade sighed. *That's the danger of shifting units around, though. Sooner or later you will create a gap that you can't fill.* In the gloom, he spotted an enemy formation moving toward the gap he was in.

He looked again back toward Cemetery Hill. *The First Corps must have received my orders to come up in support. Where are they?* Another glance toward the enemy. *They are definitely coming toward us.* The brigades on the left and right of the gap opened up with a crash of rifle fire, tearing holes in the advancing Confederates, but the line closed up and continued to advance. Meade scowled. *They are coming right at this gap. They can't be stopped.* He looked again for the First Corps. *Still no sign of it. If the enemy gets here first, they will split us in half.*

Meade lowered his head and slouched in despair. *Is this the way it ends after all this fighting? To be broken in two in the last few minutes of daylight? Is this the end of the battle and our country as well?*

The enemy line kept coming, despite the pounding it was taking. Meade straightened in his saddle. *I will do my duty like every other soldier.* He looked at the distance separating the enemy from the gap. *There will be a time when a group of horsemen, charging that line, could cause it to pause and lose its concentration,* he told himself. *That will give the units on the flanks more time to pour fire in and maybe enough time for the First Corps to get here. We will all be killed, of course.* Meade slowly drew his sword. Behind him, his staff did the same.

Meade thought about his staff. *Good men, all. Hope they are prepared for this.* He felt a quick sense of panic. *George—is he behind me?* Meade remembered he was off on an errand. *Good. He will be spared to comfort his mother. I'm sorry, Margaret. I'm sorry that it had to end this way. God, forgive me, but I cannot run away from death after asking my men to stand toe to toe with it!*

Meade felt at peace. He waited as the line came closer and closer. *Soon it will be time! How much extra time will a dead major general gain? They will all have to stop and gawk. Maybe ten minutes? Will that be enough time?*

An aide coughed nervously behind him. The din of battle engulfed him.

"Look, there they come, General!" an aide shouted.

Meade looked to his right. A long column of blue was moving at the double-quick toward him, with General Newton in the lead. *The First Corps—they made it! We made it!*

Newton pulled up next to him. "What are your orders, General?"

Meade pointed toward the rebel line, now no more than one hundred yards away. "Drive those people back across the Emmitsburg Road!"

Newton nodded and barked orders to an aide. He then pulled a flask from his pocket. "Care for a libation, General?"

Meade grinned. "Yes, that would be wonderful." He took a mouthful from the flask. A shell exploded nearby in the ground, showering the pair with dirt. He couldn't care less, though. This was something to celebrate.

A crash to his left caught his attention. A line had formed in the gap while he was waiting. This line, probably a regiment, had just fired a volley.

With a loud hurrah, they lowered their bayonets and charged the enemy line.

Newton's skirmishers came up as the rest of the line advanced. Meade pulled off his hat and pointed it at the rebel line, which hesitated as it reached Gibbon's line. "Come on, gentlemen!" he called, and spurred his horse toward the enemy line, following the skirmishers. After a brief hesitation, the rebel line broke and ran back toward the Emmitsburg Road.

Hancock watched Randall's regiment go in. *They timed that perfectly!* He followed the line as it swept down the slope after the retreating rebels. To his right, some of Gibbon's troops were counterattacking as well.

About halfway down the slope, he found the regiment had paused to collect a large group of prisoners. Randall was trying to get the group organized. "Don't worry about these prisoners, Colonel," Hancock called out. "I will take care of them for you. Just go on ahead!"

The colonel saluted, and the regiment plunged after the fleeing enemy.

A loud hurrah rose from the ridge behind him. Turning, Hancock saw Humphreys's division, still defiant, charging down the slope toward the Emmitsburg Road. Hancock smiled. All around him, the Union line was counterattacking. His eyes filled with tears. He had never seen anything more beautiful in his life.

Meade watched the blue lines charge into the semidarkness and sighed in relief. They had done it. His staff and commanders of nearby units joined him to watch the flashing lights of the counterattack, pushing the enemy back toward the Emmitsburg Road.

"Well, General Meade, things did look pretty desperate for a while," one of the group said.

Meade nodded. "Yes, but it is all right now. It is all right now."

Chapter 15

Evening of July 2, 1863

HANCOCK WATCHED THE MUZZLE FLASHES sparkle in the distance along the Emmitsburg Road. The counterattack had driven the rebels out beyond the road, and he had ordered his units to set their picket lines and return to the ridge. As the pickets took their positions and brushed with the rebels engaged in the same task, a little jostling was expected.

"General Hancock, we have a report from General Caldwell." Gibbon was beside him.

"OK." He sighed. "Let me have it."

"Caldwell reports he has reformed to the east of the ridge along the Taneytown Road. His division has sustained very heavy casualties, including many senior officers." Gibbon hesitated.

"Yes, go on," Hancock said impatiently.

"All but one of the brigade commanders were wounded. Cross is said to be near death. Zook is also mortally wounded. Brooke was wounded but is expected to recover."

"Cross..." Hancock struggled to form the question.

"The report states that Cross was wounded in the abdomen while leading his men forward. The surgeon declared the wound mortal as soon as he saw it."

Hancock nodded, his eyes watering. "He knew he was to die. He told me as much as he marched his brigade off."

Gibbon shook his head. "It's hard to explain. Sometimes men are granted a glimpse of the future in order to prepare themselves for the inevitable." He touched Hancock's arm. "He was a good man, Win, I'm sorry. I know you thought highly of him."

Hancock murmured an answer and hung his head. *They can't keep dying like this—all the best ones.* A boom of cannon and the crash of concentrated rifle fire made him snap his head upright. "Where is that coming from?"

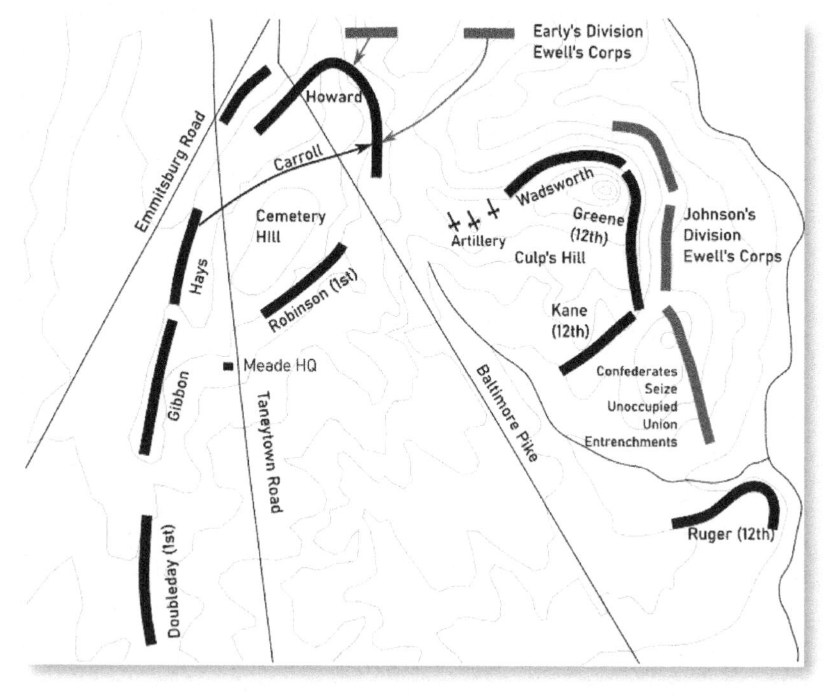

SITUATION—CEMETERY HILL EVENING OF 2 JULY

Gibbon cocked an ear. "Over on the other side of the hill. The Eleventh Corps, I think."

Hancock listened for a moment and nodded in agreement. "That's a full-scale attack. We have taken the First Corps away from them. They have no support. If they don't hold, there will be no one to stop the rebs."

Gibbon made a face. "Based on the Eleventh Corps' performance so far, there is a high probability that they will not hold."

The roar became louder, more insistent. Hancock thought for a moment. "We had better send someone over there." He paused again to consider the best man for this assignment. Of all the brigades in the Second Corps, only two had not seen action earlier. The vision of the fiery red-haired commander of Hays's first brigade flashed into his mind. "Better send Carroll," he said.

Gibbon turned and began shouting orders. Hancock swung up onto his saddle and turned his horse. "Gibbon," he called out, "I'm going to find General Meade. We need to get this line in order before the rebs attack again!"

Henry Taylor stepped gingerly in the direction of the ridge. The ground was littered with dead and wounded, and Henry could barely see anything in the dark. Somewhere, up ahead, the regiment was reforming on the colors. They had remained in position in the swale as the counterattack drove the rebels back. Only then did the orders come to fall back.

"First Minnesota, fall in here!" a voice called insistently.

Henry followed the shouts to their source and found a small group of men milling about. "E Company?" he shouted.

"Over here," came a voice.

Henry worked his way over to the voice and found several privates standing alone. "Is this all there is of E Company?" Henry asked.

"So far," came the voice.

As they waited, a few more figures wandered in. Henry looked at the small group huddled together in the darkness and counted heads. There were two corporals and five privates. *My God, eight of us! Is this all that is left? And where are Lieutenant Demarest and the first sergeant? Am I the ranking man?* He swallowed hard at the thought of being in command.

"Is this E Company?" a strange voice inquired, and a dark form moved closer.

"Yes, E Company," Henry replied.

"This is Captain Messik, G Company," the dark form said. "I am the ranking officer left in the regiment. Who is in command here?"

Henry swallowed again. *In command…such a strange concept.* "That would be me, sir…so far. This is Sergeant Taylor."

"OK, Sergeant Taylor, here is what we are going to do. We have not received any orders, so we will wait here for a while and give the rest of the regiment a chance to assemble. In the meantime, I need a few volunteers from your company to help with the wounded. Oh, I need your strength report as soon as possible."

"Captain," Henry said, "right now E Company has eight men. How many do you reckon the whole regiment has now?"

"At this time, assembled around the colors, probably no more than forty or fifty. I don't know how many more are going to show up, so that number may go up a bit."

"And what was our strength when we started?"

Captain Messik paused. "As I remember the adjutant's report, we had somewhere around two hundred and sixty present for duty this morning. That's not counting the provost guard detail and other details, though."

Henry paused, stunned. "We lost over two hundred men in a quarter of an hour?"

The captain was silent, perhaps considering this terrible truth. "Here's what we need to do, Sergeant Taylor," Messik replied, changing the subject. "Send out as many people as possible to help with the wounded. I must go tell the other companies." Messik moved off, leaving Henry in silence.

Henry turned to his small company, the size of a squad. When asked, they all wanted to go help with the wounded. Henry left several to guard the equipment and led the others back down the slope toward the dead and wounded.

The procedure developed quickly and naturally, born out of the experience on other battlefields. On approaching a form, a member of the group would ask, "First Minnesota?" If the form responded, they would ask for name and company and how badly they were wounded. In some cases, the wound was mortal and the unfortunate had only a few minutes to live. Several men were left to take down the man's last words and collect personal effects to be sent home. If the wounded man was capable of being moved, two men would lift him onto a stretcher made from blankets and rifles and carry him up over to the far side of the ridge, where a large stone barn was being used as a hospital.

Down in the swale, Henry approached a form. He called out the question "First Minnesota?"

"Yes, here," came the response. Henry could tell the voice belonged to Colonel Colvill. "Who are you?" Colvill asked as Henry knelt over him.

"Sergeant Taylor, sir, E Company," Henry said. "Where are you wounded?"

"They got me in the shoulder and ankle," Colvill rasped, "I can't walk."

"Don't you worry, Colonel, we will get you out of here." Henry called for Private Cundy, who was nearby. Together, they lifted the colonel onto the stretcher and carried him toward the hospital.

They carried the stretcher mostly in silence, except for the moans from Colvill when they jostled the stretcher while stepping over uneven ground. Finally, the colonel spoke. "How many are left, Sergeant?"

"Can't really say, sir. It was too dark to get a count," Henry lied.

Colvill persisted. "What about your unit, E Company?"

"Last count was eight, sir, but I expect more to show up."

"And what was your strength when you started?"

Henry paused to think. "Somewhere around forty, sir—officers and men."

"My God." Colvill sighed. "Who's in command, Captain Muller still?"

"That would be me, sir. Captain Muller is dead, I saw him go down. Lieutenant Demarest is missing." Henry hesitated before he spoke again. "Just lay still, sir. You need to conserve your strength. There will be time to ask questions once the surgeon has seen you."

After more than an hour's work, they had collected up all the wounded they could find. The whole regiment, exhausted and near collapse, gathered around the colors. As they lay on the ridge, waiting for orders, Henry moved around the small group, asking about Isaac. Corporal Austin said he had seen Isaac just after the order to fall back. No one had seen him afterward or taken him off as wounded. Henry returned to his meager company and collapsed onto the grass. "Isaac, where are you?" he whispered. "Have you wandered off somewhere?" Finally, realization hit him. *Isaac's dead. Otherwise he would be here or among the wounded.* Fatigue and grief overcame him, and he wept silently in the darkness.

Rustling around him caused him to look up. Captain Messik came by. "Fall in, boys. We've been ordered to take up defensive positions."

The regiment clambered to its feet and fell in to line.

George Meade stood outside his headquarters and looked toward the north and Howard's Eleventh Corps positions. Flashes illuminated the crest, and the crashing of gunfire volleys confirmed significant action in that area. *What Lee is up to, launching an attack on my right so late?* he wondered.

"General Meade!" a voice called out. Meade could tell instantly that it was Hancock.

"Yes, General Hancock," he replied.

"The enemy has attacked Howard's position. I have sent Carrol's brigade to reinforce."

"Yes, I already ordered General Newton to return General Robinson's division to his previous reserve position behind Howard. That should be sufficient in case Howard needs more assistance than just Carrol's brigade." Meade stopped to consider the situation. "It does seem odd, though, that Lee would launch an attack so late. I mean, even if they did achieve success, it would be too late to follow up on it."

"Perhaps it's a supporting attack that got started way too late?" Hancock said. "That and the attack on Culp's Hill at the same time we were attacked on our left would have seriously impacted our ability to reinforce the left."

"Yes, I suppose, so." Meade cocked an ear toward the north. "It sounds like the firing is tapering off." The pair listened to the sound for several minutes, and then Meade said, "Yes, it is definitely falling off." In a few more minutes, the firing receded to intermittent popping. A little while later, the popping ended, leaving an eerie quiet. Meade shook his head. He still didn't understand the reason for that attack.

"We need to take this opportunity to rebalance our lines," Hancock said. "Today's action has created quite a jumble."

"I agree," Meade said. "I have already ordered the Twelfth Corps back to their positions on the right. Please coordinate with Gibbon and Birney to ensure that we have adequate coverage all along our lines. The enemy most probably will attack us again tomorrow."

"I will take care of it," Hancock said. He turned his horse and rode off.

Meade walked away from his headquarters and headed up the hill toward the crest of Cemetery Ridge. The rising full moon provided sufficient light for his steps. Once on the ridge, he could see the campfires of the enemy on the far ridge. To his front lay the dead and wounded of the day's action. The moans and cries of the wounded were nearly unbearable. Lanterns illuminated the Ambulance Corps orderlies making their way among the prostrate forms.

Meade bowed his head in prayer. *Dear God, they have fought so hard today. I am afraid, though, that they will have to fight another day. Lee is not yet through. Give them strength, Lord. Give these men strength to fight another day.* Meade looked again toward the rebel line. *What will you do tomorrow, General Lee? What is the logical thing to do?* A picture of the rebel line surging toward the gap flashed in his mind. *That's it! Lee has attacked both flanks of our army today, causing us to weaken the center. His commanders have no doubt told him of the lack of troops on this ridge. He will attack here tomorrow. That is the logical thing to do. He will expect victory, but we will be ready.* Meade turned and walked back to his headquarters. There was much to do to get ready for tomorrow. He needed a little time to think through this concept of an attack on his center. As he walked slowly back, he turned the thought over and over in his mind.

Warren and Hunt were on the porch when he arrived. Warren wore a bandage on his neck. "Warren, have you been wounded?" Meade asked.

"Yes, but only slightly. The ball nicked me, just enough to draw blood."

Meade examined his friend. Warren looked a little pale but otherwise seemed fit. He nodded. "OK. Please take care of it."

He drew both men together. "I believe that Lee will try our center tomorrow. He has tried both flanks today and was unsuccessful. The center is stretched thin and he knows it, so he will try to break us in half at the weakest point."

The two generals thought about this idea. Warren was the first to respond. "Wouldn't a turning movement be the more logical alternative for Lee? We are vulnerable to a turning movement on both flanks, especially the left now that Longstreet's corps is so far to the south."

Meade shook his head. "No, Lee has suffered a serious setback today and will be eager to set it right. He will try to force a decision tomorrow; he is far from his base and can't afford to wait too long. Lee must have a victory tomorrow, or he must consider retreat."

Hunt and Warren considered his arguments and finally nodded in agreement. "Shall we strongly reinforce the line?" Warren asked. "If we place artillery hub to hub on that ridge, we will blow them apart if they try to attack."

"No," Hunt said. "That might cause Lee to call off an attack."

"I agree," Meade said. "We do not want to discourage them from attacking our center. Of all the options Lee has, it is the one most favorable to us." He waited for agreement from the pair. "The Second Corps is there and in a very favorable position," he said. "With preparation, the positions can be made very strong. Warren, coordinate with Hancock and Gibbon to have fieldworks constructed along their line."

Warren made a face. "The infantry is limited in pioneer equipment, General Meade. Most of it is in the supply trains back in Westminster."

"Well." Meade sighed. "Have them do the best they can. Any prepared position will increase our advantage."

"What about the artillery, General?" Hunt asked.

"You are the expert, Henry. What would you advise?"

Hunt thought for a while before answering. "Lee will precede his assault with a strong cannonade. We must have sufficient cannon on the ridge to answer this. The main objective of our artillery during this artillery assault must be to knock as many of the enemy pieces out of action as possible. This will reduce the enemy's ability to support the infantry during the assault."

Meade nodded. "This cannonade will no doubt be very hard on the batteries engaging the enemy. If their fire is effective, it will force the enemy to concentrate on your artillery instead of the infantry. General Hunt, you must have batteries ready to replace those on the ridge as they are rendered ineffective. We must have sufficient firepower available when the enemy infantry begins its assault."

"I will form the replacement batteries behind the ridge," Hunt said. "They will be ready to move where needed while remaining invisible to the enemy."

"Good," Meade said. "Now, Warren, we must find positions for our reserves that will allow us to respond quickly to any enemy breakthrough. We should not assume that the enemy will only attack us in the center. The dispositions should allow reinforcement of any part of the line. Please reconnoiter positions behind the ridge and give me your recommendations."

Hunt and Warren nodded and departed to begin their tasks.

Major Ludlow appeared at the doorway of the headquarters. "Is there anything I can help you with, sir?"

Halleck, Meade thought. *I haven't reported to them today. They must be frantic for news!* Meade had heard stories of President Lincoln sleeping at the telegraph office, waiting on any reports from the front. "Yes, Major. I need to send a telegraph to General Halleck. Can you take down a message?"

"Certainly, sir." Ludlow pulled a small notebook out of his pocket.

"The enemy attacked me about four p.m. this day, and after one of the severest contests of the war, was repulsed at all points," Meade said. "We have suffered considerably in killed and wounded. General Zook was killed, and General Sickles, Barlow, and Graham, were wounded. Oh, and General Warren was slightly wounded. We have taken a large number of prisoners." Meade paused to consider what he should say about his plans. "I shall remain in my present position tomorrow," he said, "but I am not prepared to say, until better advised of the condition of the army, whether my operations will be of an offensive or defensive character." He looked at Ludlow, who was finishing writing. "Got all that?" Ludlow nodded. "Clean it up a bit and send it out as soon as possible." Ludlow turned to leave. "One more thing, Ludlow," Meade said. "Send word to all my commanders to meet me here at this headquarters as soon as possible."

Meade watched Ludlow depart and sat back to wait for the arrival of his subordinates.

Hancock and Gibbon arrived first. Meade brightened as they entered the room. "Come in, gentlemen. The rest of the group should be along shortly."

The room was small and sparsely furnished. A large bed occupied one corner, and a small table with half a dozen rush-bottomed chairs sat in the center of the room. A wooden pail with a tin drinking cup adorned the table, and a single candle stuck to the table created dancing shadows on the walls. It was soon filled; every chair and the bed were occupied. The air in the room quickly became clouded with cigar smoke.

As the last arrival found a place, Meade looked around the room and began. "I sent a message to General Halleck earlier this evening. I reported our success in resisting the enemy's attack today, and I told him we would remain in this position tomorrow. Whether our operations tomorrow will be offensive or defensive in nature, I could not tell him. This all depends on the situation of the army. I have called you together to discuss the condition of the army and our general situation. General Butterfield, could you poll the group as to present for duty strength?"

Butterfield quickly tallied up the numbers given to him by each corps commander. He looked up at Meade with the answer. "Fifty-eight thousand, not counting the artillery and cavalry."

"Fifty-eight thousand?" Meade repeated. "That's nearly thirty thousand less than when we started the battle two days ago!"

"We must remember," Hancock said, "that not all this thirty thousand are casualties. We will, no doubt, be able to reduce this number as units reform. Besides, I believe that the enemy has suffered as well. They have maintained the offensive for two days of heavy fighting, and they are probably in a similar condition as our army."

Meade nodded and looked around the room. "What do the rest of you think?"

General Newton was the first to answer. "I can't speak much as to the casualties today, but the First Corps suffered heavy casualties yesterday. We are certainly in no condition to engage in any offensive operation."

"The Third Corps is in much the same situation," Birney said. "We were pushed back from our forward line by overwhelming enemy forces and lost nearly a third of our strength in the struggle and the subsequent withdrawal. I consider the Third Corps used up and not ready for any further action. I am not sure we can even stay and fight it out."

"Well, the Eleventh Corps also suffered heavy casualties," Howard said. "But this is a good position, and we should make our stand here, heavy casualties or no."

Meade nodded. *Good. That's the spirit!* "What about the Second Corps, General Gibbon?"

Gibbon cleared his throat. "Aside from Caldwell's division and Willard's brigade of the Third Division, which we reckon both suffered between thirty and fifty percent casualties, the corps is in pretty good shape for defensive operations. In my opinion, though, it is in no condition to attack."

Meade pondered that for a moment. *They suffered more heavily than I imagined. Perhaps an offensive move is out of the question.* He shifted his questioning to Sykes. "How did the Fifth Corps fare down on the left, General Sykes?"

"We held that hill at all hazards, General, as you ordered." He turned around to look at the group. "Where is Warren?"

The group turned to Warren, asleep on the bed. He was overcome from the day's exertion and loss of blood from his wound. Sykes shrugged. "I wanted to tell everyone about what he did on that hill. His actions saved the position. I have no doubt about that."

"What do you mean, George?" Hancock asked.

"Just this. Before my troops reached the area, General Warren was on the hill. He found that there were no troops on the hill, and it was not certain if there were enemy troops in the woods to his southwest. One of his aides, Lieutenant Roebling, told me about this. Warren had a cannon fire over the woods and watched for any flashes from the woods. As the round went over, the rebel infantry turned, and the sun flashed off their weapons. That way, Warren knew the rebs were in the woods in force. He went down and found the lead brigade of Barnes' division, Colonel Vincent's brigade, and rushed it up the hill. They arrived just a few minutes before the rebs. A few minutes later and we would have lost the hill."

"Certainly was a tremendous bit of luck!" Meade exclaimed.

"Well, there's more," Sykes said. "The rebs worked around Vincent's left and right flanks. The left flank was handled very well by the Twentieth Maine. They managed to extend their line and contain the rebs. The right flank was exposed on the western face of the hill and took a tremendous beating. As the rebs overlapped their flank, they were not able to compensate for it because of their losses. Colonel Vincent tried to rally his right but was mortally wounded in the process. At this point General Warren saw the danger and rode back down to find reinforcements. He found a regiment of Weed's brigade, the Hundred and Fortieth New York, and brought them up on his own authority. The New Yorkers came over the hill just as the rebs were coming up the other side. They held off the attack and drove it back across the valley, losing their commander, Colonel O'Rorke, in the process. Weed brought the rest of his brigade up the hill and extended the line. Weed was later killed by a sniper." Sykes paused, overcome with emotion.

"Take your time, George," Meade said.

Sykes straightened. "No, I'll finish my report. The other half of the left flank was held by General Ward's and Colonel de Trobriand's brigades of the Third Corps. They held on for a long time against vastly superior enemy forces but began to run out of ammunition. General Caldwell's division of the Second Corps came up, and I ordered them in to relieve the Third Corps brigades. For some reason, General Caldwell sent his brigades in piecemeal, and they were driven back in succession. I was finally forced to send in General Ayres's regulars to support Caldwell. The Third Corps line collapsed near the peach orchard, and our line was flanked and rolled up. Ayres's boys took a real pounding, but they withdrew steadily under fire. I finally ordered Crawford's Pennsylvania Reserves to counterattack. This drove the rebels back across Plum Run and finally stabilized our position." He stopped and sighed. "We are in a good defensive position, but two of my three divisions have taken heavy casualties. I don't think we can participate in any offensive action."

Meade looked to General Williams of the Twelfth Corps, who spoke up. "My corps is in good shape. They have engaged in some action, but it has not been too severe. I do worry about rations, though. My men are starting to run out. We left our wagon trains back in Westminster, and the boys only have what they carried in their knapsacks."

Several voices agreed with Williams.

"Is it possible," Meade asked, "to supplement the rations on hand with cattle and flour obtained from local farmers?"

"I think that is possible, at least for a while," Williams said.

"We could probably eke out a few half-fed days and stay here," said Slocum.

"Well I, for one, think this is no place to fight a battle," Newton boldly said.

The group, including Meade, looked at Newton with surprise. He was respected by all of them as an experienced soldier and engineer. "What makes you say that?" Gibbon asked.

"Our left," Newton said, "is exposed to an enveloping movement, which Lee can attempt by shifting a whole corps secretly at night while still occupying the present lines. That is exactly what I expect them to do. Lee would not possibly be fool enough to attack our front after two days of fighting that has only resulted in our consolidating into a very strong position."

"I agree that is a danger," Meade said. "We do have cavalry screening to our south now, and any envelopment would be detected. Still, such a move would flank us out of this position. If we are forced back, it might allow us to take up a position that would be much straighter and require fewer men to occupy. This current position is very irregular. We could establish a line from Wolf's Hill along the east bank of Rock Creek, just several miles to the east of here."

"Would it not be better to retire to the Pipe Creek line in light of the deficiencies in this present position and our lack of supplies?" someone suggested.

Several voices responded at once to this suggestion, both pro and con. The discussion went on for several minutes. Meade glanced at Butterfield. He had been fidgeting previously but now was writing furiously.

Butterfield finally looked up. "Ahem. General Meade, may I make a suggestion?"

"Yes, go ahead," Meade said.

"It seems to me that there are three basic issues we must resolve. I have taken the liberty of writing these issues down as I see them." He waited for a nod from Meade and then continued. "The first issue is, considering the existing conditions, should the army remain in its present position, or should it retire to another one closer to its base of supplies?"

"OK," Meade said. "What's the second?"

"If the army remains in its present position, shall the army attack or wait for the attack of the enemy?"

The group nodded in agreement. "Go on," Meade said.

"Finally, if we wait for the attack, how long shall we wait?"

Meade smiled. *A very logical analysis.* He turned to the group. "Are there any comments?"

"General," Butterfield said, "I believe it is time to call the question. It's getting quite late. In the interest of time, we should take a vote on the issues right now."

Meade hesitated. *Why is a vote needed? Didn't we answer these questions already? Why should there be any confusion? Still, if I don't allow a vote, will some claim later that their counsel* was *ignored? Is there any harm in taking a vote? I do value their opinion, after all.* He nodded to Butterfield. "Please proceed."

Butterfield smiled and asked the first question: stay or retreat. Hancock was the first to respond. "Let us have no more retreats! We should stay here and fight it out!" Murmurs of assent followed. The group voted unanimously to stay, with some expressing a desire to correct the position of the army.

The second question was asked. All votes were to await an attack by the enemy.

The third question, how long to wait, evoked more diverse answers. The general agreement was that the army couldn't wait more than a day for the enemy to attack.

Meade considered the answers. *They do mirror my own thoughts. I didn't know the army had taken such a beating in the past two days. Given this, an attack is out of the question. This is a strong position. Why should we withdraw? Let Lee come after us. We have the upper hand, the central position. React to his moves; he must be desperate. Let him make the mistake and react to it.* Meade looked at the group and nodded. "Such then is the decision."

The meeting broke up, and Meade moved toward Gibbon. He had not had a long conversation with the younger officer for a long time. "Gibbon, I'm glad you were able to attend the meeting. I want you to be ready. If Lee attacks tomorrow, he will attack in your front."

"Why do you say that, General Meade?" Gibbon asked.

"Because he has tried both of our flanks and was unsuccessful. He will try the center, which is logically weakened."

"Well if he does, General Meade, we will whip him!" Gibbon nodded good evening and left the room.

Newton approached Meade as the group was breaking up. "General Meade, I think you ought to feel much gratified with today's results."

Meade was stunned. "In the name of common sense, Newton, why?"

Newton smiled and said, "They have hammered us into a solid position they cannot possibly whip us out of."

Hancock walked glumly away from Meade's headquarters, his eyes on the ground. He couldn't get Sykes's report out of his head. *My division, driven from the field. I can't believe it!*

A person moved close to him. "You OK, Win?" It was John Newton who was two years his senior at West Point. They had known each other since they were young men.

Hancock shook his head. "Yeah, I'm OK."

"You don't look OK. What's bothering you?"

Hancock sighed and stopped walking. "It's my division—or, rather, Caldwell's division now. You heard what Sykes said. They didn't do well today."

"I didn't hear that at all, Win. What I heard was that the line was pushed back by overwhelming numbers and by the collapse of the Third Corps line to the west."

"I should have been there, John. The first time I wasn't with them since Antietam. If I had been there today, maybe I could have saved some of them. Maybe they could have done better."

Newton shook his head, barely visible in the feeble light from the cottage. "You can't blame yourself; you can't be expected to do everything. How does that saying go—'sometimes the biggest danger is in the duty of another,' or something like that."

"Yes." Hancock nodded. "You're right, but I can't help thinking that I could have done more. I just sent them off and let them go without direction."

"Well, Win, we will no doubt get another chance tomorrow." Newton shifted a bit and called to another form. "General Gibbon, could we see you a moment?"

Gibbon came up, and the three men stood in the near dark. "I heard Meade tell you he thought the attack will fall on you tomorrow."

"That's right," Gibbon said. "I don't know what to think of it, though. You presented a very strong argument that Lee will try to envelop our left flank."

"I do believe an envelopment is the most logical course of action for the enemy. However, a frontal attack is certainly not out of the question."

"I believe Meade is right," Hancock said. "By now, Lee's officers must have told him how bare the ridge was this afternoon. He must know it is our weak spot. He will be drawn to it, like a wolf to blood."

"If that is so, the Second Corps will have some hard fighting to do tomorrow."

Hancock clenched his teeth. "When they come, we will be ready for them." He called for an aide. "Send word to all commanders to begin entrenching at first light. Be prepared for an enemy assault on our front."

"Do you gentlemen have a place to sleep?" Newton asked.

They didn't. Time had not allowed for the preparation of such luxuries. Hancock considered the prospects of sleeping on the ground; he suddenly realized how tired he was.

"I have an ambulance at my headquarters, and there is room for the two of you. I intend to sleep there myself."

"Sleeping in an ambulance. Isn't that a bit morbid?" Gibbon asked. "And besides, there is something not quite right about a Virginian offering us a spot in an ambulance."

"Perhaps." Newton chuckled. "But I guarantee it is the best bed you will find on the battlefield."

The group, trailing their aides, made their way to the ambulance. After a few orders, they climbed in. Hancock lowered himself onto the stretcher. He felt a sudden chill but dismissed it. He was too tired to find another place to sleep.

The last aide with the last message finally left. Meade sighed and rubbed his eyes. He suddenly felt very tired. *I should be tired,* he told himself. *I haven't slept more than a total of four hours in the past three nights!* He rose from the table and shuffled to the bed. As he pulled off his boots and eased back onto the mattress, he thought of all the things they would have to do tomorrow. I'll take care of them all; I just need an hour of sleep.

"General Meade?" Hands shook him. It was the orderly on duty. "Sir, there is an urgent message here from General Slocum."

"What is it?" Meade asked groggily.

The corporal motioned an officer toward the bed. "Sir," the officer said, "General Slocum has forwarded a report from General Williams. When they returned to Culp's Hill, the Twelfth Corps found that their trenches to the south of the hill had been occupied by the enemy during their absence. General Greene still holds the hill itself, though. General Williams has requested approval to launch an attack at first light to regain his works. General Slocum has forwarded the request for your approval."

Meade nodded. "Tell General Slocum he has my permission to retake the works. He should not take unnecessary risks, though. I think we can do without those trenches if we have to."

The aide saluted and left. "Do you need anything, sir?" the orderly asked.

Meade shook his head. "Oh, yes, I do. I want to be awake when General Williams begins his attack. Please make sure I am awake about thirty minutes before first light." Meade lay back and closed his eyes.

The firing on his left was intense, but he could not see what was happening. Large trees blocked his view. Above the treetops, a huge column of smoke billowed toward the clouds. Cross led his brigade toward the smoke.

"Cross," Hancock cried, "I thought you were dying!"

Cross turned toward him and smiled. Then he motioned to his troops, and they moved off at the double-quick. Behind him was the Irish Brigade, its green flags snapping as they trotted after Cross's lead brigade.

"Stop. I need to come with you!" Hancock called after them. The troops appeared not to hear him.

"General, look to the front!" a voice called.

From the ridge to the front, line after line of gray troops marched toward him. The blue soldiers around him ran toward the battle on the right. Hancock looked around. He was alone. He tried to stop the troops from leaving, but he couldn't move. The rebel lines came closer and closer. A gray skirmisher rose up in front of him and pointed his rifle at Hancock. The rifle smoked and Hancock tried to yell...

He awoke with a start. His heart was pounding, and he was short of breath. Hancock looked around in the dark. He was in the ambulance, safe. Newton and Gibbon were snoring peacefully in the adjacent stretchers.

Hancock lay on his back and stared into the dark. Was this what Cross had experienced, why he had known he was going to die?

Chapter 16

Morning of July 3, 1863

The crash of batteries firing simultaneously caused the entire house to rattle. Meade woke with a start. Opening his eyes, he could tell it was past first light. "Damn," he said. "They didn't wake me up!" Pulling on his boots, he rushed out the door onto the porch. All his aides were waiting there.

"Why didn't you wake me as I ordered?" Meade demanded.

The aides exchanged glances. George, his son, took a half step forward. "We discussed this matter with Dr. Letterman. You had no sleep the night before and hardly two hours a night since you assumed command. We were all worried about your health, and Dr. Letterman agreed, so we decided that you should have some extra sleep...sir."

"Besides, sir," Ludlow said, "Generals Slocum and Williams are quite capable of planning and conducting this attack on their own. We would have let you know if there were any issues that came up."

Meade clenched his jaws, trying to check his anger. *They have a point,* he admitted. *I am of no use if I collapse from exhaustion. Still, I did leave explicit orders.* He looked his aides over. "Have my horse saddled," he snarled.

"It's already saddled, sir, and ready for you right here," Ludlow said.

Meade grunted and proceeded toward the horse. George was looking down with a sheepish look on his face. "Don't do that again," Meade ordered.

The group rode toward Slocum's headquarters in silence, Meade still seething. Major Biddle was the first to break the silence. "I heard from one of General Slocum's aides what his response was when he learned the rebs had taken our works." Biddle paused for effect and then continued. "He said, 'Hell, drive them out at daylight!' How about that?"

The group chuckled, and even Meade had to smile. *Good for you, Henry. That's the spirit!*

By the time they reached Slocum's headquarters, Meade was in a little better mood. Henry Slocum greeted Meade with a salute as the group arrived. "What do you have to report?" Meade called out.

"We began our attack at first light, as planned," Slocum said, "starting with a fifteen-minute artillery barrage. Our plan was to attack as soon as the barrage was finished. The rebs, however, attacked first. They appear to be concentrating on taking the crest of Culp's Hill. George Greene's brigade is up there. He has his boys dug in with well-prepared defenses. They fought off a series of attacks last night, and I'm sure they can do the same this morning. We will stay on the defensive for the time being, but I will order an attack as soon as I see an opportunity."

"That's good," Meade said. "Keep Greene well reinforced. As long as we hold that hill, the enemy can't advance." He considered the situation. "How about your right?"

"General Williams has his division ready to attack on the right."

"Meade considered this. "We should make sure his right flank is covered in case the enemy tries to get around it." Turning to his aides, he said, "Send word to General Pleasanton to have a cavalry force cover the Twelfth Corps' right."

Turning back to Slocum, Meade nodded a goodbye and said, "Keep me informed of what is going on. If you need reinforcements, I will send them to you. I'm off to check the disposition of the other corps." With that, he spurred his horse off toward the Eleventh Corps.

Reaching the crest, Meade could see the effects of the last evening's fight. It was as if a huge wave had crashed over the hill all the way up to the crest where the artillery was positioned and then had receded, leaving debris and flotsam of battle. Discarded weapons lay scattered about, and details of men were beginning to collect them and stack them in piles. The dead, both blue and gray, were being carried to rows for eventual burial. Meade looked away.

Near one of the artillery batteries, he found Major Osborn, the Eleventh Corps chief of artillery. "What happened here last night, Major?" he asked.

"We were attacked at nightfall, General," Osborn said. "The enemy was up on us before we saw them. They overran the infantry lines down at the base of the hill and made it all the way up to the guns. My gun crews had to fight them off with rammer poles and hand spikes. Fortunately, the Second Corps reinforcements showed up at the right time and drove the rebs back down the hill."

Meade grunted and scanned the Eleventh Corps infantry spread along the stone wall at the base of the hill. *My fears were confirmed,* he thought. Behind him, over the brow of the hill, he could hear the First Corps regiments preparing for the day.

Good. They're back in place. I'll have to keep them there. Can't afford to chance another Eleventh Corps rout. Turning back to Osborn, he asked, "Are your batteries ready for action?"

"They will be soon, sir," Osborn said. "We are working with General Hunt to get as many guns ready as possible."

"Good," Meade said. "I expect an attack soon. Make sure you are ready." He turned his horse and rode off toward the First Corps units.

Meade found the First Corps units, Robinson's division, massed and apparently ready to move. General Robinson acknowledged him with a salute. "We can hear the fight over at the Twelfth Corps. I got the boys formed up in case we are needed for reinforcements," Robinson said.

"Very good," Meade exclaimed. "Stay ready. They may need you." He shot a nervous glance toward Osborn's guns. "Keep an eye on the Eleventh Corps, though, and do not leave this position unoccupied without my personal orders." With that, he continued his ride along the western side of Cemetery Hill.

Here the line was occupied by the Second Corps. Meade noted with satisfaction that Hancock had his regiments hard at work entrenching their positions. Nearing a small clump of trees, he spotted Webb, now a brigadier general. "General Webb, I'm glad to see you here!" he called out. "If the enemy attacks, they will be coming right at you."

"We'll be ready for them, General!" Webb replied.

Hancock was nearby and rode toward him as he was speaking to Webb. "Good morning, General Meade," he called. "Do you still think the enemy will attack my line?"

"I do," Meade said. "But I do think that Newton may be right about an attack on our left. In either case, I believe we are prepared. The left is well reinforced, and I have ordered Sedgwick to have his reserves in a central position so that he can reinforce any part of the line as needed, especially your part of the line."

"Any ideas as to our next move if the enemy attack here on our center fails?"

Meade had thought about that possibility. "We are heavily weighted on our left with Sedgwick and Sykes there. In the event that the attempt to pierce our center fails, I will order the Fifth and Sixth Corps to attack on the left."

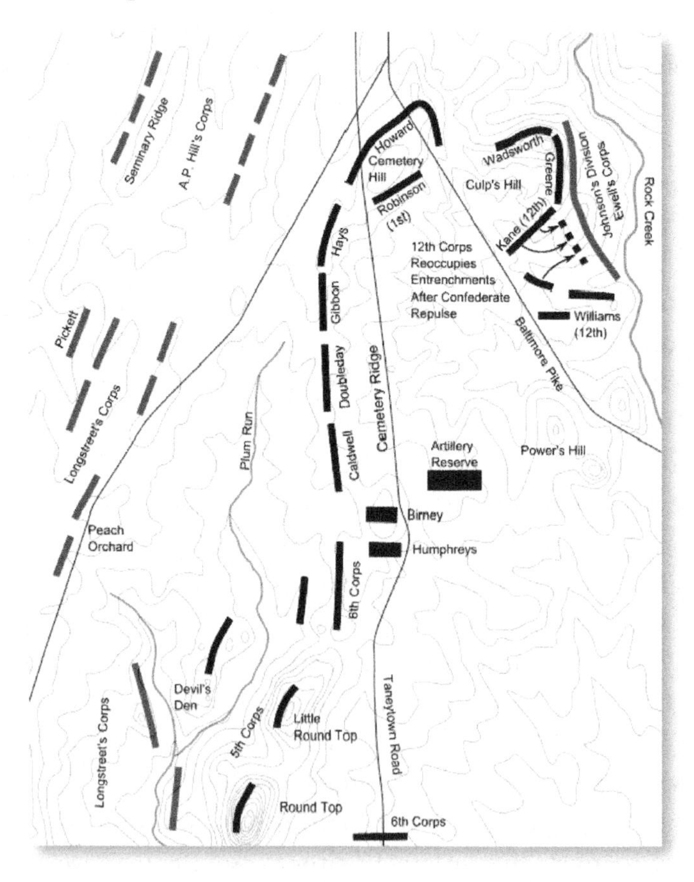

Situation—Morning of 3 July

"I like that idea," Hancock said, nodding. "They will no doubt drain forces from their right for the attack, and the center would be disorganized after a repulse. We could roll them up from the left!"

"Yes," Meade said. "We just need to make sure we repulse their attack."

Hancock slapped his gloved hands together. "Don't worry, General. We will stop them!"

Meade returned Hancock's salute and continued his ride. Doubleday's division of the First Corps was next in line, and Newton was waiting for him. "General Newton," he called. "What news this morning?"

Newton spread his arm out toward his forward line. "As you can see, General Meade, we are entrenching our line down here." He made a face. "I must tell you that I am concerned about how scattered my corps is. I have three divisions in three different places with three different missions. It does make commanding my corps quite difficult."

Meade held up his hand in acceptance. "I agree with you, Newton. John Sedgwick has the same problem with his corps. The chaos of yesterday has jumbled us all up. I would love to be able to move units around so that all commands are back together again, but I cannot chance it. If the enemy were to attack while we are moving units around, it would be a disaster. We will just have to make the best of it for now." Meade motioned with his head toward the south. "Who do you have on your left flank?"

"I'm not sure who is supposed to be down there. We have a gap of about a half a mile between my left flank and George Sykes's right flank. As far as I can tell, it is currently wide open."

A burst of continuous fire erupted from behind them in the direction of Culp's Hill. Meade jerked his head in the direction of the sound. "OK," he said, "coordinate with John Sedgwick, and get some troops from the Sixth Corps to plug that gap. I need to get back over to the right to see what is going on over there."

Henry Taylor rubbed his burning eyes. He had not slept all night. Not that he hadn't tried, but every time his head started to nod, a moan from the field to his front or the crack of a nervous picket's rifle jerked him awake, and his mind went back to worrying about his missing brother.

In the east, the sky was just starting to lighten, and Henry's eyes were growing heavy again. Suddenly, the sharp cracking of rifle fire and the booming of cannon split the gloom. His head snapped up, instantly alert, judging the direction of the sound. It was off to the right and behind them, from the area the locals called Culp's Hill. The sound continued to increase in intensity. *Something big is happening over there.*

A few heads popped up around him in response to the noise. Reassured that the attack was not directed toward them, they went back to sleep, at least for a little while. Soon, an officer came down the line announcing reveille. The scrap of a regiment stretched and yawned and scratched itself awake.

As dawn rushed toward them and the lightening sky allowed more of a view, Henry looked down toward the swale where they had bled and died the evening before. The lowest areas were still blanketed in mist. On the slope rising up from the mist, Henry could see dark forms, bodies, lying in grotesque positions. He looked away. *Oh, Isaac, where are you? Our luck really did run out yesterday!*

Henry did not have time to dwell on this for long. Captain Messick soon came down the line, telling company commanders to prepare breastworks in anticipation for an imminent enemy attack. The men did not need any instructions. They were veterans who knew how to build field fortifications. The problem was, though, that they were lacking entrenching equipment. It had all been left behind with the wagons as excess gear when they rushed to reach Gettysburg.

Henry sent a couple of members of his small company out to gather up brush, branches, and stones. They would pile them up along with fence rails in front of their position. The remainder he set to digging up the ground. Bayonets were used to clear the ground and loosen the soil. The men scooped up the dirt with tin mess plates and dumped it onto the wood and stone pile, filling the gaps with the soil. The few shovels that they had on hand were used to pry up stones, and there were plenty of stones in this soil. It was slow, hard work, but in a couple of hours, they had a mound several feet high. It was not much, but it was enough to stop bullets with the soldiers crouched behind it.

Captain Messick walked down the line with General Harrow, the brigade commander. After a brief conversation, the breastworks were proclaimed sufficient, and the men were given word to stop scraping up dirt. It was just as well; the sun was up above the trees, and the day was growing hotter by the minute. Henry wiped the sweat out of his eyes as Captain Messick ordered them to prepare for an inspection of their rifles and ammunition. They cleaned their weapons and refilled cartridge boxes. Some men had extra muskets they had collected from the battlefield, and Henry made them clean those as well. They would provide extra needed firepower in the first volley. With the regiment inspected, Captain Messick allowed the companies to start rotating men back to the rear in small numbers for coffee and a hot breakfast.

While he was waiting for his men to come back from breakfast, Henry looked out over the valley. He noticed that several men had been allowed to go back down to the swale, and he decided to ask Captain Messick for permission to go find Isaac. A clanking noise drew Henry's attention. A man was carrying coffee up to the officers, who would wait until all the men had been fed before they ate. Henry recognized the man; Snow was his name, from G Company; he was friends with Isaac. Private Snow delivered the coffee to Captain Messick and, after a brief conversation, turned toward Henry. He spotted Henry and acknowledged him with a quick lift of the chin.

Snow walked up the hill. "Sergeant Taylor, they told me you were looking for Isaac. I think I seen your brother."

Henry stared up at him. "Where…when?"

"Last night, I seen him get hit. I think he was killed."

Henry's heart sank. He looked at Snow dumbly.

"I can show you where the body is if you like."

Henry nodded and rose. They made their way to Captain Messick, who was sipping a cup of coffee. "Captain," Henry said, "Private Snow here thinks he knows where my brother's body is. Request permission to go down there with him and find the body."

Messick looked back with sad eyes and nodded. "If you find him, Sergeant, you have permission to take a small burial party down there to bury him. Just be back soon. And keep an eye on what is going on. We could have a reb attack at any time."

Henry saluted and mumbled his thanks. He followed Snow down to the swale with growing apprehension.

They approached the area where blue bodies littered the ground, and they walked through them nearly to the swale. Henry could not bear to look at them. Suddenly they stopped. "There he is, Sergeant," Snow said.

Henry followed Snow's gesture to a body lying on its side. Even from the back, he could tell it was Isaac. Henry swallowed and nodded.

Snow moved closer to the body. "Looks like he was hit in the top of the head by a piece of shell...came down and out his back. Look, it cut his belt in two."

Henry nodded, not able to look.

Snow put his hand on Henry's shoulder. "It wasn't such a bad way to go. Much better than most, I suppose. He probably didn't even know what hit him."

Henry finally found some words. "Thanks. I appreciate you bringing me down here. I couldn't stand not knowing." He approached Isaac, rolled him over, and quickly removed the contents of his pocket—a watch, his diary, a pocketknife, and his wallet. Henry straightened. "We'd better go back up. I need to find a shovel to bury him."

The pair silently walked back up the rise toward the Union lines. Henry found a spade and told the men gathered around about finding Isaac. Privates Brown and Cundy volunteered to come with him to help bury his brother.

Henry walked numbly back down to the swale, followed by Brown and Cundy.

They laid Isaac out in a proper fashion with his arms folded across his chest. Henry bent down to close Isaac's lifeless eyes. Cundy unfolded a shelter tent and covered Isaac with it.

Henry gazed down at the form cloaked by the canvas sheet: a soldier's burial shroud. "Well, Isaac, all I can offer you is a soldier's grave." He bent to pick up the shovel and began to scrape away the grass from the patch he would make Isaac's grave. He stopped, an incredible sadness gripping him. A sob escaped from his lips, then another. Soon, he was weeping uncontrollably.

His two comrades took him by either arm and led him gently to a low stone wall, where they sat him down and left him to weep. Cundy started to dig. Private Brown walked off but soon returned with a piece of board. "For Isaac's headboard," he said. Henry, in the fog of his grief, could only nod.

As the two privates took turns digging the grave in the rocky ground, Henry used his pocketknife to inscribe the headboard. He quickly carved Isaac's name, unit, and date of death on one side of the board, and then he sat looking at the result. There was something not right, but he couldn't figure it out. Then it hit him. *An epitaph—that's what's missing. I need to write you an epitaph, Isaac.* He flipped the board over, thought for a few minutes, and then began to carve the words of an epitaph:

No useless coffin enclosed his breast,
Nor in sheet nor in shroud we bound him,
But he lay like a warrior taking his rest,
With his shelter tent around him.

By the time Henry finished with the headboard, Cundy and Brown had finished digging Isaac's grave. It was only a shallow pit several feet deep, just large enough to accept the body's full height. They laid the shelter tent in the grave, lowered Isaac's body onto it, and folded the ends of the canvas over the corpse.

Henry held the headboard in place as his comrades filled the grave with dirt. He took the shovel and patted the earthen mound smooth, then took one last look at the grave. "Rest in peace, brother," he muttered.

Hancock rode toward the right of his line: Sandy Hays's division. To the west, a barn and farmhouse were aflame, sending plumes of black smoke high into the increasingly humid air. He came upon Hays, who was issuing instructions to aides. Hays looked and acknowledged him with a nod. Hancock motioned with his eyes toward the burning farm buildings.

"I ordered it burned," Hays said, responding to the silent question. "My skirmishers have been scrapping over it with the rebs all morning. It can't be held, and I've taken too many casualties over it already."

"Just as well," Hancock said. "If we have an attack on our lines, it would only restrict our fields of fire and provide a strongpoint for the enemy to support the attack. It's best to have it out of the way."

Hays grunted and cocked an eye toward Hancock. "An attack on our center—is that still the thinking?"

"Well, Meade certainly thinks so. It's either that or a run around our left flank."

"If they attack us here, we will be ready for them!" Hays exclaimed.

Turning his horse, Hancock prepared to leave. "I have no doubt of that. We will keep you informed of what is happening." He rode back down toward the left and Gibbon's division, where he had been invited to a meal hosted by Gibbon. Soon, the two generals were seated on stools under the shade of a small tree, with a mess chest serving as a table. Their staff, along with

General Newton and General Pleasonton sat cross-legged, holding their plates in their laps. Gibbon looked up to see General Meade riding by. "General Meade," he called out, "why don't you join us for lunch?"

Meade shook his head. "No thank you, General Gibbon. I have too much to do."

Gibbon would not hear of it. "General Meade, I insist. How long has it been since you have had anything to eat?"

Meade paused. "Sometime yesterday."

Gibbon nodded, satisfied. "General, you must keep up your strength. Please, join us; we have plenty to go around."

Meade murmured a grateful acceptance and slid off his horse. An orderly offered a wooden cracker box for his stool, and another orderly handed him a plate filled with stewed chicken.

After lunch, the generals retired to a nearby tree and lit cigars. Meade was the first to speak. "Newton, I've been thinking about what you said last night. It does make a great deal of sense. Lee always likes to try the flanks. He may well do it again today."

Newton nodded and looked at Pleasonton. "Any sign of movement to the south?"

Pleasonton shook his head vigorously. "None whatsoever. I have patrols out as far west and south as possible, in light of what you said last night, General Newton. There is no sign of any rebel movement."

"Well," Meade said, "that means the attack will come somewhere along our left: from here on down to the Round Tops. We can only wait for the enemy to show their hand. I think we are prepared for an attack wherever it comes."

The commander of the provost guards came by, an infantry captain in his dress uniform. Hancock and Meade watched the officer. Meade was the first to speak. "You know, Gibbon, the coming battle will no doubt involve some very desperate fighting. These provost guards are good men, and it is better to have them in the ranks firing rifles than trying to round up stragglers who would not be much use in the ranks anyway. Why don't you send them back to their regiment, temporarily, until the attack is over?"

Gibbon nodded and motioned to the captain. "Captain, did you hear that?"

The captain nodded. "Yes, sir, I did."

"You are released, then, to go back to your regiment. First Minnesota, isn't it?"

"Yes, sir, First Minnesota. Very well, sir." The captain saluted and left to round up his company.

The conversation continued for a while, with Meade growing more anxious until he finally rose. "Gentlemen, I must take my leave," he said. "The enemy may well show their intentions, and I must be in a position to see it." He mounted his horse and rode over to General Hays's positions. The rebel lines were the closest there, but he could not see much. The burning buildings and the smoke obscured much of what lay beyond. Meade turned his horse and trotted off toward Little Round Top. As they rode to the south, they were approached by a rider with red artillery piping on his uniform. *One of Henry Hunt's lads,* Meade thought.

"Sir, General Hunt reports that the enemy artillery is massing on the ridgeline opposite us," the orderly called as he pulled up.

Meade shot a quick glance toward the west. He could see artillery unlimbering along the ridgeline. "Let's go!" he called to his aides as he spurred his horse to a gallop. When they reached Little Round Top, the horses had to be left to the rear of the crest, and the men walked the rest of the way, climbing up the steep slope. General Hunt was on the top of a large rock, observing the activity on Seminary Ridge with his field glasses. "What do you see over there?" Meade asked, scrambling up onto the rock next to Hunt.

"They are lining up battery after battery out there, all facing toward our center," Hunt replied, not interrupting his surveillance of the enemy line.

"Hmm," Meade said. "Your thoughts on what this means?"

Hunt lowered his field glasses. "I can think of two scenarios. The first is that they are planning a move around our left flank and will use the artillery to protect their denuded center."

"And the second?" Meade asked.

"The second is that they are planning to blow hell out of our center with the artillery and then follow it up with a massed infantry attack."

"Will our artillery be able to counter this?"

"We spent all last night reconstituting our batteries and refilling gun chests. I personally checked the condition of all the batteries this morning. We have enough ammunition to effectively respond to the enemy artillery barrage, but we cannot waste it in useless cannonades. As we spoke last evening, General Meade, I believe we should carefully ration our ammunition so that we have enough to use on the infantry when it advances toward our line. I have instructed the batteries not to fire for fifteen to twenty minutes after the enemy batteries begin firing. They are instructed to then concentrate fire on a specific battery, with the objective of knocking it out of action. After achieving this, they will shift fire to the next battery. This will have the effect of conserving our ammunition while reducing the number of pieces the enemy can utilize for the support of the infantry assault."

"Good!" Meade exclaimed. "I agree with that plan."

Hunt motioned toward the crest of the hill. "Warren is up there; perhaps he has some ideas as to the enemy's plans."

Meade found General Warren on the summit, with his small band of aides. They had a large tripod-mounted telescope trained in a northwesterly direction toward the enemy lines on Seminary Ridge.

"Ah, General Meade," Warren said. "There is something that you should see." He motioned to the telescope.

Meade stooped and looked through the eyepiece. He saw the wood line along Seminary Ridge, magnified many times. Between the trees, he saw rows of gray figures. "Infantry?" he guessed.

"That's right," Warren said. "At least a division. We have been watching them file in to position for nearly twenty minutes."

Meade paused to consider this information. "Then they mean to attack the ridge, Hancock's sector," he said. Meade whirled to his aide. "Go find General Hancock. Tell him I will be at my headquarters, and I want to see him right away." He turned to Warren. "Stay up here and give me reports on what is happening. We may expect the attack at any time." He paused for a moment and then continued. "If the enemy does attack and we repel them, we should be prepared to counterattack. Have the Fifth and Sixth Corps prepare plans for a joint counterattack here on the left flank." Meade remounted and galloped back toward his headquarters.

Henry Taylor sat a few yards behind the earthworks, his weapon cradled in his lap. Around him, his men lay about, trying to sleep in the late-morning heat. He looked out toward the swale and Isaac's grave. The field in front of him was littered with equipment and dead bodies. He thought again about Isaac. *Your men need you. Got to snap out of it,* he told himself.

Henry noticed that the battle noise from the right was much less intense than earlier in the morning. They had almost become used to it, so the gradual reduction was hardly noticeable. The firing tapered off to scattered popping, then stopped completely. An eerie silence hung over the battlefield. The men around Henry, alerted by the sudden silence, sat up and looked at one another. *Have the rebs broken through?* Henry asked himself.

Cheering began over on the right and rose in volume. "They did it," Henry said, realizing the significance. "They beat off the rebs!"

The elation was short lived, though. Once the cheering ended, the regiment settled back down to dozing in the sun. Henry glanced up at the sun in the near-cloudless sky. *Only going to get hotter,* he told himself.

Corporal Austin broke the silence. "We found Lieutenant Demarest last night. He was badly wounded in the hip. I hope he makes it!"

"Hope so too!" Henry replied. "I understand First Sergeant Trevor was killed."

"Jock McKenzie was wounded too...legs, I think. He is not doing well."

"I seen Beer Keg last night," Cundy said. "He was wounded in the foot. Some boys from B Company were helping him."

Henry nodded sadly. He and Cundy had seen Private Berry on their way back to the hospital with Colonel Colvill. Berry had been wounded in the foot but was making his way back on his own. *Such a great sacrifice. I hope it's all worth it!*

Chapter 17

Afternoon of July 3, 1863

Henry Taylor let out a soft groan as he slowly shifted to his other side. You never got used to lying on the hard ground. He had to be careful not to disturb those dozing in the heat around him. More importantly, though, he had to minimize his exertion in the broiling sun. Holding his cap out, he squinted at the sun. *It has to be at least noon. Good God, it's hot!* He shifted to look over the earthworks toward the rebels. There was nothing going on, as far as he could see. *It's all up to the rebs,* he decided. We *will just have to wait for them to make a move.*

"What're the rebs up to, Henry?" Corporal Austin eyed him from beneath a pulled-down cap.

"Nothin'," Henry murmured. "They've got to be just as hot as us."

"Well, at least they got shade over there."

"Yeah." Henry closed his eyes. Talking was too much effort. Sweat ran down his forehead and into his eyes. His shirt was soaked. *It's too damn hot!*

The thump and rattle of marching men disturbed him somewhat, but he was too hot to look.

"It's C Company," Austin said.

Henry lifted his cap an inch and turned his head slightly to see. A column of men had halted about ten yards away; Captain Messick was in conference with another captain, the C Company commander.

"Thought you boys had provost guard," the talkative Corporal Austin said.

"General Gibbon released us. Said we were needed more back here. Said to expect an attack at any time," a sergeant answered. He looked slowly around at the pitiful remains of the regiment. "Is this all that's left? We heard you took some heavy casualties, but *damn*, where's the rest of the regiment?"

No one answered for the longest time. Finally, Austin spoke up. "They're either in the hospital or buried out there." He waved a finger toward the swale.

The men of C Company somberly spread out to form a second line. *Good*, Henry thought. *We can sure use a reserve line.* With the arrival of C Company, the regiment's strength had nearly doubled.

The regiment resumed its silent sweltering in the midday sun. Henry was too tired to grieve for Isaac. He slowly drifted toward sleep. A cannon's boom jerked his eyes open. A second boom raised him up. Instantly, the entire rebel line exploded in massed artillery. Shells screamed overhead, exploding all along the ridge. The regiment scrambled toward the meager safety of the earthworks.

Henry huddled behind the small pile of dirt and wood with the rest of the regiment. *Well*, he told himself, *the rebs have finally decided to make a move.* He had forgotten all about the heat.

Hancock and Meade looked up from the map they were studying and listened to the cannon fire. Explosions came one after another in rapid succession. "That's pretty heavy fire," Hancock said. "They must be using all their guns."

Meade cocked an ear and listened. "Yes," he said. "This is it. They're coming at you, General Hancock!" A shell whistled overhead and exploded in a field beyond the Taneytown Road.

"I'd better get up there and see what's going on," Hancock said. He moved to his horse and swung up into his saddle.

Meade reached for the horse's reins and moved closer. "General Hancock, you must hold at all costs. I will send whatever reinforcements you need. We are in a very good position to support you. Let General Hunt know if you need any more artillery, and he will supply it from the Artillery Reserve." Meade squinted up at him. "Lee must be about finished. If we can hold off this attack, I think we probably will have him beat. You have to hold on!"

Hancock drew himself up and cracked a wry smile. "You're talking about the Second Corps, General Meade. We *will* hold that position." As he saluted, Meade released the reins. Hancock spurred his horse toward the ridge.

He had already decided where he would go. Brooke's brigade occupied a position on the left of his line. From there, he could get a much better view of the entire rebel line. From Gibbon's position, the Codori farm buildings blocked a portion of the line.

Brooke, though wounded, was there to greet Hancock when he rode up. Hancock painfully noted the thin lines of Brooke's brigade. "Get ready, Brooke," Hancock called out. "The enemy will be advancing soon."

The men, huddled behind the breastworks, raised their heads to look at him.

Brooke nodded. "We're ready, General. When the rebs come, we will give them a very warm reception."

Hancock grinned and pulled out his field glasses. He could see the rebel artillery, or at least the smoke and flame, quite well. Every piece they had was blazing away as fast as the gun crews could load them. Strange, though—he couldn't see any effect of return fire from the Union batteries. Hancock lowered his field glasses and looked at the batteries to his left. They were not firing. To the north, farther up the ridge, his own corps artillery was not firing either.

Enraged, he spurred his horse over to the nearest battery. Colonel McGilvery was there. "Colonel," Hancock bellowed, "why in hell aren't you firing back?"

"General Hunt's orders, sir. We are to hold fire for at least fifteen minutes and then return fire slowly, concentrating on destroying enemy pieces."

"Goddamn it!" Hancock shouted. "How in hell does he expect my men to stand up to this bombardment when our own guns do not even fire back? Colonel, I am ordering you to start returning fire and at a rate that matches the enemy."

McGilvery hesitated "With all due respect, General, I am in the Artillery Reserve and I report to General Hunt, the chief of artillery. I must take my orders from him."

"Fine!" Hancock whirled and pointed at an aide. "Get up there and order all Second Corps artillery batteries to return fire immediately."

Hancock fumed as he left the silent battery. *What does some artillery general know about how infantrymen think? It's idiotic to expect men to lie under this fire with no sign of resistance from their own side.*

Up along the ridge, his men were facing the full fury of the rebel artillery. The air was full of white puffs of exploding shell and case. Solid shot made huge geysers of dirt as they struck the ridge. Hancock noted that it was all directed toward his corps, his men. *Maybe Meade was right,* he thought. *Maybe they are coming at us. If they are, it will be at my boys. They cannot flinch at this time, not when everything is in the balance. If they break under this artillery barrage, the whole position will be lost. I must show them there is nothing to fear. If am to die today, this must be it.* Hancock reined his horse toward the north and rode along the front of Brooke's lines.

He was suddenly aware of his aides following close behind him and turned to look at them. *It will be dangerous up there, probably deadly. No reason for them to die as well.* With a few words, he sent them all off on errands, and he was soon alone with only Private Wells, the corps standard bearer. He sighed. The corps standard must accompany him—there was no other way. "You ready for this, Wells?"

The stocky Irishman shifted in his saddle and nodded. "Yes saar, oy am."

"Let's go, then." Hancock pressed his knees together and the horse moved forward. After only a short distance, several nearby explosions startled his horse. It reared its head and stopped. Hancock nudged the horse forward. The sorrel would not move. "Come on, dammit!" He used his spurs, and still the horse would not budge.

"He's spooked for sure, Gin'ral," Private Wells said. "Funny ting, he's always been steady under fire befahr."

Hancock grimaced and dug the spurs in even harder without any response from the horse. It was as if the horse knew what was waiting for them both up there on the ridge. Hancock swore. If he couldn't get the horse moving, he would not be able to keep up the spirits of his men. He was also keenly aware of all the eyes on him at this moment.

"Would you care to borrow my horse, General?"

Hancock looked hopefully in the direction of the voice. A young captain was holding out the reins of a tall, light-colored bay with a white patch on its face. "Yes, that's very generous of you, Captain," he said with relief. Hancock traded reins with the young officer and swung up onto the bay. It was a strong horse with no signs of fear, and it moved off immediately when Hancock pressed his knees together.

The two men resumed their ride along the breastworks toward the clump of trees that marked the center of Gibbon's division, the corps standard fluttering behind them. A regimental band began playing. Hancock's chest swelled as he heard the first few notes of the "Star Spangled Banner." He pulled off his hat and waved it as he rode in front of the earthworks, smiling at his men and calling to his officers.

Many of those officers were stunned and horrified to see him riding through the middle of the barrage. Hancock ignored those looks. *This is what I have to do,* he told himself.

Harrow, one of Gibbon's brigadiers, ran up to him. "General, it is too dangerous to remain mounted. You are too exposed, sir. A corps commander should not risk his life this way!"

Hancock shook his head. It was not about him; it was about the men and the cause. He was asking them to stand firm even though it might mean sudden death, and he was prepared to show them that he would do the same. "There are times when a corps commander's life does not count," he told Harrow. Hancock turned from the brigadier and rode on.

The explosions and screaming shells compounded by the roaring cannon behind them created a mind-numbing din. Henry Taylor pressed his face into the musty dirt of the breastwork and prayed for the firing to stop. They were exposed and could not move from their position—not to advance on the enemy, and not to retreat out of the direct line of fire. Even the wounded could not be moved back without risk of being killed. They could only lie behind the breastwork, knowing that at any time one of these screaming shells could reach out and touch them with the white-hot finger of death. *Just like Isaac,* Henry thought.

Someone elbowed him on the arm. Henry turned to look. Corporal Austin motioned with his head and said something.

"What?" Henry shouted. The noise was so great, he could hear nothing.

Austin moved his lips close to Henry's ear. "Look, over there. It's Hancock!"

Henry looked to his left and caught his breath. Hancock, followed by an orderly carrying the Second Corps standard, rode slowly toward them from the south. Despite the howling and whirring projectiles and constant explosions, Hancock rode on, seemingly unconcerned, smiling and waving at his troops.

Henry cheered with the rest of his regiment, yet he watched with half-dread as Hancock rode by. It was impossible to believe that anyone could ride through this storm of steel and not be struck down, yet Hancock still rode, straight and calm as if he were reviewing his troops.

Henry blinked back tears. He was proud of that man and proud of the whole Second Corps. The barrage suddenly didn't seem quite so important anymore!

Meade looked at his watch and frowned. It was after two o'clock. The enemy barrage had lasted nearly an hour, and there was still no sign of a letup. To make matters worse, the shelling had nearly destroyed his headquarters, and he had been forced to move its location twice. General Butterfield was slightly wounded in the barrage and had left to be treated. Meade felt weary, with a vague gnawing sense that he was out of touch, too far away from the action.

"I'm going up to Cemetery Hill," he said and rode off toward the Baltimore Pike. As he rode past the cemetery gate, Meade could see that the Eleventh Corps was not in any danger. The men lay behind the stone walls, watching for any sign of enemy movement. The barrage was not directed here, and officers walked about with little regard for what was happening only a few hundred yards away on the other side of the hill.

Meade turned his horse and rode through the cemetery and over the crest of the hill. What he saw was beyond imagination. Exploding shells blanketed the entire length of Cemetery Ridge. Meade's heart sank. How could anyone hope to stand up to this terrible beating? He grimly pulled his field glasses out and scanned the position to judge the extent of the damage.

Things were much better than he could have hoped. The infantry lay motionless behind their stone and earth fieldworks, but they appeared relatively unaffected by the fury. The artillery batteries, on the other hand, were taking the full weight of the enemy's barrage. Wrecked caissons, dismounted cannon, wounded horses writhing and kicking in agony, and dead and wounded men scattered around their pieces testified to the intensity of the attack.

Meade watched the barrage for a while. Many of the rebel shells missed the ridge entirely and exploded in the fields behind the ridge. He could see a pattern in the shelling: it was clear that the enemy was targeting Gibbon's division. Meade spotted General Newton surrounded by a group of officers and rode toward them.

Newton spotted him as he rode up. "General Meade," he called, "you should see this. The enemy is concentrating their fire on the area around that clump of trees."

"That's Gibbon's division," Meade said. "The rebels may not realize it, but they are telling us exactly where they intend to attack."

"That's my opinion also." Newton motioned to an aide with a map, who held it up. "When this cannonade ends, we will have a brief time to adjust our troops before the enemy infantry attacks. I have some ideas on how we might adjust our deployment, if you would care to look."

"Yes, I would!" Meade dismounted and moved to the map. It was a copy of the map Captain Paine had made two days ago, updated with the latest troop deployments.

"The way you have us deployed right now is just right," Newton said. "In my opinion, we are in very good shape to react to any breakthrough. With Birney down behind the southern part of the ridge and two divisions of my corps behind the northern end of the ridge, we can move quickly to counterattack any penetration on both flanks. Now that we know where the enemy will attack, we can optimize our defensive arrangements."

Meade stroked his beard. "What do you have in mind?"

"When the enemy attacks, they will no doubt do it on a wide front to mask the actual point of attack. General Hays's right flank is connected to General Steinwehr's division of the Eleventh Corps. That flank is, uh, vulnerable, shall we say. I suggest we move one of my divisions, Robinson's, forward to protect

Hays's flank. I would position Robinson far enough back to allow them to participate in the counterattack if needed."

"An excellent suggestion," Meade said. "How about some support for Gibbon? We should back his second line up with another line."

Newton hesitated. "That would require three good-sized regiments. I'm not sure if the First Corps has any of those left. Stannard's brigade fits the bill, but they are already down on the line south of General Gibbon. We certainly have a chopped-up line."

"Can't be helped," Meade replied. "Looks like the regiments should come from the Third Corps. I don't want to weaken Robinson's division." Meade considered the options. "Right," he said. "I will notify General Birney to send those reinforcements."

Newton nodded and looked back at the map. "You know, I believe Birney should move the rest of his corps behind the left of Gibbon's division. That will shorten the response time for a counterattack."

"Agreed, and I will have Shaler's brigade from the Sixth Corps back up Birney. Shaler was over at Culp's Hill this morning. I ordered him to reinforce you, but with Birney supplying those regiments, he could use some help. As soon as this barrage lifts, they will be able to move into position." Meade studied the map some more, then said, "I think we are ready for them. Let them come on."

Several horsemen arrived—Hunt and his staff. "General Hunt," Meade called out, "the Second Corps batteries are badly battered."

"Yes, General Meade," Hunt said. "I know. I have ordered three batteries up from the Artillery Reserve to replace the ones rendered out of action."

"Excellent!" Meade clapped his hands together. "When the enemy infantry comes out, I want to have plenty of artillery to welcome them."

The roaring had continued for so long that they were strangely becoming accustomed to it. Hancock looked at his watch and then toward Gibbon. "It's been nearly an hour and fifteen minutes and no sign of a letup. I have never seen anything like this in all my years in the army. Tell me, Gibbon; you're an old artillerist. What do you make of this extremely long and intense bombardment?"

Gibbon rubbed his stubbled chin and squinted into the smoky haze. "Artillery theory gives two cases where you would use a sustained heavy bombardment. The first is to break up enemy infantry positions before an attack. The second is to mask a retreat." He looked at Hancock. "I believe in this case it is the latter. Lee will most certainly withdraw—he is probably doing it right now."

Hancock was stunned. "Withdraw? Everyone else expects the rebs to attack. What is your logic?"

Gibbon offered a wry smile. "Lee can't possibly hope to successfully attack this position in the center. It's over a mile of open ground, and we would rip him apart. Any attack would be suicide. Besides, the rebel artillery isn't concentrating on our infantry. Most of the rounds are passing overhead. If they were planning an attack, I would think that the artillery would take care to aim so that every round would hit the mark."

Hancock was unsure. "Well, rebel artillery is notorious for firing high."

"True," Gibbon said. "But they can't be this inaccurate. It looks like they are not even taking time to aim—just firing as fast as they can. That's why I think they are masking a retreat."

"You may have a point, Gibbon. The infantry has taken few casualties, despite the heavy shelling." Hancock raised his field glasses. The rebel positions were shrouded by smoke. "We can't afford to be wrong about this, Gibbon."

Gibbon nodded slowly. "I know. If they are in fact retreating, we must make ready to advance to catch them before they get away."

"And if they are preparing to attack," Hancock said, "we must be ready for them. We cannot do both, and doing the wrong thing will bring disaster. That is the dilemma."

The two watched in silence for a few minutes. Finally, Hancock spoke. "If we could spot infantry massing in the woods behind the rebel artillery, then we could be sure that the rebs are planning to attack. By this time, there should not be any large bodies of infantry there if Lee is withdrawing."

"Agreed," Gibbon said. "But how can we do that? You can't see a thing through the smoke."

"Well." Hancock slapped his hat against his thigh. "I'm going down to Brooke's position. Maybe I can see more from down there. If not, I'll try the Little Round Top." He mounted and rode down the crest toward Caldwell's division.

The view from Caldwell's division was not any better. Here McGilvery's cannon were in front of the infantry, and thick clouds of smoke from these batteries blocked the view. Hancock noticed some of the artillery officers dropping to the ground after every shot to see the effect of the fire. If he could only get lower, he would have a better view. That meant riding farther down the slope.

As he rode down to the end of the batteries, the ridge fell off sharply. The view here was slightly better, but a farmhouse perhaps one hundred yards beyond the left flank of the batteries and somewhat forward promised a much better view. Hancock and his staff galloped out to it.

An aide handed him a telescope, and Hancock scanned the wood lines to his front. There they were—lines of gray spilling out of the woods, hugging the ground. This was no withdrawal. They were clearly going to attack.

Hancock handed the telescope back and looked down and then up at his aides. *This is it, then.* "Gentlemen," he said, "after this artillery fire is over, it will be followed by an infantry attack upon our lines. This battle is the turning point of the war. If we win this fight, the war is practically over." He looked down at his gloved hands and then back at his officers. "We cannot tell where any of us may be when this day is over. Before leaving you, I wish to say that I speak harshly sometimes. If I have at any time ever said anything to offend or hurt the feelings of any one of you, I wish now to offer an apology."

"Why don't they just attack?" Meade growled with frustration. "It's been near an hour and a half, and they're still banging away as hard as ever!" He looked around at Slocum and his staff. Sustained fire had forced him to abandon his headquarters for Slocum's headquarters on the right of the line.

General Slocum stroked a well-manicured mustache in thought and shrugged. Though a West Point graduate, Slocum had left the army to become a successful lawyer. Careful and correct, Slocum was somewhat lacking in military experience—like most of the volunteer generals in the army.

After considering the matter for a while, Slocum offered an opinion. "Perhaps the enemy is working around our flanks and using the cannonade to keep us distracted."

"Well, that might be possible," Meade said. "But I have placed cavalry out as a screen on both flanks. In addition, I instructed the signal stations on all the hills to keep a lookout for any movement. If the enemy was moving, we should have received some reports. We have received nothing."

"Well, that does seem to rule that out," Slocum said.

Meade looked directly at Slocum. "You know, I do want Lee to attack. We have the best position possible, and we can make him pay dearly for such a rash move."

"A repulse now, after yesterday's failure and the losses sustained here on the right, would be a very severe setback to the rebels."

"That's correct," Meade said. "Lee will not be able to remain in this exposed position for long after such losses. He will be forced to withdraw, and when he does, we will have our victory."

Slocum, the lawyer, was quickly back to the point. "So how do we induce General Lee to rashly attack our position?"

"I only wish I knew the answer to that question." Meade shook his head slowly.

One of Slocum's aides approached and excused himself—he had a message from Warren.

Slocum gave him a questioning glance, and Meade said, "Warren is at the signal station on Little Round Top. I told him to report anything he considered significant." He turned to the aide. "Go ahead with the message."

The aide held up the slip of paper and began to read. "Our fire does not appear to be having much effect on the enemy artillery. It is only filling the valley with smoke, which will help to conceal the enemy infantry when they advance. Recommend you cease fire to induce the enemy to do the same. Warren."

"Cease fire?" Slocum asked. "How can you do that? Wouldn't it expose the artillery and infantry to enemy fire without the consolation of return fire? After ninety minutes of pounding, who knows what that would do to morale?"

Meade did not answer immediately. He was considering Warren's advice. Further firing would only deplete his long-range ammunition and make it more difficult to counter the attack when it came. "No," he finally answered. "I think the troops will be all right. Besides, the enemy must be worried about their ammunition, just as we are."

"So you think that the rebs will stop firing if we do?" Slocum asked.

"Yes. At least I hope so." Meade took off his glasses and rubbed his eyes. "If we're lucky, this might prompt them to launch the attack."

"Then we would have the result we are hoping for," Slocum said.

"Yes, we would." Meade motioned to his aides. "Go find General Hunt. Tell him to order all batteries to cease fire. We will try to get the enemy to stop firing and draw out the attack."

Hancock watched as one of Meade's aides raced across the ridge on horseback. The aide spotted him and quickly rode over. "Have you seen General Hunt, sir? I have an urgent message for him from General Meade."

"Not for a while," Hancock replied. "If I do see him, shall I give him the message?"

"Yes, sir, tell him that General Meade directs all batteries to cease firing in order to draw out the rebel attack."

"Very well. I will let General Hunt know."

The aide raced off, and Hancock considered this new order. There was no sign of the enemy stopping. *What would compel them to stop if we were to stop?* Hancock was skeptical, but these were the orders. He motioned to an aide to spread the word among the Second Corps artillery batteries.

One by one, the federal batteries fell silent. Exhausted cannoneers fell panting to the ground among their dead and wounded comrades.

Still, the rebel cannons continued to fire at a furious pace. Hancock paced nervously as minutes passed with no sign of any slackening in the enemy's fire. Now he was sure this wasn't such a good idea. He called for Captain Hazard, his corps chief of artillery. As Hazard rode up, Hancock checked his troops. They were huddled behind their works, still showing few effects from the long bombardment.

To his left, Brown's battery slowly limbered up, the task accomplished by the handful of artillerists remaining standing. The battery slowly pulled out, leaving dead and wounded men and wrecked equipment strewn about.

Hancock watched the battery leave. They were too badly damaged to remain in position. A shell exploded nearby. The rebels were still firing. *Perhaps I should send to Meade for permission to resume the firing,* he told himself.

Captain Hazard interrupted his thoughts. "Sir, I think the enemy fire is easing up."

Hancock cocked an ear and listened to the firing. In a few minutes he could tell that Hazard was right. "Yes," Hancock said. "The tempo is decreasing."

"You wanted me, sir?" Hazard asked.

"Hmm, it's not important now." Hancock looked back over the wreckage of his corps' artillery. "Captain, make sure the batteries are ready. The rebs will be coming soon." He waved Hazard off and turned to locate his horse.

By the time he found his horse, the firing had stopped completely. It was an eerie silence, broken only by the groaning of the wounded men. There was still too much smoke in the valley to see what the rebs were up to, but Hancock knew what was coming. There wasn't much time to get ready either. He quickly mounted and surveyed the ridge.

A battery clattered up to replace Brown's shattered battery, their sleek black barrels glistening in the sun. Hancock frowned: they were ordnance rifles, small, light, and accurate but firing smaller projectiles. They would not be able to fire as much canister the heavier Parrott and Napoleon cannon could.

"Why do you bring those guns?" he shouted as he rode up to the battery commander. "I don't want those popguns! Tell General Hunt to send me some Napoleon guns."

The officer reddened at this insult to his guns, hesitated, and turned to stop his rapidly deploying guns.

"Stop," Hancock barked. "I will see General Hunt myself." The battery was here, and he might as well use it.

Hancock rode south along the ridge. He found General Hunt with a battery commander peering into a caisson. They were discussing how much long-range ammunition was left.

"General Hunt," Hancock called out, "I have come for some artillery support. My batteries have been badly damaged during this bombardment, and I need some more batteries."

"I am bringing batteries up as quickly as possible to support you. They have been ordered up and are on their way."

"These batteries, General—I need heavy guns, Napoleons. We need to hit the rebs with a wall of canister when they get within range. You have sent up a battery of ordnance rifles. Those are no good against infantry."

"You also need longer-range guns to take the enemy under fire when they emerge from the woods, General Hancock. Napoleons would be firing at maximum range. Ordnance rifles will be more accurate at that longer range."

"But when the enemy comes in close, we need the firepower of the Napoleons," Hancock said.

"I will send you Napoleons, General. They are on their way."

There was a shout, and both men turned toward the west. A breeze had blown the smoke away, and they could see the woods along Seminary Ridge, just emerging from the woods, northwest of the Codori farm, was a long line of gray infantry.

"Get them in place quickly, General Hunt," Hancock said. "We are going to need every gun we can get."

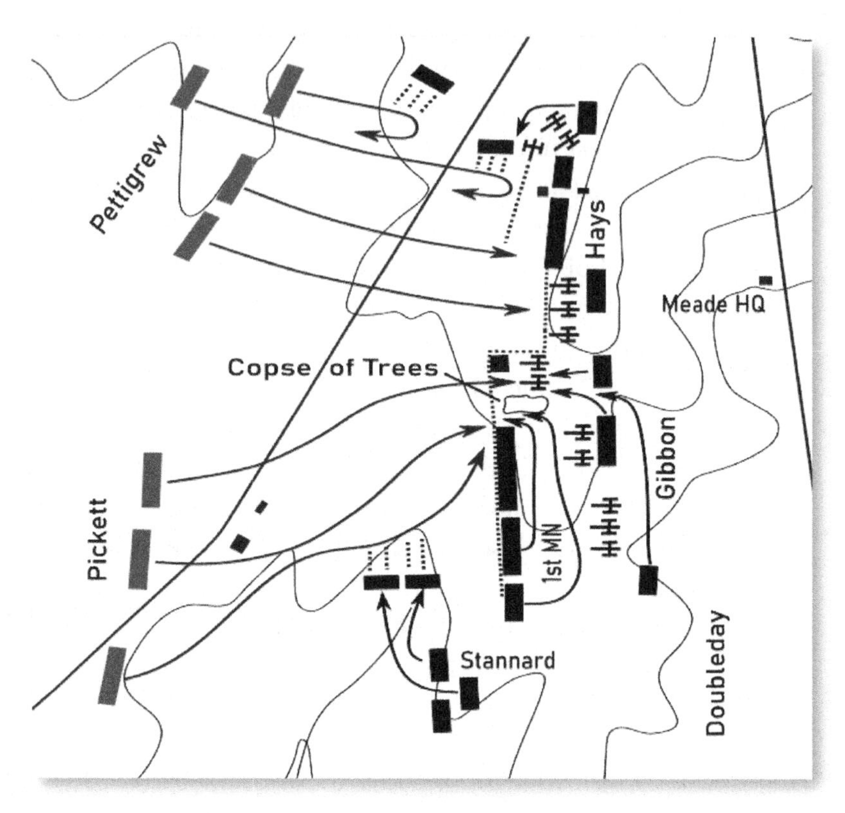

CONFEDERATE ASSAULT—AFTERNOON 3 JULY

As the last Confederate shell whistled past and a profound silence set in, Henry raised his head and looked at his men. All of them were uninjured. Henry shook his head—his ears were still ringing from the near two-hour pounding.

"Thank God it's over," someone nearby said.

"Just wait and see what's coming," Henry said.

The men raised their heads to look over the breastwork. A slight wind picked up and caught the flags as they were unfurled. Every pair of eyes strained to make out the wood line across the valley. As the wind blew the smoke away, the woods grew more distinct.

"Here they come," a voice yelled.

Henry could see a line of skirmishers advancing through the haze and behind them, stepping through the tall wheat, long lines of gray infantry. Red flags flapped as the lines moved forward. Henry watched in awe as the enemy advanced. He had never seen anything like it.

On the ridge, there was no sound. They were all veterans and knew what was coming and what was needed to get ready. Men slid their cap boxes around to the front of their bodies and opened cartridge boxes. Every little thing was done to make loading faster. Hammers clicked as nervous fingers pushed them back to feel for caps. All else was silence and waiting, each man alone with his thoughts and fears.

Guns opened up as the enemy line emerged fully from the wood line. The batteries down on Little Round Top were the first to fire. Greater elevation gave them an unobstructed view of the rebels. Shells exploded in white puffs above the gray lines. Even at a mile's distance, Henry could see that the shells were doing great damage. Gaps opened as each shell burst, only to be dosed quickly as the enemy soldiers moved rapidly to maintain a solid line.

General Gibbon rode past them, as nonchalant as if they were on a drill field. "Don't hurry, men, and fire too quickly. Let them come up close before you fire, and then aim low and steady." He repeated this advice as he progressed down the line.

Henry set his jaw and nodded. *Good advice—always worth repeating.* He grasped his weapon a little tighter. They all knew what to do, and they certainly had a score to repay. He harbored a fleeting thought of Isaac covered with the shroud.

The rebel line reached a swale near the Emmitsburg Road, and the batteries on Little Round Top slackened their fire. Henry guessed the enemy was slightly concealed from these batteries by the swale. The gray line paused and straightened itself—dressing and closing gaps, as if on parade. With the lines perfect once more, they stepped off.

As the line reached the Emmitsburg Road, it executed a left oblique movement and headed off at a forty-five degree angle from the original direction of march.

Henry caught his breath in hope. *Maybe they are headed for Cemetery Hill. Maybe they won't attack us.*

This movement presented the batteries farther south on Cemetery Ridge with a direct shot on the right flank of the line. Batteries on Little Round Top increased their fire, and soon McGilvery's guns were roaring as well, firing directly down the rebel line. Each shot tore gaping holes in the formation. Still, that line did not waver. Gaps closed and the line pressed forward, dead and wounded sprawled in its wake.

Henry watched the enemy formation on the left join with the one on the right and execute a right oblique movement so that they were again headed straight at him. This time, the rebs were a solid mass. His heart sank as he realized that they would not escape this attack.

Now the rebs were getting close—into canister range. The batteries behind them opened up, spewing smoke and spraying clusters of one-inch steel balls toward the gray mass. Stannard's forward regiments on Henry's left front opened up with a sheet of musket fire as the rebel right flank marched past their position. More gray forms fell, but the line marched forward, seemingly oblivious to the carnage.

At last there was movement in the Union line. They were ordered forward a few paces to adjust their position. Henry cast a longing glance back at the meager breastwork. He would sure like to fire from behind it, but its short height made that impractical.

Henry judged the distance. *Nearly three hundred yards away now. Not much longer.* The order soon came to take aim. Muskets clattered as they were brought to the shoulder.

Captain Messik offered a final piece of advice. "Make sure you aim for their feet, boys." His regiment strained to hold their weapons on their aiming point, awaiting the order to fire. The enemy marched forward a few more paces. At the order to fire, the whole brigade exploded in unison, sending a sheet of flame and smoke toward the rebels. The first rank of the rebel line fell, twisting, pitching, and slumping to the ground. The second rank pressed forward, seemingly unconcerned, and paused to return fire. Men around Henry jerked and fell. The rebels broke into their wailing yell and rushed forward.

Henry and the men around him were firing as fast as they could. The rebels ran toward them, losing man after man at every step. The attack lost its momentum no more than thirty yards in front of Henry and the First Minnesota. As the enemy paused to regroup, the blue line continued to pour fire into them. Groups of rebels rushed forward, but they were instantly cut down.

Smoke obscured everything above the knees. That was enough to aim at. It was all mechanical motions, like an automaton: load—aim—fire; load—aim—fire. From time to time, Henry would pause to push a soldier into a gap—keep the front rank closed. Then he returned to the automatic movements: load—aim—fire.

Henry could see that the rebel line in front of the regiment was getting thinner. He could also see the rebel feet sidling to his right. He knew what that meant—they were concentrating on some point farther up the ridge. *Have the rebels broken through up there?*

Hancock had also watched the rebel lines emerge from the woods along Seminary Ridge. Two divisions, he concluded—rebel divisions, though, much larger than the normal Union division, probably fifteen or twenty thousand men. If they concentrated against one of his divisions, they could outnumber it by two or three to one.

He rode along the length of his line, from Hays's division near Ziegler's Grove to Caldwell's division at the south end of Cemetery Ridge, making small corrections in the deployment of his forces and preparing them for the inevitable. Finally, he was satisfied. It was a good position, and the troops were deployed as well as they could be. Not that there weren't flaws in the position. Hancock was concerned about the forward position of Stannard's regiments and with the ninety-degree angle in Webb's line formed by a jog in the stone wall. He cast an anxious look at the angle again. This was the weak point in the line, and he knew it. If the enemy attack hit this point, the infantry behind the wall would face fire from two directions. Still, he had placed plenty of reserves behind the line to plug any gaps. Now he could do nothing but wait.

Hancock watched those gray lines come on. He judged the rate of advance and concluded that the rebel left flank would contact Hays's division first. In fact, the enemy's leftmost brigade had already brushed up against one of Hays's regiments out on a skirmish line. Hancock had watched with satisfaction as the concentrated artillery fire from Cemetery Hill and the flanking fire from the forward regiment caused the rebel brigade to break and stream to the rear.

That retreat left the remaining rebel line too short. Hays's right overlapped the enemy left, and Hays was quickly moving troops into position to take advantage of it. The rebel left grew closer and closer to Hays's line. When the enemy reached a wooden fence about two hundred yards away, Hays ordered his men up from behind the stone wall. Three ranks of blue-coated infantry trained their rifles on the enemy brigade struggling to make it over the fence. At Hays's command, several thousand rifles and a dozen cannon roared at once. The rebel front rank disappeared in a cloud of smoke.

On the left of Gibbon's division, Harrow's brigade thundered its first salvo. Hall's brigade in the middle was next to fire, followed by Webb's brigade on Gibbon's right. The entire line was blazing at the enemy, and smoke quickly blocked Hancock's view of the enemy line. By standing in his stirrups, though, he could see the crimson tops of the rebel battle flags rising above the layer of smoke; they were still coming on.

Hancock rode toward Hays's part of the line to see how it was holding up. As he rode closer, he could see Hays waving his hat and shouting, his reddish hair blazing as he hurried his right flank regiments forward. Hancock smiled as he realized what Hays was doing: a flanking movement. The regiments would move ninety degrees to the main line and be able to fire directly down the enemy line.

Artillery pieces were moving as well. Hancock turned back toward the south. Hays had things well under control.

A thought suddenly hit him. If the rebels were concentrating on the northern end of his line, then perhaps he could do the same flanking maneuver in the south. Stannard's brigade was in a perfect position to do that. He galloped to the south.

As he rode along the crest, he could see the rebel flags had concentrated in front of the angle. They had found the weakest part of his line, and Hancock knew he urgently needed to take the pressure off. An officer on foot in front of him was shouting and waving his hands. As Hancock pulled up, he recognized the man, a colonel in Hall's brigade. Leaning closer, Hancock could hear what the colonel was shouting over the roar of the battle.

"General," the officer shouted, "they have broken through—the colors are coming over the stone wall—let me go in there!"

Hancock looked over his right shoulder. Above the smoke, tops of rebel flags were at the wall, waving in triumph. A few dozen federals broke through the smoke, headed for the rear. It was a breakthrough. An immediate counterattack was needed. No time for planning—just react, or it might be too late.

Hancock turned back to the Colonel and nodded. "Right. Go in there pretty goddamned quick!"

The colonel shouted to his troops and to the regiment on his right. Together, they charged toward the gap with a long yell.

Hancock looked around for more troops to throw into the gap. A mounted officer had succeeded in halting the retreating men and faced them about to face the enemy. Hancock recognized the officer—it was Haskell, one of Gibbon's aides. Behind them, a regiment was moving forward, led by General Webb. *This is under control for the moment,* Hancock told himself. *Better get down to Stannard—a flank attack will help ease the pressure at this breakthrough.*

He found Stannard mounted, shouting directions to his soldiers. Hancock called to him as he rode up. "General Stannard, I want your brigade to attack the rebel flank immediately!"

"We are already in position and ready to attack now," Stannard shouted back.

Hancock peered through the smoke at the lines forming. "Send them in fast and hard, Stannard. Gibbon is being pressed hard up there near the clump of trees." He reined his horse back toward Webb's brigade. *Time to get back up there and see if they need more help. Can't let the enemy have a toehold.*

Suddenly, a searing pain cut into his right thigh, causing Hancock to double over. Through the pain and lightheadedness, he realized that he had been wounded. *Not now,* he thought. *Not when they need me the most!* He started to swoon.

Hands lifted him from the saddle and laid him on the ground. Hancock fought the nausea and felt for the wound. His upper thigh was sticky and the pain was incredible, but Hancock found the wound and placed his fingers over the hole. His fingertips touched something hard. Hancock felt a touch of fear. If it was bone, it meant his leg was broken and he would probably lose his leg. His fingers closed around the hard object, and he raised his hand up so he could see it. His hands were covered with blood, but he sighed with relief when he saw the object. It was a tenpenny nail, bent but still recognizable. "They must be pretty hard up if they are shooting this," he said weakly.

One of Stannard's aides was talking. Hancock forced his reeling mind to concentrate on what he was saying. "...very bad bleeding. General, don't know if it is mortal."

*Mortal...*Hancock swallowed hard at the thought.

"Well," Stannard snorted, "it will be mortal very soon if we don't stop the bleeding." He dismounted and pushed the others away. Quickly fashioning a tourniquet, he tightened it around Hancock's thigh above the wound. "This should hold you until we can get you back to a hospital," he told Hancock.

Hancock shook his head. "No hospital! Don't worry about me; I'll be all right. Tend to your troops." He reached to grasp Stannard's arm. "Drive them off the field, Stannard!"

Henry squinted through the smoke, trying to make out the enemy line in front of him. The smoke was so thick that he could barely make out the dead and wounded marking the rebel line. Orange flame in the middle of the smoke testified to the presence of at least some Johnnies still in fighting condition.

Henry fired and looked again, stooping slightly for a better view. It wasn't his imagination; the amount of orange flames coming from the enemy was much less than only a few minutes ago. Concentrated fire had driven many of the rebs to the right—those who weren't dropped from the ranks. He reloaded and glanced quickly at the forms littering the position around him. *Not that the rebs haven't done a job on our own boys.*

A hand on his shoulder caused him to start. Captain Messick was shouting into his ear to be heard. "Enemy has broken through up by that clump of trees—we must attack."

Henry nodded, and Messick scrambled off to spread the order. By grabbing each man and shouting in their ears, Henry prepared his tiny company.

Almost at once, the regiment was running, with Captain Messick in the lead. Someone started a cheer, but it came out as a deep, low-pitched growl: a primal sound, like a wounded animal about to strike out.

They quickly lost structure as they ran, turning into a mass of growling, screaming men following the other regiments toward the breakthrough at the clump of trees. Just before the clump of trees, the mass of men was stopping. Henry had his first view of the situation—beyond the clump of trees, the rebs were over the wall, some struggling to turn the cannon there around for use against the blue tide surging to seal the breakthrough. A group of the gray infantry saw them coming and fired. Captain Messick stumbled and fell. The regiment rushed forward, howling, past their commander's prostrate form and into the blue mass crowding the enemy penetration.

The bigger men shouldered their way to the front of the firing mass. From the back of the crowd, Henry craned to see what was happening. It looked like several hundred rebels had made it over the wall and up to the cannon some twenty yards behind it. This small number was taking fire from two sides and losing men every second. Already, scores of gray-jacketed dead and wounded lay around the guns. To Henry's front, on the far side of the wall, more rebel infantry was crowding their way toward the breakthrough point.

A man went down in front of Henry, and he squeezed his way forward into the gap. It was a clear shot from this position, and Henry snapped his musket up and fired. Twisting to the side while he reloaded, Henry let someone behind him poke his weapon through the space and fire. Then Henry fired again and again, gray forms dropping in the murderous fire. Henry, shouldered back by two burly privates, managed to poke his musket through a gap and fire. As he reloaded, Henry suddenly realized he was shouting. A quick gaze around told him that everyone else was shouting as well. The shooting, clubbing, yelling, and killing continued in a mindless melee.

Behind the wall Henry could see more rebels, but the federals raced into the group of enemy still standing. The two groups recoiled slightly at the impact and then closed again. Swinging rifles as clubs, the front rank battled the rebels across the wall. Unable to reach the enemy, the rear ranks threw rocks over the heads of their comrades or fired over shoulders into the faces of the enemy.

Then something happened—something Henry had never seen before. Some of the rebels turned and ran back toward the wall while others dropped their weapons and raised their hands in surrender. The blue mass rushed forward with a roar, chasing the rebels away from the wall and overwhelming those who did not flee.

The firing to the right slackened, and Henry looked nervously over to see the reason. He recognized General Hays riding through the smoke toward the wall, a rebel battle flag dragging behind his horse. Hays was shouting at the men as he rode. The firing dropped off as the general rode forward. When Hays was almost on top of him, Henry could finally make out what the general was shouting.

"Stop firing, you goddamned fools! Can't you see it's over? Stop, stop, stop!"

They all lowered their weapons and looked dumbly about. *Is it possible that it's over, that we've won?* The few enemy remaining in their front had dropped their weapons. The rest were streaming back toward the Emmitsburg Road. *Yes, it's possible.* Henry collapsed onto the stone wall. *We did it—we won.* He suddenly thought of Isaac, lying buried only a half mile away. *We did it brother*; we *finally won.* "Clubs is trumps," he whispered. Tears streamed down his powder-blackened face—tears of joy, tears of relief, tears of an avenged death.

Hancock winced at the flash of pain as he lifted his head slightly to get a better look. From his position on the ground, he could see very little of what was happening. Private Wells noticed his pain and offered water from his canteen. Hancock gratefully filled his mouth with the lukewarm water and slowly swallowed it. "Tell me what's happening, Wells," Hancock said.

The private stood to get a better view. "Stannard's boys are going in, Gin'ral, fast and hard like you told 'im."

Hancock set his jaw against the pain and nodded. "They do all right for ninety-day men. What about Gibbon—the breakthrough?"

Wells hesitated. "I can't see dhat part so well, saar, with all dhe smoke, it looks like Harrow's and Hall's brigades have left dheir position to counterattack. Dhere's a big fight up dhere fahr sure."

"Look for our flags, Wells. Where are they?"

Wells looked again. "Dhey are down at dhe wall."

"Down at the wall? You sure about that?"

"Yes, saar. Positive."

Hancock sighed with relief. *They have regained the wall. That means the breach is sealed.*

Wells squinted into the smoke. "Here comes Major Mitchell. Maybe he's got some news."

Hancock turned his head gingerly, trying to avoid disturbing his throbbing leg. "Mitchell, give me your report," he said in the firmest voice he could muster.

Mitchell gaped at Hancock's wound and started to say something. Then he hesitated, nodded, and began. "We counterattacked the rebel breakthrough and drove it back, sir. Every one of them who came over the wall is now either dead or our prisoner."

Hancock nodded with satisfaction. "Major Mitchell, I want you to take a message to General Meade." Hancock thought for a moment, searching for the right words. "Tell General Meade that the troops under my command have repulsed the enemy's assault and that we have gained a great victory. The enemy is now flying in all directions in my front. It's time to launch our planned counterattack."

Mitchell was off in a flash, and Hancock relaxed just a bit. The heat and his wound made him light headed, but he fought it off. *No, I need to stay alert; it may not be over yet.*

The sounds of battle seemed like they were miles away. Wells put the canteen to Hancock's lips, and he took another mouthful. Waves of nausea washed over him. Hancock closed his eyes.

"Captain Bingham is here, saar." It was Wells speaking.

Hancock opened his eyes. Wells hovered above him, and beyond was Bingham's horrified face. Hancock swallowed and nodded. "Your report, Captain."

"Sir, a report from General Hays," Bingham said. "The enemy has broken and is in full retreat. We are collecting many prisoners. One of them says he knows you, sir. It's a General Armistead."

"Armistead?" Hancock asked. "Is he all right?"

"No, sir, he is mortally wounded. I spoke to him personally." Bingham hesitated. "He said to tell General Hancock that he has done you and all of us an injury that he shall regret the longest day he lives."

Hancock closed his eyes from the pain and sorrow for his old friend. He could only nod.

There was a silence as neither man could come up with anything to say. Finally Hancock spoke. "What about our casualties?"

"No formal report yet, sir. From the number of dead and wounded, I would say that casualties in Gibbon's division are high."

Major Mitchell was back. "Sir, I have brought you an ambulance. Can we take you to the hospital now?"

Hancock was satisfied he could do no more and was no longer needed at the front. "Yes," he whispered. "I'll go now."

Meade looked up at his aide and shook his head. "No! Go back and tell General Shaler that he is to report to the Third Corps, not General Newton. I want General Humphreys's division as strong as possible to provide a force to deal with any possible breakthrough."

The aide saluted and rode off. Meade clenched his jaws and looked around for aides. They were all off, carrying messages or leading units to new positions where they could support Hancock in case he needed assistance. Ever since Gibbon sent a message saying that the enemy attack was coming directly at him, Meade had been adjusting unit positions to provide the Second Corps with maximum support. He was satisfied that the new deployment was sufficient, but he was frustrated at the lack of information.

He spotted George returning from an errand. Meade smiled at his son. "Hello, George. I'm glad you're here. You must stick by me now—you are the only officer left." As George dismounted, Meade continued his pacing.

After some time, Meade stopped his pacing to listen to the sound of the battle raging on the far side of Cemetery Ridge. *No cannon fire for some time,* he thought. *Still sustained rifle fire. Has it slackened a bit?* He turned to George. "Do you think there is a letup in the fire up there?"

They both stood silently, listening to the gunfire. After some minutes, George said, "Yes, I do think it has fallen off a bit."

Meade looked toward the ridge for any sign of a messenger from Hancock. He had been forced to move out of his headquarters during the artillery barrage. With that position dangerous and impractical, he decided to move his headquarters near Slocum's headquarters on the right of his line. It was safer there for his staff, but he was nearly a mile away from the center of Hancock's line. Even so, he did need a secure location where he could keep an eye on his flanks, just in case this barrage was a cover for an end run. After the worst of the barrage ended, he moved to an open field just down the hill from his original headquarters.

Meade turned his head to listen. The fire was definitely lessening. "You know, I do think it is letting up." After a few more minutes, it had reduced to a pattering, and then it finally stopped completely. *What could it mean?* Meade looked again for a messenger. *Nothing!* "George, Let's go up there and see what's happening," he said.

Meade mounted his horse and rode toward the ridge, followed by George, his sole available aide. "We better check at the headquarters first. Maybe the messenger went there by mistake," he said to George.

The white headquarters building, perforated with shrapnel holes and surrounded by dead horses, was vacant. Meade motioned with his head, and the pair continued to ride up toward Gibbon's division.

As they left the white headquarters building behind them, Meade spotted a rider galloping toward him. A little closer, and Meade could make out that it was Major Mitchell, Hancock's aide.

Mitchell pulled up in front of Meade and snapped off a quick salute. "Report from General Hancock, sir! He has been seriously wounded but wishes to report that the enemy attack has been completely repulsed."

"Wounded?" Meade asked. "How serious is it?"

"We're not sure, sir. He was wounded in the upper thigh. We don't think an artery was severed, but so far no doctor has looked at it. General Gibbon has been wounded as well, but I do not have any word on his condition. General Hancock refuses to be evacuated until the action is over."

"Yes, that does sound like Hancock." Meade thought for a moment. "Do you say the attack has been repulsed?"

"There was some scattered firing when I left him, but the enemy was definitely retreating."

Meade clapped his hands together. "Good, good!"

"Oh, one more thing, sir," Mitchell said. "General Hancock said now is the time to counterattack as you planned."

"Yes, it is," Meade said absently. *That supposes the enemy is not ready to launch an attack elsewhere or follow up with another wave,* he thought. A picture of his Achilles heel, the Eleventh Corps, flashed into his head. "Thank you, Captain," he said to Mitchell. "Now go and get a doctor for your general!" Turning to George, he said, "Let's go and see for ourselves!"

Once they crested the hill, however, Gibbon's line was shrouded in smoke, and Meade could see nothing. He scowled and looked around. Over on the right, Hays's division was relatively smoke free. He spurred his horse in that direction.

They came across a young artillery lieutenant whose section was firing canister down a farm lane. "Where is General Hays?" Meade asked the lieutenant.

"Down there, sir." The lieutenant pointed toward the front line.

Meade looked in that direction. Hays was beyond the stone wall on his horse, dragging a rebel battle flag behind him. "Has the enemy turned?" he replied.

"Yes. See, Hays has one of their flags, sir."

"I don't give a damn about the flag," Meade snarled. "Has the enemy turned?"

"Yes, sir," came the reply. "They are turning now."

Meade grunted and turned back toward Gibbon's line, the point of the enemy attack. That would tell the story for sure.

The pair rode along the western slope of Cemetery Ridge. Meade pulled up sharply. A large group of gray-clad soldiers was moving toward him. His panic was relieved when he realized that none of them had any weapons.

They looked up at him. "Where should we go, General?"

Meade pointed toward the far side of the ridge. "Go down there, and you will be taken care of." He watched the group move off. *Prisoners. That's a good sign,* he told himself.

A lone horseman rode toward them. Meade squinted, trying to make out who the person was through the smoke. "Who is that, George?" he asked.

"That's Lieutenant Haskell, one of Gibbon's aides," George replied. "I was talking to him this morning when we had the meal at Gibbon's headquarters."

As Haskell neared them, Meade called out, "How's it going here?"

"I believe, General, the enemy's attack is repulsed" was the reply.

Meade rode closer to the lieutenant and skeptically looked him in the eyes. "Is the attack *entirely* repulsed?"

Haskell nodded vigorously. "It is, sir!"

Meade looked out over the slope, over the expanse of dead and dying men and horses, the wrecked batteries and abandoned equipment. In the distance, he could make out gray infantry fleeing back toward the woods on Seminary Ridge. "Thank God!" was all he could say. He reached up and pulled off his hat to cheer, but stopped himself. All this death and destruction was nothing to cheer about.

Meade turned his gaze back toward Haskell. "Lieutenant, I understand both Generals Hancock and Gibbon are wounded. Who is in command now?"

"Well, sir, General Caldwell would be in charge of the corps, and General Harrow is in charge of the Second Division."

"Yes, where are they now?" Meade paused for barely a second and then continued. "Never mind; I will give my orders to you, and you can pass them on to Caldwell and Harrow. The troops need to be reformed as soon as possible and kept in position. The enemy may be crazy enough to attack again. If the enemy does attack, you are to attack him in the flank and sweep him off the field. Is that clear?"

He waited for acknowledgment from Haskell and then turned his horse in the direction of the cemetery. He still needed to ensure that Howard's line was secure.

The Eleventh Corps commander was on the crest near Osborn's guns when Meade approached. Spotting him, Howard called out, "Congratulations, General, on a great victory!"

"Thank you," Meade replied cautiously. *It's not a great victory until it is over,* he said to himself. "How are things to your front, Howard?"

"Very quiet. Not a sign of any enemy activity."

"Hmm." Meade raised his field glasses and scanned the fields and ridgelines to his front. There were no artillery batteries visible and no massed infantry to be seen. *Perhaps that was the main attack on Hancock after all,* he mused. "Very well, Howard. Let me know immediately if anything changes!" Turning around, he found that George was no longer with him. "Well then," he said. "I need to get to Little Round Top." More aides rejoined him as he galloped toward his southern flank, and soon he was followed by a rather large group of horsemen.

Soldiers soon recognized him and began to cheer. Meade, embarrassed at first, took off his hat and acknowledged the cheers by waving his hat. *They are the ones who deserve the cheers,* he thought.

He suddenly remembered his conversation with Hancock earlier in the day. The attack had certainly been repulsed, and it was time to counterattack. He turned to an aide. "Ride ahead and find General Warren. Tell him to have Sykes and Sedgwick attack immediately as we discussed!"

Epilogue

Epilogue

BUT SYKES AND SEDGWICK DID not attack immediately. Later, they would claim that they never received orders to plan for such an attack. By the time scattered units were organized and set into motion, it was already late in the day. Nearly, two brigades of skirmishers moved forward at that time and quickly pushed the rebel defenders back until a stronger line was encountered. There, the attack faltered and, with nightfall closing in, all action ceased. The overwhelming opinion among the senior officers that evening was that the army had achieved a great victory and that it would be foolhardy to risk the success of the day with any further action.

Henry and the rest of the Second Corps had no time to savor victory after the repulse of the rebel attack. They were immediately ordered back to their original positions in anticipation of another attack. There was no time to tend to the wounded; the ambulance corps would have to see to them. Before exhaustion forced Henry to collapse into sleep, he found time to write an entry in his diary: "I feel that I have partially avenged the death of my brother."

Dan Sickles had spent the night before in a field hospital behind the lines. His leg had been amputated above the knee, and the shattered leg was packed in ice and sent as a specimen to the Army Medical Museum in Washington. In the morning of July 3, Dr. Sim, the Third Corps medical director, judged it was too risky to have him remain in the field hospital and ordered him evacuated. Judging that an ambulance ride would possibly cause fatal bleeding, Sim and Tremain organized a stretcher detail to carry Sickles to the nearest rail depot in Littlestown, some eight miles away. The detail consisted of ten teams of four soldiers each, what constituted the better part of a regiment in the now-shattered Third Corps. Dr. Sim accompanied the detail. It is unclear whether he did this voluntarily or if he was ordered to do so. Regardless, the Third Corps wounded lost the services of an experienced surgeon. The detail reached the rail depot on the morning of July 4, and Sickles, along with his aides and Dr. Sim, were loaded onto a train ultimately bound for Washington.

Hancock was treated on the field and loaded onto an ambulance. He stopped the ambulance at least once to dictate a message to Meade. Later, once his wound had been stabilized, he was evacuated by ambulance to Westminster. From there, he was carried by train to Baltimore and then on to Philadelphia where he arrived around noon on July 4. Doctors examined the wound there and forbade any further travel until his condition improved.

Meade returned to his shot-up headquarters and found that it had been converted into a field hospital. He moved his headquarters about a quarter of a mile down the road to an open area strewn with rocks. There he sent a cautious report to General Halleck in Washington. "After the repelling of the assault, indications leading to the belief that the enemy might be withdrawing, an armed reconnaissance was pushed forward from the left, and the enemy found to be in force. At the present hour all is quiet. My cavalry have been engaged all day on both flanks of the enemy, harassing and vigorously attacking with great success, notwithstanding they encountered superior numbers both of cavalry and infantry."[5] There was no indication in the message of the great accomplishment which the army had achieved.

During the night, Lee decided to retreat to a better place from which to conduct a defensive battle. He shortened his lines by drawing his left in away from Culp's Hill and onto hills to the north and west of Gettysburg. Once there, his troops were ordered to entrench. Lee also gave orders for his wagon trains full of wounded, captured booty, and supplies to get underway on their move back toward the Potomac River.

Sometime in the early morning, well before dawn, a torrential rainstorm struck. It appeared that God and all of the Heavenly Host were weeping over the absolute carnage on the battlefield and the manifest sinfulness of mankind. The rains continued on and off all day, washing off the blood-soaked grass and inflicting more misery on the wounded still stranded between the lines.

As daylight came, pickets in the Twelfth Corps began to detect that the rebels were no longer to their front. Meade ordered the Eleventh and Twelfth Corps to advance troops to determine the enemy location. This reconnaissance revealed that the town and area around Culp's Hill had been abandoned by the enemy. Movement to the Emmitsburg Road, however, evoked heavy fire from the Confederate positions; the rebels were still there in force.

Meade considered these new lines and concluded that either Lee was either planning a defensive battle or was masking a withdrawal. If it was a defensive battle that Lee wanted, Meade stated that he would not oblige the enemy by storming fixed positions as the army had done previously at Fredericksburg. They would pursue the enemy, however, if Lee was planning a withdrawal. While his corps commanders advised caution and expressed fears of a trap, Meade ordered Warren to lead the Sixth Corps on a reconnaissance in force commencing at dawn on the next morning.

The rest of the day on the fourth was uneventful, with both sides waiting for the other to make a move. Each army was too battered from the previous three days of fighting to make any offensive moves. For the federal troops, the thunderstorms and torrential rains of the day were brightened by the arrival of supply wagons from Westminster, bringing rations and other supplies. Henry Taylor took advantage of the calm to place stones around Isaac's grave.

Meade sent a series of cautious reports to Halleck that day, reluctant to claim victory. Unbeknownst to him, a thousand miles to the southwest, General Grant was at that time accepting the surrender of the entire garrison and city of Vicksburg. These twin victories, one in the east and the other in the west, extinguished any hope of the South's recognition by the European powers.

On the morning of the fifth, in the gray light of dawn, men of the Sixth Corps advanced cautiously toward the rebel lines. Skirmishers reaching the lines occupied by the Confederates the day before found them empty. Signal stations reported a large body of troops deployed to the west. Uncertainty evaporated—the enemy was in retreat. Meade ordered his pursuit plan into action. He would utilize the relatively unscathed Sixth Corps, his largest corps, to pursue Lee's army and apply direct pressure.

The rest of the army would be the encircling force, marching in parallel to Lee through the Boonsboro pass to the south in a race to beat Lee to the Potomac River crossings.

It was also during the day that Meade issued a general order to the army. It was one whose wording Meade would later regret. He began by congratulating the army for the "glorious results of the recent operations" and then reminded them that their task is not yet complete, for he "looks to the army for greater efforts to drive from our soil every vestige of the presence of the invader." President Lincoln, on reading the general order, remarked "Is that all?" He had been expecting much more aggressive action and to have the Army of the Potomac annihilate what he supposed to be Lee's decimated army before it crossed the Potomac. Characteristically, Meade ended the general order by crediting the Almighty for the victory.

Late in the afternoon of July 5, Dan Sickles received word that the president had arrived to see him. Sickles had found lodging in a boarding house on Eighth Street, where Dr. Sim and a team of orderlies oversaw his care. The president was concerned about Sickles's condition and quite eager to hear more details concerning the battle. Sickles used the opportunity to spin his side of the story. As he described it, Meade did not want to fight at Gettysburg; he had had no plan, and Sickles had sent his own corps forward to precipitate a battle to prevent Meade from retreating. Lincoln listened intently and departed even more concerned that Meade was not going to be aggressive enough. Sickles must have smiled as the president left. As a lawyer, he knew that the story heard first was the one most likely to be believed.

Sedgwick, wary of a trap, cautiously pursued the rebel army until he reached the Fairfield Gap. There he ran into heavy resistance. After a brief fight, he drew back and reported to Meade that he thought the rebel army was going to make a stand in the Fairfield Gap, just east of the Monterey Pass. Meade, hampered by his orders to keep his army between the enemy and Washington, was forced to suspend his encircling move until he had a clearer picture of the enemy's intentions. After midnight on the sixth of July, Meade directed Sedgwick to push a reconnaissance into the gap to more accurately determine the enemy intentions.

At first, Sedgwick was reluctant to advance, but he finally did so after prodding from Meade. A subsequent message was sent to Meade confirming that only a small force held the gap, and Sedgwick expected it to retreat when pushed. Meade received this message late in the afternoon and immediately ordered his encircling movement to resume. Unfortunately, a full day had been lost in the race to reach the Potomac.

Meade pushed his army forward with forced marches—some units marching over thirty miles in a day. On the seventh of July, torrential rains turned some of the roads into quagmires, making the roads nearly impassable and slowing progress to a crawl. Not only was the weather hindering his movement, but his army was operating with a shattered command structure and had taken over twenty-three thousand casualties. His two most trusted and aggressive corps commanders, Reynolds and Hancock, were gone, as well as two division commanders and a dozen brigade commanders. Some depleted regiments, with all of their senior officers dead or wounded, were being commanded by captains.

The heavy rains continued on July eighth, so units were not able to concentrate at Middletown until the ninth—two days later than planned. By the evening of the ninth, however, they were over the last set of mountains and into the Cumberland Valley.

Meade had learned that Union cavalry sent from Frederick by General French had destroyed the rebels' only pontoon bridge across the Potomac. Additionally, the heavy rains had raised the water level of the Potomac to flood stage. It appeared that Lee's army was trapped with its back to the impassible Potomac. There was more good news for Meade on the eighth; General Humphreys joined Meade's staff that day as chief of staff, replacing General Butterfield.

The Union army moved forward toward the Potomac behind a screen of cavalry. Their progress was stubbornly resisted by Confederate cavalry backed by infantry support. By the twelfth, all of Meade's corps had reached the main rebel defensive line located east of Williamsport on the Potomac. Lee had selected defensive positions on a series of ridges, and Meade ordered a reconnaissance in force for the thirteenth. He reported to General Halleck by telegraph his intentions for the next day. In preparation, he called his corps commanders together for an evening conference to gather more details and to finalize plans for the operation.

While both Warren and Humphreys agreed with Meade that an attack should be conducted the next day, his corps commanders certainly did not. Only two of them sided with Meade; the others argued strongly that no attack should be made without a thorough reconnaissance. Following an all-too-common pattern in that highly politicized army, Meade allowed a vote, thereby turning his commanders' conference into a council of war. He was voted down and reluctantly agreed to postpone the attack until a proper reconnaissance could be made. The vote also forced him to telegraph Halleck announcing the delay—news not very well received in Washington.

The next morning, Meade and Warren rode along the line to inspect the terrain and the enemy lines. Convinced that an attack could be made, Meade ordered the operation to go forward on the next morning. The troops advanced the next day, alerted by skirmishers that the positions might no longer be occupied. As they reached the Confederate positions, their suspicions were confirmed—the rebels were gone.

Lee had conducted a masterful retreat over a ten-day period, and his engineers had achieved the near-impossible task of constructing pontoon bridges from pieces of barns and warehouses. Advised that the Potomac water level had dropped, Lee gave the order to withdraw around the same time Meade was conducting his reconnaissance. During the night of the thirteenth, Lee's divisions had silently left their positions and filed to the crossing points over the Potomac. After discovering the enemy retreat, Union troops rushed toward the river but were only able to bag stragglers and some of the rear guard.

Upon inspecting the abandoned rebel fieldworks, most Union officers believed that it was a very good thing not to have attacked those positions. They realized the positions were much too strong and it would have resulted in a blood bath. Such carnage could have very well offset the victory won at Gettysburg. Disappointment over Lee's escape was tempered by the realization of the enormous price that would have been paid in the attempt to capture his army.

This sentiment, however, was not shared in Washington. President Lincoln was apoplectic, believing Lee to have been next to helpless after his battering at Gettysburg. All that was needed, he argued, was for Meade to reach out his hand and gather up the shattered Southern army. Halleck dutifully transmitted to Meade via telegram the full measure of Lincoln's dissatisfaction over the enemy's escape. This was too much for Meade to accept; he knew that Lee's army, though badly damaged, was still an intact force and still extremely dangerous. Meade also knew what Herculean efforts his army had made to defeat the enemy at Gettysburg and pursue him to the Potomac. He fired off a response to Halleck, asking to be relieved of the command he had not asked for in the first place. Halleck quickly changed his tune, explaining that the president was only disappointed, not dissatisfied. This mollified Meade, at least for the time being.

That day, the fourteenth, the Army of the Potomac began to cross the Potomac in pursuit of Lee's army. Cavalry units crossed at Harper's Ferry and began a reconnaissance operation. Infantry units crossed beginning on the seventeenth. Conscious of his supply lines and his orders to stay between the enemy and Washington, Meade followed Lee south, looking for an opportunity to attack the retreating columns. One finally presented itself near Front Royal, Virginia. Meade had the chance to split the retreating rebel columns in two if he could break through a pass. Slow movement and timid response on the part of one of his corps commanders stymied Meade's plans, and the enemy got away. The pursuit finally ended up at the Rappahannock River, where orders arrived from Washington for Meade to take up a "threatening position" there but not to advance against the enemy.

Meanwhile, trouble had been brewing in New York City. Publication of the Gettysburg casualty lists combined with the draft calls had stoked enormous anger in the white working class of that city. Rioting broke out among the primarily poor Irish and German working class, who were the recipients of the draft calls and who did not have the $300 needed to buy a substitute. Buildings were burned, Blacks were beaten and lynched, and homes and offices were ransacked. To quell the riots, the militia was called in, and the draft was suspended in the city.

The war, however, had an insatiable hunger for manpower. Not only did casualties need to be replaced, but whole units were being discharged as their terms of enlistment expired. Lincoln and the War Department faced mounting pressure to resume the draft in the city and turn back on the manpower spigot upon which the army so desperately depended. To this end, Meade was ordered to send veteran regiments to New York to maintain order when the draft was reinstated. Henry and the First Minnesota were among the units sent north for this duty.

Washington was roiling as well, but it was of an insidious political nature. Dan Sickles was happily spinning his version of the events at Gettysburg and opining what steps should be taken going forward. Politicians were openly expressing their chagrin at the events and Meade's apparent unwillingness to crush Lee. Newspapers wove all this information into an anti-Meade narrative. Joe Hooker, sensing the direction in which the political wind was blowing, began to lobby for a way back into command of the Army of the Potomac.

In the midst of all this, General Howard wrote a personal letter to President Lincoln, attempting to set the record straight. Howard's abolitionist bona fides were well established, so his opinion was one that Lincoln could rely on as not being biased toward Meade. This letter praised Meade's handling of the army before, during, and after the battle and attributed victory primarily to Meade's efforts. Lincoln replied to Howard with a letter expressing his gratitude for what Meade had accomplished as well as his confidence in Meade. Howard showed this letter to Meade, and it must have provided some consolation in the face of all the negative press swirling about.

In early September, Meade's intelligence service reported that Longstreet's corps had been withdrawn and sent to the Western Theater. Meade immediately spotted the opportunity and sent his cavalry out followed by his infantry. Good forward progress was made, and a movement around Lee's left flank was about to be conducted when an order was received from Washington halting any further movement. Help was needed in the west, and the Army of the Potomac was called on to supply the necessary manpower. Meade was ordered to send the Eleventh and Twelfth Corps west. There, they would be consolidated into the Twentieth Corps and placed under the command of General Hooker. These troops would eventually remain in the western army for the rest of the war.

Now Meade was the one at a disadvantage. Lee spotted the weakness and was quick to act, ordering an advance. Meade learned of these plans through an intercepted message that was also confirmed by scouting reports. He quickly set the army into motion, staying ahead of Lee's advance. At Bristoe Station, Meade's rear guard ambushed A.P. Hill's corps, inflicting two thousand casualties. Meade entrenched on high ground soon thereafter, daring Lee to attack. The position was too strong, and Lee could not remain there with his supply lines extended, so he was forced to retreat back to the Rappahannock, where he planned to form his winter lines.

Meanwhile, things were happening in Gettysburg. Governor Curtin, the Soldier's Friend, visited the battlefield soon after the combatants left. He appointed a prominent local attorney to act as an agent to select and purchase a plot of land for a soldiers' cemetery and began to lobby the other northern governors to participate in the creation of a national cemetery. By the end of October, land had been purchased and a contract let to disinter the bodies of Union soldiers scattered around the battlefield and to reinter them in the new cemetery located next to the Evergreen Cemetery on Cemetery Hill. President Lincoln was invited to attend the dedication, and the contractor was under pressure to reinter as many bodies as possible for that dedication. By mid-November, almost 1,200 bodies had been reinterred when President Lincoln arrived for the ceremony. There he gave what is considered by many to be the greatest speech in the English language, known as the "Gettysburg Address."

In October, Dan Sickles left Washington to travel to Meade's headquarters, where he reported himself fit to resume duty as the Third Corps commander. Rumors had been swirling around Washington that Sickles was bucking for command of the army. Meade turned him away, however, saying that he was not yet healthy for a command. Although Meade and most of the other senior officers in the army would have preferred to court-martial Sickles, they all knew that it would be impossible to do so to a battle-wounded, politically connected general. Sickles left this meeting with the realization that he would never have a command so long as George Meade remained in command of the Army of the Potomac, and he promptly set out to remedy that situation.

While Sickles had experienced a speedy recovery, Hancock was not so fortunate. His wound continued to drain, and his doctors advised him that the bullet, or some other foreign object, was still in his body. Medical procedure in the era before x-rays was to probe with metal rods to find the bullet—an excruciating procedure. Several specialists were called in to probe for the bullet, with no success. In the meantime, Hancock was growing weaker, and there was a mounting concern that this wound would eventually take his life. Finally, an army surgeon home on leave called on Hancock to see if he could be of assistance. The doctor had Hancock sit in a chair in the same position as when he was wounded. Using forceps, the doctor was able to remove the bullet with a minimum of pain. Once the bullet was removed, the wound began to slowly heal.

Meade was facing increased frustration during this period. Halleck constantly pestered him by telegraph with injunctions from the president to "attack Lee somewhere and hurt him." When plans to attack the enemy were presented, however, they were rejected. There were no suggestions from Washington on what type of plan they would approve, nor was there any overall strategic direction for Meade's army forthcoming from Halleck.

Lee had destroyed the rail line during his retreat after Bristoe Station. Since the railroad was his only supply line, Meade was forced to rebuild the line as he moved forward. This considerably slowed his advance, much to the consternation of Washington. At last, Meade arrived at the Rappahannock, where Lee had encamped his army for the winter.

Cavalry reconnaissance identified two vulnerable fords across the Rappahannock, and Meade decided to attack them. In a series of swift moves, including a rare night attack, both fords were seized, and over two thousand casualties were inflicted on the rebels. Lee was forced to fall back to the Rapidan, and the Army of the Potomac followed.

Meade, eager to keep up the pressure, spotted an opportunity to turn Lee's right flank. In great secrecy, they planned a move. Lee, however, was tipped off when he received information that Meade had ordered ten days' rations for his troops. Slow movement by some of Meade's commanders and a series of blunders gave Lee time to select and prepare a strong defensive position. As Meade's army closed on the heights at Mine Run, they could see just how imposing these positions were. Many soldiers, believing they would be killed in the anticipated attack the next day, wrote their names on slips of paper and pinned them to their tunics. That way, they reasoned, their bodies would be able to be identified. Convinced by subordinates that an attack was suicidal, Meade reluctantly called off the attack. The army was ordered to withdraw, with Meade convinced that he would finally be relieved of command. When Meade's official report reached the president's desk, Lincoln realized that Meade had done the right thing, so no criticism came from that quarter.

And with this, both sides moved to their winter camps. The campaign from the Gettysburg retreat down to Mine Run appeared more like an eighteenth-century war of maneuver than the bloody slugfests earlier in the year. At the same time Meade was withdrawing, Grant was achieving a great victory at Chattanooga. While Grant was lionized in the papers, Meade was villainized.

As the army settled into its winter camp, Meade had a more important concern than the political turmoil in Washington. The enlistments of many of his veteran regiments were expiring in the spring, and Meade needed them to reenlist if he was going to have any kind of an army for the next year's campaigning. His spirits were raised by the arrival of Hancock in late December. Still not completely healed, Hancock was well enough to report for duty and was quickly reappointed Second Corps commander. After a short stay in camp, Hancock was sent to Pennsylvania for recruiting duty.

The First Minnesota was heavily courted for reenlistment as well, with offers of large cash bonuses and extended leaves. Some decided to reenlist, but many, including Henry Taylor, decided not to do so. With Colonel Colvill gone, many were dissatisfied with the new regimental commander. In the end, not enough men reenlisted, so the regiment was slated to be disbanded.

The New Year brought an increase in political turmoil and intrigue, if that was even possible. Congress decided to award medals to recognize the military successes of the previous year. Grant was an obvious choice, but when it came to Gettysburg, the political maneuvering began. Sickles loudly insisted that he was the one who provoked the battle on the second day and insinuated that it would have been over on that day if he had been properly reinforced. Besides, he argued, Howard was the one who chose the site, not Meade. Hooker maintained that he had led the army as far as Frederick and had planned the movement into Pennsylvania, so he should get the credit. Everyone had their champions—Hooker was the darling of the Radical Republicans, Howard was an abolitionist, and Sickles had the War Democrats. Meade had no one to promote his cause. In the end, medals were awarded to Hooker, Howard, and Meade in that order. Sickles had too many enemies, so he was dropped from the list.

The Radical Republicans were not content with just issuing a medal, however. They wanted Fighting Joe Hooker back in command of the Army of the Potomac. To this end, they started out to discredit George Meade, and their chosen instrument was the Joint Committee on the Conduct of the War. Dan Sickles was the lead-off witness once the hearing was convened. In two days of testimony, Sickles testified his oft-repeated line that Meade had never wanted to fight at Gettysburg and that he, Sickles, had been primarily responsible for the victory by taking the initiative on the second day. He also gave ample testimony rehabilitating Hooker's reputation. Sickles was followed by other witnesses, each of whom had an ax to grind with Meade.

Relieved of command by Meade for one reason or another, these disgruntled officers testified to Meade's lack of fitness for command. When the committee felt that it had sufficient evidence to damn Meade, they adjourned and sent a delegation to present their case to the president, suggesting that General Hooker would be an acceptable replacement for Meade.

President Lincoln, however, was in no hurry to change commanders. He had a plan to change the overall command structure and had requested Congress to revive the grade of lieutenant general. Upon approval by Congress, Lincoln appointed Grant to be commanding general of the armies with a rank of lieutenant general. Grant thereby outranked every other Union general officer, including Halleck. When the congressional delegation personally presented the evidence concerning Meade, Lincoln suggested that it might be better if both sides of the issue were presented. Their plan stymied, the delegation reluctantly returned to the capitol and called Meade to testify.

Meade appeared before the committee and countered every charge by reading the details of official reports into the official record. With their case completely destroyed, the committee adjourned in silent defeat.

Meade also had other important business at that time. He had long complained to Secretary of War Stanton that his army corps were understrength and that there was a lack of aggressive leadership. Stanton's suggestion was to consolidate the army corps by disbanding the First and Third Corps and incorporating their units into the Second and Fifth Corps. The ablest leaders would be selected for this new organization. Once implemented, this organization would serve the Army of the Potomac for the coming hard campaign and on to the end of the war.

Frustrated by the failure of the plan to oust Meade, Sickles hatched another plan. A long article was published in the *New York Herald*, penned under the pseudonym Historicus. In it, the military virtues of Dan Sickles were lauded, while the failures of the indecisive Meade were presented in full detail. Historians debate who Historicus really was. Some say Sickles, others Tremain. Whoever the author was, the effect was to permanently tarnish George Meade's reputation.

About this same time, General Grant reported to Washington to assume his new position. During meetings with Secretary Stanton, he was given authority to move all the armies as he saw fit and to make whatever changes in command he thought necessary. Visiting the Army of the Potomac, Grant met with Meade, whom he had not seen since the Mexican War. Meade suggested that Grant might want another commander, one from the Western Theater, with whom Grant was more familiar. He suggested General Sherman as a replacement. Grant, perhaps impressed with Meade's willingness to step aside, told him that he needed Sherman in the west and that Meade would stay in command of the Army of the Potomac.

Grant's strategy for the coming campaign season was simple—he would have all his armies advance simultaneously, thereby depriving the enemy of the ability to shift forces around to counter various threats. His instructions to Meade were simple as well: "Lee's army will be your objective point; wherever Lee goes, there you will go also." He also made it clear that he would be accompanying the Army of the Potomac during the upcoming campaign.

In early May, the army moved across the Rapidan and into the same jumble of trees and overgrowth in which they had fought a year earlier. Grant was intent upon seizing and maintaining the initiative and seemed to be following the president's idea of striking the enemy and hurting him. He would turn the army into a blunt weapon to beat Lee's force into submission. In a series of battles, including the Wilderness, Spotsylvania, and Cold Harbor, Grant inflicted punishing losses on Lee's army. The corresponding cost in Union dead and wounded was mind boggling, renewing Grant's sobriquet of Butcher, earned at Shiloh two years previously. In the one-month period between entering the Wilderness and the end of the battle at Cold Harbor, the Army of the Potomac suffered nearly fifty-five thousand casualties. Grant and his staff from the western army had learned that the Army of Northern Virginia was deadlier and more resourceful than any of the Confederate armies in the west had been.

A surprise end run and brilliant crossing of the James River put the army before the city of Petersburg, but capture of the city slipped through their fingers. By late June the campaign had devolved into a siege, presaging the brutal trench warfare of the First World War.

Hancock at this point was forced to go on medical leave. His Gettysburg wound had reopened, discharging fluid and pieces of bone. He was also emotionally spent after the loss of friends and many of his Second Corps soldiers. Sandy Hays had been killed in the Battle of the Wilderness, and John Sedgwick was killed by a sniper at the Battle of Spotsylvania. As for his beloved soldiers, Hancock remarked after Cold Harbor that the Second Corps lay buried between the Rapidan and the James. Hancock did not return to duty with the Army of the Potomac during the rest of the war.

The summer languished into fall and then fall into winter, with each side desperately trying to break the siege. Despite trying different stratagems, including extending the lines, breaching attacks, and even a gigantic Union cratering charge, the siege lines held. Finally, in the early spring of 1865, with General Sherman advancing north through the Carolinas, Lee realized that he could not remain in his lines protecting Petersburg and Richmond. Once Sherman arrived, the Union would have enough manpower to cut Lee off from his last supply lines. After the success of a Union turning movement on his right flank, retreat was the only option, and in early April, Lee slipped his army out of their trenches and started a withdrawal toward the west.

Upon discovering that Lee had abandoned his lines, Grant ordered an all-out pursuit, sending Sheridan's cavalry and Union infantry to cut him off. Lee reached Appomattox Court House and found his path blocked by Union cavalry backed up by infantry. With the Second and Sixth Corps pressing him from behind, Lee realized he had no other option but to surrender. On the seventh of April, he sent Grant a message requesting terms of surrender.

Grant accepted Lee's surrender on the ninth, but neither Meade, nor any of his officers were invited to the ceremony. When Meade announced the surrender of the Army of Northern Virginia later in the day to his troops, they wildly cheered and called his name, just as they had done on the third day at Gettysburg. The next day, Meade obtained permission to cross the lines to visit Lee, whom he had known in the Mexican War. When Lee asked him what he was doing with all the gray hair in his beard, Meade said, "You have to answer for most of it!"

The newspapers rejoiced in celebration over the surrender. All the credit, however, was heaped upon Sheridan's independent cavalry command. The yeoman work done by the Army of the Potomac was neglected, and in fact, the army was rarely mentioned in the articles. The entire army was disgusted by this treatment, and Meade wrote to his wife, "I don't believe the truth will ever be known and I have a great contempt for history."

Lee's surrender to Grant did not end Meade's and his army's work. Joe Johnston's army was still unsubdued in North Carolina, blocking Sherman's army on its move north. It was not until two weeks later that Johnston surrendered to Sherman. Only then was Meade able to march his army north toward Washington and the great victory parade planned there. There was, of course, a victory parade in Richmond on the way: the goal of the Army of the Potomac since 1861. Meade took the time while he was in Richmond to see Lee and urge his friend to take the Oath of Allegiance, believing that it would begin to help heal the wounds caused by the conflict. Lee refused, wanting to wait to see what would happen to the other high officials of the defunct Confederacy.

The parade route in Washington was lined with cheering crowds and festooned with banners when the Army of the Potomac marched in review. Meade led his army along Pennsylvania Avenue, the crowd chanting "Gettysburg, Gettysburg" as he rode by. Reaching the reviewing stand, Meade dismounted to join the reviewing party. From there, for over six hours, he watched rank after rank of his blue-coated boys march past, some ninety thousand strong. A group of ambulances followed each brigade, with the blood-soaked stretchers attached to the side of each ambulance giving silent testimony to the hidden price of the victory parade.

This was the last official act for most of these soldiers. The next day they started on their way back to their home states, where they would be mustered out of the army. Once they arrived home, some units conducted elaborate celebrations, and in early June, Meade attended one of these in Philadelphia.

These festivities were over soon enough, and Meade was called back to Washington. Serious discussions were taking place over how the postwar army would be organized, particularly in light of the demands on the army for occupying the former Confederate states and for overseeing what came to be known as "reconstruction." Military districts were formed, each being subdivided into military divisions. These districts were to be commanded by major generals, and assignments were to be determined by rank. Meade, being the third-ranking major general, was given command of the Military District of the Atlantic.

By early 1865, Hancock had recovered sufficiently to return to duty. General Grant placed Hancock in command of the "Middle Department," based in Winchester, Virginia. After Lee's surrender, Hancock negotiated the surrender of John Mosby's Rangers, the only Confederate military force left in the Shenandoah Valley. While in Winchester, Hancock learned of Lincoln's assassination and was immediately ordered to Washington since the capital city fell within his military district. There, he took personal command of the garrison and helped restore a sense of calm after the public chaos following the assassination. He was also responsible for overseeing the sentence of the military court that had tried the Lincoln assassination conspirators. While the three men sentenced to death for their part in the plot were clearly guilty, Hancock had serious reservations concerning Mary Surratt, the owner of the boarding house where the assassination plot was hatched. In a revenge-driven rush to judgment, the court found her guilty of conspiracy with rather flimsy evidence. While he could not affect the carrying out of the sentence, Hancock placed horsemen at intervals between the White

House and the place of execution, just in case President Johnson would issue a pardon or commutation. None came, however, and Mary Surratt was executed along with the others.

Henry Taylor had spent most of the previous year trying to readjust to civilian life. He was discharged in May of 1864, married, and returned to his home in Belle Prairie, Minnesota. After ten months, however, he found himself too restless and enlisted in the Veterans Corps as a lieutenant. His job was to train new recruits, and he served in that capacity until the spring of 1866. While serving and away from home, he received word that his wife had died. Upon discharge, Henry returned to his family home in Prairie City, Illinois, and found a job teaching school. Still restless, he moved to Cass County, Missouri, in the spring of 1867, where he taught school and farmed. He remarried and eventually had seven children. In 1875 he entered the insurance business and later became an associate judge for Cass County and an elder in the local Baptist Church. In 1907, at the age of sixty-eight, he died of pneumonia. Noting his passing, a local newspaper stated that the county had lost "one of its most estimable citizens. He was honored and respected by everybody for his manhood and his broad intellectual capacity. No higher tribute can be paid his memory than the encomium that he was a good citizen. His life and the manner in which he lived is a eulogy in itself."

The Lincoln assassination injected more political turmoil into the capital. President Lincoln had selected Andrew Johnson, a pro-Union southern Democrat from Tennessee, as his running mate on a national unity ticket. Johnson supported the same even-handed approach to southern reconstruction that Lincoln had espoused. The trouble was the Radicals in Congress were hell-bent on meting out harsh retribution to anyone even remotely associated with the rebellion. Secretary of War Stanton was on the side of the Radicals, and General Grant, already eyeing an 1868 presidential run, threw his lot in with the Radicals. Directions on reconstruction policy from the president were routinely countermanded by Grant and Stanton. After the 1866 midterm election, the Radicals gained a supermajority and began to enact veto-proof legislation to enhance congressional power while reducing the power of the presidency. This culminated in the unsuccessful impeachment of the president in 1867.

Such was the toxic political soup into which the military commanders were thrown. The Southern states were divided into military districts, with federal troops in place to keep order and dispense justice with the use of military tribunals. The economy in the Southern states was flat on its back, and the social structure had disintegrated, along with law and order. Mob violence and bloodshed was common, with groups of ex-Confederate veterans and dispossessed Blacks roaming the streets of Southern cities.

While the army was concerned with challenges in the Southern states, Meade's most serious problem was in the north. After the war, prompted by events in Ireland and by Canada's perceived pro-Confederacy position during the war, an Irish American group calling itself the Fenian Brotherhood began to attract a large following. Consisting primarily of veterans, the group's goal was to force England into recognizing an Irish republic by attacking and seizing British army forts and customs posts in Canada.

Clashes and cross-border incursions had already begun when Meade received orders to deal with the problem. He shuttled between flash points along the US-Canada border from Eastport in Maine to Buffalo and Ogdensburg in New York, using a combination of governmental actions and personal persuasion. Many of the veterans were his former troops, and they cheered him when he appeared. His personal appeals for them to disperse and go home were no doubt helpful in defusing the situation. Finally, Meade had the leader of the group arrested, and the movement fizzled out.

It was after this affair that President Johnson appointed Meade to the command of the Third Military District. Composed of the states of Georgia, Florida, and Alabama, this district was in an uproar after General Pope, the district commander, had taken a series of highly controversial actions. The president, no doubt impressed by Meade's handling of the Fenian issue, was eager for someone to restore order in the district. Meade was able to use an even-handed approach in resolving the problems and restoring order.

After Grant was elected president in 1868, the army experienced a change in top leadership. Sherman, who was in command in the west, was promoted to Grant's old position. Meade, as the next senior major general, expected to be assigned to Sherman's command in the west. He was severely disappointed when Grant bypassed him and appointed Sheridan, his junior, to the command. Meade was ordered to return to command the Military District of the Atlantic.

When he returned to his old command, Meade was not a well man. He was suffering from recurring bouts of pneumonia, which kept him bedridden for weeks at a time. Doctors believed that the condition was a complication of his seriously war-wounded lungs. Meade was able to carry on in command of the district until late October 1872, when he suffered another bout of pneumonia. This bout was more serious, and the doctors were powerless to treat it. On November 6, the day after the election, Meade passed away at age fifty-six.

The funeral was a spectacle, with President Grant, General Sherman, and many cabinet officers attending. Thousands marched in Meade's funeral procession, including many veterans of his old commands. The *Philadelphia Inquirer* labeled it as "one of the grandest ever witnessed in the country." He was laid to rest at Laurel Hill Cemetery in Philadelphia. On his grave is the simple epitaph "He did his work bravely and is at rest."

George Meade's legacy is a mixed one. Tarnished by the accusations of Sickles and others, his achievements still stand out. He was able to organize and lead his army in a great victory while only in command for a few days. He showed great skill in maneuvering his army against a very wily foe, and his use of maneuver and entrenching indicate he perceived the tactical changes required due to the impact of rifled weapons. Perhaps Colonel Theodore Lyman, who joined Meade's staff in the early fall of 1863, summed it up best in a letter to his wife:

"During a long campaign he has handled an army...under circumstances very trying...that is to say, obliged to take the orders and tactics of a superior, but made responsible for all the trying and difficult performance...I undertake to say that his handling of the troops...has been a wonder, without exaggeration, a wonder. His movements and that of Lee are only to be compared to two exquisite swordsmen, each perfectly instructed and never erring a hair in attack or defense...He has done better with the Army of the Potomac than McClellan, Pope, Burnside, or Hooker; and—I will boldly and without disparagement to the lieutenant General—better than Grant!...I don't say he is Napoleon, Caesar, and Alexander in one, only that he can handle 100,000 men and do it easily—a rare gift!"[6]

Hancock was appointed by President Johnson to command the Fifth Military District in Louisiana and Texas, over the objections of General Grant. After meeting with the president to discuss policy in his military district, Hancock issued the famous General Order 40. This restored civil liberties in the district and reinstated the handling of crimes by civil tribunals.

This order evoked great relief throughout the South and approval by many in the North, who saw it as an end to the tyranny of military occupation. The Radicals, however, were outraged. They pressured Grant to do something about Hancock. Grant responded by harassing Hancock and overturning decisions until Hancock was compelled by frustration to resign. Johnson reluctantly accepted the resignation, assigning Hancock instead to serve under Meade in the Military District of the Atlantic. In 1866, Congress finally got around to recognizing Hancock for his achievements at Gettysburg.

Even though Hancock did not campaign for the nomination, he still received 144 votes at the 1868 Democratic Convention. Grant was nominated by the Republicans and eventually won the 1868 election. Hancock's brief brush with politics, however, increased Grant's hostility toward him. Hancock was subsequently passed over for promotion and then essentially banished by Grant with an appointment to the Military District of the Dakotas, the least desirable of all the army commands. When Meade died, Hancock was the senior major general in the army and was entitled to command the Military District of the Atlantic, which he took. He moved the District headquarters to Governor's Island, New York, where he remained in command for the last fourteen years of his life.

During this period, he was often visited by veterans, many down on their luck. Hancock always greeted them warmly and made sure they left with some money, even if he could not afford it. Some, his aides complained, were clearly imposters. Regardless, Hancock helped them all.

In 1880, Hancock was nominated by the Democratic Party for president, but lost to the general turned politician James Garfield. Many believed that Grant's failures as president led many voters to be wary of electing another general with no political experience. Garfield's margin of victory was only seven thousand votes, and there were accusations of voter fraud. Hancock, though, would hear none of it and refused to contest the election. Perhaps he recalled the turmoil caused by the disputed Tilden-Hays election four years earlier and did not want to see a repetition.

When Grant died in 1885, Hancock was assigned the responsibility of organizing the funeral rites for the man who had shown him so much postwar animosity. As was his nature, Hancock handled the task with professionalism and respect. It was a pageant that is believed to have surpassed the most elaborate burial rites in American history to that time.

In 1886, Hancock suffered from a painful boil on the back of his neck. It was treated, but the boil became infected, and sepsis set in. Despite the best efforts of the doctors in the age before antibiotics, the infection spread to his blood, and Hancock's condition became critical. He died on the ninth of February, just five days before his sixty-second birthday.

Hancock's funeral was simple, without military pomp or dirges, just as he had wished. His friends from West Point, the army, and the Second Corps attended to honor the man. After the funeral, the body was transported by train to Norristown, Pennsylvania, for internment. The streets were lined with aging veterans, eager to pay their respects to their old commander.

The next day, Dr. John Paxton spoke about Hancock from the pulpit. Paxton had been a captain in the Second Corps and became an ordained minister after the war. His words echoed what many of his old comrades were thinking:

"They buried yesterday my old commander—the ideal soldier—the pure patriot—the noblest man—the stainless name—gentle as a woman, with voice low and caressing as love in the camp and at the fireside, but heroic as Cid, and with a voice of thunder in the battle to inspire and command.

"And I shall see his face no more. But while life lasts he will live in my memory, admiration and love as the grandest figure I ever saw...For three years I followed him—from Fredericksburg to Appomattox—my hero, lofty and superb! ...Glorious Hancock—countryman and comrade in arms! I see you now at Gettysburg, thrilling me with the accents of command. I see you in the Wilderness, inspiring me with your dauntless courage... my hero—my leader...farewell!"[7]

Dan Sickles learned of Lincoln's assassination while he was in Colombia on a diplomatic mission. The president, perhaps realizing that Sickles would never be given another military command, sent him on a series of missions as a personal representative. This would get him out of Washington, where he was continuing to stir up controversy.

Returning to Washington, Sickles was nominated by Stanton to be the military governor of South Carolina. He moved to Charleston to take command and the next year was appointed to the newly formed Second Military District, which included North and South Carolina. Sickles's decisions, however, began to ruffle feathers. While Grant supported him, he had run-ins with the attorney general and President Johnson. Finally, Johnson dismissed Sickles in the late summer of 1867.

After his inauguration in 1869, President Grant retrieved Sickles from the political wilderness by appointing him minister to Spain, a rather important diplomatic post. The administration was keen on getting Spain to cede Cuba to the United States, and Dan Sickles's powers of persuasion and Tammany Hall–style use of political bribes were thought to be useful for this purpose. Turbulent Spanish politics, however, with its frequent changes in government, made this mission quite difficult. Even if a current government might be "persuaded" to sell Cuba, which they probably would not, they might not stay in power long enough to get the deal done.

Sickles managed to keep himself occupied during these trying times by conducting a series of high-profile affairs, including one with Isabella II, the deposed Queen of Spain. As word of this affair became known, the newspapers began to mock Sickles as "the American King of Spain." This mocking found its way back to the US, where doubts were expressed as to Sickles's suitability for his post. Somewhere in the middle of all this, Sickles married a young Spanish woman.

Finally, Dan Sickles's penchant for doing things his own way got the better of him once again. A diplomatic incident in Cuba flared up when Spanish forces intercepted and executed the passengers and crew of an American ship trying to smuggle guns into the island. Sickles, without instructions from Washington, closed the American embassy in protest. Secretary of State Fish began to deal directly with Spain, cutting Sickles out entirely. Sickles left his post soon afterward, moving to Paris with his new wife, his mother, and his daughter from his first marriage. Paris was his home until 1879, when he left to go back to America. His wife and two young children left him to return to Spain.

Sickles's desire to be back in America was based on the upcoming 1880 election. His friend Grant was planning a political comeback for an unprecedented third term. The convention turned out differently, however, with Garfield receiving the nomination. Sickles had no hope of any government position from a man he did not know and against whom he had worked.

Sickles devoted the succeeding decade to the battle of Gettysburg. Various memoirs began to emerge, some supporting Sickles's decision to move forward to the peach orchard, while others criticized it. Sickles waded into the fight, writing his own defense and reasons why Meade should not receive any credit. During this time, New York State appointed Sickles to the chairmanship of its Monuments Commission, in charge of the design and installation of monuments for New York regiments at Gettysburg. This was a position that would occupy him for most of the rest of his life.

He ran for Congress in 1892 and won, but he lost his reelection bid in 1894. Congress paid him an honor in 1897 by awarding him the Medal of Honor for his bravery on July 2. His citation reads, "Major General Sickles displayed the most conspicuous gallantry on the field vigorously contesting the advance of the enemy and continuing to encourage his troops after being himself severely wounded."[8]

In 1912, the Excelsior Brigade was planning the construction of a monument. This was Dan Sickles's original brigade; the one he had recruited and had won him his first general officer's star. The monument was planned to have five columns that surrounded a statue of Sickles. During construction, however, it was discovered that $28,000 was missing from the construction funds. An audit discovered that Sickles was responsible for the missing funds, and an arrest warrant was issued. While he was arrested and released on bail, Sickles was never prosecuted. The Excelsior Brigade eventually finished their monument, but without the statue of Sickles.

Sickles suffered a cerebral hemorrhage in April 1914. In an ironic twist of fate, the man who spent his entire adult life using and then discarding women was left helpless and had to be nursed by one of these discarded women—his estranged second wife—for the last two weeks of his life. Sickles died at age ninety-four, one of the last of his generation. He was buried in Arlington National Cemetery with full military honors. His gravestone has a simple epitaph: "Medal of Honor." Sickles's severed leg is still preserved at the National Museum of Health and Medicine in Silver Spring, Maryland. Legend has it that Sickles used to visit his leg every year on the anniversary of his wounding.

Following the November 1863 dedication and President Lincoln's address, the reinternment process in the Soldier's Cemetery continued through the fall and winter. By March 1864, the last of the battlefield dead had been relocated to the cemetery. This included over 3,500 soldiers; nearly 1,000 of whom were listed as unknowns. Despite careful supervision from the cemetery committee, identifying the dead was not an easy task. Most units, when burying their own dead, took care to mark each grave with the soldier's name and regiment written on or carved into a wooden headboard. No doubt some of these were trampled during the Confederate attack of the third of July. Others were damaged by weathering or by wild animals disturbing the shallow graves. Errors or sloppiness on the part of the reinternment crews may also have played a part. Whatever the cause, many bodies arrived at the Soldier's Cemetery without proper identification and had to be listed as unknown.

As work on the cemetery progressed, monuments began to be erected around the battlefield. The First Minnesota Memorial Urn in the cemetery was the first monument to be placed on the battlefield. Dedicated in 1869, the Soldiers' National Monument sits at the center of the semicircle of graves, consisting of a column topped by a statue depicting Liberty mourning her dead. Construction on the cemetery was completed in 1872, and the grounds were transferred to federal control that same year. Remains continue to be occasionally found on the battlefield and are reinterred in the National Cemetery. The last such set of remains was transferred in 1997.

Shortly after the battle, its magnitude began to be realized. David McConaughy, a prominent local attorney and civic leader, donated parts of his property that were part of the battlefield. He encouraged others to do the same and began to sell subscriptions for the purchase of battlefield land. The Gettysburg Battlefield Memorial Association was chartered in 1864 to acquire and preserve land associated with the battle. The association transferred property rights to the federal government in 1895, and the Gettysburg National Military Park was created.

Veterans groups raised money after the war to commemorate the participation of their units in this momentous battle. State legislatures approved money to erect statues to the senior officers who showed exemplary leadership. These monuments and statues now dot the landscape throughout the park. Hancock sits astride his horse on the brow of Cemetery Hill, just as he did on the afternoon of July 1, his hand out, coolly giving orders and restoring order. Meade's statue on Cemetery Ridge depicts him at the moment of victory when he sat on his horse observing the retreating Confederates on July 3. The First Minnesota has two monuments; one depicts a charging soldier near the spot where they began their charge on July 2, and the other identifies their position in line during the assault of July 3.

In the National Cemetery, there is a different set of monuments. They are small granite blocks; each identifying the grave of a participant who, in the words of President Lincoln, offered their "last full measure of devotion" and never left the battlefield. Somewhere under one of these blocks is the grave of Isaac Taylor with the simplest, yet most tragic epitaph of all—"UNKNOWN."

Direct Quotations Used in this Novel

1. George Meade, *The Life and Letters of George Gordon Meade, Major-General United States Army*, George Gordon Meade, Ed., chap. 5, pages 4-5, www.perseus.tufts.edu/hopper/text?doc =Perseus%3Atest%3Atext%3A2001.05.0134%Achapter%3D5 %3Apage%3D4

2. Meade, Life and Letters, chap. 5, page 5

3. Meade, Life and Letters, chap. 5, pages 13-14

4. Meade, Life and Letters, chap. 5, page 18

5. Meade, Life and Letters, chap. 5, pages 111-112

6. Freeman Cleaves, *Meade of Gettysburg*, (Norman, University of Oklahoma Press), page 299

7. "A Tender Tribute to Hancock" New York Times, February 15, 1886. https://croniclingamerica.loc.gov/lccn/sn83030214/ 1886-02-15/ed-1/seq-3/

8. Daniel E. Sickles Medal of Honor Citation. www.cmohs.org/ recipients/daniel-e-sickles

Suggested Further Reading

Cleeves, Freeman. *Meade of Gettysburg.* Norman: University of Oklahoma Press, 1991.

Coddington, Edwin B. *The Gettysburg Campaign.* New York: Charles Scribner's Sons, 1984.

Keneally, Thomas. *American Scoundrel: The Life of the Notorious Civil War General Dan Sickles.* New York: Anchor Books, 2003.

Moe, Richard. *The Last Full Measure: The Life and Death of the First Minnesota Volunteers.* New York: Avon Books, 1994.

Tucker, Glen. *Hancock the Superb.* Dayton: Morningside Bookshop, 1980.

Made in United States
Orlando, FL
20 March 2022